To
Rebuild
A
Life

Enjoy!

Nancy Feldkuhn

Other books by Nancy Feldbush…
To Repay A Debt

To Rebuild A Life

Nancy Feldbush

Moose Run
Productions
Clinton Township, Michigan

Published by...
Moose Run Productions
22010 Highview • Clinton Township, Michigan 48036
moose-run.com

Publishing History...
First Edition—Originally published as *Written in Sand, Written in Stone,*
    © 2002, original ISBN: 1-59129-554-8
Second Edition—Revised, © 2005

Manufactured in the United States of America

ISBN-13: 978-0-9766315-1-4
ISBN-10: 0-9766315-1-2

Library of Congress Control Number: 2005925791

Cover design by Nancy Feldbush
Printed in Michigan on recycled paper

This book is dedicated to those who made it possible for me to pen the words "the end."

To my Lord Jesus, my inspiration. "Thank you" just doesn't say enough... You've blessed me with a second novel, and I praise You for Your graciousness.

To Ann and Julie. Your enthusiasm, gentle prodding, and careful editing kept me inching toward my goal—even when I didn't want to move. Thank you.

To Colleen, Jim, Julie, and Ken, my "prereaders," who meticulously reviewed my manuscript. Your comments were enlightening, and I know the story is stronger because of them. Thank you.

To Henrik, Lars, and Tom. Thank you for helping me with my research... you gave so generously of your time and knowledge when others closed their ears to my questions.

To my dad, my personal salesman, who probably sold more copies of my first book than I did, and to my mom, my companion on many research excursions. Thanks for your cheers and support.

❦Preface❦

Wally Burke glanced skyward and chuckled at the canopy of dark clouds. "I told 'em it was gunna rain today," he said with a lilt of pride in his voice. "I told 'em." Gazing over his shoulder, Wally squinted as he tried to check the progress of the two horse-drawn vehicles behind him, but they had disappeared into the dust created by his own wagon. "They better keep up," he mumbled, turning around to face the front. "Least the rain'll wet down these roads."

Examining the stormy summer sky again, Wally shook his head—this time he found no humor in the gloomy ceiling. "I told 'em and told 'em it was gunna rain today," he repeated sourly as more murky clouds began elbowing their way into the overhead mass. He knew his horses were plodding along as fast as they could, but he also knew if three wagonloads of rain-soaked lumber arrived at the train depot, he'd receive all the blame. "They should've listened to me and covered the wood," he announced to the horses. "I told 'em it was gunna rain today."

As if in agreement, one of the horses snorted and bobbed its head. Bolstered by the animal's apparent sympathy, Wally smiled and carefully scanned both sides of the road while reaching inside his jacket. Then, after searching once more for any unwanted witnesses, he pulled out a small flask, unscrewed the cap, and raised the bottle to his lips.

Suddenly, the wagon's left-front wheel slid into a deep rut, and Wally's arm violently jerked, causing him to douse his beard with the contents of the flask. "Burke, you fool! That's a waste of good gin!" he muttered, wiping his sleeve across his face.

Determined to have a drink, Wally surveyed his surroundings once again. But, this time, he spied a distant figure standing beside the trees that lined the west side of the road, and reluctantly, he recapped his bottle and slipped it back into his jacket. Irritated by his lost opportunity, Wally eyed the newcomer with annoyed indifference—until the man strutted into the middle of the road. Instantly, disinterest changed to concern, and Wally slowed the horses' gait.

Dressed in a fine black suit, the stranger also wore a beard, mustache, gold-rimmed glasses, and a black top hat, which sat slightly crooked upon his bald head. Wally grinned at the lopsided hat and considered asking the newcomer why hair stayed on his face, but not his head. Then the rifle, which the stranger held at his side, came into focus, and Wally's chiding remark faded from his thoughts. Holding up his hand, the bald man yelled, and Wally brought the wagon to a stop, leaving only a few yards of road between them.

"Unhitch the horses and take them over there," the man hissed, using his gun to point to a clearing on the right side of the road.

"We ain't carrying no money," Wally tried, his heart pounding against his chest.

"Unhitch the horses and take them over there," came the crisply repeated answer.

Wally didn't move. The situation, along with the stranger's request, made no sense. Then, in one swift motion, the bald man cocked the rifle and aimed it at Wally's head—immediately, everything made sense and he leaped from the wagon and started to unhitch his horses.

"Tell them to do the same," the gunman put in, nodding toward the approaching wagons.

"What's goin' on, Mister?" Wally questioned.

"Tell them to do the same!"

Coldness emanated from the stranger's dark eyes, and Wally decided that arguing was not the smartest route to take—especially when the source of that coldness held a Winchester rifle. "Yes Sir," he offered with a hard swallow.

"What's the hold up?" the second wagon's driver bellowed as he tugged on his reins. "If the guy won't move, just run him over."

Wally moistened his lips and peered at the stranger. "I'm gunna go tell him what to do…okay?"

Only silence answered him.

Edging over to his fellow teamster, Wally motioned to the clearing. "Morgan, take your horses over there."

"What?"

"Just do it, Morgan! This guy's crazy as a loon. He's got a rifle and I think he wants an excuse to use it…tell Bob to do the same when he gets here," Wally returned and hurried back to his wagon.

In time, the three drivers stood with their horses in the clearing. And, as they waited, Wally's curiosity began to poke at him. Raising himself up on his toes, he twisted his body to and fro, but he still couldn't get a view of the stranger's latest actions. Spurred on by bewilderment, Wally inched his way toward the road—only to face the bald man's Winchester once again.

"You getting a notion about stopping me?"

"I…uh…no," Wally stuttered, regretting that he had left the clearing. "We got the horses where you wanted 'em…what do we do now?"

"I'll tell you what you do now," the gunman rasped as he lifted the rifle above his head. "You watch."

Seconds after the signal, two adolescent boys, carrying buckets, galloped out of the forest. Then, with mischievous delight, they emptied their pails onto the wood and flicked lit matches at the kerosene-doused lumber. Slowly, a sly grin spread across the bald man's face as he watched the yellow-orange flames blanket each of the wagons.

Wishing that the impending rain would magically come and save his precious cargo, Wally cast a quick glimpse upward—but the overhead scene made him frown. The clouds had obviously changed their minds about producing the much-needed downpour and were parting company. There was no hope now for wood or wagon.

The two fire-starters stood motionless for a moment, viewing their handiwork, then they threw their pails onto the flaming vehicles and congratulated each other on a job well done. Finally, the shorter of the two gave his partner a shove, and both boys marched over to the stranger. "We done just what you asked, Mr. Dearborn," the taller boy announced. "You said five dollars—each."

The bald-headed Dearborn stared at the boys. "I said you'd get a quarter eagle each."

"Naw uh. You said half eagle."

"Did I now?" Dearborn murmured. And, as he surveyed the three bonfires, an icy smile parted the hair on his face. "Well…you two did okay. I guess I can part with the extra money," he said, handing the boys their fee.

With yelps of joy, the fire-starters tightly wrapped their fists around their coins and darted back into the forest.

Pivoting toward Wally, Dearborn let out a devilish laugh and gestured toward the lumber with a grand sweep of his arm. "All yours, my good man."

"But…but why?" Wally wondered aloud.

Without an answer, Dearborn circled around and vanished through the grove of trees.

Wally shook his head in confusion. Why would a well-to-do dandy take so much pleasure in destroying cut maple?

✳One✳

"If I take both sets today, I think I could have them back to you...um, by Wednesday," Maxwell Green offered, surveying a round pedestal table. "If you really need them back tomorrow...I guess I could do that," he added as he inspected the carefully painted roses that decorated the center of the tabletop. "Remarkable work," he whispered. Then, leaping onto a nearby chair, Max rubbed his chin and considered the table from above. "I've got it, Peter...I've got the perfect environment for each set."

"Environment? I thought we talked about taking simple pictures," Peter Leighton remarked—but his words went unheard. With a sigh, Peter smiled and shook his head, knowing that it was too late. Max's creative spring had already catapulted the photographer into his own, preoccupied world.

"This one," Max said, jumping down from the chair, "yes, definitely, this one needs a parlor-type background. Something that will complement the elegance of the table but won't divert the eye from the floral design."

"Max, we discussed plain photographs...remember?" Peter tried again.

"And the other one...yes, a solarium. Good...good. That would accentuate the painted wildflowers—especially on the chairs."

Peter watched with amused admiration as the photographer's bushy, silver-haired head bobbed up and down around the furniture. The creative mind always bewildered and intrigued him—he never understood how some people could take pieces of nothing and artfully mold them into something grand. And, as he continued to observe his friend's antics, Peter wondered if he would ever find an outlet that would allow his imagination to soar like that. "Max, we do have a budget for these catalogs."

"I'd like to take one picture with the table alone, then a second with the chairs... sakes alive, Peter, you didn't tell me these sets also come with a matching bookcase!" Max exclaimed as he hurried toward the six-foot-tall piece of furniture. "Fabulous," he murmured, fingering the brushstroked flowers that cascaded down the side of the bookcase.

"No, the sets are only the table and two chairs. That's just a one-of-a-kind…the Jaye girls painted it to demonstrate their skills," Peter returned as he joined Max.

"But you must let me photograph this…that was the whole idea of the picture catalogs, wasn't it? To show what your company can produce?"

"Yes…it's just…I…we don't have the money for a lot of elaborate settings…every time I get a dollar in my hand, something comes along and snatches it out," Peter replied, then he clenched his jaw shut—he had not planned on voicing his financial woes to his friend.

"We'll work something out, Peter. I mean, these pictures will be a kind of advertising for my studio too. Let me take the two tables, their chairs, and this bookcase…and let's just see what happens."

Peter started to object, but the bell over the front door sounded, and his attention was drawn to the entrance of the showroom. "May I help you?" Peter called, walking toward the visitor who had just entered.

"Yeah, I heard you was lookin' for help."

"Yes, we are, Mr.…?"

"Manning Cole," the man answered as he thrust out his right arm.

Shaking Cole's thick, filthy hand, Peter asked, "Have you worked in a furniture factory before, Mr. Cole?"

"I guess."

The man's response caused Peter's eyebrows to instantly raise. It was true, his company desperately needed help, but it also needed men who could remember if they had worked in a furniture factory or not. "You'll have to speak to my partner, Mr. Jaxson Averill. He's the foreman and does the hiring," Peter explained, deciding to give the unkempt Mr. Cole a chance. "Mr. Averill's at the factory now…the building's a couple of miles from here—northeast of the train depot on the other side of the river."

"You mean this ain't the factory?"

"No, Mr. Cole, we just showcase the finished pieces here."

"Oh…so I still gotta go someplace else?"

"Yes, I'm afraid you do."

"You think I should go over there now?"

Peter grinned politely. "You can go anytime you want to."

Manning Cole nodded, then rubbed his nose with the cuff of his shirt. "They just better have somethin' I like to do," he mumbled and tramped out of the showroom.

As he stroked his mustache, Peter exhaled deeply—he had an odd feeling that he would regret sending Manning Cole to the factory.

"Are these the only flower designs that your decorators paint?"

Pivoting on his heel, Peter found the photographer, once again, standing on a chair—this time studying the tables through a square he had made with his fingers. "Max, what are you doing?"

No answer came.

Peter grinned at his friend's obsession with the brushstroked furniture. "Yes. Right now, those are the only designs…well, no, we've been working on a huge order with a completely different motif, but you won't be able to photograph any of those tables."

Max Green lowered his hands and stepped off the chair. "Why not? If you're worried about the extra cost…"

"No, it's not that. The order's for James Wild. He wanted a design that would be exclusively his…he even made sure that stipulation was in the contract."

"Yep, that sounds like Wild all right," Max said, nodding his head so zealously that his bushy, silver mane danced in the air. "Is he refurnishing his hotel already? The place just opened."

Peter forced a smile. He did not enjoy discussing James B. Wild, the third—or the man's numerous assets. In fact, every time he heard the man's name, it felt as if a thorn were being pushed into the back of his neck. "No, the furniture's for a hotel he just bought in Grand Rapids…he's refurnishing that one."

"He bought another hotel?"

"Yep."

"You know what I heard?" the photographer continued as he leaned on the back of one of the painted chairs. "And this is from Mark Johnson himself…Wild wants to buy into the cycle shop…I mean, what does a man like James Wild want with a bicycle store?"

Tilting his head from side to side, Peter tried to release the tension that had crawled into his shoulders. "Probably the same thing he wanted with the clockmaker's store."

"Exactly!" Max shouted. "That man is buying into just about everything. And—you won't believe this—Mark said that the newspaper has already decided to name Wild as 1889's Man of the Year…sakes alive, the year's only half over. I wonder how much he paid *The Chronicle* for that one."

"Evidently enough," Peter returned with a smirk.

"You never have much to say about Wild," Max remarked, straightening up from his propped position. Then, pulling the chair away from the table, he settled onto the seat. "How come?"

"Well, my opinion about Wild is rather divided, so it's better if I just keep my mouth shut." Peter hoped his brief reply would satisfy his curious friend, but Max slouched down in the chair, stretched out his legs, and crossed his ankles—obviously readying himself for a more lengthy answer. "This company is very obliged to Wild," Peter went on as he slowly ambled through the showroom. "You see, when we finally had the new factory up and running, we couldn't get any orders."

"Why? Because of all that rubbish last year?"

"Yep. People just shied away from us. It was Wild who ended up breaking through all the apprehension. He came in one day and ordered some desks for his hotel here in town. After that, people started to follow his example and business began trickling in."

"I never knew you had that kind of trouble," Max said, sitting up straight.

"I never really let anyone know…so, you see, on the one hand I'm grateful for what Wild did—that first order set the factory into motion."

"And on the other hand?"

Peter stopped meandering and gazed intently at the photographer. "And, on the other hand, I'm ready to ride him out of town on a rail because he won't stop buzzing around my fiancee."

"Still?"

His jaw clenched, Peter just nodded.

"I thought Anna's father was going to talk to Wild and make him quit his sparking."

"He did speak to him…and I've spoken to him…even Anna's spoken to him. It seems the more difficult things get for Wild, the more he enjoys them."

"Sakes alive, I wonder what will make him stop?"

"I don't know," Peter offered, but inwardly, he did know what would stop James Wild from continuing his pursuit of Anna Spreyer. And it was his greatest fear… Wild's chasing would end when the man had finally stolen Anna's affections.

Reaching behind him, Peter massaged the complaining muscles in his neck, and as he did, he realized that his hair was hanging over his hand. Glancing into one of the long mirrors that lined the showroom walls, Peter gasped—never in his life had he allowed his hair to reach the length it was in his reflection. Still not fully believing his eyes, Peter combed his fingers through his dark, uncivilized mane. He knew he had been busy the last few months—each day melting into the next—but how could he have overlooked such an obvious necessity? And, he wondered, what else had he neglected in that time?

"Your hair's been the topic of many gossip sessions lately," Max chuckled.

Peter spun around to face his friend. "It has?"

"Uh huh…because of that crowning glory and the soft felt hat you wear now, some of the girls say you could be a character in a dime novel."

"Well, I've had worse things said about me."

"No, they're really fascinated with you," Max countered. "One girl said that you'd make the perfect hero for one of those stories because you had all the right features—tall, strong, handsome, and a bit mysterious."

"And how, exactly, did you hear all this? Have you joined a quilting bee?"

Max Green roared with laughter and pushed himself from his chair. "When I get behind my camera and under that black drape, people forget that I still have ears," he explained with a hearty laugh. "I think I'm going to change the title of my profession to 'photographer and official hearer of gossip.'"

Peter joined in with Max's chuckling. "Well, the gossips will have to find something new to talk about...I'm going to see my barber—today."

"Oh, I'm sure the women won't have a problem with—"

Suddenly, the door's overhead bell jingled once again, and both men turned to greet the youth standing at the threshold.

"I'm looking for Mr. Peter Leighton."

"Here."

Maneuvering around the pieces of furniture, the young man walked over to Peter. "I have a telegram for you, Sir."

"A telegram?" Peter quietly echoed as he exchanged a coin for the note.

"Thank you, Sir," the lad chirped, wrapping his hand around his tip.

Staring at the unexpected message, Peter hesitated—he knew, in his spirit, that it was not good news. With a trembling hand, he slowly opened the note, and as the telegram's abbreviated lines drew him into a trance, he barely heard the bell sound as the delivery boy departed.

"What is it?"

The question jolted Peter from his daze, and he peered into the photographer's inquiring eyes. "It's another dead end in my maze," he answered with a sharp bite of sarcasm in his voice.

"What do you mean?"

"Nothing."

"Is it bad news?" Max persisted.

"It's nothing," Peter mumbled as the weight of the telegram's words pulled at his shoulders. But the answer was a lie...it was something all right.

"Peter," Max returned sternly, "I may talk a lot, but what's said between you and me—stays between you and me."

Peter's brow furrowed as he tried to decipher his friend's statement, then his eyes widened as he realized that his hesitation had been interpreted as mistrust. "I'm sorry, Max...I didn't mean to imply that it wouldn't stay between us."

"So what is it?"

As he let out a deep breath, Peter fingered his mustache. He never liked discussing business with those outside his company, but now, to sooth Max's ego, he knew he'd have to confide in the photographer. "We were supposed to receive a load of lumber today…the telegram's from the lumberyard. It seems that while the wood was being transported to the depot, the teamsters were stopped by a highwayman…he and two accomplices set fire to the wood…it's gone."

"Well, can't they just refill the order?"

Stuffing the telegram into his waistcoat, Peter absently combed his hand through his hair, then slumped onto one of the rose-decorated chairs. "No, they have a small yard…that was all the dry maple they had."

"I don't understand, Peter. Just go to another lumberyard," Max replied, taking a seat on the other brushstroked chair.

"It's not that easy to find what we need."

"Maple? In Michigan?"

Peter smirked. "Scandals produce quite an interesting legacy…they make people, both customers and suppliers, very leery of doing business with you—even after a year…yes, for us, dry maple has become very scarce in Michigan. I tell a sawmill or lumberyard that I'm from Rheinhardt Furniture, and suddenly, they don't have any wood available."

Max shook his head in disbelief. "If the name's causing that much trouble, why not change it?"

"Because my partners want the company's reputation absolved—and so do I."

"I wish I could help."

"I wish you could too," Peter returned with a half-smile as he carefully glided his finger over one of the painted roses on the table in front of him. Then, glancing up at the silver-haired photographer, he offered, "I'm afraid I've wasted your time this morning…I can't even think about doing the picture catalogs now."

"Peter, I can still—"

"No. If I can't get any lumber, we're not going to be able to finish Wild's tables," Peter declared, and as he said the words, a twinge ran through his temples. The thought of telling his nemesis that the factory could not fulfill the order pained him more than his budding headache.

"Just let me take the rose set first, then I'll—"

"No, Max, we'll just have to wait until—"

"Peter, you should know by now that I'm going to continue to insist—and that you will eventually give in to shut me up…so save us both a lot of trouble, and help me get this table into my wagon."

Surrounded by two valises, a small wooden case, and a tapestry bag, Lynette Chesnay stood on the crowded depot platform and watched the parade of train cars leisurely lumber toward their next destination. As the last car passed, Lynette drew in a deep breath and gently touched her son's shoulder to quiet his bouncing enthusiasm.

"Did you see, Mama? Did you see the train man wave at me?"

"Yes, I certainly did," Lynette returned, trying to sound as cheerful and carefree as her son.

"Where are we, Mama?" the boy asked as he turned to face his mother.

"We are in a city called Sandorville."

"Is this where God said to come?"

Lynette smiled and rumpled her son's dark-brown hair. "Yes, William, this is where He wants us."

"I'm hungry, Mama. Can we eat lunch soon?"

Instantly, tears formed in Lynette's eyes, and as she furiously blinked them away, she stroked the small handbag that hung from her waist. How could she tell her son that the few coins she had in the bag were not enough to buy lunch…or supper…or a room for the night. "I know you are, Sweetheart, but we have to wait for the Lord to show us where to go next."

William nodded his understanding.

"Why don't we go sit over there," Lynette said, pointing to a bench near the depot.

William bobbed his head again, picked up the tapestry bag, and galloped toward the seat. By habit, Lynette stacked the little wooden case on top of one of the valises, then, grabbing the handles of the two large bags, she hoisted them off the platform. The luggage, barely three inches off the ground, pulled at her petite frame, and as she reached the bench, Lynette gratefully dropped her load. How? she wondered. How was she going to drag the heavy valises to…to…

"Where is our journey's end, Lord?" she whispered. "Where are we supposed to go from here?"

As if answering, a slight gust of wind danced around her and flittered through the pages of a newspaper that lay abandoned on the wooden slats of the bench. Sliding the paper to one side, Lynette lifted William onto the seat, then shoved the two large valises under him with her foot. Suddenly, her tears returned, and as she struggled to keep them under control, she placed the small case and fabric bag on top of the newspaper. Finally and with a long sigh, Lynette settled down between her son and the luggage, sitting back as far as her bustle would allow.

"How long do we have to wait?" William questioned as his empty stomach voiced its unhappiness with a loud growl.

Lynette shook her head. "I don't know," she answered, and with her words, she lost the battle against the tears, and they rolled down her cheeks. Hoping to hide her weeping from William, Lynette pulled a few strands of her black hair from under her bonnet, then nonchalantly wiped at her face.

She knew she was where God wanted her to be—His words had been so clear in her heart…

'Go as far as your money will take you, then I will take you the rest of the way.'

Doubt had constantly whispered in her ear, telling her to keep enough money for a meal and a room—but she had learned, long ago, that even when God's paths were rutted and rock-filled, they always led to a beautiful valley. And, even now, as doubt reminded her of how foolish it had been to spend all but a few cents on the train tickets, Lynette knew she had followed His will.

"What a darling boy."

The comment tugged Lynette from her thoughts, and glancing up, she saw an elderly couple standing in front of them.

"And what is your name?" the gray-haired woman inquired.

"William."

"Are you waiting to go on a train, William?"

He shook his head. "We just got off one."

The older gentleman looked at Lynette. "May we be of assistance?"

"No, thank you. We're waiting for…for someone."

"Would you like some cookies, William?" the lady asked, holding out a little paper bag.

William's eyes opened wide and he reached for the pouch, then, hesitating, he gazed at his mother. "Can I, Mama?"

"I made them for my grandson, Graham. They're mincemeat cookies," the elderly woman explained. "My little grandson gets very fidgety on the train, so I made him some cookies…but he said he didn't want them."

"You're very kind, thank you," Lynette offered.

With a sad smile, the gray-haired lady placed the bag in William's outstretched palm. "I hope you like them."

Carefully, William peeked inside the pouch, removed a cookie, and took a bite. Then a broad smile bloomed on his face, and he clutched the little sack as if he had been given a bag of gold. "They're real good," William murmured as he bit into the cookie a second time. "Your little boy was silly—he should've taken them."

"Thank you again," Lynette announced, trying to draw attention away from her son's unexpected commentary. "The cookies are very much appreciated."

"We're just glad they won't go to waste," the gentleman added. And, after saying their farewells, the couple strolled, arm in arm, toward their tethered carriage.

Stuffing his hand into the pouch, William pulled out another cookie. "Here, Mama."

"Thank you, Sweetheart," she said, stroking the boy's hair. Then, as Lynette nibbled on the mincemeat snack and surveyed the train station, weariness wrapped itself around her. Like the older man and his wife, the crowd had departed, and except for a group of people trying to squeeze themselves onto an already overloaded horsecar, she and William were alone. So very alone, Lynette silently repeated. Had she made a wrong decision somewhere along the way? Had the Lord abandoned her?

Looking at the morsel in her hand, Lynette suddenly smiled. God, too, had heard William's hunger—and He provided. Once more, tears flooded Lynette's eyes, but this time, they were grateful tears—she had not been forgotten. "Thank you, Lord, for this food. May it nourish our bodies as Your word nourishes our souls. Amen."

"Amen," William agreed as he munched on his next cookie.

On the tail end of the prayer, another warm breeze encircled them and rattled the newspaper that had been trapped beneath the wooden case. Beckoned by the flapping pages, Lynette pulled the paper from under her luggage and studied the text that wanted so badly to be set free.

"What's that, Mama?"

"The local newspaper, see…*The Sandorville Chronicle,* Sunday, July 14, 1889," Lynette read, pointing to each word as she said it. "It's yesterday's paper, but it still might help me find a better place for us to wait." And, more important, she added voicelessly, it might help me find a church or home that will give us shelter for the night.

Skimming through the paper, Lynette stopped as she reached the Want Columns, and immediately, her eyes were drawn to an advertisement near the bottom of the page…

'Wanted—Christian female to care for ailing woman. Also needed to cook, clean. Room and board, plus wages. Apply to Dr. O. Spreyer, Highview St. west of Market St.'

Lynette's heart raced and she reread the advertisement. It seemed perfect—as long as they didn't mind having a child around. "William, Sweetheart, finish up your cookies…we're going to be leaving soon."

"Did God show you where to go?"

"Yes, I think He has," she replied, hoping that it was truly the Lord she was following and not her own desperation.

❧

Peter Leighton started climbing the stairs that led to the offices on the second floor, but after a few steps, he paused and surveyed the showroom. He wasn't sure why, but the room's interior seemed dimmer than usual. Maybe it was just a passing cloud eclipsing some of the sunlight…or maybe, it was the missing rose-painted table and chairs.

Leaning on the banister, Peter stared at the emptiness that had replaced the table, then his eyes drifted to the wildflower set. He had to admit it—the decorated pieces were exceptional. It continually amazed him how a little paint could transform a simple, sturdy table into a piece of fine furniture. But, he corrected himself, it wasn't the paint…it was the decorators' talented brushstroking.

Slowly, a guilty grin spilled onto his face, and Peter fingered his mustache, remembering that it was he who initially refused to have the company produce any decorated merchandise. Now, he was thankful that his partners had overruled his decision. The new line of painted pieces was quickly becoming Rheinhardt Furniture's new specialty, and it was also erasing some of the tarnish from the factory's reputation. Yet there still remained a small part of him that was against the decorated line…or rather, against its dependence upon two people—his decorators. If he ever lost them…

Peter laughed sarcastically, recalling the telegram stuffed into his waistcoat pocket—if he didn't find some more wood, losing the decorators would be the least of his worries. It had been nearly impossible to locate a lumberyard that didn't sneer or cringe at the name Rheinhardt Furniture…now, he had to find another one—and soon. It would only take a few days for the factory to devour its meager inventory of maple wood.

As the predicament pounded through his head, Peter sat down on the steps, and resting his elbows on his knees, he folded his hands. "Lord, I'm losing my hope," he murmured. "Why did You allow the wood to be destroyed? And where do I go to get more?"

Tilting his head to the side, Peter gazed at the precisely positioned furniture through the staircase railing—and a touch of pride welled up inside him. When his company did make furniture, it made very good furniture. His company, he repeated inwardly. He would have never guessed, when he stepped into the Rheinhardt Showroom last July, that he'd end up the managing partner a year later…the partner responsible for the firm's successes and failures. And, lately, there had been a flood of the latter. He continually tried to drag Rheinhardt Furniture out of the muck it had stumbled into, but every time he made a little progress, something came along and added its weight to his burden…such as losing his wood to a fire-breathing highwayman.

With the lumber problem refreshed in his mind, Peter closed his eyes and bowed his head. Instantly, he let out a long groan as the movement strained his stiff muscles.

Then, as he reached up to massage his temples, he moaned again. Not another head-ache, he voicelessly prayed. Please, Lord, not today—I have to…

Hearing footsteps on the stairs behind him, Peter jerked alert, then relaxed—in the midst of his pain, he had forgotten about his two employees upstairs.

"You should go home, before your headache gets worse."

Using the banister to pull himself erect, Peter circled to face his bookkeeper. "No, Del, I can't…maybe it'll go away."

The bookkeeper's expression of doubt told Peter that his friends knew his head-aches all too well.

"It was so quiet down here," Del went on as he descended, "I thought maybe you had left."

"No, I was on my way up…but I got sidetracked."

Del paused on the step above Peter's, and for the first time, the two men stood almost eye-to-eye. "Go home, Peter. You shouldn't work until the headaches make you sick."

Ignoring the remark, Peter pointed to the gap created by the missing painted table. "If he has time today, would you have Josef move the furniture around to fill in that hole?"

The bookkeeper nodded, rapping his fingers on the railing. "No problem. He was going to finish hanging the mirrors anyway…then the showroom will finally be done."

"Finally," Peter echoed. Even though he and his partners had made altering the showroom a priority, the lack of both time and money had greatly hindered the remodeling—making him doubt if the project would ever be completed.

"Everything looks good," Del put in. "I like the changes…to be honest, I never really liked having my office behind that curtain, but Karl had insisted."

Peter grunted his agreement as he inspected the room's interior again. Yes, he liked the changes too. He never understood why Karl Rheinhardt had partitioned the first floor into two sections—it had accomplished only one thing…creating a cramped showroom. Now, with all the offices on the second floor, the entire down-stairs was spaciously dedicated to showcasing their merchandise.

"At least now," Peter replied, grinning, "our customers can move around—with-out having to walk over any furniture."

Del Franz laughed as his tapping fingers started to pet the railing instead.

"I'm just sorry," Peter continued, "that we can't afford to have a clerk down here to watch the floor. I hate to make you keep running up and down the staircase to wait on customers."

Del shrugged and began polishing his pocketwatch with his sleeve. "It's fine with me…I don't mind one bit."

Peter stifled a laugh. In the past year, he had become very familiar with his friend's incessant need to keep in motion and was quite sure that the wiry book-keeper relished the idea of having a reason to dart between the floors.

"I'll have Josef move the furniture this afternoon, as soon as he finishes the banking," Del said as he pocketed his watch.

"You have quite a remarkable son there…I have to tell you, I have nothing but praise for Josef's work."

Rocking back and forth on his heels, Del's face gleamed with pride. "He's always been a quick learner…soon you won't even need me."

Peter rubbed his tired eyes. "No, Del, I need all the loyal employees I can get."

"You should go home," the bookkeeper returned, placing a fatherly hand on Peter's shoulder. "Joe and I can take care of things here."

"I can't," Peter countered. "I have to get over to the factory. I told Jaxson I'd fill in for—"

Once again, the overhead bell interrupted, announcing a visitor. And, as the showroom's front door swung open, Peter glimpsed a familiar sight—and his heart sank. The ornately carved, ivory walking stick meant only one thing…

"James Wild…just what I need," Peter whispered under his breath. Then, a sec-ond after he said the name, his lanky, long-haired rival followed the fancy stick into the room.

"I'll wait on Mr. Wild, if you'd prefer," Del quietly offered.

"Thanks, but I'll take care of him."

"Are you sure?"

Peter nodded. "Yeah." And, while his bookkeeper trotted back upstairs, Peter drew in a deep breath and descended the few steps to the floor. "James, what can I help you with today?"

James Wild leaned his ivory walking stick against the hat stand by the door, then brushed at the sleeves of his frock coat. "The dust in this town is insufferable."

"I suppose," Peter mumbled as he joined his nemesis.

Removing his top hat, Wild cleaned off the brim, then placed it on a hook. "Of course, you are probably used to it, with all the time you spend working amidst the sawdust in your factory."

Peter knew the statement was meant as an insult, but his head hurt too much to be offended. "Is there something I can help you with, James?"

Wild flicked his long, sandy hair behind his shoulders and smoothed the lapels on his coat.

"James?" Peter tried again, growing tired of the methodical preening.

"Yes? Oh, yes. I just thought I would pop in and see how my tables are pro-gressing."

"Everything's fine," Peter remarked. Then he added silently, for now.

"Are you sure? No problems?"

His jaw clenching, Peter shook his head. "No, we're right on schedule."

Reaching into his waistcoat pocket, Wild pulled out a small, decorated cylinder, and as he twisted one end, a gold toothpick emerged from the other. "You would inform me if there were problems, correct?" he asked, scraping his teeth with the toothpick. "Remember, the grand opening of my hotel is dependent upon those tables and chairs."

Peter's jaw clamped down tighter as his mind raced. This visit was no coincidence—Wild knew. Somehow the man knew about the damaged wood. But how? Did Wild have something to do with the lumber being burned? Or did he just get wind of the telegram? "We are on schedule, James. Your tables will be delivered by September first, as agreed."

Abruptly, the front door flew open, and a breathless Manning Cole stormed into the showroom.

"You," Cole spit out as he pointed at Peter. "I was just here looking for a job, you remember?"

Peter nodded. "Yes, Mr. Cole, I remember. I sent you to talk to my foreman."

"Yeah, ya did…the guy's black!" Cole fumed, his face turning red behind the dirt and stubble.

"So?"

"So I don't work for no black man."

"Then I guess you don't work for me," Peter replied, sprinkling his words with sarcasm.

"What?!" Cole exclaimed. "You're gunna keep his kind over hirin' me?!"

James Wild chuckled and twisted his gold toothpick back into hiding. "I mentioned to you before, Peter, that retaining Averill as your foreman might cause this kind of problem."

Peter looked from the tall, lanky Wild, to the thick-chested Cole, then back again. He wasn't sure if it was the throbbing in his head or having to deal with the two narrow minds standing in front of him, but either way, his patience had vanished. "Yes, I'm going to keep his kind…loyal, hardworking employees are difficult to find," he snapped.

Cole responded with a curse, then bolted out the door.

Peter shook his head. He had been right—he did regret sending Manning Cole to the factory.

"You should have hired him, Peter," Wild offered as he returned the toothpick to his waistcoat pocket. "I know how badly you need laborers."

"Do you?"

"Of course…when the owner of a business spends so much of his time toiling with the rest of the hired help, the need for employees is quite evident," Wild quipped, grabbing his hat and walking stick from the stand. "I do hope that this manpower shortage will not delay my tables."

"They'll be done on time."

"I certainly hope so," Wild declared as he exited.

Staring at the door, Peter forced himself to release the tension in his jaw. Conversations with James Wild were always unpleasant and annoying—but he could usually shrug them off. This time was different. Wild's words kept poking at him…and the more they poked, the angrier he became. Wild knew a lot about the factory's troubles—much more than he should. And, Peter wondered, did the man's knowledge of their misfortunes go even deeper?

Pivoting away from the doorway, Peter headed back toward the stairs, and with each stride, anger and worry fought inside his mind, adding their battle to his escalating headache. How could the company survive if James Wild and his money were against them?

Upon reaching the foot of the staircase, Peter looked up and breathed in deeply. "If God is for us, no one can be against us," he reminded himself as he began to trudge up the stairs once again.

<hr/>

With a satisfied sigh, James Wild pulled the showroom door closed. Then, smoothing back his hair, he replaced his hat and strutted toward the covered carriage waiting in the street.

Upon seeing Wild, the coachman hopped down from his perch and opened the carriage door. "Home, Sir?"

"Not yet, Aaron…did you see a man dart out of this building just a few moments ago? A stout, dirty man? He wore a plaid jacket and a tattered derby."

"Yes Sir."

"Which way did he head out?"

"I saw him turn the corner onto Main."

"Was he on foot or horseback?"

"Foot, Sir."

"Excellent," Wild murmured, a smile forming on his face. "Find him. I want to speak with him. Now!" he continued as he climbed into the coach.

"Yes Sir!" the driver crisply replied and latched the door.

As the carriage bounced over the rutted dirt road, James Wild smirked contentedly as if he were a cat that had just cornered a mouse. He enjoyed having Peter

Leighton as an opponent—the man absolutely refused to raise a white flag. And that tenacity made the game much more challenging...

Without warning, the carriage jolted, tearing Wild from his thoughts. "Finally, a civilized road," he whispered as the coach rolled from the dirt onto brick paving. But, almost immediately, the brougham slowed, ending his smooth ride. Glancing out the window, Wild chuckled—Cole was just yards away. This tactic, he mused, would be one of his best.

At first, the driver passed by the dirty man, then, steering the coach toward the sidewalk, he reined in the horses and jumped from his seat, landing with a thud directly in front of Cole. "Mr. Wild would like to speak to you," the coachman announced.

"I don't know no Wild," Cole muttered, shoving the driver aside.

"My dear Sir," Wild called from the carriage window. "You and I were both in the Rheinhardt Furniture Showroom just moments ago...I understand that you are seeking employment."

"Huh?"

Wild grinned—he had found the perfect pawn. "You are looking for a job, correct?" he asked again, trying to simplify the question as much as he could.

"What if I am?" Cole answered as he swaggered over to the coach.

"Well, I need the right kind of man to do a job for me—a job that pays very well. Are you interested?"

"Doin' what?"

"I would rather discuss that privately, here in my brougham," Wild explained, pushing the door open.

Stepping back, Cole shook his head. "I dunno..."

"I will pay you ten dollars a day."

"Ten dollars?! Every day?!"

Wild nodded. "Each and every day you work for me...so are you interested?"

Cole responded by leaping into the carriage and sprawling on the seat opposite Wild.

As the coachman closed the door, he peered at his employer through the window. "Where to, Sir?"

"Home, Aaron...I think my new assistant might enjoy a nice gourmet luncheon."

"He'd like any kind of lunch," Cole added, moistening his crusted lips.

The coach rocked side to side as the driver took his seat, then it slowly resumed its quiet hum over the brick-paved road.

"This is some rig you got," Cole offered as he surveyed the inside of the carriage.

"It is a double-brougham," Wild corrected. "Not a 'rig.'"

Rolling his eyes, Cole snorted. "Well? What do I gotta do for my money?"

"First, I need to know a little about your ethics."

"My what?"

Wild exhaled deeply—communicating with his new pawn was going to be a challenging game in itself. "How do you feel about doing things that might be…well, let me put it this way…things that the law may frown upon?"

"Wouldn't be the first time."

"Good. And, of course, you would…um…keep your mouth shut about the things you do for me, correct?"

"I ain't stupid!"

"Of course not…I just wanted to make sure that you are the right man for the job."

"Look, Mr.…Wild, was it? For a gold eagle a day, I'll do just about anything… 'less it's killin'…that's more."

"I am not seeking an assassin—I am seeking someone who will do my bidding."

"For a gold eagle, I'll make any bids you want."

A broad smile appeared on Wild's face. "I think you will do just fine."

"So what's the job?"

"It is simple…I would like you to take a position at the Rheinhardt Factory."

Cole cursed. "I said I'd do just about anything…but takin' orders from that foreman ain't one of them."

Wild held his index finger up to his lips. "Hear me out first…I would like you to take the job at the factory and do what you are asked to do. And, while you are working, I want you to observe the various activities and relay the information back to me."

"Do what?"

"I want you to tell me what is going on at the factory," Wild began, reminding himself that he was speaking to a simpleton. "Things such as new orders to be filled, or lumber shipments coming in, or new people being hired…do you think you can do that?"

Wiping his nose with his sleeve, Cole nodded. "Sure, but I still don't wanna work for—"

"Look at it this way…not only will you be making even more money because of your wages, but every time you tell me something, it will be as if you were spitting in that foreman's face—and Peter Leighton's."

"Who?"

"The man you talked to at the showroom…the man who prefers to have a black employee over a white one."

Cole smiled, revealing a mouthful of crooked, stained teeth. "Yeah, okay, you got a deal, Mr. Wild."

With a pleased grin, Wild gazed out the window of the brougham, then his smile quickly faded. The carriage had slowed to a crawl—so much of a crawl that they were actually being passed by a man walking on the sidewalk. Reaching up with his carved walking stick, Wild tapped on the ceiling of the coach.

"A milk wagon has overturned, Sir. It's a real mess," came the coachman's voice from outside.

James Wild groaned. Normally, he would not care about the delay, but the odor emanating from his guest was making the large carriage feel smaller and smaller. "I was going to wait until our luncheon to discuss something else, but since we have some time on our hands, we will talk about it now…I have a very special task I would like you to do, Mr. Cole, and I am prepared to offer you a bonus for doing it."

Cole's interest perked up and he leaned slightly forward. "A bonus…for what?"

"I will give you a half eagle every time you can persuade…um…talk any of the men into leaving the Rheinhardt Factory."

"You mean scare 'em away?"

"No, it would be unwise to try that kind of strategy—especially now. Just tell the men that the Sullivan and Smith Furniture Company in Grand Rapids will pay any Rheinhardt employee ten cents an hour more than they are making now…that should set their greedy little minds into motion."

"How do you know they'll pay more?"

"Because, my good man, I am part owner of the Sullivan and Smith Company."

"Yeah? Then how come it ain't called the Sullivan, Smith, and Wild Company?"

"The 'why' of my business ventures is never up for discussion. You will just have to be content knowing that I am a partner—even though my name is not on the placard."

Chuckling, Cole reclined against the side of the carriage and lifted his legs onto the seat. Then, digging into his jacket pockets, he pulled out a crumpled pouch.

"No," Wild snipped, upon seeing the sack.

"Huh?"

"No chewing. Not in my carriages. Not in my homes."

Cole grumbled out a few angry words and replaced the pouch.

"And that goes for—" Realizing that the coach had come to a complete stop, Wild interrupted himself and thumped on the ceiling with his walking stick once more.

"Everything's at a standstill, Sir," Aaron shouted in return.

With an exasperated sigh, James Wild turned his face toward the window and gulped in some badly needed fresh air. And, as he did, his eyes were drawn to a petite, dark-haired woman, whose beautiful, delicate features dripped with perspiration as she struggled to maneuver her luggage through the mass of people that had gathered to watch the milk wagon commotion. Returning his attention to the now dozing

Cole, Wild frowned. He would not be able to offer his carriage to the lady—not with scum covering one of the seats. "Wake up," he demanded and nudged his new employee's leg with the ivory stick.

"Yeah?" Cole mumbled, wiping at his eyes.

"There has been a change of plans. Take this," Wild said as he held out a silver coin, "and rent a room in the Besyrwan Hotel. It is just east of here, on the corner of Cherry Street. I will meet you there to discuss the complete details of your job."

"But how you gunna know what room I'm in?"

"Because it is my hotel."

"And what about my gor…gour…my lunch?"

Wild sighed. "I will have something brought up from the restaurant…now, after I leave, wait a few minutes, then go," he ordered and stepped out of the carriage. Then, to the coachman, he added, "Aaron, when you are able, pull over to the side of the road."

Bobbing his head to and fro, Wild searched for his wilted flower among the myriad of people on the sidewalk, then, finally, he caught sight of her lavender walking-suit and feathered hat. Slowly, a triumphant expression spread across his face, and Wild strutted toward his damsel while parting the crowd with his walking stick. "Please, allow me," he offered and gently lifted the valise from her left hand.

"No, please, I don't—" she returned, trying to pull the case back.

"Madam," Wild interrupted as he took the other pieces of luggage from her grasp, "this kind of labor is a man's duty—not a delicate woman's." Setting the first valise down, he touched the brim of his top hat. "James Besyrwan Wild, the third. I would like to loan you the use of my carriage," he said, motioning toward his now empty coach, which sat at the edge of the street.

"Thank you, Mr. Wild, but it wouldn't be proper…not without a chaperon."

Wild waved his hand. "Not to worry, my lady. My brougham is at your disposal. From here, I can walk to my destination." And, before she could object again, he picked up the valise and headed toward the waiting carriage. "Aaron!" Wild beckoned as he neared the coach.

Once again, the driver ejected himself from his seat and jumped onto the sidewalk. "Sir?"

"I want you to take Miss…" It was only then that Wild noticed the small boy at the woman's side, tightly grasping her skirt. "Excuse me, Mrs.…"

"Chesnay…please, Mr. Wild, I don't want to cause you any inconve—"

"Take Mrs. Chesnay's things and put them into the carriage, then take her—"

"Mr. Wild, we don't want—"

"Please, Madam, it is not an inconvenience to take care of a fragile flower like yourself."

Inhaling deeply, she nodded and eventually smiled. "Thank you. We were trying to get to…" Her voice trailing off, she removed a neatly folded piece of newspaper from her handbag. "Here," she continued, opening the paper and pointing to an advertisement, "to see a Doctor Spreyer."

Wild beamed with delight. "I know the Spreyer family quite well. Please, give my regards to my sweet Anna when you see her."

⌕

Taking the steps two at a time, Jaxson Averill bounded up the showroom stairs, and upon reaching the top floor, he headed toward the second of the three offices. Then, hearing a familiar bickering in German, he stopped at the first office and leaned against the doorjamb.

Josef Franz had been apprenticing under his bookkeeping father for almost a year, and it was quite obvious—audibly and visually—that the two men had very different methods of doing their work. Both were conscientious and precise, but Joe's methodical attention to detail clashed with Del's fast-paced urge to do everything at once.

"Hey, you two," Jaxson called from the doorway, "I keep tellin' ya…if you're gunna fight, do it in English—so the rest of us can enjoy it."

The two men looked up and smiled sheepishly at the teasing remark—they, too, were well aware of their contrasting styles.

"No, no," Del Franz returned, "you have to learn German, then you can join in."

Jaxson grinned. It had taken quite awhile for Del and Joe Franz to accept him and his position in the Rheinhardt Company, but now, he was treated as a colleague and friend—it was a nice change.

"Is Peter around?" Jaxson asked, tilting his head toward the second office.

Joe Franz nodded, but Del motioned for Jaxson to come into the room.

"Some bad news came in about the wood you were expecting," Del whispered.

"What happened?" Jaxson inquired as he perched himself on the edge of the bookkeeper's desk.

"Peter should really tell you about that…but I think it triggered a headache…he's in a great deal of pain already. I tried to make him go home, but he won't…maybe you can persuade him to go."

"Another headache?"

Del answered with a nod.

Drawing in a deep breath, Jaxson looked from Del, to Joe, then to the wall that separated Del's office from Peter's. "I'll try, but you know he ain't gunna listen to me either."

Laboriously, Jaxson pushed himself from the desk and shuffled out of the bookkeeper's office. The news about the wood troubled him, but not as much as the information about Peter. His friend's headaches had become alarmingly frequent and intense—and even though all the doctors labeled the attacks as 'migraine,' they still could find no cause...or cure. As he reached Peter's office, Jaxson raised his hand to knock, but instead, he just stood in the doorway and observed the scene in front of him.

Peter sat at his desk and sifted through some papers with one hand while rubbing his temple with the other. Suddenly, Jaxson shuddered as a familiar fear resurfaced—he could never shake the feeling that, somehow, each headache was shoving Peter closer and closer to an early grave. Death had already snatched away one of his best friends—he couldn't bear the thought of losing Peter too. Quietly, Jaxson tapped on the door, then entered the office.

Raising his eyes from the papers, Peter smiled. "Jax! I didn't expect to see you... did...did I not hear the bell?"

"Naw, I rode the bicycle over...came in the back...you've got another headache, don't ya?" Jaxson asked, although he already knew the answer.

Peter nodded slightly. "I'm getting so tired of these things. If only I knew how to keep them from happening...or how to get rid of them."

As he settled onto one of the chairs opposite Peter's desk, Jaxson nodded in sympathy. "I thought Doc Spreyer was gunna try somethin' new...usin' plants or herbs or something."

"Yeah, he's given me some to try, but with the way things are right now, I just never get the chance to take them," Peter replied, rubbing his eyes.

Jaxson slid to the edge of his chair. "Why don't ya go to Doc Spreyer's and let him give you some of that laudanum."

"No...not yet anyway...we both know you need my help at the factory."

Slouching down in his seat, Jaxson exhaled loudly. Unfortunately, it was the truth—they were already shorthanded, and without Peter's help, they would surely fall behind schedule. "Um...while we're on the subject of needing help...did Manning Cole come back to see you?"

"Who? Oh, him...yeah."

"Whatd'ya tell him?"

"What do you think I told him?"

A wide smile shined on Jaxson's face, then it transformed into a grimace. "This ain't the first man we've lost because of me...if you wanna try and work somethin' out with these guys..."

Peter placed both arms on his desk and stared at Jaxson. "No, I don't want to work anything out with them."

"We need men."

"No, Jaxson, we need good men…like the ones we have now. The ones who don't care about the color of your skin…the ones who stick by us despite all the rumors and newspaper stories…the ones who allow us to be a day or two late with their pay. If these new guys won't accept you as foreman, then they definitely won't be loyal through anything else that might come up."

Warmed by his friend's attitude, Jaxson's grin returned. After a lifetime of prejudice, it renewed his spirit to have his skin color viewed as just a difference and not a detriment. "Thanks."

"You don't have to thank me…we're in this together, Partner."

Jaxson nodded. Since last July, he and Peter had walked through one fiery trial after another—and had exited the tribulations as brothers. "I just hope Hermann Winkel's family shows up soon," Jaxson put in. "If they're anything like Hermann, we won't have to worry about being shorthanded ever again."

Peter responded with a grunt and finished dividing the papers on his desk into two piles.

"Whatd'ya doin'?"

"Just sorting our options…oh, yeah," Peter murmured as he dug in his waistcoat pocket and pulled out a crumpled piece of paper. "Here's the latest." Ironing out the wrinkled page with his fingers, Peter pushed the sheet toward his foreman.

Guessing that it was the news about the wood, Jaxson grabbed the document and skimmed over the words. "Man alive," he said, looking at Peter. He didn't know why, but he couldn't find any worry inside himself—only a little disappointment and a lot of hope. "We'll find more wood. God'll bring us through this too."

Peter studied the piles of paper on his desk, then slid the larger stack to the side. "Well, this is all the Lord has to work with," he declared as he picked up the small bundle of pages in front of him. "These are the sawmills and lumberyards that we haven't contacted yet."

Jaxson snapped his fingers. "Add Logan MacKay…no, MacColl to the list. He's in Willow Ridge."

"Willow Ridge?" Peter echoed, stroking his mustache. "That's a ways out."

"I know, but Benjamin Jaye said they've got a good-size yard and their own sawmill."

With a shrug, Peter scribbled the name on one of the sheets in his stack. "Can't hurt," he mumbled, then, with a sigh, he massaged his eyes again.

The habit pulled Jaxson to his feet—he knew how much the light aggravated his friend's headaches. And, without a word, he walked to the window behind Peter's desk and tugged at the heavy curtains until only a glimmer of daylight peeked into the office. "So what's the plan?"

Turning in his chair, Peter nodded his thanks for the darkened room. "I'm going to send telegrams to all of these," he explained, holding up the papers in his hand. "And, depending on their responses, we'll figure out where we can get our wood." Then Peter slammed the pages down and pushed himself from his chair. "But I'll tell you one thing...when I place the order, I'm doing it in person."

"How come?"

Joining Jaxson at the window, Peter replied between clenched teeth. "Because, not half an hour after I got the telegram, Wild walks in the door, asking me if there were any problems with his tables...you should have seen the look on his face, Jax... he knew about the wood."

Jaxson scratched his chin, then crossed his arms and leaned on the windowsill. "Huh, so Wild's got an ear at the telegraph office."

"Or worse," Peter added. "We were pretty vocal about who was supplying our maple...Wild could have arranged for the highwayman and the burning."

"That's quite a jump, Peter. The wood was for his tables."

"I know...I'm sure he would love for us to default on our contract with him."

"Why?"

"Why? So he'd have us in the palm of his hand...you know how much he wanted to be a partner when we rebuilt."

"Yeah, but—"

"Don't you see? If we default, we'd lose what little credibility we have. And Wild knows that...so he'd probably offer us an extension—in exchange for part ownership."

With a long sigh, Jaxson considered his partner's accusations. He trusted Peter's judgment completely—except when it came to James B. Wild, the third. Peter disliked the flamboyant Wild—with good reason—but that animosity often impaired his logic. "Okay," Jaxson yielded, "but what good will it do to place the order in person? Wild would know what yard we choose by the answers we get from the telegrams."

Peter's jaw clamped tighter. "Well, we'll just have to pray that we get back more than one positive response...then he won't know which one we choose."

Jaxson started to argue but immediately stopped himself. Even in the dim light, he could see the pain etched into Peter's face, and he had no desire to continue beating his friend over the head with James Wild. "No matter how Wild found out 'bout our wood...the thing is, he found out. I think you're right, we oughtta be more careful."

Peter's jaw relaxed and he nodded.

"Besides," Jaxson went on, "it'll do you good to get away from everything for a bit."

"Right...as it did in May?"

This time Jaxson didn't blame his partner for the sarcastic reply. James Wild always intensified his pursuit of Anna Spreyer whenever Peter was out of town. And what made matters worse was Anna's insistence that she and Peter postpone their wedding until her brother, Hans, could attend—that delay only spurred on Wild's efforts. "What about taking Anna with you?"

With his finger, Peter slowly traced the intricate pattern carved into the window's trim. "It'd be nice," he returned with a slight smile. "But I don't think it'll work out…her mum's too sick to be our chaperon, and I really don't want to ask Mrs. Arthur again."

A single chime sounded from the corner of the darkened room, and Jaxson strained to see the position of the clock's hands. "I better be gettin' back…you sure you wanna work in the factory today?"

"Yeah, I'll be there as soon as I get the telegrams sent."

"You want me to do that on my way?"

"No, thanks, I thought I'd stop at the barber shop while I was out."

Jaxson released a slight chuckle and surveyed Peter's unusually long hair. "I wondered when that mane would finally get to ya…it's almost as long as Daven's was." As he realized what he had said, Jaxson's eyes opened wide. He wished he could snatch the word 'Daven' from the air before it reached Peter's ears—but it was too late…the name had already stabbed his partner in the heart. "I'm sorry," Jaxson offered. "It just slipped out."

Silence.

"I'm sorry," he tried again. "Peter, you need to forgive yourself for—"

"I'll meet you at the factory as soon as I'm done with the telegrams," Peter cut in, ignoring Jaxson's slip of the tongue and apologies. Then, tramping over to the desk, he grabbed the small stack of papers and left the office without another word.

Circling to face the window, Jaxson shoved the curtains aside, letting the sunlight wash over him and flood the office. "Why'd you have to say that?" he quietly reprimanded himself—but he knew why.

Daven Ashby's memory had dominated his thoughts ever since the calendar turned from June to July. He missed Daven and their friendship. And, as the first anniversary of Daven's death approached, he longed to reminisce and talk about his talented friend. But that was impossible, because the only other person in Sandorville who had known Daven Ashby well—namely his stepbrother, Peter Leighton—would not even allow Daven's name to be spoken.

As Jaxson absently gazed out the office window, his thoughts drifted to the past…and to finding Daven at the South Pine River—shot and dying…and to carrying his young friend to the doctor's house—but not in time to save him…and to the worst chore of all—shoveling dirt onto the casket. Daven's death had pierced him deeply, but it had left a gaping hole in Peter, who still blamed himself for his brother's demise.

Slowly, a half-smile formed on Jaxson's face as he also recalled Daven's carefree spirit and sparkling blue eyes—and his skill as a woodcarver. With a sigh, Jaxson placed both hands on the windowsill and watched the trees dance with a gust of wind. He prayed, every day, that Peter would overcome his self-imposed guilt. Then, maybe, the healing would start, and his partner could finally remove the black arm-band that he still wore and begin to cherish the memory of Daven's life.

❆Two❆

Once again Lynette Chesnay stood surrounded by her luggage. But, instead of an ever-changing train depot, this time she faced a staunch and stable farmhouse—and, hopefully, her future.

"Do you want me to wait, Ma'am?" the coachman asked as he set the small wooden case next to her valises.

Lynette considered the question, then shook her head. "No, thank you…we're stepping out in faith."

The driver stared at Lynette with a blank expression. "Well, I…uh…I hope everything works out," he mumbled, turning toward the carriage.

"Oh, just a minute…" Lynette called as she dug in her handbag, trying to find the few coins inside.

The coachman circled and held up his hand. "It was Mr. Wild's pleasure," he announced, tipping his hat.

Lynette watched the driver climb onto his seat, then her attention refocused on the house. What now? she wondered. Should she just walk up to the door with her son and luggage as if she already had the job? Yes, she told herself, because that's what stepping out in faith was all about. Barely listening to the carriage as it rattled away, Lynette sighed and picked up her valises—praying that it would be the last time she'd have to haul the bags anywhere.

As she reached the porch, Lynette paused and studied the steps in front of her. After a few moments of consideration—and catching her breath—she hoisted the bags up the stairs, shuffled a few paces onto the veranda, and relaxed her fists, causing the cases to land on the wooden planks with hollow thuds. Taking a handkerchief from her handbag, Lynette patted at the sweat rolling down her temples, then she glanced over her shoulder, just in time to see William start climbing up the stoop with the fabric bag. "Do you want me to help you, Sweetheart?"

William shook his head while continuing his ascent.

As the tapestry sack bounced up the steps behind her son, Lynette bit at her lower lip, trying her best not to worry about the bag's contents or its finely woven fabric.

Conquering the last step, William dropped his stair-beaten load next to the valises, and copying Lynette's actions, he wiped at his face and scanned the porch. "Mama! Look!" he exclaimed as he gestured to a tiny, orange-colored kitten curled up on a wicker chair. "It's Bock!"

The kitten immediately sat up, stretched, and squeaked out a faint response.

Running over to the animal, William scooped it up into his arms and held it to his chest.

"William, Sweetheart," Lynette called, "I'm sure that kitten belongs to some-one already."

"No, he's a stray and doesn't belong to anyone...yet."

The soft, accented words startled Lynette, and she quickly twirled around, searching for the source of the gentle voice—but there was no one on the veranda or in the yard.

"Why do you call him 'Bock'?" the voice questioned.

William shrugged. "Because that's his name."

Following her son's gaze, Lynette finally located the origin of the mysterious voice—a pale yet exquisite-looking woman sat inside the house next to one of the large, wide-open porch windows.

"I'm terribly sorry if we've disturbed you," Lynette offered, walking over to her son's side.

Reaching through the window, the woman rumpled William's hair, and as she did, her thin arm disappeared into the folds of her sleeve. Guessing that this was the 'ailing woman' referred to in the advertisement, Lynette smiled. She didn't know why, but she liked the tranquil, soft-spoken lady.

"A child's love for an animal is never a disturbance."

The woman's German accent was unmistakable—and so pronounced that some of her words became lost in Lynette's untuned ear. "I've come in response to your advertisement," Lynette explained as she removed the piece of newspaper from her handbag. "I hope the position is still open."

The woman laughed softly. "Yes, it is," she answered, then, turning from the window, she said a few words in German. Within seconds, a pretty, golden-haired girl crouched next to the woman and peered through the window.

"Hello," the girl chirped in a dovelike voice. "Please come in."

Lynette tapped William on the shoulder. "Put the kitten down, Sweetheart. It's time to go inside."

Carefully, William replaced the kitten on the wicker chair and patted him on the head. "You stay here, Bock," he whispered. "I'll be right back."

Grinning at her son's parental remark, Lynette lightly placed her hand on William's shoulder and guided him toward the door.

The golden-haired girl, in the meantime, had stepped out onto the veranda and held the screen door open for them. As they neared, Lynette realized that the girl was not a girl at all, but a lovely young woman. Then Lynette noticed her luggage, which she had left carelessly strewn about. "I'm sorry…I shouldn't have left my belongings in such a mess," she apologized, biting her lower lip.

"They're fine," the young woman returned, smiling tenderly. "You must be very tired from your journey. Please, come in and rest, then we can take care of your valises."

"Thank you," Lynette said as she looked up at the woman's pretty face, which glowed with a sweet innocence. Once inside the house, Lynette smiled and breathed in deeply. The delicious aroma of cooking food scented the air, causing her mouth to tingle. But, unfortunately, the fragrance also reminded her of how long it had been since she and her son had enjoyed a hot, home-cooked meal.

"My name is Anna Spreyer," the young woman began. Then, stepping through a doorway to the right of the entrance, she continued, "And this is my mother, Irene Spreyer."

Lynette entered the room and headed toward Anna's mother. "Mrs. Spreyer, it's a pleasure to meet you," she declared, taking the woman's hand in hers. And, as she did, Lynette immediately loosened her grip, fearing that she would break Irene Spreyer's frail limb. "I'm Lynette Chesnay, and this is William, my son…your advertisement said I was supposed to see a Doctor Spreyer."

Anna nodded. "He'll be busy with patients all day today, but my mother and I will be happy to talk with you. Please, sit down and…oh, my goodness…the biscuits!" Anna exclaimed and rushed from the room.

"I'm sorry," Irene Spreyer offered. "My daughter worked at the hospital this morning, and she arrived home later than usual. I told her not to worry about making a large afternoon-meal for just the two of us, but she—"

"Mama, look…it's her," William said as he pointed to the painting easel in front of Mrs. Spreyer.

For the first time since entering the room, Lynette noticed the short easel that sat on a low table in front of Irene Spreyer's chair. Shifting her position to fully view the self-portrait, Lynette spied her own reflection in the mirror that Irene was using—and she immediately shuddered. Although she was tired to the core, Lynette had not realized how much her weariness had grizzled her features. And adding to her haggard appearance was the soot and soil that many, many hours of travel had deposited…everywhere. Even her hair, once tightly braided and rolled into a bun, had untied itself and now framed her face with unruly wisps of black.

Turning away from her travel-worn reflection, Lynette surveyed her surroundings. By the furnishings in the room, she surmised that this had become Irene Spreyer's home within a home—serving as bedroom, sitting room, and painting studio. And, even though a few manly toiletries lay scattered about, the decorations stated that the chamber definitely belonged to the quiet, ailing woman. As she continued her study, Lynette spotted an open Bible lying on the bed and inwardly sighed—the book's ragged edges and loose pages told her more than words ever could. In her heart, Lynette knew Christ was welcome in this home, and she hoped, even more, that she would be accepted for the position.

"Do you see, Mama?" William called out a second time, tugging on her skirt. "She's painting herself."

With a shake of her head, Lynette dragged herself from her reverie and gazed at the portrait again. "Yes, I see, William…Mrs. Spreyer, you are a wonderful art—"

"I'm so sorry, Mrs. Chesnay," Anna announced, reentering the room. "I apologize for my rudeness. I'm running late with our noontime-dinner, and I needed to get the biscuits into the oven. You and William are more than welcome to join us…you both look as if you could use a good meal."

Lynette started to refuse, but her son's pleading eyes and her own grumbling stomach forced her to reconsider. "We would be very grateful…and if you don't mind, I prefer Lynette, instead of Mrs. Chesnay."

"All right, Lynette…please, have a seat," Anna went on as she tried to brush the multicolored cat hair from two upholstered chairs at the foot of the bed. "We have a bit of time while the biscuits are baking—and there is something that we should discuss right away."

The seriousness in Anna Spreyer's voice pressed down upon Lynette, and as a lump formed in her throat, she guided William to the chairs, thankful that she could sit and rest her wobbly legs. "I know you probably didn't expect anyone with a child," she started while twisting the ruby ring on her right hand. "But he's a good boy. He's quiet and—"

Anna shook her head. "I apologize again. I didn't mean to be so vague. William is very welcome. I have six nieces and nephews—believe me, this house is used to children," Anna said, sitting on a large trunk near the painting easel. "No, what we need to discuss is my mother's illness…she has tuberculosis—consumption. Many of the women who've come here have walked out when we mention the consumption…so we've learned to put that matter first."

Lynette nodded and considered Anna's words. She knew how deadly the disease was and that it could pass from one person to another—particularly children. But, without knowing why, she was completely at peace with the prospect of being so close to the ailment. "That's not a problem for us," Lynette replied as she continued to turn the ring around her finger. "And you're sure that William won't bother you?"

With a smile, Anna shook her head again. "Not at all. We have two adjoining rooms upstairs that will be perfect for both of you," she returned. Then, leaning forward, Anna placed her elbows on her knees and asked, "How old are you, William?"

"Five," he answered and stretched out his open hand to confirm the number.

Lynette gently touched his leg. "You'll be five on August fifth…right now you're four."

William nodded, then folded his thumb to his palm and thrust out the remaining four fingers.

As Anna and her mother talked with William, Lynette sighed inwardly. She felt very at ease with both women, and her heart yearned to be a part of their family—but if that was going to happen, they had to know the truth…

Slipping her ruby ring on and off her finger, Lynette tried to gather the right words in her head. "There is something you should know," she declared quietly. "I…I was married, but I'm not a widow…I divorced Mr. Chesnay a year and a half ago." Silence filled the room and Lynette's pulse quickened. "It was not an easy decision to make. I know what the Bible says about marriage, and divorce was the last thing I wanted. But Mr. Chesnay did not believe in obeying God's Commandments—he was unfaithful several times…I don't think William and I…" Lynette hesitated and looked at her son—she hated to put him through the story again.

Suddenly, a soft squeak pulled everyone's attention to the window behind Irene Spreyer—and to the tiny orange kitten that had climbed onto the sill.

"Bock, what are you doing?" William questioned as he hopped off his chair and skipped over to the kitten.

"What did he call him?" Anna asked.

"Bock," Lynette replied sheepishly. "I'm afraid my son just adopted your kitten."

Anna laughed and joined William at the window. "Bock has some food on the back porch…you can take him to his bowl, if you want. Just follow the veranda all the way around and you'll see his dish."

William's face lit up with excitement, and he ran from the room.

"Walk!" Lynette cried, but William had already darted out the front door and onto the porch. Figuring that it was too late to apologize for her son's exuberance,

Lynette watched in silence as William scooped up the kitten and galloped around the corner of the house. "Be gentle with him," she called.

Hopping to a standstill, William peered through one of the side windows. "I will. I promise," he said, then, turning from the window, he began to sing a whispered tune into the kitten's ear.

Lynette tried her best to decipher the words but soon gave up—the song, obviously, was only understood by little boys and kittens.

"You have quite a precious child there, Lynette," Anna offered, propping herself on the now vacant windowsill.

"He's been a wonderful gift…and thank you for giving him a reason to leave the room…William knows what happened—he lived through it—but I just hate making him relive it all the time."

"You're welcome," Anna returned with a luminous smile. "The divorce must have been very hard on him—and you."

Lynette lowered her eyes. "Not as hard as it was to live with Mr. Chesnay. As I said, I know what is taught about marriage, but I don't think William and I would have survived if we had stayed with Mr. Chesnay…and that must have been true, because the Lord opened the door for us to leave…if you need to know more details about what happened…"

Irene Spreyer lifted her hand. "You only have to tell us—" she rasped out before an attack of coughing cut her off.

"Mama?" Anna softly inquired, placing her hand on her mother's shoulder.

"I'm…all…right," Mrs. Spreyer answered between coughs. Then, as the hacking subsided, she continued, "You only have to tell us what you feel comfortable telling us."

Instantly, Lynette's eyes flooded with grateful tears. "Mr. Chesnay can't hurt me the way he used to—but he still causes me quite a bit of grief…he or someone he's hired has to be following my journeys, because he always knows where I'm at. And he sends letters to the boarding house where I'm staying or to my employers…and I soon find myself being snubbed, ridiculed, and jobless."

"How awful," Anna soothed. "I promise you—that won't happen with us."

"But when others learn about my divorce—which I know they eventually will—your family could be placed in the middle of a scandal because of me."

Anna and her mother exchanged sad but amused looks. Then, as her lower lip started to quiver, Anna replied, "God has taught our family how to stand when the winds begin to blow…and we'll stand by you."

Irene Spreyer turned and spoke to her daughter in German. The action caused Lynette's heart to jump into her throat, and she nervously tugged at her ruby ring. Was Mrs. Spreyer disagreeing with Anna's statement? Or was she…

"Are you sure?" Anna questioned her mother.

Irene Spreyer nodded.

Her face aglow, Anna proclaimed, "Mrs. Ches…I mean, Lynette, we would like to offer you the job…we want you to join our family."

Upon hearing the words, Lynette's ring tumbled from her trembling fingers. "But…but…don't you want to check my references or…or something?" she stuttered as she leaned over and picked the ring up off the floor.

Another bout of coughing hit Irene Spreyer, and she patted her daughter's hand.

"We have the only reference we need," Anna said, speaking for her mother. "We have a Heavenly reference—my mother felt in her spirit that you would be coming today."

A chill ran up Lynette's back as the Lord's words resounded in her head…

'Go as far as your money will take you, then I will take you the rest of the way.'

Yes, God did take care of the rest—and she thanked Him for His faithfulness.

"Come," Anna continued, "I'll help you with your things, and while you and William get settled, I'll get our meal ready."

Lynette sat in stunned silence. Her blessings had come so quickly—and perfectly—that she wondered if she was really asleep on a train somewhere, dreaming. "Thank you," she murmured as she rose unsteadily from the chair. "Thank you both…I've seen many miracles in my life—and this is definitely one of them."

❀

Anna Spreyer entered the kitchen and inhaled deeply. "Lynette, what's baking? It smells so good!"

"Just a molasses fruit cake…a sort of thank you—from me to you and your parents."

"You didn't have to do that," Anna returned, settling onto one of the chairs surrounding the kitchen table.

"Yes, I did. You've made us feel so welcome today, and after that wonderful noon-dinner, I wanted to do something special for our supper."

Anna smiled. "Again, you didn't have to…but I must admit, I can't wait to try some of that cake!"

Lynette laughed. "It's one of my favorites…my Aunt Noelle created the recipe," she replied as she rolled some bread dough between her hands.

"And what are these?" Anna inquired, pointing to the little balls of dough on the table.

"Eventually, they'll be cloverleaf herb rolls. My aunt used to make these too."

"Lynette, you shouldn't be going to all this trouble—not on your first night here."

"It's no trouble. I love to bake and it's been a long time since I've been able to make anything—living in boarding houses and all," Lynette said as she took the inch-round sphere she had been forming and placed it next to the others.

Leaning forward, Anna sniffed the herbed dough-balls. "Oh, these smell delectable…your aunt must be an outstanding baker."

"She was," Lynette beamed, pulling more dough from the bowl in front of her. "She even owned her own bakery in Detroit."

"Really?!" Anna exclaimed as she also grabbed some of the mixture and began rolling it between her palms.

Her face still sparkling, Lynette nodded. "Creating edibles has always been a part of my family's heritage…when my grandparents first came to America, they opened a small tavern, and eventually, it was passed along to my father, who expanded it into a very nice restaurant. But Aunt Noelle wasn't interested in the restaurant life—her passion was baking…so, single and scared, she stepped out in faith and started a bakery. She told me that the family just laughed at her. Thankfully, God blessed my aunt with the ability to make foods that people just loved—and the bakery flourished…she ran it until the day she died."

"My goodness…what a lady," Anna sighed, setting her dough-ball on the table.

"Anna, I appreciate your help, but you don't have to…I know you have other things you need to get done."

"I just feel guilty having you in here doing all the work."

"Isn't that why you hired me?"

Anna half-smiled—it was exactly why. Her parents had always said that they didn't want her to bear the burden of caring for her mother and the house all by herself. They wanted her to have the chance to do other things…such as helping at the hospital or at the church…or continuing with school or becoming a seamstress…or enjoying time with her betrothed. She was thankful for Lynette—yet it still felt awkward to have someone else preparing the evening meal.

"Yes, Lynette, you are needed very much, but I'm afraid it's going to take awhile before I'll be able to fully relinquish any of my chores," Anna finally admitted as she picked up more dough. "Besides, I've taken Mrs. Arthur's dress as far as I can. She'll have to try it on before I can finish. It's amazing how much sewing you can get done when you don't have to worry about burning the supper at the same time."

With a chuckle, Lynette patted Anna's hand. "I understand."

"I can't wait to try these rolls," Anna announced, sniffing the fragrant dough once again. "Did you work with your aunt in her bakery?"

Lynette bobbed her head slightly and started to turn the dough-covered ruby ring on her right hand. "My family said I disgraced them when I walked away from my husband, and they wanted nothing to do with me after that. Aunt Noelle was my only supporter. She took William and me into her home, and during that time, she taught me all she knew."

"Thank goodness she was there for you."

"I agree…I wouldn't have made it without her."

"Your aunt's passing must have been very difficult."

"Yes, it was. I miss her and the bakery so much. But Aunt Noelle lives in my heart whenever I make one of her recipes or look at the ring she gave me," Lynette said as she held up her hand.

"What happened to the bakery?"

"Mr. Chesnay happened…my aunt died unexpectedly a few months after my divorce, and he did whatever he could to make things miserable for me—he even charmed the landlord into raising the rent…I just couldn't continue with Mr. Chesnay hovering over me like that."

"That's dreadful," Anna gasped.

"The worst part was the fact that my family cheered his every move."

"I can't even imagine what it was like having your family abandon you like that."

"It was pretty lonely," Lynette returned. "Things are better between us now, but there's still a lot of tension."

After brushing a few strands of hair away from her face with the back of her dough-coated hand, Anna shook her head sympathetically. "How awful for you…I know how much it hurts when my sisters come against me—and you went through so much more."

"Your sisters have hurt you?"

"Yes, at times…oh, they've never pulled their love away as your family did, but they are extremely critical of the things I do…although, I sometimes think they do it just to harass me."

"That's surprising…you and your parents are so close and open, I just figured that…that your whole family would be that way."

"Not always," Anna murmured. "My sisters are a unique foursome. When they find something they don't like, they'll just peck it to death. And, to make matters worse, they've recently developed a real love for the society life…if you know what I mean."

"Quite well. I've dealt with my share of 'Pharisees' since my divorce."

"Yes!" Anna exclaimed, sitting up straight. "That's exactly what they act like… right now they keep picking at my fiance. But Peter's been very patient with them. He says he's been criticized so much lately that he just tosses my sisters' remarks in the garbage with all the others."

Placing another little ball of dough on the table, Lynette looked quizzically at Anna. "Peter?"

"Yes, Peter Leighton, my fiance. He should be coming by later for supper…I'll introduce you then."

"You…you're not seeing a man called James Wild?"

"James Wild? Goodness, no. Why did you think that?"

"When I was in town, trying to find my way here, he came up to me and offered me his carriage. He asked me to give 'my sweet Anna' his regards. I just assumed that you two were courting," Lynette replied as she gathered the last bits of dough from the bowl.

Anna exhaled loudly, and as she stood, she took the empty bowl from the table and cradled it in her arms. "James Wild is a very kind man, but we aren't courting. I met him last year at a party. We had one dance, and since then he keeps acting as if he were my beau—and he keeps ignoring the fact that I already have a fiance."

"Have you tried to talk to Mr. Wild?"

Strolling to the dry sink, Anna placed the bowl on the counter. "Yes. And so has my father and Peter has too," she said, pumping some water into a small metal tub in the sink. Then, as she immersed her hands and rubbed the bread dough from her fingers, Anna's thoughts drifted to the long-haired James B. Wild, the third. At first, she had been flattered by his misguided attention, but the man's constant chasing had become annoying—like a giant gnat that she had to keep shooing away. "James Wild comes from a very wealthy family, and he's used to getting his way," Anna went on. "He just doesn't seem to understand the meaning of the word 'no.'"

Joining Anna at the sink, Lynette also plunged her hands into the cold water and scrubbed the dough from her hands. "Be careful with Mr. Wild," she offered. "From what you've told me, he's a young, arrogant man with a child's outlook and a ready supply of money—that combination can be dangerous."

"No, James isn't like that. He's definitely spoiled, but at the same time, he's extremely considerate and generous…such as when he offered you his carriage or when he donates money to the hospital and churches here in town. Because of him, Sandorville now has two more doctors and a new apothecary…James is a good man—he just doesn't know when to quit."

Wiping her hands on her apron, Lynette nodded, but her expression remained skeptical. "I found the cake pans in there," she said, pointing to a cupboard near the stove. "But I didn't see any muffin pans...do you keep them someplace else?"

Anna frowned and dried her hands with a towel. "They should have been...oh, that's right," she continued, snapping her fingers. "My sister Marion borrowed them, and I'll bet we'll find them over here." Moving to the cupboard next to the dry sink, Anna reached down and yanked at the doors until they opened. "We don't use this cupboard in the summer because the doors stick...but Marion puts things where she wants to put them, not where they belong," Anna explained as both she and Lynette knelt on the floor and peered into the cupboard.

"Here they are," Lynette proclaimed, grabbing the tins. Then, as Anna pushed the doors closed, Lynette added quietly, "Please...keep your eyes open around Mr. Wild."

Anna smiled and shook her head. "He's a sweet man...really," she returned, not understanding why Lynette had suddenly become so concerned about James Wild. "But I do know that James' chasing does have to end...it makes Peter so angry—and he has enough to deal with right now."

"Yes, you said that Peter was facing a lot of criticism."

"And he deserves none of it."

"Why? What happened?"

Pain instantly etched itself into Anna's features as scenes from the past year flashed through her head. What happened? If only the answer could be as simple as the question.

"I'm sorry," Lynette put in as she pulled herself to her feet. "I didn't mean to pry."

"No, it's not that," Anna said, also standing. "It's just that so much has happened, I'm not sure where to begin." And, as she and Lynette returned to the table with the muffin tins, Anna considered the task of summarizing the last twelve months—and shuddered. All the events had combined to form one giant storm that whirled around her, and it was almost impossible to see the individual pieces anymore. "You see, a year ago, Peter exposed some wrongdoings in a factory here in Sandorville."

"That was good...wasn't it?" Lynette asked as she started to grease the muffin tins.

"Oh, yes, it was. And I'm so proud of what he did—Peter helped a lot of people out of a horrible situation. It's just that...well, since then, we've had one dreadful thing after another come at us...legal battles and newspaper stories and gossips...it's like a continuous barrage of waves. Those waves have changed our lives—and they're still rushing at us..."

"My goodness! Why...why have you had so much trouble?"

"Because Peter ended up uncovering much more than he or anyone else ever expected…"

Lynette's jaw dropped open. "What…what did he find?"

"He found evil…and lost his brother."

"I don't understand…Anna, what happened?"

With a faint groan, Anna resumed her seat at the table. "Last year, Peter and his brother, Daven, came here to help out a friend—the owner of the factory I told you about—Karl Rheinhardt…" As Anna heard the story emerge from her own lips, the spinning storm that surrounded her began to slow for the first time in a year—and it felt good. "Mr. Rheinhardt believed that someone was using his company's name to sell their own furniture, so Peter came to find out what was going on. He worked as Karl's assistant, and Daven went to work in the factory—but they didn't let anyone know that they knew each other. That way, they could attack the problem from both directions."

"Did you know Peter before he came here?" Lynette inquired as she dropped three of the little spheres of dough into each of the buttered muffin cups.

"No…the Lord brought us together soon after Peter arrived…I don't mean for this to sound trite, but I loved him the minute I saw him. And I think there was a reason for that…I think God had us fall in love so fast because He knew Peter would soon need the love and support of a family."

"So what did Peter and Daven find out?"

"Well, the culprit ended up being Karl's own daughter, Lorelei. She was secretly working with the salesman and the foreman to make special pieces of furniture on the side…they had a miniature business going on inside the factory."

"Why would she do that?"

Anna shrugged. "Lorelei said she wanted to prove to her father that she had as much business sense as her late brothers and that she was capable of running the company."

"Too bad she didn't have enough common sense to know right from wrong," Lynette muttered, squeezing the last three dough-balls into a muffin cup. Then, pushing the filled tins together, she covered them with a thin towel. "And Mr. Rheinhardt had no idea that his daughter was doing this?"

"No, he was blind to all the atrocities that were going on."

Sinking onto one of the kitchen chairs, Lynette's brow furrowed in confusion. "All the atrocities? There were more?"

Anna bowed her head. "Lorelei was only a small part of the problem. Peter also discovered that the foreman, Quentin Fetch, was doing even more things on his own—worse things. Mr. Fetch would cheat the men on their wages, then beat them or threaten their families if they told anyone…or he'd offer the men loans, then attach so many conditions that they ended up owing him double."

"Didn't…didn't anyone try to stop him?"

"They wanted to, but Mr. Fetch ran the factory like a prison. He even hired two men, Frank Hallam and Leland Bryce, to act as guards and keep the men from trying to get out of their jail…Mr. Fetch had no intentions of giving up his power—even if that meant committing murder."

"Oh, my goodness!"

"And that's exactly what he did…Mr. Fetch found out that Daven and Peter were working together to stop him…so he…he…" Anna quickly blinked her eyes, trying to keep the tears from forming.

"What'd he do, Anna?"

"He shot and killed Daven," she answered, her voice faltering. Then the tears began to fall as she remembered the moment her father closed Daven's crystal-blue eyes—forever.

Lynette gasped and the kitchen filled with silence, except for Anna's sobs.

Finally, with a heavy sigh, Anna raised her head and wiped her face. "Daven was a very sweet and talented man," she put in. "That's his portrait hanging in the parlor…Peter still blames himself for his brother's death…it's been so hard on him."

"The poor dear."

"Please, Lynette, don't mention Daven's name around Peter…it…it upsets him so much."

"That's not a healthy way to live—for either of you."

"I know," Anna replied with a deep, quivering breath. "It's just easier right now…in the past year, while he's been trying to revive the factory, Peter's had to endure courtrooms and prosecutors and newspaper men and whispers behind his back…I just don't have the heart to force Daven on him."

"All of that must have been difficult for you too."

Anna nodded and dabbed at the last of her tears with her apron. "At times, very difficult…but Peter's used himself as a shield and kept most of it from ever reaching us…I worry about him so."

"Just remember that Christ—not your worry—will keep Peter safe."

Her eyes opening wide, Anna exclaimed, "My mother told me the same thing right before you came! Well, she used different words, but it was the same message."

"Then you have been worrying too much…about Peter—and your mother."

With a sad smile, Anna averted her gaze.

"How long has your mother been sick?"

"All her life it seems. She's lived with consumption for a very long time, but since May, she's taken a turn for the worst."

"We'll take some time later and pray for her…then you won't have to fret so much."

Anna heard the genuine concern in Lynette's voice and was warmed by it. She missed being able to share her concerns and fears with her usual confidant—her mother. And, ordinarily, she could confide in her father, but lately, he kept his thoughts and prayers about her mother's failing health to himself. Peter, also, had volunteered to listen, yet she declined, not wanting to burden him with more problems. With a deep breath, Anna looked upward and voicelessly thanked God for sending Lynette into their midst.

"I appreciate the offer," Anna returned as she slowly rose from her chair and stepped over to the stove. "It's almost time for Mama's tonic. I'll show you how to make the tea—she should have a cup in the morning and one in the evening."

"Her tonic?"

"Yes, my father and brother have been experimenting with different teas, trying to find something to help her fight the consumption," Anna explained, moving the kettle from the back of the stove to the hot burners over the flames.

"Is your brother a doctor too?"

"He's studying to be one…he was going to school in Ann Arbor but decided to continue his education in Germany instead."

"And has the tea helped your mother?"

"Very much. Papa's also making sure that she gets plenty of fresh air. That's why we moved their room downstairs—that corner room has the best ventilation. And, every evening, they go for a short stroll, then sit on the porch swing until supper…this has been one of Mama's best years—except for the last couple of months."

"Your father seems to be a very devoted husband."

"He is," Anna replied with a lilt of pride in her voice. "He's making sure that they spend as much time together as possible…I think they both know that there isn't…"

With the kitten draped around his neck like a stole, William meandered into the kitchen, and Anna decided to let her last comment remain unfinished.

"Is supper ready?" William asked. "Bock's hungry."

Anna glanced at Lynette and winked. "Bock's hungry."

Lynette smiled in return.

"The rolls have to rise and then bake," Anna went on as she walked over to the boy and tousled his hair. "Have you been having fun with Grandpa Otto and Grandma Irene?"

William nodded, stroking the kitten's paws. "We all went for a walk. Then they watched me play with Bock—that's when Peter came and I showed him my new kitten."

"Peter?" Anna asked, gazing down the hallway. "Is he here?"

"Uh huh, he's talkin' to Grandpa Otto and Grandma Irene about a fire…Mama? Can me and Bock go watch the chickens 'til supper's ready?"

"May Bock and I watch the chickens," Lynette corrected. "And, yes, you may… but I don't want you—or Bock—to leave the yard."

"We won't…I promise," William declared as he ambled toward the back door.

"Well, I guess Peter's here," Anna said with a smile. "Come, I'll introduce you."

As she led the way to the front of the house, Anna could hear Peter talking to her parents, then she glimpsed his tall, muscular frame through the screen door—and her heart skipped a beat. Even after a year of knowing Peter Leighton, her skin would still goose-pimple at the sight of him—but this time, something new sent an excited shiver through her…

Peter's once mustached face was now clean-shaven, and that, along with the slight dusting of premature gray in his freshly barbered hair, made him more dashing than she had ever seen before.

"Is that your Peter?" Lynette whispered as they lingered at the door.

Anna nodded.

"He's very handsome."

Anna bobbed her head again.

"He's older than you, isn't he?"

"Yes…why?"

"How many years?"

"Eight…why?"

"Hmm…oh, no reason…you two complement each other very well."

Anna smiled, yet she still wondered why Peter's age was such a concern for Lynette. Then, returning her attention to her fiancé, Anna noticed that he kept his right hand hidden behind his back as he rested against the porch railing. The concealed arm sparked her curiosity, and Anna started to push the screen door open but froze when she caught a fragment of his conversation. Suddenly, as she realized that there had been more trouble, the storm circling around her intensified, and fear wrapped its cold arms around her shoulders. Would they ever get a reprieve from the turmoil that constantly plagued them?

"Are you okay?" Lynette asked in a hushed voice.

With a slight nod, Anna took a deep breath and pushed the door open. "I think you left something at the factory," she announced, touching her lip.

A smile spread across Peter's face, then it immediately fell into a frown. "You don't like it," he said, stepping away from the porch railing.

"Yes, I do—but you never said you were going to get rid of the mustache."

Peter shrugged. "I just didn't want to look like a character from a dime novel anymore."

"I think he looks very charming," Mrs. Spreyer proclaimed from the porch swing. "So do I," Anna added. "Your hair looks nice too."

Peter responded with a boyish grin, and bringing his right hand from behind his back, he held out a bouquet of flowers.

Anna released a squeal of delight as the flowers—and Peter's thoughtfulness—melted the fear that enveloped her. With a happy, unsteady hand, Anna grasped the flowers. "What's...what's the occasion?"

"You."

Anna smiled at the word, but it was Peter's steady gaze that sent a tingle of delight racing through her body. Raising the bouquet, Anna hoped to hide the blush that she felt spreading across her face. Then, as she breathed in each flower's fragrance, she heard her father speak a few gruff words in German. Not quite hearing, Anna lifted her eyes and studied her parents, who sat, hand in hand, on the swing. Quietly, the doctor repeated his statement, and this time, Anna let out a small gasp, realizing that she had completely forgotten about Lynette. Circling, Anna grabbed her friend's hand. "I'm sorry," she murmured.

Lynette beamed with understanding. "It's all right," she whispered in return. "I know what it's like to be in love."

"Peter," Anna went on, trying to divert everyone's attention from her impropriety, "this is Lynette Chesnay. She came in answer to our advertisement...Lynette, this is Peter Leighton, my fiance."

As the two greeted each other, Anna moved next to the swing and took her father's outstretched hand. "Lynette also has a son," Anna put in.

Peter grinned. "Yes, we've met...I'm glad the kitten found a friend."

"He certainly has," Lynette laughed. "Those two have been inseparable since we arrived."

Still enamored with her fiance's new visage, Anna continued to stare at his every move. And, as she saw him rub his temple and squint his eyes, she knew he was being tortured, once again, by a headache. Immediately, Anna glanced at her father, who squeezed her hand—he had also noticed.

"It's been so nice to meet you, Mr. Leighton," Lynette remarked, "but I need to check on our supper...and my son."

"Thank you for helping us," Peter replied, and lifting Lynette's hand to his lips, he gave her a light kiss.

"I'm the thankful one," she returned. Then, pivoting toward Anna, Lynette questioned, "Would you like me to take your flowers inside and put them in some water?"

The word 'water' poked at Anna, and as she suddenly remembered that she had placed the kettle on the hot burners, she exclaimed, "Goodness! I forgot about the tea!" Realizing that her statement made little sense, Anna added, "I was going to show Lynette how to make Mama's tea."

"Maybe, when you're done with that, we could take a short walk before supper?"

Peter's unexpected invitation thrilled Anna to the core—time alone with her fiance had become almost nonexistent in the past few months. And now, with Lynette's arrival, she could actually say yes...but was it fair to leave Lynette alone on her first day?

"I'll be fine, Anna," Lynette murmured in her ear.

Surprised, Anna turned to face Lynette. "How did you..."

"Tell him yes."

With a bewildered but pleased smile, Anna nodded and circled back toward Peter. "I'd love to go for a walk with you...the tea won't take long."

As he watched Anna and Lynette disappear into the house, Peter inwardly sighed, grateful that someone had finally come to offer his fiancee some relief. Anna had become increasingly overworked since the recent decline in her mother's health, and his offers of assistance were refused or misunderstood. He just couldn't figure out what kind of help Anna wanted or needed, but thankfully, God knew.

Closing his eyes, Peter massaged the left side of his face. He realized the walk with Anna would increase the throbbing in his head—and that each step might push him into losing his meager lunch—but he had vowed to himself, as his long hair drifted to the barber shop floor, that he would no longer neglect the people or the things that he cared about. It was a promise he planned to keep, in spite of his headaches.

"Do you want some laudanum?"

The voice yanked Peter from his thoughts and his eyes sprang open. Eventually, his vision cleared, and he peered at Doctor Spreyer, who now stood in front of him. He hated relying on the doctor's laudanum, but it was the only thing that would ease the pain. "Yeah...I'll take it home though."

Slowly, a smile emerged on the doctor's husky, bearded face. "I also have a surprise for you. I sent away for something...and I think they'll help."

"More herbs?"

Doctor Spreyer shook his head and smiled again. "You'll never guess," he replied, then vanished into the house.

Peter looked to Mrs. Spreyer for an explanation, but she only answered with a grin. Patting the empty seat next to her on the swing, she beckoned, "Pay-ter, come...sit."

Stepping over to the swing, Peter sat next to his future mother-in-law. "How are you today?" he inquired, taking her hand.

"Very good. I'm happy that Lynette has come."

"At least something good happened today," he mumbled in return.

"Just remember, Pay-ter, all things work together for good to them that love God."

"So having our lumber burned was a good thing?"

"No, it doesn't mean that all things will be good…but they will work toward good. God can take any wicked act, turn it around, and make it work for His purpose."

Peter nodded.

"Sometimes the Lord will reveal to us why things happen the way they do…and sometimes he won't. We might never know the 'why' of things until we're in Heaven with Him. But we need to trust that God knows what He is doing."

Peter half-smiled and nodded again.

"And when the Lord needs us to go down a certain path, He will first show us the way, then wait for us to walk down it on our own…" she continued until a bout of coughing interrupted her.

While Mrs. Spreyer struggled to get her cough under control, Peter slid sideward on the swing so he could face her. Between his headache, her heavy accent, and the imagery, he was finding it very difficult to keep up with the meaning of her words, and he hoped the new position would help his concentration.

"But, if you tarry," she finished in a raspy voice, "God may give you a push to get you started down His path…and you might not like how He pushes you."

Peter's smile faded as Irene Spreyer finished speaking. As difficult as it was to understand her story, he clearly heard her switch from the generalized 'us' to the very personal 'you.' His eyes narrowing, Peter crossed his arms and shook his head. "I've tried to walk where the Lord wants me to go," he muttered. "I know the factory can't survive without God's help—that's why I've always tried to follow His guidance with every decision I make for the business. I don't understand what you're saying…I haven't procrastinated," Peter went on, his voice rising. "If the burning of my wood was supposed to push me down a certain path—"

"No, Pay-ter, I'm not talking about the factory," she cut in, laying her hand on his arm. "I'm talking about your unwillingness to remember Daven."

The name hit Peter like a slap across the face, and he pulled away from Irene's grasp. First Jaxson…now Mrs. Spreyer…why couldn't they just leave things as they were?

"You need to accept the bad, so you can remember the good," she went on.

Without answering, Peter stood up and stared at Irene Spreyer with anger, hurt, and dread. Jaxson's slip of the tongue had been accidental, but Mrs. Spreyer said his brother's name on purpose…she knew something was going to happen…

"Here you go, Son," Doctor Spreyer's voice boomed from behind him.

Startled, Peter spun around.

"What's wrong?" the doctor asked.

Finding no words, Peter just shook his head.

"Come into my office and let me take a look at you."

"No," Peter choked out, then, looking at Mrs. Spreyer, he said it again—firmly. "No!"

Instantly, the doctor's eyebrows knitted together. "Did I miss something?"

Peter forced a smile. "No, everything's fine," he lied, "but I think I should go home…my head's about to explode."

"You can stay in my office for the night…both beds are free."

"No."

Doctor Spreyer sighed. "All right—I know better than to fight with you…here's your laudanum."

Peter took the small, brown bottle and slipped it into an inside pocket of his frock coat.

"There's enough in there for one dose."

"Thanks."

"And here," Doctor Spreyer added as he gave Peter a hand-size, rectangular case.

"What's this?"

"The surprise I told you about. They just came today. You'll have to let me know if they do you any good."

Peter's forehead furrowed and he peered at the doctor. "What is it?"

"Well, open it," Doctor Spreyer laughed.

Carefully, Peter lifted the case's hinged cover. "Spectacles?" he questioned, removing the wire-rimmed eyeglasses from the case.

"In a way…try them."

Snapping the cover closed, Peter shoved the case into his pocket with the laudanum, then he slid the glasses onto his face. Immediately, day turned to dusk as Peter looked through the dark-colored lenses.

"Until we figure out what's going on with your headaches, I thought these eyeglasses would help relieve your light sensitivity."

"How do they feel?" Mrs. Spreyer called from the swing.

"Good…thank you, Otto," Peter said with a genuine smile. Not only did the glasses ease his strained eyes, but they also distracted Mrs. Spreyer from their previous conversation.

As Peter scanned the darkened front yard, he noticed a carriage slowing in front of the house. Eventually, the coach halted and a young blonde-haired man stepped out. At first, Peter thought nothing of the newcomer, but then his attention was drawn to the stranger's mannerisms. Walking to the edge of the porch, Peter lowered his tinted glasses and continued to watch as the young fellow extended his hand and helped an elderly—and oddly familiar—gentleman exit the vehicle.

It took the old gentleman a few minutes to get his balance, but in time, the two men strolled onto the plank walkway. And, as they inched their way toward the house, a chill shivered through Peter. He wanted to turn away from the approaching visitors, and yet he couldn't stop staring at their rugged features…and their crystal-blue eyes. Suddenly, the words that Irene Spreyer had spoken, just moments before, repeated themselves in his head…

'God may give you a push to get you started down His path…and you might not like how He pushes you.'

Her prophesy, as usual, had come true. Peter knew, in his heart, that the new-comers were his 'push,' and Irene was right—he didn't like it. He didn't want to be shoved into remembering his brother…not yet. That was one memory he longed to keep tightly locked away.

"Those eyes…could they be…" Doctor Spreyer mused aloud in amazement.

"There's little doubt," Peter mumbled as he began to massage his left palm with his right thumb.

"Good day," the young blonde-haired man announced as he and his companion reached the porch's stoop. "My name is Erik Hanson and this is my uncle, Lars Nilsson," he continued with an unmistakable Swedish accent. "We are looking for a man named Peter Leighton. Do you know where we may find him?"

Why Lord? Peter wondered. Why now? Why did these men have to come today? Then a thought leaped into this head…he could just say he didn't know Peter Leighton…

A nudge from Doctor Spreyer dragged Peter from his reverie, and he realized that he had no choice but to confront Erik's question. "I'm Peter Leighton."

The young man smiled and spoke to his uncle in Swedish. Lars Nilsson nodded, then also smiled.

"Welcome to our home, gentlemen. I'm Otto Spreyer. Please, join us," the doctor put in, motioning for the two visitors to come up onto the veranda.

As young Erik helped his uncle climb the porch steps, Doctor Spreyer jostled Peter's arm. The gesture, Peter guessed, was a silent reprimand for his rudeness. Glancing at the doctor, Peter shook his head. He had no desire to meet the two Swedish men with the azure eyes—they were, beyond a doubt, relatives of his late stepfather, and they would force him to awaken the memories he had worked so hard to keep dormant.

Once on the veranda, Erik shook Peter's hand. "We tried to find you in Bradlee, but your neighbors told us that you moved down here, to Sandorville… luckily for us, the carriage driver we hired at the depot—I think he said his name was Charlie—said he knew of you and that you'd probably be here at this time…and you are!"

"Yes," Peter returned, his jaw clenching, "I'll have to remember to thank Charlie for that."

"We are so happy that we found you…we were hoping you could tell us where Anders Nilsson is."

Peter's brow crinkled in confusion. "Who?"

"Anders Nilsson…Anders is my other uncle," Erik answered, then, placing his hand on Lars' shoulder, he went on, "and his younger brother. We know, from Anders' letters, that he came to Michigan and that he had a wife and son, but she died. And then he and his son moved to Bradlee, where he later married a widow named Lorraine Leighton, who had a son named Peter. We searched for Anders in Bradlee, but no one knew him…that's when we decided to find—"

Lars Nilsson interrupted his nephew with a few lines of Swedish while pointing at Peter.

"My uncle fears that we have made a mistake…you are the Peter Leighton that we've been seeking, aren't you? Anders did marry your mother, didn't he?"

Peter sighed resignedly. If only the doctor and Mrs. Spreyer weren't behind him on the porch…he could so easily be rid of Erik and Lars with a simple 'no.' "Yes, he was my stepfather," Peter replied, thumbing his palm again, "but he must have changed his name…I knew him as Tait Ashby."

"Ahh…so that's why we couldn't find Anders Nilsson!"

With a hard tug at Erik's sleeve, Lars once again chattered at his nephew.

"I'm sorry," Erik explained, "my uncle doesn't understand English. Please give me a moment to tell him that we have found our Peter."

As Erik translated the news, Peter slowly removed his dark glasses and slid them back into their case.

"We are both so happy," Erik announced. "When you didn't recognize Anders' name we thought—"

Waving his hand, Peter cut off his stepcousin. "I knew you were related to Tait, uh, my stepfather. The family resemblance is unmistakable…and those eyes—they're a very prominent legacy."

Erik nodded and laughed. "Where is he? Your Tait Ashby and our Anders?"

Peter moistened his suddenly dry lips. "Tait died…seven years ago."

The smile fell from Erik's face, and his crystal eyes started to water. "No…no…my uncle needed to speak with him…how…how did he…"

"His heart just stopped."

Lars grabbed Erik's arm and shook it again. Gazing sadly at his uncle, the young man haltingly translated Peter's revelation. As he listened, Lars' countenance paled—

and without warning, he lost his balance, prompting both Erik and Peter to reach out and steady him.

"Uncle Lars is not feeling well," Erik said quietly. "He needs to rest. We should go and find a hotel or boarding house."

"Nonsense," Doctor Spreyer declared. "You both can stay here."

"No, we couldn't impose on—"

"Mr. Hanson, I'm a doctor. I'll be able to tend to your uncle, and besides, we are all family…Peter is engaged to marry my daughter."

Erik hesitated, then, looking at his uncle's sagging shoulders, he nodded. "Thank you…if you'll help Uncle Lars, I'll give leave to the driver and get our things from the carriage."

While Doctor Spreyer pulled the screen door open, Peter wrapped his arm around Lars and guided his stepuncle into the house.

"Take him to my office," the doctor directed.

Tightening his grip, Peter pointed down the hall toward the kitchen, and the older man bobbed his head in understanding—but as they shuffled past the parlor doorway, Lars yanked himself from Peter's grasp and hurried into the room.

"What's wrong?" Doctor Spreyer asked as he and Irene joined Peter at the parlor entrance.

"I don't know…he just pulled away." Then Peter realized why. Lars had seen the painted portrait of Daven that hung above the parlor fireplace. Rubbing his left palm, Peter closed his eyes as the old man pointed at the picture and wildly yammered in Swedish.

"What's going on?" Anna questioned as she and Lynette emerged from the kitchen. "Who is that?"

Peter's eyes fluttered open. "Why that's Tait Ashby's brother," he said with a touch of angry sarcasm.

The announcement caused Anna to shudder, and she almost dropped the teacup she was holding. "His brother! But how…how did he—"

"Is there something wrong with Uncle Lars?" Erik chimed in as he dropped his luggage and crammed himself into the hallway with the others.

"And that's Tait's nephew," Peter added, using his thumb to point at Erik.

"All right. All right," Doctor Spreyer bellowed. "I don't think Mr. Nilsson needs all six of us watching him and standing here like sardines. Anna, why don't you and Lynette take Mama into the kitchen, so she can have her tea in peace. And, Erik, would you please try to calm your uncle and find out what he's saying?"

As everyone dispersed, Doctor Spreyer entered the parlor and motioned for Peter to follow. Massaging his hand, Peter shook his head and remained in the doorway—he just couldn't get his legs to move inside the room.

"Uncle Lars wants to know who this is," Erik proclaimed as he gestured toward the portrait. "He says it looks like his brother, Anders…many years ago."

Peter lifted his eyes and gazed at the picture for the first time in almost a year. "That's Tait's, uh, Anders' son…my brother, Daven," Peter choked out, averting his eyes from the accusing picture.

After Erik's translation, Lars then pointed to four different pieces of carved furniture—the only remnants of Daven's remarkable talent.

"And he wants to know who carved these two tables, the bookcase, and those shelves," Erik continued. "Uncle Lars says that it looks like Anders' work."

Peter shook his head again. "Daven."

Understanding the name, Lars nodded and caressed the finely carved handiwork.

His eyes darting from one carved piece to the next, Peter tried to swallow the growing knot in his throat. He had been so grateful that the Spreyers had asked to shelter his brother's furniture—their parlor kept the pieces safe…and out of his sight.

Shuffling over to the doorway, Lars faced Peter and motioned toward Daven's portrait while speaking in Swedish. Scrutinizing his stepuncle's weathered features and sad, sky-blue eyes, Peter frowned. He knew what Lars wanted to know—even without Erik's interpretation. Then, in Peter's mind, Lars' visage slowly transformed into Tait's…

'Why?' his stepfather's voice echoed inside his head. 'Why did you involve Daven in such a dangerous task? Why didn't you protect your brother? Why did you let Quentin Fetch kill my son?'

"My uncle wants to know where Daven is…he would like to meet him."

"What?" Peter murmured as he came out of his trance.

"My uncle wants to know where Daven is…he would like to meet him," Erik repeated.

Each word stabbed at Peter's aching head, and he looked pleadingly at Doctor Spreyer.

The doctor cleared his throat. "No…you need to tell them."

Peter's jaw clenched tightly. He was getting extremely tired of everyone telling him what he 'needed' to do regarding his brother's memory. And, as he peered at the three men who anxiously waited for him to speak, he decided that he had been pushed far enough for one day. Whipping around on his heel, Peter stomped to the front entrance, shoved the screen door open, and stepped out onto the porch.

Finally free—and ignoring both the doctor's shouts for him to return and the pounding in his head—Peter marched down the stairs and onto the plank walkway.

He knew that he was being rude and selfish, but with each hollow thud of his boots, he became more and more determined to keep the memories of his brother undisturbed.

❊Three❊

Grabbing the thin rail, Lynette tried to steady herself on the wagon's seat as it rattled along the decaying wooden road.

"It will end soon," Doctor Spreyer hollered over the wagon's chatter. "The brick paving starts right up ahead."

Lynette grinned and glanced over her shoulder. William, who was sitting in the bed of the wagon, wildly giggled as he bounced around like water on a hot griddle. Her smile widening, Lynette shouted back, "It's fine…I think my son is actually enjoying it." Finally, the wagon turned a corner, lurched one last time, then settled into a smooth roll.

"I apologize," the doctor offered, "but that's the only road to the Taylor house."

"That's quite all right," Lynette returned, adjusting her bustle so she could sit farther back on the seat.

"That was fun!" William called. "Can we do it again?"

The doctor laughed. "I don't think this wagon will survive many more trips on that road…I think whoever decided to pave a road with wooden blocks should have to travel over that one—forever!"

Lynette nodded in agreement.

"Now there, in that empty field," Doctor Spreyer continued as he gestured with his hand, "is where the open-air market takes place every Saturday."

"The open-air market?"

"Yes, it started out as a place where the local farmers came to sell their produce, but now, we have games, a brass band, homemade goods…and of course, lots of food. It's becoming quite an all-day event…people from all over the area come to enjoy the festivities."

"It sounds wonderful."

"We try our best to never miss it," he replied, then, reining the horse to a stop on the edge of the road, the doctor swept his arm from side to side. "That's Second Street."

"I thought things were looking familiar," Lynette said. "That means the depot should be straight ahead."

The doctor nodded and pointed to the right. "The Post Office is down Second on the corner of Cherry Street...I can take you—it's not that far."

"No, Doctor Spreyer, we're fine. I should learn my way around my new home."

"I didn't get to tell you last night, but I'm very happy that you've joined our family. Anna's been so busy with Mama and all...I'm glad she finally has someone to help her."

"I'm honored to be a part of your family, Doctor."

"Please, it's Otto...I just wish your first day hadn't been so...so eventful...and I wish I could tell you that yesterday was an unusual day, but...well, we've had a very trying year."

"Anna told me some of what's happened."

"I hope it won't change your mind about us."

Lynette turned slightly and studied the doctor. She knew, from his tone, that he and his family must have experienced a great deal of snubbing because of their troubles—just as she did because of her divorce. "No, it won't change my mind," she said firmly. "I know what it's like to have tribulations and how it feels to have people desert you because of them. I wouldn't do that to your family."

Doctor Spreyer smiled broadly. "My wife was right about you...you do have a warm spirit." Dropping the reins, the doctor climbed down from the seat and walked to the other side of the wagon. "You should really have an escort," he remarked, holding out his hand.

The edges of Lynette's lips curled upward at the doctor's comment—it wasn't a rebuke or a demand, just a statement from a traditional gentleman who had learned to live with independent women. "But I do have an escort...William," she returned as she took the doctor's hand and worked her way down from the seat.

The doctor chuckled. "Ah, that's right," he replied, moving to the back of the wagon. "I bet you take good care of your mama, don't you?" And, as he asked the question, Doctor Spreyer lifted William out of the wagon's bed and placed him next to Lynette.

"Yep," William answered as he put his hand into Lynette's. "Me and God take real good care of her."

"God and I," Lynette added.

"God and I take real good care of her," William repeated, correcting himself. "And now, Bock can help too."

The doctor frowned and studied William. "You did leave that kitten at home, didn't you?"

Wide-eyed, William looked up and tried his best not to smile. Then a large lump under his jacket began to move and he giggled.

"William!" Lynette scolded. "You were told to leave Bock at home."

"But he wanted to come, Mama."

"Thankfully, we don't have many places to go to," Lynette sighed.

"Next time," the doctor said, lightly tapping William on the shoulder, "Bock stays home."

Instantly, as if he heard his name, the kitten's orange head popped up over the top button of William's jacket.

"Do you understand?" Doctor Spreyer continued as he scratched the kitten between the ears.

"Yes, Grandpa Otto."

"Should we set a place for you at the luncheon today, Doctor Sprey…Otto?"

He nodded. "I'm making my rounds of the homebound this morning. Unless something comes up, I should be there…I want to check on Mr. Nilsson anyway."

"He's not well, is he?"

"I'm afraid not."

"Do you think Peter'll come back to talk with him?"

"I really don't know," Doctor Spreyer replied with a shrug. "That poor boy's been through so much…I think it would do him some good to talk about Daven, but he may not be ready for that yet." Tipping his hat, the doctor climbed back onto the wagon and picked up the reins. "If anything should happen while you are in town, just head north on Main 'til Oak Road and go to the Rheinhardt Furniture Showroom. Whether Peter's there or not, they can get word to him." Then, with a light tap of the reins and a few words of German, the doctor urged his horse to a slow walk. "Be careful," he called as the wagon glided down the street.

Lynette smiled and exhaled. It had been a long time since she felt the soothing warmth of a father's concern. Her divorce had created such a deep rift in her relationship with her father. And, although the gap had been eventually bridged, there were still, unfortunately, some weak spots between them.

Opening her handbag, Lynette pulled out the letter that had taken her most of the previous evening to write and clenched it tightly in her hand. After witnessing the Spreyers' closeness and deep love for each other, Lynette hoped and prayed that the letter to her parents would be a soothing salve—one that would help heal her broken family. She longed for the day when she could talk openly with her relatives about her divorce…and for the day when she could be confident, once again, that they loved and respected her…and for the day when she could stop ending her letters with the words 'please don't reveal my whereabouts to anyone—especially Mr. Chesnay.'

A quiet 'meow' drew Lynette's attention to William. The kitten had, once again, poked his head outside of William's jacket and was licking him on the chin. She wanted to be angry with William's disobedience, but she couldn't. They had lost so much in the past few years that his attachment to the kitten was understandable.

"If you do this again, William," she said sternly, "the kitten will not sleep in your room for a whole week…do you hear me?"

William replied with a quick, worried nod.

"Now, let's go find the Post Office."

<hr />

With a steadfast march, Peter headed toward the Rheinhardt Factory as quickly as he could. Although he knew a horsecar or carriage would be faster, he just couldn't resist a brisk walk—especially when it was headache-free. He had been both pleased and surprised that he had awakened with no pain. His headaches usually didn't depart so easily, and he wondered what made the difference this time. Was it the dark glasses? Was the laudanum stronger than usual? Or was it the fact that he had stepped away from his Swedish tormentors the night before? Either way, his headache had subsided, and he was determined to do everything to keep it from returning—which included using his new glasses and keeping plenty of distance between himself and Lars Nilsson.

As he entered the factory's front yard, Peter paused and gazed at the two-story brick building. Through the large and frequent windows, he could see the men inside rushing from one station to another trying to keep the furniture projects on schedule. He wanted, so badly, to reward his employees for all their efforts, but even paying them their wages had become difficult.

Grabbing a twig lying near his boot, Peter absently snapped the stick into tiny segments. Why was the company still struggling to survive? he wondered. What was he doing wrong? Every fiber within him yearned to make Rheinhardt Furniture more successful than it had ever been—but he was beginning to wonder if God still supported that wish. Were all the obstacles and setbacks God's way of telling him to abandon his desire? Was he truly following the Lord's aspirations? Or his own?

Then, as he studied the structure in front of him, Peter shook his head. He had to be on the right path…God would not have provided such a grand building if the company was supposed to fail. Suddenly, Irene Spreyer's words jumped into his head…

'God can take any wicked act, turn it around, and make it work for His purpose.'

Tossing the last piece of his twig into the air, Peter nodded in silent agreement. The new factory definitely proved that God had quite a knack for bringing good out of evil.

Although he tried and tried to keep his thoughts on the present, they still, uncontrollably, wandered back to the old building—and to the fire that had devoured it. Then, as Peter started to massage his left palm, the memories flooded into his head…

The incessant flames…the lost livelihoods…the hopelessness of starting over… the battles with the law…the invasion of newspaper men…and lastly, the telegram informing Karl Rheinhardt that his brother-in-law's illness had turned deadly…

The barrage of miseries seemed endless, but with one simple maneuver, the Lord transformed them all into a miracle. Peter knew it was only by God's urging that Karl's brother-in-law decided to devote all his remaining time to his family…and to stop the production of his Sandorville wagon factory…and to sell the nearly completed building to Karl.

Peter grinned and looked toward the sky. "Thank you…I never realized…You were working on getting us a new building even before the old one burned down, weren't You?" His mind then drifted to the factory's more recent problems, including the charred lumber—he just had to trust that God would bring some good out of them too.

With renewed hope, Peter finished his trek to the factory. Bounding up the loading platform's steps, he walked through the wide, propped-open doors and was immediately greeted by screeching saws, rotating belts and pulleys, suffocating sawdust—and the friendly smiles and waves of his employees. Lifting his hand, Peter returned the greetings as he surveyed the various faces around him. Not seeing Jaxson, he ambled over to Hermann Winkel, the thin, wiry German who had become one of his most loyal allies. "Hermann, how are you?" Peter asked, raising his voice to be heard over the saws.

Hermann Winkel reached up and pushed a lever to one side, disengaging his saw from the forever revolving overhead shaft. "Sehr gut, danke," he bellowed.

"That's good to hear," Peter replied, smiling. He always reminded his men that he didn't know any other language than English—yet at times, they forgot. Thankfully, over the past year, he had learned enough to understand the basics, including Hermann's 'very well, thank you.' "Do you know where Jaxson is?"

Hermann pointed to the second floor. "Moving the tables for the decorators," he answered with a wink.

Peter chuckled. It was a well-known secret that Jaxson enjoyed the company of Holly, one of the decorators, and he would often work in the assembly room upstairs to be close to her. Nodding his thanks, Peter started to move toward the stairs when Hermann grabbed his arm.

"Are you all right?" Hermann inquired, his brow creased with concern.

The unexpected question shook through Peter and dredged up the events from the night before. How did Hermann know what happened?

"Are you all right?" Hermann repeated, this time pointing to Peter's tinted glasses.

With a nod, Peter sighed in relief. "They're from the doctor…they're supposed to help with the headaches."

Hermann smiled in return. "Ah, that's good…I've been praying for something to help you."

"Thank you, Hermann…right now I—" Spotting a new face among the workers, Peter interrupted himself and peered at the man over his dark lenses.

"He just started this morning," Hermann put in. "His name is—"

"Manning Cole," Peter announced, his jaw muscles visibly tightening.

"Then you know him?"

Peter pushed his glasses back in place. "Yeah, I know him. He came to the showroom yesterday looking for work—but he had a small problem with the color of Jaxson's skin."

"He must not care anymore, because he talked with Jaxson this morning, then started working right after that…he's good at lifting the heavy lumber pieces, but he's not too strong up here," Hermann replied as he pointed to his head.

His anger mounting, Peter barely heard Hermann's response. "You didn't have to hire him," he mumbled, voicing his displeasure to the absent Jaxson. Then, taking a deep breath, Peter realized that he wasn't angry at his partner for hiring Cole—he was angry that Jaxson had to sacrifice his pride to keep their factory running.

⚜

Leaning over the freshly painted tabletop, Jaxson whistled. "I think you ladies are gettin' even better…if that's possible."

"Well, those pedestal bases you made really help…it's so nice to be able to walk around the whole table, especially when we do the scrollwork."

As Jaxson moved to examine the fine, golden scrollwork that trimmed the outside edge of the table, he bumped into one of the decorators. Jerking upright, he spun around and stared at the beautiful, dark-skinned girl that he had collided with. "I'm awfully sorry, Miss Holly."

Holly Jaye smiled, causing her upturned nose to crinkle. "You're the only one here, other than our pa, who can tell me and Bonnie apart," she commented as she stepped next to her twin sister. "Why is that?"

Jaxson shrugged. "It's just luck," he replied, wishing he could tell Holly the truth…he could tell them apart because she was the sister who made his pulse race and palms sweat…she was the sister who had captured his heart.

"Luck, yes, that must be it," Bonnie Jaye teased as she gave her sister a light jab.

Worried that his constant ogling would betray his secret, Jaxson returned his attention to the table. "I'll get this one outta your way," he mumbled, placing his hands under the tabletop. Then, lifting the maple circle off its base, Jaxson carried it into a separate room and carefully placed it on a long counter, which held four other brushstroked masterpieces. Stepping back from the drying tabletops, Jaxson glanced out one of the wide windows behind the counter—and his love-struck smile immediately disappeared. Although he was relieved to see Peter in the front yard, he was not happy to see his friend's palm massaging—the habit only appeared when Daven's memory surfaced. With a sigh, Jaxson pivoted from the window…if only he hadn't blundered yesterday and said Daven's name…

"Is somethin' wrong?"

The question gently tugged Jaxson from his thoughts. "What?"

"You got so sad when you looked out the window just now…is there somethin' wrong?" Holly asked, entering the drying room.

"No…I just…" How could he explain to her about what he had said to Peter? Especially when he couldn't even talk to her about the weather without stumbling over his words. "I was just gunna stoke the embers and make sure they didn't go out," he offered as he headed toward the small box stove that kept the room warm and dry.

Walking to the counter, Holly stood up on her toes and looked out the window. "That's Peter down there, isn't it?"

"Yeah," Jaxson answered, squatting in front of the stove and swinging the door open.

"Are you mad at him?"

"No."

"That sounded convincing."

Jaxson half-smiled and studied the simmering pieces of wood inside the stove. "I ain't mad…I just said somethin' that I shouldn't have," he answered as he closed the stove door.

"What'd you say?"

From his squatting position, Jaxson tilted his head and gazed up at Holly. Once again, his heart began to hammer against his chest, and he wondered if it was the stove or her beautiful smile that was making the sweat roll down his back. "Well… I…I reminded him of somethin' he wants to forget."

Holly nodded. "You mean what happened to Daven."

The name knocked Jaxson off balance, and he unsteadily rose to his feet. "How do…how do you know about that?"

"Jaxson, we all know…Hermann told us what happened."

"But nobody's ever said nothing."

"Because we're all like you—we don't wanna cause Peter any more hurt."

Jaxson shook his head. "I don't know…I think it's hurtin' him more, keepin' it all quiet."

"Why?"

"Peter's always felt that it was his fault 'bout Daven gettin' killed. But now, the guilt's built up so bad that sayin' Daven's name is like hittin' Peter with a hot branding iron…I just wish I knew what to say to make him forgive himself and set Daven free…and when I should say it."

Strolling over to Jaxson, Holly tenderly grasped his hands. "God'll let you know when it's the right time to talk to Peter, and He'll give you the words to say…but you can't make Peter forgive himself—that's only up to him."

Holly's touch and the warmth of her words sent a thrill tingling through Jaxson—which he enjoyed for a moment—then he shook his head and forced his mind to concentrate on their conversation. "I, uh…I know it's up to Peter. I just wish he'd let Daven's memory live…I gotta tell ya, ol' Helpful would hate all this."

"Who's 'Helpful'?"

"That's what I used to call Daven," Jaxson chuckled. "He would've hated being cooped up inside of everybody like this."

"You must miss him."

"Yeah, Daven was a good kid…he was the one that brought me back to the Lord," Jaxson replied, then, realizing that his conversation with Holly had been their longest one yet, he grinned.

"Well, I'm thankful that Daven lived up to his nickname," she returned, squeezing his hands tighter.

"Me too," he whispered as he gazed at Holly's pretty face and bright, brown eyes. And, as he continued to stare, he wondered if someone so lovely would be happy with his plain features and meager assets.

"Jaxson?"

"Hmm?" he murmured, becoming completely lost in the thoughts of holding and kissing Holly.

"Uh…am I interrupting?"

The deep voice yanked Jaxson from his daze, and pulling his hands from Holly's grasp, he looked sheepishly at Peter, who stood in the drying room doorway. "No… no…I…I was just moving the tables for…what kinda eyeglasses are those?"

Peter grinned. "Doctor Spreyer ordered them. They're supposed to help with the lights when I get a headache."

"You still got the one from yesterday?" Jaxson asked worriedly.

"No, thank God…I don't know if the glasses did anything to get rid of it or not, but I've been wearing them in the hopes that they'll ward off any more."

Jaxson nodded, inwardly praying for the same thing.

Heading toward the counter, Peter gestured at the maple circles. "I see you got some more tables done."

"Speakin' of getting more tables done, I better get back to my painting," Holly volunteered, then, with a slight wink, she continued, "before the boss gets mad."

Peter smirked at the teasing. "You ladies are doing a wonderful job...thank you, Holly."

"Now, was that a good guess? Or are you startin' to be able to tell Bonnie and me apart?"

"A little of both, I guess."

"Pretty soon you'll be as good as Jaxson...he always knows which one of us is which," she said, patting Jaxson's shoulder. "You'll just have to keep practicing, Peter."

"I reckon...I did learn a few words of German, so I guess anything is possible."

"And Bonnie and me will make it even easier for ya," she put in as she started to leave.

"How's that?"

Stopping, Holly turned back and giggled. "We won't trade places on ya."

A wide smile parted Peter's lips. "Well, thank you, Holly. I appreciate that...hey, would you mind closing the door on your way out?"

"Sure...and I'll keep everybody away, so you two can talk."

Jaxson scowled at Peter's request. "What's goin' on?"

Waiting until the latch clicked, Peter inquired quietly, "Have you asked her out yet?"

The question hit Jaxson like ice water. "What?"

"When are you going to ask Holly out?"

"What...what makes you think I want to ask her out?"

"Because you don't drool when you look at the other one."

Realizing that his hidden attraction to Holly wasn't so hidden, Jaxson's spine stiffened. "I don't drool," he snapped, then, as an embarrassed grin spread across his face, he added, "that much."

"So ask her."

"I will...when the time is right."

"It's the right time, my friend...so do it."

Peter's statement poked at Jaxson, and he took a step back as Holly's words flashed in front of him...

'God'll let you know when it's the right time to talk to Peter, and He'll give you the words to say.'

Was this Christ's way of telling him to talk to Peter? It seemed as if he was being prodded, but he still wasn't sure...

"Peter, I'd like to talk…about what I…about what happened in your office yesterday." Jaxson waited for a response, but none came. Usually, he could read Peter's mood—but this time, the dark glasses made it impossible.

"So are we on schedule with the tables?"

Sighing at the obvious diversion, Jaxson nodded. "Yeah, we're doin' fine. Whatever the girls added to the paint to make it dry faster sure is working."

Peter lowered his spectacles and studied the freshly painted tabletops. "I just hope this decorating won't be more trouble than it's worth."

Crossing his arms, Jaxson leaned against the drying room wall. No matter how much he tried to convince Peter that the painted furniture was a good and worthwhile product, his partner still had reservations about the new line of merchandise…and about becoming too specialized…and about placing the factory's hopes on the abilities of two young decorators.

At that thought, Jaxson bowed his head. He knew, in his heart, that he was partly to blame for his friend's uneasiness—he had ignored Peter's arguments and sided with Karl Rheinhardt in favor of producing the decorated furniture. Although he had talked himself into believing that his decision was based on good business sense, the truth still nagged at him…the painted furniture kept Holly Jaye within his sights. "The tables look great, don't they?" he put in, trying to ease his guilt.

"They're outstanding," Peter replied as he slid his glasses back into place. "Oh, yeah, I've got some good news for you."

"What?"

"When I arrived at the showroom this morning, we already had some replies to the telegrams I sent out yesterday."

"And?"

"And, believe it or not, we had two positive responses."

"Who?" Jaxson prompted, pushing himself from the wall and joining Peter at the counter.

"A lumber yard just outside of Grand Rapids and that place in Willow Ridge that Benjamin Jaye told you about."

"So which one you wanna go with?"

"The Grand Rapid's yard is a lot closer…but I like what MacColl had to say about his place in Willow Ridge…I just think the Lord's pushing me to go there."

"I thought the same when Benjamin told me about it…I say let's try Willow Ridge…when ya goin'?"

"Today…this afternoon."

Even though Jaxson heard a bit of pain in his friend's tone, he still couldn't see Peter's expression behind the tinted spectacles. "Why so soon?" he tried.

A shrug was his only answer.

"If it's because of what I said yesterday…"

Peter laughed sarcastically. "Believe me, it's not because of what you said."

"Listen, I know I hurt ya when I—"

"Why did you hire Manning Cole?"

"What?" Jaxson returned, thrown by Peter's sudden detour.

"I saw Cole downstairs. Why did you hire him?"

"Because we need help."

"I thought I made myself clear that we don't need a bad egg like him."

"Yeah, I know he was in a pucker yesterday…but he came here this mornin' all sorry and beggin' for another chance."

"But he's not—"

"We need the help, Peter," Jaxson cut in, wiping the sweat from his forehead, "especially if you're leavin' town today…did you ask Anna to go with you?"

"No, there isn't time."

"Why? What's the all-fired rush?"

"I just want to get out of town…to get the wood."

Jaxson blew out a deep breath. Both the drying room's warm air and Peter's attitude had evaporated his patience. "Look, you can talk to me about Daven either now or when you get back—I don't care which—but we will talk about him."

Peter's jaw clenched and he backed away. "This has nothing to do with what you said yesterday…I know you didn't mean to say his name…it's fine."

"No, it ain't!" Jaxson shouted. "And take off those dang-it-all glasses. I want to talk to you, not them."

Slowly, Peter slipped the eyeglasses off his face and into his coat pocket.

"You gotta let Daven go…he'd hate bein' all shut up inside your heart."

Silence.

"Peter, I wanna be able to say Daven's name without sendin' you into a frenzy."

"I do not go into a frenzy!"

"Yes, you do. You're doin' it right now—your jaw's clamped tighter than a bear trap."

Peter visibly tried to relax his jaw muscles and shook his head. "I don't want to discuss this right now, Jaxson," he said, then headed for the door.

Reaching out, Jaxson grabbed Peter's arm and pulled him back—if his friend left now, it would be days before he could get him alone again so they could talk. "Well, I do wanna discuss it."

Angrily, Peter yanked himself free and resumed his retreat.

Rushing forward, Jaxson caught Peter's wrist just as he was reaching for the latch. Then, spinning his friend around so they were face-to-face, Jaxson pushed him against the door. "I'm sorry, but this time you're gunna listen," Jaxson announced, praying that God would truly give him the right words to say.

"Leave it alone," Peter seethed and shoved Jaxson away.

Once again, Jaxson slammed his friend against the door. "I'm just as strong as you are," he continued as he clutched Peter by the shoulders. "You can fight me all you want, but you ain't goin'—not yet anyways."

"Jaxson...don't. You don't know what happened last night."

"So tell me."

"No."

"Fine. We'll just cook in here along with the tables." Then, through his grip, Jaxson felt Peter tense. "Come on—talk to me!" he urged.

"Tait's brother and nephew showed up yesterday," Peter finally choked out. "They came all this way, looking for a man who's been dead for seven years."

The news shook through Jaxson and he released his hold. "What'd they want him for?"

"I don't know."

"Well, what'd they tell you?"

Silence.

"Sakes alive, Peter. Didn't you even talk to them?"

"Sure I talked to them," Peter snapped with a bite of sarcasm. "I had the joy of telling them that Tait was dead and so was his son."

"You gotta go talk to them."

"I don't have to do anything."

"Ya know what, Peter? Fetch may have been the one who killed Daven, but you're the one who's smotherin' his life."

"What?!"

"Daven could still live...through our memories and stories about him."

"No, I—"

"Peter, I know you got cheated out of being able to share your life with your brother and you got cheated out of being there for him in his last hours and you got cheated out of burying him because of your busted arm and you got cheated out of mournin' for him because of all the trials and court stuff...but you're the one who's cheatin' yourself out of his memory. I know you're hurtin' because of Daven, but you gotta stop blamin' yourself...it's not your fault that a madman shot him. It's time you took that idiot black band off your arm and remembered Daven's life...go and talk to Tait's brother."

Peter slumped against the door. "I can't."

"You're the only one who knows anything about Tait—and Daven."

"You knew Daven."

"For a couple of weeks. You watched him grow up…there's gotta be some good memories in all those years…something you'd wanna remember and keep with you…"

"If only I hadn't involved him…he'd still be alive."

"You don't know that."

Peter's eyes filled with tears. "Yes, I do."

"If you knew he was gunna be killed and still involved him, then you'd be to blame, but you didn't know…what would Daven say if he were here right now?"

"I don't know."

"Yeah, you do," Jaxson went on. "He'd tell ya to let him out of the crate that your brain's got him hidden away in…he'd tell ya that there was a reason why it all happened…he'd tell ya that he's okay, that he's with the Lord now."

"How can I be sure?"

"Because Daven loved the Lord. And the Lord loved Daven—even more than you did. Jesus was with him the whole time."

"I wish I could be as sure as you are."

"One day you will be…so are you gunna go talk to Tait's brother?"

"I don't know…are you done slamming me against the door?"

"I don't know…are you done actin' like an idiot?"

Peter half-smiled and rubbed his forehead. "I don't know."

Jaxson laughed. "Come on…let's get outta this heat."

With a nod, Peter grabbed the latch and pushed the door open. As the cooler air hit them, both Jaxson and Peter realized that the decorators and assembly men were frozen in place and staring at them with wide, questioning eyes and mouths hanging open…obviously, their scuffle had been very audible.

"It's all right," Jaxson announced, placing a brotherly hand on Peter's shoulder. "We had a little trouble stoking the fire, but everything's fine now."

❧

Haltingly, Peter climbed up the Spreyers' front stoop. He still had no desire to speak with Lars Nilsson, but ever since his shoving match with Jaxson, an itch had developed inside his gut, and he knew the meeting had to take place. Taking a deep breath, Peter walked the few steps to the screen door and wrapped his fingers around the long, thin handle. Suddenly, a twinge crawled up his forearm, and with a silent wince, he released his grip. Shaking the cramp from his arm, Peter grasped the handle again, but the movement caused the ache to return. As he rubbed his right forearm, he shook his head. Great, just great, he thought…if it wasn't one reminder about his brother, it was another…

"Is somethin' wrong with your arm?"

Turning toward the porch swing, Peter smiled as he located the questioner. Surrounded by some brightly painted wooden blocks, William sat on the veranda, building a fort around his sleeping kitten. As he ambled over to the swing, Peter answered, "My arm was broken last year and sometimes it still hurts…especially when it's going to rain."

William lifted his left arm. "See," he declared, pulling his sleeve up to reveal his bare limb. "Mine's all better."

"Was your arm broken too?"

"Uh huh…how did yours get broke?"

Peter drew in a deep breath. "Well…someone hurt my brother…and I wanted to…I wanted to stop that man from hurting anyone else and to bring him to the police for what he did, but when I tried to do that, he got very angry and broke my arm."

"That's what I tried to do too," William said as he stroked the kitten.

His curiosity piqued, Peter sat down on the swing, and placing his elbows on his knees, he leaned forward and asked, "What did you try to do?"

"One time, when Papa was hurting Mama, I tried to make him stop, and he got mad at me."

"Did your papa break your arm?"

William nodded. "Mama said he didn't mean to do it. She said he was drunk and didn't know what he was doing."

"Well, I'm sure she was right," Peter returned calmly—but he was far from calm on the inside. Lynette and William's obvious abuse hit a protective nerve, and his entire being was filled with outrage. "Where is your papa now?" he put in, trying to muffle his anger.

"Back where we used to live. Mama has a paper that says we don't have to live with him anymore."

"That's good to hear," Peter replied, somewhat relieved. But, as he considered the situation, he decided to expand his guardianship and keep a watchful eye on Lynette and William.

"And where's the man that hurt your brother?" the boy inquired.

Peter half-smiled—clearly, God was determined to make him confront Daven's memory.

"He died," Peter said as he absently began to rub his left palm with his right thumb. "When I chased after him, he tried to escape, and he fell from the second floor of a building."

"And is your brother all better now? Like Mama and me?"

"William, that's enough."

Surprised by the third voice, Peter turned and saw Lynette standing next to the swing. In his preoccupation with William, he never even heard her come out onto the porch.

"You've questioned, Peter…um, Mr. Leighton quite enough," Lynette added.

Standing, Peter tipped his hat. "Peter's just fine."

Lynette smiled. "I just kept hearing your name so much last night that it became so familiar. I apologize, Mr. Leighton, it wasn't appropriate."

"No, as I said, Peter's fine," he persisted, then, as he thought about her words, he frowned. "Sounds as though I was the main topic of the evening."

Her grin fading, Lynette bit at her lower lip. "After Mr. Nilsson rested and had something to eat, he was very curious about…about everything. We talked for quite awhile."

"Oh."

"I hope William didn't bother you with his questions."

"No. I'm guessing that, by what he asked, William didn't hear the discussion last night?"

Lynette shook her head. "No, he didn't. As you've witnessed, he tends to be a bit of a parrot—like most four-year-olds. I thought it best, for everyone concerned, to have him play with Bock—upstairs."

"Thank you."

"I…I did overhear what William told you just now…you've probably assumed that I'm divorced from my husband."

Peter nodded, and remembering Jaxson's complaint about the dark lenses in his spectacles, he removed his glasses and pocketed them. "Did the boy tell me something he shouldn't have?"

"Oh, no…the Spreyers are aware of my divorce, and I know Anna had plans to tell you yesterday, but…"

Peter grinned at Lynette's polite way of bringing up his abrupt and ill-mannered departure the previous night.

"I hope my divorce won't…that you…that it won't…" Lynette nervously stuttered as she twisted her ruby ring.

Holding up his hand, Peter shook his head. "It was a very brave thing to do."

"It may cause you some…some trouble or embarrassment."

"Lynette, I'm sure you know by now, I'm quite used to dealing with those things."

"But I don't want to add—"

"You won't. And, if anyone harasses you, please, let me know."

"Thank you, Peter," Lynette said, smiling once again. "May I get you something to drink? I've just made some fresh lemonade."

"No, thank you…by the way, where is everyone?"

"Mrs. Spreyer was in very good spirits this morning, and she wanted to go for a ride, so she and Anna went visiting. And Mr. Nilsson and Mr. Hanson went to the cem..."

"The 'cem'?" Peter questioned, his brow furrowed.

"The cemetery."

Peter slowly exhaled, and for the first time, he realized how much his avoidance of Daven affected those around him. Lynette had been with the Spreyers only one day, and she was already conditioned to dodge the subject of his brother. "When did Mr. Nilsson and Mr. Hanson leave?"

"Awhile ago...they shouldn't be gone too much longer."

Twisting his watch chain between his fingers, Peter studied Lynette. Her statement sounded very prophetic and 'Irene Spreyer-like'—and he knew, from experience, that the prophesy would probably manifest itself very soon. "Well, I suppose I can wait." Then, glancing over his shoulder, Peter noticed that William had resumed his fort building around the kitten. "William?" he called.

Wide-eyed, the boy looked up. "Yeah?"

"To answer your question," Peter said, his voice breaking, "my brother didn't get better—he was hurt very badly and he...he died."

"He's with God?"

"Yes."

"That's good...Aunt Noelle won't be alone then."

Blinking back the tears, Peter nodded. It took a child's faith to remind him that there were many in Heaven watching over his brother—the Lord, Tait, and the mother Daven had never known. Then Peter's thoughts drifted to his own parents... they, too, were with Daven. Gazing upward, Peter scanned the now cloud-dotted sky. He knew he had to trust that Daven was safely with God—but he still wished that he could know for sure.

⚜

Standing in front of Daven's portrait, Peter massaged his palm and examined the picture. Guilt had always made him avoid the painting, but now, as he thoroughly studied it for the first time, he marveled at how Mrs. Spreyer had captured his brother's essence—Daven's light-blue eyes, handsome face, and long sandy-blonde hair seemed almost real. And, somehow, her remarkable talent had also brushstroked Daven's kind, carefree spirit into the painting as well.

Although the portrait still generated a deep sadness within his heart, Peter was thankful that he had the colorful, lifelike remembrance, instead of the postmortem photograph that Max Green had taken at the wake. As he recalled the gray, mournful picture and his brother's lacerated, stiff face, Peter's eyes started to water. That was not how he wanted to remember his brother, and even now, he was not sorry that he had tossed the photograph into the fireplace and let the flames swallow up the horrible image.

Shaking his head, Peter refocused on the painting, and a small smile came to his face. Irene Spreyer had met his brother only twice—and that was after Daven had been beaten and his hair cut short. Amazingly, she and her paint brushes had recreated the stubborn, long-haired, undisciplined, wonderful, young man whom he had helped raise—and whom he had dragged into…

"Uncle Lars says that Anders had that same habit."

The announcement tore Peter from his reverie, and he circled to find Erik and Lars standing in the parlor entranceway. Silently, he laughed—Lynette's prophesies were as accurate as Irene Spreyer's. "I'm sorry," Peter replied, "I didn't hear what you said."

"Uncle Lars says that Anders used to rub his left palm like that," Erik returned, pointing to Peter's hand. "He used to do it when he was troubled."

Twitching the habit from his hands, Peter half-smiled. "Daven must have inherited it from his father, and I guess I inherited it from Daven…listen, Mr. Hanson, I want to apologize for my behavior yesterday. It was very disrespectful. Please extend my regrets to Mr. Nilsson."

After a short conversation with his uncle, the young Swede nodded and smiled at Peter. "And we are sorry for stirring things up—and for our poor timing."

"You're not to blame. You had no way of knowing what happened…my rudeness was uncalled for."

"Uncle Lars says it's all forgotten—as long as you stop being so formal. We may be distant family, Peter, but we are still family."

"Yes, that we are," Peter offered with a sigh, then, reluctantly, he motioned to the sofa. "I reckon it's time to talk…Erik, Uncle Lars, please, have a seat."

As he converted English into Swedish, Erik led his uncle to the sofa, and when he reached the words 'Uncle Lars,' a grin appeared on the older man's face. Lars responded with a few sentences, then Erik bobbed his head. "Uncle Lars asked me to translate his words exactly. He doesn't want me to use 'Uncle Lars said' anymore. He wants me to say 'I' and 'me,' so he can feel that he is really speaking to you…and if you don't mind, he wants me to do the same with your words."

"That's fine," Peter murmured as he sat on a chair opposite his stepuncle. "I…I don't really know where to begin…"

"Please, tell me about Anders," Lars said through Erik.

Placing his elbows on the arms of his chair, Peter folded his hands and released a deep breath. "I, unfortunately, don't know that much. Tait…I'm sorry…I just can't get used to calling him Anders…well, he and I didn't exactly see eye-to-eye on things—especially on what was best for Daven—and it put quite a wedge between us. Anders and I were together for a year, then I left for college…he died while I was away at school…Anders was very, very closemouthed about his past."

Lars just grunted.

Then, leaning forward, Peter stared into Lars' crystal-blue eyes. "There were some rare moments when Tait and I actually got along…and during one of those times, I asked him about his past. He said he couldn't bear to remember what had happened…Uncle Lars, what did happen? What happened that made him change his name and shun his past?"

Lars held up his hand but said nothing.

Peter glanced at Erik for an explanation, but his stepcousin remained motionless, waiting for the words to interpret.

Finally, Erik began to speak, translating his uncle's response. "After our parents died, I tried my best to take care of my family."

Nodding sympathetically, Peter studied his stepuncle's somber, weathered face—and immediately, he felt a bond develop between them…one that only a firstborn son could comprehend.

"And Anders tested me often," Erik continued, repeating his uncle's words in English.

Peter smiled in full understanding.

"Anders was an unruly, impetuous young man—and a bit selfish—but he also had a carefree sweetness and charm that made you overlook those things."

"That doesn't sound like the Tait, um, Anders that I knew," Peter said, his face creased with confusion. "The man who married my mother was reserved, mild, and very giving…the person you're describing sounds like Daven," he finished and pointed to the portrait.

Lars gazed at the painting and laughed sadly. "Yes, I'm sure that you had your hands full too. It appears that Daven inherited his father's wild spirit," he returned, then lowered his eyes.

"I still can't envision my stepfather having a 'wild spirit.'"

A faint smile appeared on Lars' face. "Anders was quite impetuous…and he was not very fond of working on our farm. I would give him a task, and later, I'd find him sitting under a tree, carving something out of a piece of wood. I suggested he get an apprenticeship with a master carver, but he always declined—saying he didn't want to be chained down. Anders was a stubborn, wild stallion who refused to be tamed…but please don't misunderstand, even though I complain, I still loved him very much."

With a slight smile, Peter nodded.

"I just wanted Anders to settle down…to become more responsible," Lars and Erik went on. "Our homeland was going through some difficult times, and if Anders was going to survive as an adult, his attitude needed to change. So I pushed him to be more mature…like…like…" Lars' voice trailed off and he closed his eyes.

"Are you all right?" Peter asked.

After Erik translated the question, Lars' eyes opened and he bobbed his head. "I honestly thought I was doing it for his own good…that I was helping Anders. But, as I looked back just now, I realize that…that I was jealous…Anders was so carefree—and I was not."

Peter slumped against the back of his chair, completely sledgehammered by Lars' words. He had made the same mistake with Daven—and for the same reason.

"From what you've told me," Lars added, "I see that my efforts to change Anders accomplished only one thing—killing his spirit…why didn't I just let Anders be the man that God wanted him to be?"

Peter bowed his head—whether it was in English or Swedish, grief still sounded the same. He understood his stepuncle's anguish, probably more than anyone else ever could. Although God did open his eyes and soften his heart before he crushed Daven's spirit, the metamorphosis, unfortunately, came only days before Daven's death. He had spent so many precious years trying to tame Daven and push him down the wrong path—just as Lars did with Anders…

Suddenly, Peter sat upright. That was why his stepfather had been so lax with Daven's discipline and allowed the boy to do whatever he wanted. And it was also why he and his stepfather constantly butted heads over the subject. Peter swallowed hard—he regretted that he had become another 'Lars' in Anders' life.

"You didn't do the damage that you think you did," Peter tried, searching for the words that would ease some of Lars' guilt. "Tait, um, Anders still had many of the traits you spoke of. He approached life with a very joyful, light-hearted attitude— which did cause some problems when it came to business. But Anders was always kind and giving, and he treated me with respect…much more than I ever gave to him. I think a lot of his shyness came from the fact that he didn't speak English very well…I rarely saw him unhappy, and when he was, he'd always go to his Bible…I just don't understand why he'd change his name because of what you've told me."

"I'm sure he changed it because of something else that happened between us," Erik said as he translated his uncle's barely audible words. "Something that happened on a terrible Sunday in June."

"What…what happened?"

"It started out as a fine day…after our Sunday worship my family and the family of Sven Gustavsson—from a neighboring farm—decided to go for an outing. We were very close to Sven's family…he had died the previous year, and we helped his wife and children tend their fields. Before he died, Sven promised his only daughter,

Nilla, to me in marriage…she was quite young—very close to Anders' age—but I cherished her with all my heart…we planned to have an October wedding…"

As Lars' voice drifted off, Peter relaxed somewhat, enjoying the brief respite from his stepuncle's emotion-laden story. And, knowing how difficult it was to relive the past, he just let the older man rest in silence, until finally, Lars took a deep breath and proceeded with his tale.

"We had a good meal, and my sister, Johanna, had baked a huge cake—which Anders ate most of," Lars explained with a chuckle. "I also presented Anders with a pocketwatch that day…I knew I shouldn't have spent the money—especially during that rough year…but I thought the timepiece might help my brother become more responsible…Anders wasn't always mindful of the time."

Peter smiled—he knew that particular watch very well.

"It was later," Lars and Erik continued, "that…that I noticed both Anders and my Nilla had disappeared. Her oldest brother, Axel, and I went looking for them… and we found them…together…"

Lars' revelation shook through Peter and he leaned forward. "You mean 'together'?"

Lowering his eyes, Lars nodded. "When I saw them, I knew Anders had forced himself on Nilla, and God forgive me, I wanted him dead. Axel tried to hold me back, but I was in a blind rage…I was going to make Anders pay for what he did to my Nilla."

Sitting on the edge of his seat, Peter stared, wide-eyed, at Lars—he still couldn't believe that the story being told was about his shy stepfather.

"It was Nilla's pleas that stopped me from killing Anders that day," Lars put in softly. "As she defended him, I realized that Anders did not attack her. My brother had fallen in love with Nilla—and she with him…" Once again Lars became mute, and removing a handkerchief from his pocket, the old man wiped at his eyes.

As Peter digested Lars' story, he surveyed his stepuncle's pale face, then he noticed Erik's equally pained expression. Obviously, dredging up the family history was taking its toll on everyone. "Uncle Lars, would you like to rest for awhile and have something to drink?" Peter questioned.

"No, if I stop now, I don't think I will ever be able to start again," Lars returned, then, as he squeezed Erik's shoulder, the older man went on. "Anders begged me to forgive him and let him explain, but all I could think of was how he had disgraced us all…and how he had taken my Nilla from me. I told him things…things that I'm still too ashamed to repeat. Then I took his new pocketwatch and threw it as far away as I could. I told him to go pick up the watch and, once he had it, he could just keep walking…for the first time in his life, Anders did exactly what I said…I never saw or heard from him again…" Both grief and guilt pressed at the elderly man, and losing his voice, he began to sob into his handkerchief.

Peter shook his head and leaned back in his chair, feeling as if he had just finished a suspense-filled, 900-page novel—but this story wasn't fiction, it was his stepfather's life. He never imagined that the quiet man he knew as Tait Ashby had harbored such terrible and intense secrets. Then, as he thought about his young stepfather venturing out into the world with nothing but his God-given talents and the clothes on his back, Peter frowned. "Didn't…didn't the rest of your family or Nilla's family question Anders' sudden disappearance?"

Lars sighed deeply. "Of course they did, but Nilla's brother and I took care of all their inquiries with one simple—and horrible—lie…we told everyone that Anders had raped Nilla and that, when Axel and I tried to stop him, he ran away."

Peter's jaw fell open in disbelief. "So…what…whatever happened to Nilla?" he asked, still trying to overcome the shock of Erik's latest translation.

"Without Anders, she had no allies, so she went along with the story. I told Nilla's mother that I still loved her daughter and planned on going through with the marriage—even after what my brother did…Nilla hated me for all the lies and told me she would never marry me because of what I did to Anders…but something…something eventually happened that changed her mind, and she agreed to marry me."

"What happened?"

"Nilla realized that she was with child."

The words 'with child' swirled in Peter's head, and he stood as he fit the new piece of information into the puzzle of his stepfather's life. "Anders' child?" he murmured.

Lars bobbed his head.

With a shiver, Peter gazed at Daven's portrait. There was another child…Daven had a half-sibling. Then he looked at Erik and the chill returned. "You?"

Erik smiled sadly, then shook his head. "No, I'm Johanna's son," he said, answering the question himself. "Anders and Nilla's son was stillborn."

"Oh," Peter replied, not quite knowing why he was so disappointed at the news. "Uncle Lars, did you ever tell Anders about the child?"

"No," Lars answered as the conversation resumed through Erik. "As I said, after that day, I never heard from him again."

"But yesterday you said you knew to go to Bradlee because of his letters."

"He wrote to our sister—not to me…Johanna shared the letters with Nilla, but they were kept from me—until a few months ago." Reaching into his coat pocket, Lars pulled out four pieces of worn, yellowed paper. "In his first letter," Erik began as Lars unfolded the paper, "Anders wrote that he took an apprenticeship with a wood-carver in England…it seems I pushed him down many unwanted paths…" With a deep breath, Lars opened the second piece of paper and continued, "In here, Anders says he moved to America, to Michigan, where he became a lumberjack…and the letter also says that Anders married a young woman named Eva."

"Eva," Peter echoed. "Eva. Tait never spoke about his first wife…my brother never talked about her either…I had no idea what her name was."

"The third letter is only one sentence…it just says that Eva died after giving birth to a son. Anders wrote nothing more—not even what he named the boy." Then, with an unsteady hand, Lars carefully opened the fourth piece of paper. "This is his last letter," Erik announced as Lars held up the tattered page. "It is the longest and most detailed one…this is where he told Johanna about moving to Bradlee and about you and your mother." Handing the letter to Peter, Lars went on, "It was the first time he ever said where he was living, so Johanna tried to write to him, but like us, she addressed the letter to Anders Nilsson, not Tait Ashby…if only he had told her that he had changed his name."

Settling back down on his chair, Peter studied the yellowed letter in his hand and the familiar handwriting. Except for the names, the words were foreign to him, but he could still feel his stepfather's warmth and love in the scribbles. With a long exhale, Peter looked up and noticed that both Erik and Lars were peering at him, waiting for him to speak.

"I guess it's my turn now, huh?" Peter questioned, returning the letter to Lars. "Back then I…I really didn't like Tait, uh, Anders that much…oh, he was good to me and Mum…I just felt, well, that we didn't need him. But I think my mum needed him a lot more than I realized…my father had been gone only a year and three months when she married Tait, uh, Anders—which really sent the society women into a conniption fit. I didn't exactly like it either, but Anders made Mum happy and took away her loneliness, so I accepted him as best I could."

Lars grinned kindly. "In his letter, Anders wrote that you were a very strong-willed, independent young man—but that you also had a kind heart."

Peter laughed sarcastically and shook his head. "I wasn't that kind to him…as I said, we had our differences, and most of them concerned Daven," he replied, rubbing his palm. "Anders and I worked together for a year. We owned a small general store in Bradlee, and I taught him what I could about the business before I left for college…he died while I was gone." Pushing himself from his chair, Peter walked over to the fireplace and continued, "After Tait's funeral, I reviewed his bookkeeping and realized that he had been a lousy businessman…he put us rather deeply into debt. I worked for years trying to fix his errors and pay off all our obligations…I hated him for a long time for what he did." As he combed his fingers through his hair, Peter glanced at his brother's portrait, then quickly averted his eyes. "My anger," he went on, "hurt Daven a lot…it wasn't until last year that I finally found forgiveness and dropped my grudge against Tait."

As Erik translated Peter's words, Lars lowered his face into his hands.

"I'm sorry that there isn't a better ending to the story," Peter added.

Lifting his head, Lars wiped at his eyes and mumbled a response. But, instead of translating, Erik answered his uncle in Swedish, and the two had a short conversation before the young man looked up at Peter. "Uncle Lars wants me to tell you," Erik declared, "that he appreciates all of what you've told him—it has filled in many holes. He also asked if I would finish for him, so he can rest."

"If he's tired, we can stop for a—"

"No," Erik interrupted, "I asked him if he wanted to continue later, but he said no. He just wants to rest for a few minutes."

"All right."

"You see," the young man said, "my Aunt Nilla died a few months ago, and with her last breath, she begged Uncle Lars to find Uncle Anders and make things right… Lars wanted, so badly, to ask Anders to forgive him—now that can't happen."

Peter stared at his stepuncle's worn expression and sagging shoulders, wishing he could do or say something that would lighten the man's burden—he knew, from experience, just how heavy guilt could be to carry around. Sliding his elbow onto the fireplace mantel, Peter's arm touched a small wooden box, and as it did, a marvelous thought sprang into his head. "Erik, tell Lars that Tait, I mean Anders…tell him Anders did forgive him."

After hearing the translation, Lars glanced at Peter, then shook his head.

"He did," Peter insisted as he opened the wooden box and pulled out the pocketwatch he had entombed a year ago. "This proves it." And, holding the watch by the chain, Peter walked over to his stepuncle.

Lars absently gazed at the watch—then, suddenly, his eyes gleamed with recognition. Pushing himself from the sofa, Lars reached out and carefully took the silvery timepiece from Peter's hand.

"That's the watch you gave Anders…isn't it?"

Standing up behind his uncle, Erik whispered into the older man's ear. Lars nodded and caressed the timepiece's smooth, silver case, then, as he opened the cover, a tear rolled down his cheek and landed on the watch's face.

"How did this get here?" Erik questioned, translating his uncle's muddled words.

"Tait carried it with him wherever he went, and when he died, Daven carried on with the tradition. And, when Daven d…when Daven died, he gave it to me…that watch proves that Tait forgave you."

"How?" Lars asked through Erik.

"It keeps lousy time, but there's enough silver there to make it valuable… don't you see? When he walked away from you that day, he had nothing but that pocketwatch—and yet he never sold it…he never gave it up. If he still hated you, why would he keep a reminder of you?"

"To remember the hate."

Peter shook his head. "He never looked at that watch with any kind of animosity…he cherished it."

With tear-filled eyes, Lars stared at Peter, then, tightening his hand around the timepiece, he nodded.

"You are welcome to keep it," Peter murmured.

"No, Daven gave it to you."

"Really, I wouldn't mind," he tried again, hoping to find a new home for the keepsake, which naggingly reminded him of his brother's death.

"No…it's more important that you keep it."

Peering into Lars' sky-blue eyes, Peter conceded. He wished he could make his stepuncle understand that the pocketwatch constantly made him remember Daven, and that was why it was buried in the little wooden box.

"Now…tell me about Daven's life," Lars said through Erik as he pushed the watch into Peter's hand.

Instantly, Peter's heart fell into his stomach. He thought that maybe, just maybe, Lars had grown weary of the past, especially after their lengthy conversation. But his stepuncle's request squelched that hope. With a long exhale, Peter shook his head—he still couldn't summon the strength to delve into his brother's demise.

"Please?" Erik begged for his uncle. Then Lars repeated the English word himself, and placing his hand on Peter's shoulder, he said it again. "Please, Peter."

"Excuse the interruption," Lynette called from the parlor doorway, then, entering the room with a tray of lemonade-filled glasses, she added, "but I thought you gentlemen could use some refreshments."

"Thank you," Peter replied, grateful for the diversion. Even though he knew the discussion about Daven would inevitably come, he was still glad to have it delayed for a few minutes more.

Setting the tray on the low table in front of the sofa, Lynette asked, "Will you be staying for the farewell luncheon, Peter?"

"What farewell luncheon?"

"Uncle Lars and I will be leaving tomorrow," Erik explained. "I'm going to accompany him back to Sweden and stay there until he…until I'm not needed any longer, then I'll return to Minnesota."

"If your departure has anything to do with my behavior yesterday, I—"

"No…no…it just took us much longer to find you than we had anticipated. We need to leave tomorrow if we are going to make it to the ship in time…and…and,"

Erik stuttered, glancing at the older man, "Uncle Lars' health is declining quickly. I think he needs to get home…soon."

As Peter scrutinized Erik and the ailing Lars, his thoughts drifted to his overworked men and to the painted tables that constantly called his name. He knew he should return to the factory, but he also knew that he would probably never see his stepuncle again. "Thank you for the drinks, Lynette…and yes, I'll be staying for lunch."

Lynette smiled. "Good…I'll set a place for you right now."

Squeezing the pocketwatch still in his hand, Peter sighed, then slowly walked to the mantle and returned the timepiece to its box. "I did love Daven," he offered as he looked at the portrait of his brother, "and I tried to be everything for him…but I could never get it right. When he needed me to be a friend, I'd act like his older brother, and when he wanted a brother, I'd react like a father." Turning from the painting, Peter faced his stepuncle, who had resumed his seat on the sofa. "If I knew then, what I know now, I would have tried harder with Daven…but as I said, we were in a lot of debt, and I did just about anything to get us out of it…I sold what I could…we opened our house to boarders…I worked two jobs…I didn't exactly have the time to be patient with Daven."

While Erik finished converting English into Swedish, Peter stepped over to the table and grabbed one of the glasses of lemonade. Without stopping for a breath, he gulped down the cold liquid, but it didn't offer his parched throat much relief. "To help us out," Peter went on, setting the empty glass on the tray, "a friend of mine—Karl Rheinhardt, who lives here in Sandorville—loaned me enough money to pay off our debts. That money saved us from losing everything." As he went on with his narration, guilt began to peck at the back of his neck, and Peter started to pace, hoping that the stabbing pain would not evolve into a headache.

"So last year," he said as he meandered around the parlor, "when Karl asked me to help him with some trouble at his furniture factory, I just couldn't say no. My mum had passed away, so there wasn't that much holding us in Bradlee—and I honestly thought it was a good opportunity. You see, Daven and I had talked about starting a business, and I figured that working for Karl would be a quick way to find out if we could put up with each other. And, since Karl insisted on paying us, we'd also have some capital to get started with…but things…things didn't exactly turn out as I had planned."

Slipping into silence, Peter quit pacing and blankly stared out one of the parlor windows. With the dam now broken, the memories flooded back into his head full-force, and he tried to blink away the tears that the long-suppressed scenes brought to his eyes. "I'm sure the Spreyers told you what happened," he put in, his voice breaking with sorrow. "We found out that the corruption in the factory was controlled by the foreman—Quentin Fetch…but while we were trying to stop him…he…he found out that Daven and I were really brothers…he killed Daven to punish me…"

This time he couldn't prevent the tears from coming. Wiping his face dry, Peter shook his head. It had taken a lot of time, but with God's help, he had forgiven Quentin Fetch for taking his brother's life—yet the memory of Fetch's retaliation still pierced his soul. Feeling a hand on his shoulder, Peter circled and faced his stepuncle. "I'm sorry," he whispered. "I'm sorry."

Lars grabbed Peter, and hugging him tightly, he spoke quietly in Swedish. "It is not your fault," Erik murmured from behind Lars.

Pulling away, Peter swallowed hard and nodded, even though he didn't believe the words.

"It is not your fault," Erik said again. "All your intentions were good—to help your friend…to make things better between you and your brother…to stop the trouble that was going on in the factory. You made your decisions with good intentions…you cannot hold yourself responsible for another man's actions."

As he peered into his stepuncle's watery, azure eyes, Peter recalled Jaxson's words from only a few hours ago…

'I know you're hurtin' because of Daven, but you gotta stop blamin' yourself…it's not your fault that a madman shot him.'

He understood the message from both men—he even believed it…but acceptance was another matter.

Grasping Peter's shoulder again, Lars continued, "I intentionally hurt Anders…I wanted my brother to suffer for stealing away the woman I loved. I am to blame for what happened to Anders…you are not to blame for what happened to Daven," he said, then Lars' grip tightened. "You said this Fetch person killed Daven to punish you."

"Yeah."

"If you refuse to forgive yourself, then you will lose your battle with Fetch."

"I will lose? Fetch is dead—he's the one who's lost the battle," Peter replied, scowling.

"No, Peter, his punishment is still going on inside of you. Fetch is laughing at you—laughing that his last act of violence is slowly killing you…forgive yourself, Son, and then you will be victorious."

His stepuncle's words pushed Peter back against the parlor window, and he clutched the heavy velvet curtains to steady his balance. Was he still combating the evil-hearted foreman? Slowly, Peter's thoughts returned to the flame-infested factory…and to his bloody and final encounter with Fetch…and to the foreman's last statement about their war…

'It'll be over, Leighton, when you're dead.'

He hated the idea that Fetch could still win their fight, even though the man was rotting in his grave. But, it was the truth, Fetch was indeed killing him—emotionally anyway.

"I see I hit a bull's-eye," Lars announced through Erik.

Peter smiled as the dagger of blame in his heart shrank to a splinter. "Yes, you did. Fetch knew right where to hit me to make me fall...and to keep me down... thanks for helping me back up."

Lars grinned. "No thanks are necessary. I'm just happy that you can think of Daven without it causing so much pain...now, you will be able to tell me the rest."

"The rest? There is no more...Daven's dead."

"Yes, I know. You have told me all about his death—but I want to know about his life."

"I don't underst—"

"What made Daven happy? What frightened him? What were his dreams? What were his faults?"

Peter released a deep breath. "That will take some time."

"Please?" Lars and Erik pleaded.

As he looked into his stepuncle's eyes, then into his stepcousin's, Peter saw a sparkle in their powdery-blue gems that had not been there before—it was as if the chance to know Daven ignited a dying hope. The two men were obviously looking forward to hearing some joyful stories about Daven, and even though he felt the twinge of a headache coming over him, Peter silently admitted that he, also, wanted to hear those stories. "My brother was in his glory when he was carving," Peter began as he led the two men back to the sofa. "And Daven was talented—extremely talented—the pieces in this room are proof of that."

After Erik's translation, Lars nodded and resumed his seat.

"Daven's greatest fear was losing that talent," Peter went on, perching himself on the edge of his chair. "As for his dreams...he didn't talk much about them...he never really thought about the future. He tended to live just day by day."

"And his faults?"

A smile crept onto Peter's face. "I always thought that there were a lot, but it was just different personalities...I'm sure you can understand that."

Again Lars nodded, but this time he also chuckled.

"Daven was just like the young Anders you described...reckless, impetuous, somewhat wild...but he always had a strong faith in God."

"That's a comfort," Lars returned, then sipped at his now warm lemonade.

Glancing over his shoulder, Peter scrutinized the painted portrait of his brother. "And he was never on time for anything. That watch of his didn't help matters either," Peter offered, gesturing toward the hidden keepsake. "It didn't keep very good time."

Lars lowered his eyes. "It must have gotten damaged when I threw it away that day."

"Daven had some kind of formula he used to try and compensate for the lost time—but it never worked," Peter added, then he grinned widely. "Daven left his watch out once, so I reset it…between that and his formula, he was early for everything that day…he was as mad as a March hare because he couldn't figure out why he was constantly early." Peter laughed at his long-forgotten prank—he could still remember the look of bewilderment on his brother's face. "Daven eventually figured out that it was me and returned the favor later that week by setting my watch back."

Lifting his glass in a salute, Lars smiled. "Please, tell me more."

The merriment that now danced in his stepuncle's eyes urged Peter to continue, and for the first time in a year, he didn't mind talking about his brother.

❊Four❊

With her mother's arm looped around hers, Anna Spreyer slowly climbed the steps leading to the kitchen door, then, beaming happily, she held the screen door open and guided her mother over the threshold. It had been quite a few weeks since her mother had ventured out visiting, and as they entered the kitchen, Anna said a silent prayer of thanks for their outing—it meant, for at least this day, the consumption had loosened its hold.

"Hello!" Lynette greeted as she moved a large iron pot to one of the warming burners on the back of the stove. "How was your buggy ride?"

"Very good," Irene Spreyer replied. "We were able to call on poor Mrs. Finster. She just hasn't been the same since her little dog passed away."

Anna smiled again at her mother's sprightliness—that was something else she hadn't seen in a long time. "Mrs. Finster kept bringing us food too," Anna put in with a laugh. "I told her that we had a special luncheon planned, but I think she was so glad to have company that she just couldn't resist being a hostess."

"Well I hope you still have a little appetite left," Lynette offered, "because everything will be ready in about a half an hour."

"For your baking?" Anna returned, sniffing the deliciously scented air. "Of course I still have room."

"Would you like some tea, Irene?"

"That would be very nice," Mrs. Spreyer answered as she settled onto one of the kitchen chairs.

"I can do that, Lynette," Anna said, heading for the cupboard. "Did Mr. Nilsson and Mr. Hanson get home from the cemetery yet?"

"Yes, they've been back for quite awhile…talking with Peter."

"Peter?"

Lynette nodded.

"He…he came back?"

Lynette bobbed her head again. "He even said that he'll be staying for the luncheon."

As she picked up the small wooden tea box, Anna sighed inwardly. Her prayer had been answered—Peter had returned to face his relatives…that was the first step.

"I'll make the tea," Lynette volunteered as she slid the box from Anna's grasp. "Why don't you see how Peter's doing."

Anna mouthed a 'thank you' to Lynette and headed down the hall toward the parlor. Then, as she neared, a sound reached her ears that warmed her completely— Peter's laugh. Standing quietly in the doorway, Anna studied her fiance as he sat on the edge of his chair, telling a story about Daven. Thrilled that another prayer had been answered, she exhaled with a gasp of elation.

"Anna," Peter announced, rising.

"I'm so sorry for interrupting," she returned, entering the parlor. "Please continue."

Peter shook his head. "We've made poor Erik hoarse from all his translating. It's a good time to stop."

Erik and Lars both stood, smiled, and then shook hands with Peter. From their joy-filled expressions and the tranquil atmosphere in the room, Anna guessed that the men had conquered some demons while she had been away. "Lynette is making some tea for Mama," Anna said to Erik, "I'm sure she'll be happy to make some for you and your uncle."

Erik offered his thanks and led his uncle toward the parlor door.

"Is everything all right?" she asked as Lars and Erik left the room.

Peter grinned in response and gave her a light kiss on the lips. "How would you like to take a trip to Willow Ridge tomorrow?"

The offer—and abrupt change of subject—rattled through Anna, and she couldn't find her voice to answer.

"Why don't we go outside," Peter said, extending his arm.

Still speechless, Anna nodded and wrapped her arm around Peter's.

"I know it's sudden," Peter continued as they walked out onto the porch, "but I thought it would be nice for us to go someplace…it's been ages since we've done that."

Anna's heart jumped. The proposal was romantic and exciting—and with Lynette's help, it was even possible. But she knew she couldn't go, she had already committed the day to her mother and sisters. "Peter, I can't. My—"

"I know. Your mum's too sick to chaperon…but we could ask someone else."

"No, Peter," she put in, sitting on the porch swing, "tomorrow's Wednesday…my sisters are coming. Remember?"

Peter bobbed his head with a crestfallen grimace.

"I'm sorry, Honey. I would love to go with you. Can we postpone it until Thursday?"

"No, I have to go there tomorrow to order some wood…it's all right. The two of us can go another time."

"I'm sorry."

"Don't be," he replied as he sank onto the swing next to her. "I know I sprang this on you…it's just that we haven't…haven't had much time to ourselves lately."

"I know."

"If we were married, then…then we could be together…I wouldn't have to leave at night."

Anna stretched out her arm and grabbed Peter's hand. "I want that too."

"Then why don't we set a date…right now."

Anna shook her head. "You know I want to wait until the whole family can be at the ceremony…for Mama's sake."

"Yes, but your brother isn't helping matters…he won't even acknowledge our engagement in his letters, let alone tell us when he can come home for the wedding. What's he got against us getting married?"

Hearing the frustration in Peter's voice, Anna squeezed his hand tighter. "He's not against us…it's just hard for Hans to get away from his schooling," Anna tried, but she knew she had already burst her fiancé's hopes, and her words were not helping to ease his disappointment.

"If there's anything I've learned, Anna, it's to value the time we have with each other."

She sighed and caressed the side of his face. "Peter…" she murmured, then gently turned his face toward hers. "I love you, Peter, with all my heart. I love you and I want to be your wife more than anything, but I want my brother here for the nuptials—I want everyone in my family to be here. It might be the last time that the Spreyer family will be together before Mama…before anything happens to Mama."

Putting his hand behind her head, Peter pulled in close and firmly kissed her on the lips. His touch, as it always did, sent a thrill pulsing through her, and she held him tightly, not wanting the moment to end. Finally, as they parted, she stroked his cheek again. "If you'd like, I'll send a telegram to Hans and find out when he can come," she said softly.

Peter smirked. "No, I don't want to waste the money on an overseas telegram."

"But this is important for both of us…I'll tell him he has to make up his mind."

"Or we could set a date…then he would have no choice."

Anna smiled at Peter's persistence. She knew her procrastination irked him, but she also knew how much it meant to her parents, especially her mother, to have all six Spreyer children standing next to each other once again. Her parents had given her so much, and she wanted to give them a gift in return—the gift of having her wedding with the whole family in attendance. "I'll tell Hans that we would like to have the ceremony by the end of the year...all right? That way he can make some arrangements...coming home will take him away from his schooling for quite awhile."

Peter exhaled and nodded.

She wanted to explain further...she wanted to make Peter understand how important her brother's presence was to her and her family. But, noticing her fiancé's suddenly somber mood, she decided to switch subjects instead. "Willow Ridge is quite a long way to go for wood."

"Yeah, it is, but I keep getting an itch every time I think about it, as if God was telling me to go there...I'm just not sure why."

"How long will you be gone?"

He hesitated, then combed his fingers through his hair. "Between the stage and train schedules, I won't be back until Thursday evening...I just wish they weren't so far from the railroad."

As they fell into a silence, Anna watched Peter twist his watch chain between his fingers—it was a nervous fidget she had come to know very well in the past year. "What's wrong, Peter?"

He just shrugged.

"Are you worried about the trip?"

"No."

"Then what's wrong?"

With a sigh, Peter started to answer, but he was immediately cut off by a 'meow' from the parlor window behind them. "Well, hello there, Patience...where have you been hiding all this time?"

In response, the cat meowed again, jumped onto the swing, and pushed her head under Peter's hand. Anna couldn't help but smile at the mutual affection. The timid three-legged cat had adopted Peter last July, and whenever she heard his voice, she always came running to see him. Knowing that Patience usually soothed Peter's moods, Anna decided to make one last attempt to pry him open. "Peter, what's bothering you, Honey?"

"I...I just don't want you...I just hate being away."

"You've been away from the factory before, and everything's been all right."

"It's not the factory I'm worried about," he mumbled, looking downward.

Anna frowned. She could almost see the gray cloud that had settled over Peter's head, but she couldn't figure out what had caused the somberness to descend upon him. And, to make matters worse, the cloud was pulling him further and further away from her—not even Patience could break through the gloom that surrounded him. "You could send someone else in your place," she offered.

"No, the fewer people who know, the safer it'll be."

"The safer what will be?"

"Our lumber…that way Wild won't…that way no one will interfere with us getting our wood this time."

Even though Peter tried to cover up his slip of the tongue, Anna clearly heard the name 'Wild'—and suddenly, she understood what had created his dark disposition. "Peter, I've told you not to worry about James—" she started, then, seeing Jaxson ride up the walkway on his bicycle, she cut her statement short.

Leaping to his feet, Peter bounded down the porch steps and ran to meet Jaxson. "What's wrong?" he shouted.

"Nothing," Jaxson returned, rolling to a stop. "I just came to see if everythin' was okay."

"Hello, Jaxson. It's good to see you," Anna called.

"Miss Anna," Jaxson greeted and tipped his hat.

"You are just in time for our luncheon," Anna put in as she joined the two men. "We're having a special afternoon-meal to wish Peter's uncle and cousin bon voyage."

"Oh, no thanks, Miss Anna, I gotta get back."

"Please stay, Jaxson, I'm sure they would love to meet—" Anna said, but once again, she was interrupted—this time by a wagon that slowed, then stopped in front of the house.

"Hello," the driver beckoned from the street, "is this the home of Miss Anna Spreyer?"

"Yes, it is," Peter yelled back. "What can we do for you?"

"I have a delivery," the driver returned, and jumping down from his seat, he hoisted a crate from his wagon and marched toward them.

"Are you expecting anything?" Peter asked.

Anna shook her head, wondering what treasure was hiding in the large wooden box.

Almost as if he had read her mind, the delivery man offered, "They're pineapples, Ma'am."

"Pineapples?!" Anna, Jaxson, and Peter exclaimed in unison.

"Yep," the man replied as he joined the group. "Special delivery from Mr. James B. Wild, the third…where would you like them, Ma'am?"

"Oh, my goodness!" Anna squealed. "What a wonderful treat…please come this way. I'll have you take them straight through into the kitchen," she said, then hurried along the walkway and up the porch steps. Yanking the screen door open, Anna spun back around and proclaimed, "You must stay, Jaxson. You can't miss having some fresh pineapple."

Acknowledging the invitation, Jaxson waved as he watched the burly delivery man disappear into the house, followed by Anna. Even though he had never tasted a pineapple, he found his mouth watering for the fruit that only the very rich could afford. Then, as he recalled the source of the gift, Jaxson glanced at Peter, whose jaw muscles were bulging with tension and anger.

"He knows I can't afford to get her pineapples," Peter mumbled quietly through clenched teeth.

Guessing that his friend's statement was not really for his ears, Jaxson bent over his bicycle and fiddled with the front tire, pretending that he didn't hear the remark. "Did you get a chance to talk to your stepuncle?" he asked, hoping that the change of subject would ease Peter's animosity.

With an exhale, Peter nodded. "Thanks for the push," he said, his jaw relaxing. "I learned a lot about my stepfather that I never knew."

"Is that all you talked about?"

Peter tilted his head to the side and looked wearily at Jaxson. "No...we talked about Daven too."

Jaxson smiled upon hearing Daven's name—especially since it was Peter who said it. "That's good to hear."

"Yeah," Peter returned as he stared at the Spreyers' empty porch. "It was hard." Then, turning toward Jaxson, he added, "It was very hard...but at least the worst mountain's behind me now...I think."

The grin on Jaxson's face grew as he listened to his friend—finally, the wound of losing Daven was starting to heal.

Without warning, the burly delivery man burst through the front door, leaped off the porch, and tramped down the plank walkway. "Gentlemen," he said with a tip of his hat as he reached Peter and Jaxson. "I never thought eight pieces of fruit could weigh so much! Well, good day," he chuckled as he continued toward his wagon.

"Eight?!" Peter echoed incredulously. "How did Wild get eight fresh pineapples here in the middle of summer?"

Jaxson shrugged. "He's got money, Peter. He can do anything he wants."

"I know."

"It doesn't matter," Jaxson put in, angered by James Wild's newest tactic. "Anna's not gunna go runnin' into his arms 'cause he gave her eight pineapples."

Peter only grunted in reply.

"Is Anna gunna go with ya to Willow Ridge?"

"No."

"Well, I'll try to stop over here when I can."

Silence.

"She cares for you," Jaxson tried, "not Wild or his money."

Peter crossed his arms and released a deep breath. "Then why won't she pick a date for our wedding?"

❦

Gazing at the darkening sky, Peter stood in the Spreyers' backyard, rubbing his right arm. Although the canopy above sang of a calm night, his arm was telling him that rain was on the way—soon. After the long discussion with his stepuncle and the bon voyage luncheon, Peter had been grateful to go back to work—at least there he could escape from his thoughts. But now, in the dim twilight, the day's events played war inside his head, and every piece of new information battled for his full attention.

"I hope we aren't disturbing you."

Pulling himself from his skygazing, Peter circled and saw Lars and the man's deciphering shadow, Erik. "No...I was just enjoying the quiet."

"I wanted to thank you for letting me get to know Daven," Erik said, once again translating his uncle's exact words.

Peter nodded and grinned. "Well, I appreciate what you told me about my stepfather."

Reaching out, Lars placed a fatherly hand on Peter's shoulder. "I hope you don't mind, but I think of you as if you were my nephew by blood."

"I don't mind," Peter returned. "In fact, I'm honored...when I lost Daven, I lost my family...I just thank God that He sent the Spreyers when He did...I've learned just how precious family is."

"I thank the Lord for that too," Lars replied. "I'm happy that you have such a wonderful new family and good friends, like Jaxson. I know you'll be safe in their hands."

Peter smiled inwardly—Lars' protective nature mirrored his own.

"I've never known a man of color," Lars continued, "but Jaxson seems like a fine young gentleman."

The touch of prejudice in Lars' words grated against Peter's nerves and he lost his smile. "Jaxson is a very fine young gentleman, and I thank God for him...he's like another brother to me."

"Good. I'm pleased to know that your family is important to you," Erik translated, mimicking his uncle's suddenly serious tone. "And that you take care of those who are close to you...Peter, there is one final thing that we must discuss."

Peter slumped under the weight of his stepuncle's statement—he had trudged through enough family history for one day. It was time for both him and Lars to lay down their questions and answers and let their souls mend for awhile. "I can't. It's getting late," Peter blurted out. Then, trying to think of an excuse, he added, "I...I'm leaving town tomorrow."

"And so are we…but what I must tell you is more important than anything we have already discussed…if you care at all for Anders and his part of your family, you must listen to what I have to tell you."

Massaging his left temple, Peter cussed silently. Up until that very moment, he had been successful in fighting back the headache that loomed over him since the farewell luncheon—but his stepuncle's announcement instantly ended that success. With a sigh, Peter motioned to some willow-branch chairs under a huge, twin-trunked pine tree. "Why don't we sit down."

While Lars and Erik settled into their seats, Peter pulled a match from his waist-coat pocket and lit the lantern that hung on a chain from a low branch. Steadying the swinging lamp, Peter stared at his stepuncle and shook his head—the second round of digging into his emotions was about to begin, and he had no way of stopping it.

"There were two reasons why I came to this country to find Anders," Erik interpreted as Peter sat down. "First, to ask his forgiveness for what I did, and second, to give him a task…but with both him and Daven gone, I have no one else to turn to but you."

"Uncle Lars, I can't possibly take on—" Peter started, but Lars cut him off with a sharp gesture.

"I can't do it, Peter. I just don't have the strength or the time anymore. And Erik cannot—after I am gone, he will be busy moving what is left of our family to Minnesota. You are all I have…you must agree…please…for Anders and for me."

Peter exhaled resignedly. Although he dreaded the idea of adding another burden to his heavy load of responsibilities, he couldn't resist his uncle's pleas. "What is the task?"

"Do you remember how I told you about Anders and Nilla and my fight with him? And how, after he left, Nilla and I still married? And about the lie I told of how he had ravaged her?"

Peter nodded—it was not an easily forgotten story.

"That was not the only lie I told." Even though Lars kept speaking in Swedish, Erik abruptly stopped translating and sat bolt-upright in his chair as if ice water had been poured down his back.

"What's wrong, Erik?" Peter asked as he watched the young man's expression change from surprise, to confusion, and finally, to anger.

Oblivious to the question, Erik just glared at Lars in disbelief. Then the young man spoke to his uncle, but his usual gentle tone had become harsh and impolite. Lars replied with a few softly spoken words and patted Erik's knee, then he jabbed his finger at Peter. But, instead of speaking, Erik bowed his head and covered his face with his hands.

"What's going on?" Peter tried again.

Rubbing the tears from his eyes, the young Swede swallowed hard and looked up. "I'm sorry, Peter. My uncle's words came as quite a shock to me...please...I'll tell you in a moment."

As they sat in silence, Peter's mind raced, trying to figure out what Lars could have said that was more shocking than his earlier revelations.

"The lie about Anders attacking Nilla was not the only lie I told," Erik whispered, finally repeating his uncle's words in English. "The child that they conceived did not die."

The words shoved Peter against the back of his chair. No, he told himself, he heard wrong—the hammering inside his skull must have caused him to mishear Erik's translation. "Erik, I don't think I heard that correctly...what did you say?"

Erik sighed. "You heard correctly...Anders and Nilla had a son...a healthy son. It was Uncle Lars who told everyone that the baby had died."

Peter's eyes opened wide as the truth hit him—the boy was alive...he did have another stepbrother. "Why? How?" Peter stammered, now understanding Erik's emotional reaction.

"When Nilla realized that she was going to have Anders' child," Lars replied through Erik, "she told her mother, who told me...word of the rape had spread through our church, and Nilla had suffered tremendously because of her 'shame.' Her mother and I didn't want her to endure the humiliation of carrying and birthing an illegitimate child, so it was decided that she and I should be married right away...luckily, Nilla did not..." Erik said, then his voice broke.

"Do you want to stop?" Peter inquired, guessing that the story was doubly hard for his stepcousin to translate—not only was Erik hearing the tale for the first time, but he had to repeat it in English before he even had the chance to digest it.

Holding up his hand, Erik continued his interpreting with an unsteady voice, "Luckily, Nilla did not look as though she was with child at the wedding, so when she did announce that she was going to have a baby, everyone thought that it was mine—or they pretended that they believed it was mine. Only six of us knew, positively, that the child was Anders'...me and Nilla, Nilla's mother, her brother Axel and his wife, and my sister, Johanna...and only Nilla, Axel, and I knew the truth about Anders' so-called attack."

Peter shook his head in disbelief. "If people thought the child was yours then why did you lie about—"

"Because I didn't want the child," Lars cut in as he blankly stared at the flickering lantern that swayed slowly with the breeze. "I was such a fool...Nilla and I never had any children of our own—maybe that was God's punishment for what I did, or maybe, the Lord knew we couldn't have children, and He was trying to give us one...I'm not sure. All I do know is that, back then, my pride wouldn't let me see anything but the fact that my wife was carrying my brother's child. I felt the baby should die, but Nilla's pleas softened me some, and I told her it could live, but not in my home…Axel's wife begged for the child, so he reluctantly agreed to take the baby…they had plans to emigrate to America, to Minnesota, and they said they would take the baby with them, and it would be forever out of my sight…so when the boy was born, Axel and his wife took him and went to live with her family until they could get passage to America…the rest of us spread the news that the baby had been born too early and died…I even made a grave for it next to my parents' graves…"

Overcome by guilt, Lars lost his voice and started to cry. In the sudden stillness, Peter glanced up at the nearly dark sky and massaged his aching right arm. Lars' new tale was even more staggering and horrible than his previous story, and Peter could find nothing to say, except "Where is the child now?" And, as he said the word 'child,' he laughed inwardly to himself—Anders' son was probably as old as he was.

"When the time came for Nilla to give birth," Lars and Erik went on, ignoring the question, "Axel and his wife came to the house and waited to take the baby away. I didn't want Nilla to see the child—I didn't want her falling in love with it the way she did with Anders…Nilla begged to see the boy, but when her mother and Johanna delivered the child, they did exactly as I ordered and gave him to Axel's wife."

"So where is the child now?" Peter asked again.

"In retaliation for my heartlessness," Lars continued without answering, "Nilla took the wooden chain that she constantly wore around her neck and broke it in two. She kept half and gave the other half to Axel to give to the baby…you see, Anders carved that chain and gave it to Nilla as a gift. I think that it was her way of telling me that the child would always have a place in her heart—as would Anders."

Peter waited for a reply to his question, but when none came, he repeated it a third time. "Where is the child?"

"In his one and only letter to me, Axel wrote that his wife, who had gotten sick on the voyage over, had died when they reached Detroit. He blamed himself for her death—he said it was his punishment for all the lies he had endorsed. He also said that he couldn't bear the guilt anymore…that he couldn't even look at the boy he had stolen…so he left him at an orphanage."

Peter's heart fell into his stomach as Erik spoke his uncle's words—the only one who was blameless in the whole situation was made to suffer alone in a loveless orphanage.

"I never told Nilla," Lars said. "I knew it would crush her to know that the child had been abandoned."

"Then you don't know where Anders' son is, do you?"

"No," Lars returned, looking straight into Peter's eyes. "That is the task I am giving to you—find him."

His mouth falling open, Peter gaped at his stepuncle. "Find him?" he echoed incredulously. "Do you know how big Michigan is? And who's to say if he even stayed in this state."

"I know it will be difficult, but you must promise you will look for him."

"Difficult? Try impossible…look how long it took you two to find me, and you had a letter to help narrow your search."

"I know."

"And what am I supposed to do if the orphanage has closed or if they didn't keep records of—" Suddenly, a thought pounced on Peter's tired and throbbing head, "Axel did tell you what orphanage, didn't he?"

Lars shook his head.

Peter jumped up as if his willow-branch chair had caught on fire. "You expect me to check every orphanage around Detroit for…for…what name was the boy given?"

Lars looked away and said nothing.

A chill rippled through Peter. "You do know the kid's name, don't you?"

"No."

Although he knew the word was not a joke, Peter laughed at Lars' answer.

"Please, Peter, promise me that you'll try to find him."

"You're asking me to find a lost timber in a logjam—you realize that, don't you?"

"I'm asking you to find Anders' son and give him back the family I stole from him."

❧ ☙

Sitting in Peter's office, Jaxson slouched in his chair and listened in amazement as his friend finished recapping Lars Nilsson's incredible tale. "Man alive!" he exclaimed. He knew it wasn't the most intelligent answer, but it fit the situation perfectly. "How in Sam Hill does he expect you to find this stepbrother of yours?"

"It'll take a miracle, that's for sure," Peter murmured with a shrug.

"You'll be searching for a ghost."

Peter's eyes widened in surprise. "That's exactly what Doctor Spreyer said when I told him and Anna last night."

"So did you promise you'd try to find this ghost?"

With a humorless chuckle, Peter nodded. "Yep. Lars begged me again this morning when I drove him and Erik to the depot…I said I'd try."

Jaxson smirked at the response—it was typical Peter to promise to look for someone who might not even exist anymore. And, as he watched his careworn partner stack some papers on the desk, Jaxson shook his head. Why? he asked himself. Why did Lars Nilsson have to come and shove such an overwhelming obligation into his friend's arms? And why did Peter agree to take it?

Deciding to put an end to the foolishness, Jaxson pushed himself from his chair and joined Peter at the desk. "It ain't right what Mr. Nilsson asked ya to do, and I'm not gunna watch you chase all over Michigan for this kid, you gotta…" It was then that Jaxson noticed it—Peter had finally removed the mourning armband that he had worn since Daven's death. Maybe, he thought. Maybe Mr. Nilsson's visit had accomplished some good after all.

"I gotta what?"

"Huh?" Jaxson said, forgetting that he had stopped in mid-sentence. "Oh, you gotta…you gotta realize that you can't do it alone…I'll help all I can," he finished, inwardly laughing at his own acceptance of Mr. Nilsson's hopeless assignment.

Peter chuckled. "Thanks…but let's take care of the impossible task of getting some lumber first," he replied as he rubbed his eyes.

"Headache?"

"No, tired. After Lars and I finally finished, I ended up repeating the whole story to Anna, then to her father. By the time I got home, it was after midnight," Peter returned. "That reminds me," he continued as he picked up a thin, oblong case and placed it on his pile of papers. "I don't want to forget my glasses—the way things have been going, I may need them."

"Maybe this trip will do ya some good…it'll take your mind off everything for a bit."

Peter grunted a response and wandered over to the window. "Not everything."

"I can go, if you want," Jaxson offered, knowing that Peter hated the idea of not being around to block James Wild's advances toward Anna.

Leaning against the windowsill, Peter crossed his arms. "No…ever since last night, I've had this…this kinda jabbing inside me…I know I have to go to Willow Ridge, and I have to go today—I just don't know why."

"Well, it sounds as if God wants you there…just remember—"

"I know…our times are in His hands."

"Right," Jaxson said with a smile. He had repeated his favorite verse, over and over, whenever a new tribulation hit them—and it lifted his spirit to know that it had finally made an impression upon his friend. "It's gotta be the right time for somethin' to happen."

"Please," Peter proclaimed, holding up his hand, "I've had enough happen lately."

Jaxson chuckled at the light-hearted remark. "You goin' to Anna's before you leave?"

"No time."

"Need me to drive ya to the depot?"

Peter shook his head. "I already have a valise with me. I'll just head out from here and grab a horsecar."

As they drifted into silence, the clock in the corner of the room announced the quarter hour with a chime.

Exhaling deeply, Peter added, "I better get going…think the wood will last until we can get a shipment in?"

"There's plenty," Jaxson replied, trying to sound confident and optimistic. He knew their inventory would probably disappear by the week's end, but he wanted to relieve some of Peter's apprehension—even if that meant being untruthful.

"Just keep in mind that Emerson is due back from his sales trip on Saturday."

Moving over to the window, Jaxson placed his hand on Peter's shoulder and gave him a slight nudge toward the door. "We'll be fine…go to Willow Ridge…let me worry about the factory. I'll take care of everything, and I'll stop by and check on Anna at lunchtime."

Peter nodded. "You better make that supper time…her sisters will be there all day, and you know what it's like trying to get away from them."

"Yeah," Jaxson returned, but his answer was, once again, far from the truth. He didn't know what it was like trying to get away from Anna's sisters—because they made it very clear that they didn't want him around at all. "You're gunna miss your train…go."

⁕

With his valise in hand, Peter stepped to the edge of the sidewalk and peered down Second Street. Although it was only a dot in the distance, he was still relieved to see the horsecar waddling toward him—it was the first time in months that the vehicle was on time. Then a faint sound reached his ears…someone was calling him. Circling, he surveyed the faces of the people around him, but no one laid claim to the attention-getting call. Maybe he was wrong…

"Peter! Peter Leighton!"

This time he recognized the voice and scanned the crowd for Maxwell Green. Spotting the photographer's bushy-haired head bobbing toward him, Peter waved in return. "Max!" he shouted, casting a watchful eye on the approaching horsecar.

Finally, the photographer's face appeared as he broke through a group of people standing in the middle of the sidewalk. "Peter…Del at the…the showroom…said," Max panted out as he tried to catch his breath, "that you…you were on your way…to the depot. Glad…I caught you."

"What'd you do? Run all the way?"

"Prac…tically."

"Why?" Peter asked, now alarmed. "Is something wrong?"

Max shook his shaggy head as he gulped in some deep breaths. "No…wanted to show…you this," he announced, handing a photograph to Peter.

Taking the picture, Peter gazed at the rose-painted furniture that had been in his showroom only two days ago. The decorated set now sat in the middle of an elegant parlor setting—but somehow, Max had manipulated the lighting so that the exquisite brushstrokes and fine craftsmanship were the main focus of the picture. "Max, I'm sure the complexity of this photograph cost—"

"Forget that for a minute, Peter...do you like it?"

Glancing at the picture again, Peter smiled. "Yeah, you sure do know your craft...you've made our furniture look as if it belongs in a palace."

Max Green beamed in return and nodded so vehemently that his bushy, silvery mane danced on his head. "It did turn out well, didn't it? And, if you don't mind, I'd like to keep the furniture for a few more days."

"Sure, but why?"

Max shrugged. "I just want to try some things...experiment a little. Just to learn more for my own knowledge...so can I go ahead and make some more prints of this one?" he questioned as he pointed at the photograph in Peter's hand.

"Yes, but—"

"I know what you're going to say, but I have an idea. I learned a lot from this photograph—mainly that people like their portraits taken in this kind of scene. When I was setting everything up to take this," Max explained, tapping on the picture, "Mr. Taylor, you know, from the newspaper, insisted that his portrait be taken in this mock parlor—he thought it was the backdrop I always use. So I hope you don't mind, but I took his photograph just the way he wanted it—with your furniture."

Peter shook his head as he nervously stared at the approaching horsecar. It was within shouting distance, and if he didn't signal soon, the car would just lumber along its tracks right past him. "I don't mind, Max, but I have to get to the depot."

"I know...I know," Max replied hurriedly. "They told me you were going out of town...so here's my idea. We work out a trade—I'll take care of all the catalog pictures, and in return, Rheinhardt Furniture builds me some painted props for my studio...whatd'ya say?"

"But that's not fair to you...with Wild's order, there's no way we could make your pieces until September," Peter said as he hailed the horsecar.

"I know...that's all right...is it a deal?"

"Max, I've got to go...we'll talk when I get back." Jogging into the street, Peter grabbed the railing of the slowing but still moving horsecar and pulled himself up the step and onto the back platform. Then, without warning, the vehicle lurched forward as the driver up front, obviously unconcerned if Peter was aboard or not, urged the horse back up to speed. The movement flung Peter against the back railing, and as he tried to steady himself, he noticed that he held not only his valise in his left hand, but

Max's photograph too. Grabbing the picture with his free hand, Peter lifted it over his head and called out, "Max! Your photograph!"

"Keep it!" Max hollered. "Well? Should I make more prints? You know I'll keep at ya until you agree."

The increasing distance made Max Green's shout sound like a whisper, and Peter knew he had to answer immediately to be heard—which was not the way he liked to make decisions. "All right!" he finally yelled with a wave of his arm.

He wasn't sure if the photographer heard him or not, but then, with a chuckle, Peter shrugged off his doubt. He knew Max all too well—the man had probably planned to go ahead with the catalog pictures even if he had answered 'no.' With an exasperated sigh, Peter shoved the photograph into his valise and stepped toward the inside of the horsecar.

"Your fare, Sir."

It was only then that Peter saw the conductor standing on the back platform.

"I'm terribly sorry," Peter apologized, reaching into his waistcoat pocket. "I'm just trying to do too many things at once," he told the man as he handed him a nickel. *And, Peter added inwardly as he headed into the car, doing none of them well.*

After surveying the long seats that ran lengthwise down both sides, Peter settled himself on the right-side bench between two other businessmen and slid his bag under the seat with the heel of his boot. Then, as the horsecar rumbled and squeaked toward the train depot, Peter became very aware of two things...first, that he was the subject of a whispered conversation between the three women who sat across from him, and second, that the morning's activities had taken their toll on his already aching forearm. Trying to ignore the gawking women, Peter concentrated on his sore limb. And, as he opened and closed his right hand, he prayed that the rain would just come and go, so his arm could return to normal.

Maybe Jaxson was right, Peter thought. *Maybe the trip would do him some good—if nothing else, it would enable him to escape the endless parade of gossips that seemed to follow him everywhere in Sandorville.*

❦

"It looks delicious," Anna said.

"I just hope it tastes as good as it looks," Lynette returned. "As I said, I never made this recipe before...in fact, this is the first time I've even touched a pineapple."

Leaning over the kitchen table, both women peered at the pie that sat between them, then they looked at each other and giggled.

"There's only one way to know for sure," Anna replied, picking up the knife lying on the table.

"But it's not ready!" Lynette announced as she grasped her friend's hand. "Aunt Noelle always said that this pie should be served cold."

"Well, if we like it while it's still warm, then it'll be wonderful cold."

Lynette bit her lip and shook her head.

"Don't worry, Lyn. The refrigerator'll give it a nice chill before the girls get here."

"And what if your sisters don't like it?"

Anna laughed and sank the knife into the center of the pale-yellow treat. "Believe me, your worst pie would be better than anything those four could ever bake."

Lynette chuckled at the joke, but the humor still didn't stop the nervousness that was crawling over her. *Why am I so worried about meeting Anna's sisters?* Lynette asked herself. Then, as she considered the question further, she started to fidget with her ring—she knew exactly why she was so anxious…

Anna, Otto, Irene, and Peter had reminded her of how wonderful it felt to be accepted—without judgment or conditions. She wanted that feeling to continue, but after what Anna had said about her siblings, Lynette wondered if her good fortune would be short-lived.

"My sisters aren't really that bad," Anna said as she lifted out a piece of pie and slid it onto a plate.

Realizing that her features must be reflecting her uneasiness, Lynette blushed. "I'm sure they're not."

"Actually, at times, they can be quite civil…except for Marion—she just loves to…to agitate."

"Why?"

Easing a second slice onto a dish, Anna shrugged. "Marion's always been like that. She'll do whatever it takes to make you angry and then just sit back and watch the show," she answered, handing one of the plates and a fork to Lynette. "Well… shall we taste?"

As Lynette held up her triangle of pie and examined it, question after question ran through her head. Did she remember her aunt's directions correctly? Was the baking time long enough? Would Anna be pleased? Suddenly, her trepidation melted into curiosity, and Lynette plunged her fork into the pineapple dessert. But, even before she could scoop up a sample, Anna's moan of delight told her that the recipe was a success.

"Lyn, this is marvelous!"

Slipping a forkful into her mouth, Lynette agreed wholeheartedly—the pineapple pastry was scrumptious.

"Oh, I just had a great idea!" Anna exclaimed. "You should make more of these and sell the slices at the open-air market on Saturday…I'll bet you'll sell every piece by noon."

"Anna, I can't do that."

"Why?"

"They're your pineapples."

"Well, I'm giving them to you…besides, I would prefer to just have them gone and out of Peter's sight."

Lynette nodded in full understanding. Peter's worry and anger over James Wild's extravagant present had been extremely obvious—especially when he refused to even taste the fruit. "He's jealous," Lynette finally offered.

"Why? The pineapples were just a gift from a friend."

"No, they weren't, Anna," Lynette returned, setting her unfinished pie on the table. "They were an expensive present from another man."

"I'm sure James didn't mean it like that…he was just being kind to the family. He and Papa have been working quite closely trying to improve the hospital."

"Mr. Wild addressed that crate of pineapples to you, and he sent eight, not one."

"He's harmless, Lynette," Anna snipped, annoyance ringing in her voice.

Becoming just as perturbed, Lynette placed her hands on her hips. "Then you wouldn't mind if another girl in town started giving Peter freshly made fudge or darning his socks? And you wouldn't get the least bit upset if he accepted those gifts with nary a word of caution to the girl?"

Anna began to answer, then stopped, and after a moment of thought, she said, "I didn't really look at it that way."

"I wouldn't say all this if Mr. Wild was just a friend, but you yourself said that he has romantic notions about you."

"But James knows they are futile…he knows I'm engaged."

Lynette sighed and settled onto one of the chairs surrounding the table. And, as she placed a forkful of pie into her mouth and savored the sweetness, she tried to find the right words for her reply…

"When I first met Redmund Chesnay, something in my spirit said 'be wary of this man.' I was given many glimpses of his real personality, but I was in love and overlooked much more than I should have—I ignored the warnings…I get the same inkling about James Wild. He's a man who's used to getting what he wants, and right now, he wants you. Please, be watchful around him."

Without responding, Anna sat kitty-corner to Lynette and ate her dessert in silence.

Biting at her lower lip, Lynette prayed that she had not alienated Anna with her lecture, but she knew, deep in her soul, that James Wild had a greedy spirit and Anna's innocent, trusting nature didn't see it—yet.

Finishing the last of her pie, Anna pushed her plate away. "I trust your intuition," she finally said. "I'll try to make my 'no' much louder, so James will completely understand that I am devoted to Peter—and that way Peter will know it too."

"I'm sorry...I didn't mean to preach."

Anna smiled. "No, you spoke from your heart—just like Mama." Then Anna's brow crinkled and she gazed into Lynette's eyes. "While we are on the subject of intuition...you said something on Monday that's...well, that's been bothering me."

"What did I say?"

"When we were standing in the doorway, you questioned me about Peter's age...why?"

Lynette shrugged. "I'm sorry if that worried you...I meant nothing by it," she answered. Anna remained mute, but her intense stare told Lynette that she wanted a more detailed explanation. With a resigned exhale, Lynette put in, "I just found it curious that you and Peter are about the same ages that Mr. Chesnay and I were when we got married."

"Really?" Anna replied, her eyebrows rising in surprise. "My sisters keep telling me that the age difference is going to make it difficult for us...do you think it had anything to do with...with your troubles?"

"For me it did," Lynette confessed, lowering her eyes. "In my naivete, I was easily deceived by Mr. Chesnay's charms."

"Oh?"

Hearing the sudden alarm in Anna's voice, Lynette reached across the table and held her friend's hand. "As I told you, I had many chances to see Mr. Chesnay's true nature, but I was so lost in love that I closed my eyes to his inconsistencies...the only advice I can give you is to keep your eyes open and confront God and Peter about what you see."

Anna nodded. "Mama told me that I'd know Peter by the fruit that he bears... he's had some terrible things happen to him this past year, but his essence has never changed."

"That's good," Lynette returned as she patted Anna's hand. "And, remember, advice is just advice. Your sisters and I can only tell you our points of view—biased as they may be. It's the Lord's guidance you need to seek the most."

Anna bobbed her head as her face lit up with delight. "I know God meant for Peter and me to be together...when I first saw him at the train depot a year ago, it was as if a sign had appeared over him that read 'This Is Your Husband.' I can't explain it—I just knew. And then, a few days later, Papa and I were at the open-air market, and I went to get some honey for Mama...all of a sudden, a bouquet of flowers appeared in front of me held by a strong, sturdy hand—it was Peter."

Lynette smiled at Anna's story—and at her friend's excitement about the meeting. "It sounds as though you two had a very romantic beginning."

"Yes, but it was a rough road for awhile…Peter was a very different man back then—he was quite bitter about all the misfortunes in his life, and he didn't have a good relationship with God."

"And now?"

"Now, the bitterness has melted away, and he's become a very godly man."

Lynette sighed, and as she picked at the rest of her pie, her thoughts traveled back to Redmund Chesnay…and to the discrediting letters that he had written to her past landlords and employers…and to the hardships that she and William had endured because of him. "God's blessed you with a Christian man…that's wonderful," Lynette murmured as she fought the envy welling up inside her. "Mr. Chesnay was not a follower of Christ—nor is he now. When I agreed to marry him, I didn't think it would cause any problems—but it did. I tried to follow God's plan for our marriage…Mr. Chesnay followed his own."

This time Anna grasped Lynette's hand, and the two women exchanged heart-felt stares. Finally, Anna broke the silence. "Thank you."

"For what?"

"For listening…and for your guidance…and for treating me like an adult—my sisters don't do that…to them I'm still a child."

"I'm afraid they will always treat you like that—you're their little sister," Lynette offered with a grin, then her features sobered. "And thank you for not judging me—or my mistakes."

The corners of Anna's lips turned upward. "You're welcome…so are we going to make some pineapple pies for the open-air market?"

Her friend's tenacity made Lynette's grin return, but she still shook her head. "I don't have enough money for the ingredients."

"We'll use what we have here," Anna replied as she stood and lifted the pie tin off the table. "I better get this into the refrigerator…I want it to be nice and cold when the girls try it."

"But six more pies would use too much of your supplies…it's not right."

"It'll be fine," Anna returned, placing the pastry on a shelf in the icebox.

Instantly, Lynette began to stroke her ruby ring. Although her mouth kept saying 'no'…her heart was screaming 'yes.' She knew Anna's offer could help bring her secret dream—to open her own bakery—into reality. But she also knew that she could try and fail—and end up watching that desire crumble into ruins. "I'm sure there's a bakery in town that already frequents the market," she tried. "They probably wouldn't appreciate the competition."

"There are many bakeries in town," Anna answered as she closed the refrigerator door, "but most of them don't sell at the market, and the couple that do, well, let's just say that the people will be thankful for a different place to buy their baked goods…if it'll ease your mind, you can replace the ingredients you use with your profits."

"What if there are no profits?"

Anna laughed as she ambled back to the table. "Lynette, you tasted the pie—they'll sell…it'll be great. We'll offer those people who pass by our stand a little taste—then let them know they can buy a slice or a whole pie." As Anna stared into the air considering the idea, her eyes started to twinkle. "And," she proclaimed, "you could make some molasses cakes too—the one you made on Monday was delicious."

"Wait," Lynette said, rising. "There's no time to make the food and a booth."

"Sure there is…and if not, we'll just sell out of the back of Papa's wagon. Don't worry."

"Is there a charge to sell something at the market?"

"It's free," Anna returned, then her enthusiasm visibly faded. "If you don't want to do it, just tell me."

Releasing a deep breath, Lynette studied Anna's crestfallen expression. God was opening a door—why was she so determined to keep pulling it closed again? She could fail, yes, but the market could lead her down a new and exciting path…if only she would step out in faith and make the decision to go down that road. "I want to," Lynette said as a flutter ran through her body, "I'm just not sure if I'll be ready by Saturday."

"I'll help you."

Even though the fluttering had transformed into exhilaration, Lynette shook her head. "You are supposed to be slowing down, remember?"

"But I want to do this."

"You are too overwhelmed already."

Anna's shoulders slumped. "I know I've taken on too much, but it's the things that I haven't chosen, the things that have fallen on me and my loved ones—that's what's drowning me…do you remember those waves I told you about?"

Lynette answered with a nod.

"It's those waves that I can't take anymore…I think if one more comes, I'll go down for sure."

Clearly hearing the fear and exhaustion in her friend's voice, Lynette walked over to Anna and hugged her. "Give your worries to God…He can carry a lot more than we—"

"So this is where you are hiding!"

The unfamiliar voice startled Lynette, and she quickly circled to see a woman standing near the kitchen doorway. The newcomer's mannerisms and features mimicked Anna's, but the woman lacked her friend's kind and gentle demeanor.

"Marion!" Anna announced, perturbed. "What are you doing here?"

Marion rolled her eyes. "It's Wednesday, my dear, or have you forgotten that too?"

"Yes, I know it's Wednesday," Anna replied coolly. "I meant what are you doing here already? You're an hour early…and what do you mean 'forgotten that too'?"

"That's precisely what I mean," Marion said, fingering a large, gaudy brooch on her overly decorated visiting-suit. "You obviously forgot that we were coming at eleven today—that's what I meant by 'forgotten that too.'"

Anna's lips tightened into a thin line and she crossed her arms. "I can't forget what I was never told."

"What are you talking about? I told you the last time I saw you," Marion returned harshly as her caressing moved from the brooch to one of her equally garish earrings.

"And when was that?" Anna persisted.

"Well, I don't remember—but I know I told you," Marion muttered with a flip of her hand. "Now, the girls will be here soon, so you better get started setting everything out."

Anna's features turned deep red and clouded with anger, but her only response was a loud sigh.

Attempting to slice through the tension, Lynette offered, "We'll start right now…however, we do have some new things on the menu that will take a little extra time to get ready."

"I'm sorry, Lyn. I've neglected to introduce you again," Anna said, her expression softening. "Marion, I'd like you to meet Lynette Chesnay. She's going to be helping me with—"

"I know who she is," Marion cut in. "Mama just told me all about her." Then, without any words of greeting or welcome, Marion pivoted on her heel and left the room.

As she watched Anna's sister fly from the kitchen, Lynette raised an eyebrow. She had hoped that Anna had exaggerated about Marion's fondness for agitation—but obviously, the description was quite accurate.

"That," Anna murmured, "was Marion."

"Ah," Lynette replied, still trying to figure out why there was such a large chasm between the two sisters' personalities.

Anna laughed. "I see she also left you speechless."

Lynette smiled, gladdened by Anna's cheerier mood. Then, as she considered Marion's disposition—and the destruction it might cause—her grin vanished. "Anna?" she asked as she fidgeted with her ring. "What…what were you and your parents planning on telling your sisters about…about my divorce?"

Anna held her finger up to her lips. "That's what I plan on telling them," she whispered, "especially Marion. She wouldn't take very kindly to the news of the divorce. She's always been a thorn, but ever since she moved back here, she's developed such a highfalutin attitude."

"Moved back?"

"Yes, she and her husband, Michael, used to live in Grand Rapids, where he worked in a jewelry shop. Eventually, Michael's boss asked him to become a partner in a store here in Sandorville...I think all that jewelry has gone to Marion's head—she puts on such airs because of it."

Lynette bobbed her head in understanding, remembering Marion's blatant attempts to draw attention to her flamboyant brooch and earrings. "Does Michael make the jewelry or just sell it?"

"Just sells it. But he does have a wonderful jeweler who works for him, Jacob Moss... Mr. Moss made our engagement ring," Anna chirped, holding out her left hand.

As Lynette admired the ring, the corners of her lips curled upward—even their taste in jewelry separated the two sisters. Anna's ring, refined and tasteful, consisted of a plain band of gold and two small inlaid diamonds. And, between the gems, a small cross had been carved into the metal. "It's beautiful."

Anna's face brightened with a sparkling smile. "We told Mr. Moss our ideas for the ring, and he made them come to life," she said, then her expression changed to a smirk. "Michael said that since our ring was so tiny and unimaginative it could just be made from scraps, so he would only charge us for Mr. Moss' time to make it."

Lynette's eyes widened in amazement. "He actually said that?"

Anna sighed and nodded. "Well, I guess we better start getting the food ready...I am not looking forward to this gathering at all," she mumbled as she moved to the counter near the side window, pulled out a drawer, and shuffled through the linens inside.

"Oh? Why?" Lynette prompted, clearing the dishes from the table.

"Because these luncheons have become a farce...my sisters say that they want to spend time with Mama, but then, when we do get together, all they do is avoid her," Anna explained, removing a light-green checkered tablecloth from the drawer. "I think they are frightened by the changes they see in my mother, and they busy themselves just so they don't have to face her illness. They'll go through the whole afternoon talking and gossiping, but they'll never ask Mama how she is feeling or what they can do for her."

"If you dread these meetings with your sisters, then why don't you just..." As she heard the words come out of her mouth, Lynette paused and covered her lips with her fingers—the last thing she wanted was to pass along one of her own worst habits.

"Why don't I what?" Anna questioned as she unfurled the green cloth and waved it over the table. "Why don't I stop having them?"

"Yes," Lynette replied sheepishly, helping to even out the fabric as it floated onto the table, "that's what I was going to say, but I've learned, from experience, that's not the thing to do."

"Then what is the thing to do?"

"Talk to your sisters…use your words as a mirror, and show them how much their remarks hurt."

"I…I can't."

"Believe me, Anna, I know it's hard…I didn't have the strength to do it with my family. Whenever they came at me with their hate-filled words about the divorce or whatever, I just kept quiet. Eventually, it came to the point where I dreaded getting together with them…and instead of making my feelings known or telling them how their actions were affecting me, I just stepped away from them—emotionally and physically…it was the wrong way to handle the whole situation." Lynette waited for a response, but her friend just stood motionless as a statue, staring at the kitchen table. "Anna? Are you okay?"

Slowly, Anna nodded and looked up. "That's exactly what's been happening… and not just with my sisters."

"What do you mean?"

"I've written and written my brother, Hans, asking when he could come home for my wedding. He'll write back, but he never answers that question—he keeps skirting the issue…I don't understand…Hans and I were always so open with each other—now, he won't even talk to me. I've wanted to tell him that I feel as if becoming a doctor is the only important thing in his life."

"You've wanted to tell him…then you haven't told him?"

Anna shook her head. "I just didn't want to make any more waves for myself, but his silence is a wave of its own…I feel as though Hans has abandoned me."

"You need to tell him that."

"But what if it just makes matters worse…what if I make him angry and he doesn't come home? I want him here. I want him to meet Peter. I want the wedding to be perfect…for Mama and Papa's sake."

"Only Heaven is perfect," Lynette said with a smile of sympathy. "Love makes up for the imperfections…your parents know that."

Instantly, Anna stood up straight as if a cast-iron shawl had slipped off her shoulders. "You're right…I've been making Peter wait until everything is perfect—until all the waves stop…that's not going to happen, is it?"

"It could—the Lord can still any storm…or He may just still your heart instead, so you can cope with the waves. You need to spend—" Lynette tried to finish her sentence, but a choir of inharmonious voices from the front of the house silenced her. "I think the rest of your sisters are here," she declared, trying to be heard over the increasing din.

"Whatever gave you that idea?" Anna laughed. "Well, pick up your armor, Lyn, the battle is about to begin."

Beaming at her friend's sudden burst of resilience, Lynette winked in return. She had no doubt, now, that they both would survive the approaching luncheon because they were no longer alone—they had each other for protection.

―――

Sitting on a rough-hewn chair with his head resting against his hand, Peter exhaled deeply as he continued to wait for Logan MacColl—the man he had traveled so far to see. Slowly, his heavy eyelids closed, and as a sleepy haze engulfed him, his head suddenly bobbed forward. Jerking awake and wondering if anyone had noticed his inappropriate nap, Peter sheepishly gazed around the sawmill's little office. Seeing no one, he pushed his stiff body from the chair and stretched, trying to restore some life into his sleep-filled head.

Normally, the several-hour trip to Willow Ridge was enjoyable and relaxing, but between the overcrowded train, an army of screaming children, a drunken salesman, and a broken stagecoach, the journey had become an all-day nightmare that drained what little energy he had. And, although lumber was his main objective, all he wanted now was to find a hotel and get a few hours of peaceful sleep.

Circling, Peter surveyed the tiny office's bare interior, which offered only one item of visual interest—a photograph hanging on the wall behind the desk. Walking over to get a better view, Peter studied the picture of what must have been the sawmill's first day of operation, then his attention wandered to the bottom of the photograph where someone had painted the words 'As for me and my house, we will serve the Lord.' Rereading the verse, Peter half-smiled and hoped that Logan MacColl did indeed live according to the painted message.

His vision blurring, Peter rubbed his stinging eyes. So far, regrettably, the trip had accomplished only one thing—now, he was even more miserable. And, as he began to wonder if he had made a terrible mistake, the more forgettable events of his arduous day bounced back into his head…

The loud, inebriated salesman who tried to sell a 'cure-all ointment' to everyone on the train…leaving his dark-lensed glasses in his office, along with the work he had planned on bringing…almost getting run down by a wagon as he rushed from the Willow Ridge stage depot to the sawmill…the hasty decision to let Max Green continue with the catalog photographs…

"That picture was taken a long time ago…I'm afraid none of us look that young anymore."

The voice and the sound of the door clicking shut wrenched Peter from his thoughts, and he turned to face an older but very sturdy, red-haired man. "Mr. MacColl?" he questioned.

"Mr. Leighton, I apologize for making you wait," MacColl offered, extending his arm. "I have a few men out on deliveries, and I was filling in for them."

Shaking MacColl's sawdust-frosted hand, Peter smiled inwardly at the all-too-familiar situation. "It's okay…and I'm sorry that I've arrived so late in the day. My trip took a great deal longer than I had expected."

MacColl replied with a loud belly-laugh. "That ride from the train to here isn't exactly a Sunday morning drive, is it?"

Peter chuckled. "No, it's far from that," he agreed. "Our stage even lost a wheel on the way."

MacColl grunted with a nod. "I wouldn't doubt it—that's one rough trail…if only the railroad had laid its tracks just a little more to the east," the lumberman mused. "But, anyway, I'm glad you're here. In fact, ever since I got your telegram about the maple, I've been praying that we could do business."

"How so?" Peter asked as the comment snapped him wide-awake.

"I had a huge order come in for hundreds of board feet of maple—then it was canceled. Your need for maple is a prayer answered…we're just too small to have that kind of inventory just lying around."

'Just lying around.' The words echoed inside Peter's head—after all the challenges he had endured trying to procure lumber, all he needed was here in Willow Ridge 'just lying around.' He was thankful that he had been guided to MacColl's sawmill, but he couldn't help wondering why God had taken so long to point him in the right direction.

"What I don't understand," MacColl continued, slapping the sawdust from his clothes, "is why you came this far for lumber. I'm sure any place in Grand Rapids would have what you need."

Peter smirked cynically. "As I said in my telegram, I'm from Rheinhardt Furniture in Sandorville."

MacColl shrugged and scratched at his beard. "So?"

A bead of sweat rolled down Peter's back at the lumberman's revelation. MacColl's ignorance of Rheinhardt Furniture's past held both calm waters and raging rapids—and Peter wondered which way the lumberman would drift when he learned the truth.

"We, uh, we had a little trouble about a year ago," Peter said, meandering toward the window. "There was some corruption in the factory, and we had quite a scandal develop because of it." As he studied MacColl, Peter frowned, and another drop of perspiration crawled along his back—the lumberman just stared at the floor, completely emotionless. "The guilty parties were taken care of," Peter went on, "and the factory now has new management, a new philosophy, and a new product…but unfortunately, we have a rather tarnished reputation…one that makes people shy away from doing business with us."

MacColl abruptly raised his head and jabbed a dusty finger at Peter. "I remember now," he announced, "I read about you in the newspapers…you're the one who revealed what was going on in that factory."

Feeling as if he had just been handed a tubful of bricks, Peter winced and nodded.

"That was some story," MacColl remarked as he perched himself on the edge of his desk. "Every newspaper in these parts had tales about it."

Peter released a deep breath as some more bricks of doubt and worry landed in his imaginary tub.

"You said that Rheinhardt Furniture has new people in charge—are you one of them?"

"Yes…after all the mess was cleaned up, Karl Rheinhardt, the original owner, and I became partners, hoping to rebuild the company." Still not being able to determine if MacColl was pleased or disgusted with him, Peter decided to offer a more in-depth answer. "Well, it started out as just Karl and I—fifty, fifty. Karl decided that I should handle the reins of the company while he settled back into the role of our designer, but we still found that we hit too many impasses when it came to making decisions. So, to keep from strangling each other, we brought in our foreman, Jaxson Averill, as a third partner…Jaxson's ten percent interest has ended most of the dueling between Karl and me."

MacColl grunted again. "And the new philosophy?" he asked, crossing his arms.

Peter pointed to MacColl's photograph and the painted Bible verse. "Same as yours."

Another grunt. "It's still Rheinhardt Furniture, isn't it?"

With a confused scowl, Peter nodded.

"You said you had a new product," MacColl clarified. "You still making furniture?"

"Yes," Peter returned, then he grinned as he remembered that his valise—and Max's picture—were with him, sitting under the chair. Moving over to the unfinished seat, Peter squatted and dragged his bag into the open. "We've developed a new line of decorated furniture," he explained as he dug inside his case. Finally locating the now travel-worn photograph, Peter stepped over to the desk and handed it to MacColl. "This is why we need the maple."

Squinting, MacColl looked at the photograph, then he stretched out his arm and examined the picture from a distance. "The eyes aren't what they used to be," he laughed. "Land sakes, this is some nice-looking furniture."

As he leaned on the desk next to MacColl, Peter nodded, then cast his eyes upward and smiled. He knew that God could work miracles—he had seen them happen—but it constantly amazed him that the Lord cared enough to navigate even the smallest detail into place…such as maneuvering Max Green's picture into the midst of his meeting. "We have a great crew, and they really enjoy working on them," Peter added as MacColl continued to admire the brushstroked table and chairs.

"It shows…you must have a heck of a time meetin' delivery dates with all that paint—it's gotta slow you down."

Feeling his load of worry-filled bricks lighten a bit, Peter replied with a grin, "Somewhat, but our decorators added some kind of siccative to the paint, and it's really helped with the drying time."

With a grunt of fascination MacColl dropped the photograph on the desk and clasped his hands together. "Well, you ready to pick out your wood?"

Pushing himself upright, Peter searched MacColl's face for sincerity. "You don't mind working with Rheinhardt Furniture?"

The lumberman shrugged. "Is it the same company it used to be?"

"No."

"Then I don't mind."

Instantly, his tub of concerns evaporated and Peter grinned. "Thank you." But, as he considered his unexpected bonanza, one brick of worry reappeared and he inquired, "If we close the deal today, how soon do you think we can have delivery?"

MacColl rubbed his hand over his beard. "When do you need it?"

"Soon…very soon."

Standing up, the lumberman shook his head. "I don't know, I'll need to check the train schedule, and I gotta be honest, it's gunna take a lot to get to the depot— that road just rips my wagons to shreds."

Peter grimaced as he felt the lumber being yanked from his grasp.

"Although…there might be another solution."

"What's that?"

"The road south runs parallel to the railroad," MacColl explained, "but it's a decent thoroughfare…we could just deliver by wagon. It'll take a solid day or more, but it'll work even better for me."

"By wagon?"

MacColl bobbed his head. "The train would require loading the lumber here and then reloading it onto the train, plus getting over that idiot west-bound road. If we just load the wood and head right out, it'll end up taking less labor and save some of my wagon wheels…the only problem I see is that it might only be a partial shipment."

Rolling his watch chain between his fingers, Peter contemplated the idea. Going by wagon would create a direct line between source and destination, lessening the chances of mishaps or interference. And, if James Wild did get wind of the new lumber order, the man would never think that it would be delivered by such a simple and basic method. "Wagon sounds perfect."

"Great! I have a couple of men who might be willing to start out with the wood Sunday afternoon—they've been asking for the chance to earn some extra money. If so, we could deliver by late Monday."

"And the remainder of the order?"

"Shouldn't be any problem getting it to you by Friday."

Extending his hand, Peter declared, "I appreciate all the extra effort."

As MacColl started to reply, the office door flew open, and a mountain of books and papers entered, held by a thin, brown-haired man who could barely be seen behind his cargo. "Kyle? Is that you?" MacColl asked.

"Yeah. Here're the catalogs you wanted," the brown-haired man returned as the pile of books began to tumble out of his hands. "Uh, help…"

Both Peter and MacColl lunged for the avalanching catalogs and grabbed what they could as the stack gushed onto the desk like a mud-slide, shoving MacColl's papers to the floor.

"Sorry, Logan. Quite an entrance, huh?" the man announced, then, noticing Peter, he thrust out his hand. "Kyle Knight, court jester. And you are?"

Dropping his catch onto the desk with the rest of the fallen books, Peter shook the man's hand. "Peter Leighton."

"Mr. Leighton's a new customer. He's going to be taking some of that maple off my hands."

"Splendid!" Knight exclaimed. "Good to meet you, Mr. Leighton. Where do you hail from?"

"Sandorville."

"Sandorville, huh? Perhaps you'd like to take a few of my catalogs with—"

"Kyle," MacColl cut in gruffly, "Mr. Leighton's my customer, remember?" Then, turning toward Peter, he added, "Kyle works for a mail-order company out of Detroit."

"Hopefully not as the delivery man," Peter commented with a grin.

Knight laughed out loud. "That was funny. Really, take some catalogs with you," he urged, pointing to the spilled books. "We're branching out into all kinds of merchandise."

"Kyle, let Mr. Leighton pick out his maple before you start loading him down with your catalogs, okay?"

❦

As he rested his hand on one of the motionless saws, Jaxson scrutinized the interior of the factory, which was now illuminated by only the evening sun peeking through the windows. This was his favorite time of the day—the finale—when he could watch the sawdust settle onto the slumbering machines and congratulate his fellow laborers on a good day's work. He didn't know why, but it always comforted him to see the factory fall asleep at night. Maybe, he thought, that peace came from knowing what the Rheinhardt Furniture Company was like before Peter Leighton came…when there was no respite from the work.

Reaching up, Jaxson twisted the gas lever on the lamp above his head, stopping the flow of fuel. Abruptly, the starved flame vanished. Then, for the third time, Jaxson scanned the other hanging lights to make sure that they, also, were safely extinguished. He knew he was being overly cautious, but he figured he had a right to be vigilant—especially since the old building had been destroyed by a lit cigar.

Yet, Jaxson reminded himself, some good did come from the ruined factory—a new, vibrant, honest company had emerged from the ashes. And he thanked God that he was a part of it. Somehow, the Lord had rearranged the pieces of his life and made him foreman—and co-owner—of Rheinhardt Furniture, the place that had held him captive and tortured him for years…God was definitely full of surprises.

Glancing around the almost deserted building, Jaxson noticed that three of his workers—Manning Cole, Jasper Jennings, and Holden Miller—were having a small conference in the shadows near the front door. Normally, he would have just shrugged off the meeting, but it was the trio's fifth clandestine parley since the morning.

"They are at it again, I see," Hermann Winkel said, joining him.

The comment increased Jaxson's concern—he wasn't the only one to notice the covert gatherings. "Yep," was all he answered.

"Jennings and Miller are not the only ones that Manning Cole's been talking to."

"Really?" Jaxson returned as he peered at the wiry German.

Hermann nodded. "Do you want me to try to find out what he's been up to?"

"No," Jaxson answered with a shake of his head, "I can't ask you to do that, Hermann."

The thin German bobbed his head again. "I'll see what I can find out from the others."

Jaxson smiled inwardly at Hermann's stubbornness—and loyalty. Then his thoughts drifted to another time…a time when the only emotion between him and the spry German was hatred. No, Jaxson corrected himself silently, you were the one filled with anger, not Hermann. Sighing, Jaxson pushed the memories from his head…he was very different back then…everything was different back then…

"Hermann, I just said that I didn't want you to—"

"Ah, I may not have to ask the others after all."

Jaxson scowled at the comment, then looked to where Hermann was pointing—Manning Cole had disappeared, but Jennings and Miller were both strutting toward him. And he knew, in his gut, that the approaching confrontation would not be good.

"Mr. Averill, me and Jasper've decided to move on. We want our wages," Holden Miller announced, thrusting his chest out in defiance.

Miller's statement shook Jaxson to the bone, but he tried to keep the shock from showing on his face. "Really? I thought you boys liked it here."

"Yeah, well, we do, but we got a better offer in Grand Rapids," Miller returned, losing some of his boldness.

"You did? Is that what you and Manning Cole were talkin' about just now?"

"Uh…no, we was talking about—"

"He just asked us," Jasper Jennings interrupted, "if we wanted to go with him to get somethin' to drink…that's allowed, ain't it?"

"Sure it is. I was just wonderin' where you boys heard about this great place in Grand Rapids."

"Around," Jennings snapped. "We ain't bound to this factory…we can leave any time we wanna."

Jaxson slowly nodded. Although Jennings and Miller were far from being good employees, they were still two strong backs that he didn't want to lose. "Yeah, you can go anytime…but you sure I can't do somethin' to make you wanna stay? We really need the help."

Holden Miller laughed. "Not unless you're gunna pay us ten cents more an hour, like this other place."

"Ten cents? Where you goin' that you'd get that kind of money?" Jaxson asked, dumbfounded by Miller's announcement.

"The Sulli—"

"That's none of your funeral," Jasper Jennings cut in. "So can we get our money? We got some comin' for this week."

"Yeah, but everything's closed up for the day, you know that…I can't pay ya 'til tomorrow…I'll have your money in the morning."

"You just better have it when we come back."

"We're sorry to leave ya shorthanded, Mr. Averill," Holden Miller put in weakly. "Maybe we could stay through the end of the week…that other place don't need us 'til Mon—"

With a quick jab, Jasper Jennings elbowed Miller in the ribs. "No, we can't. Today's our last day…we'll be here in the mornin' for our money," Jennings proclaimed, then both men turned and headed toward the door.

"Man alive," Jaxson murmured, "when will this curse of bad luck go away?"

"Don't you worry," Hermann soothed, placing his hand on Jaxson's shoulder. "My brothers will arrive soon. They are good men and will work fifty times harder than Jennings and Miller ever did…and if I tell them to, they will work even harder than that."

Jaxson grinned at his coworker's consoling words. "Now, now," he teased, "you sound like Quentin Fetch…I don't think either of us want to see the factory being run like that again."

Hermann shook his head and laughed wearily. "That much is true…but my brothers will be good workers. I've told them how much we've all been through, especially Peter, and they want to help."

At the mention of Peter's name, Jaxson winced—losing two more employees would not help lighten his friend's burdens.

＊＊＊

At an unusually relaxed pace, Peter meandered down the freshly replanked sidewalk of Willow Ridge's only main street. With no factory disasters or worries about lumber to occupy his time, he had the evening free—and he was determined to enjoy it. As he neared the town's general store, Peter tipped his hat and said hello to a passing couple, then he stopped and absently perused the collection of goods on display in the store's front window. Exhaling, Peter shook his head…his life had changed so much. Growing up, he always figured that he would spend all his days in Bradlee, running the general store that had belonged to his father—never, in his wildest imaginings, did he think he'd end up partially owning a struggling furniture company.

As he resumed his aimless, twilight walk, Peter's thoughts rambled over all the twists and turns that had propelled him from those simple days in Bradlee to his complicated life in Sandorville. He had no desire to relive any of the life-changing milestones that he had gone through, but he was thankful that some wonderful people had entered his life because of them—it was those individuals that made all the tribulations worthwhile. With a deep sigh, Peter smiled. For the first time since…since what seemed like forever, he was at peace with the events of his past.

Completely immersed in his memories, Peter didn't see the gentleman that was hurrying toward him until it was too late—and he slammed into the man head-on. Dazed, Peter staggered backward and grabbed the hitching post next to him for balance. Shaking the fog out of his head, Peter rubbed his eyes, then, noticing that his victim's hat was lying near his boot, he bent down, snatched the hat from the sidewalk, and held it out to the stranger.

"I apologize," Peter said. "The collision was completely my fault…I hope I didn't cause you any harm."

The man cursed as he examined the bump on his head with his fingers. "You idiot…you nearly killed me!" he shouted.

Eventually, the stranger lowered his hand, allowing his face to come into full view. And, as Peter caught sight of the man's features, his breath caught in his throat and his hand tightened into a death grip around the hat's brim. Swallowing hard,

Peter couldn't help but stare at the man's blonde hair…and his familiar chiseled features…and his crystal-blue eyes…

"Daven?" Peter choked out in a hoarse whisper.

"No," the man snapped, yanking at his hat, "the name's Nick Anderson…now, let go of my hat, or I'll rip your arm off."

The name 'Anderson' slugged Peter in the face, and as the blow surged through him, his hand went numb and opened. Taking his hat, Nick Anderson cursed once, then twice, then continued on his way. Although Peter tried to call out, no words would come, and in stunned silence, he just watched Nick Anderson strut down the sidewalk and enter the town's saloon.

"Oh, Lord," Peter murmured, his heart pounding against his chest, "that's him, isn't it? That's the other son."

The man wasn't quite as tall as Daven had been, and he was more sinewy and weathered, but there was no mistake about it—Nick Anderson was indeed Anders' lost son—and the name confirmed it. It was an incredible coincidence…or was it? As Peter considered the events of the past few days, he shook his head. It was too perfect to be a coincidence…this meeting could have only been arranged by the Master of timing. Suddenly, everything became clear—so clear that it sounded as if God was whispering in his ear…

This was why, Peter. This was why your lumber was allowed to burn—so you would come to Willow Ridge on this day and see your stepbrother. And this was why you had to be forced into accepting Daven's death—so you wouldn't think that this man was a delusion or an apparition sent to punish you. And this was why Lars Nilsson had to come and tell you the truth about your family before you left for your trip—so you wouldn't walk away from Nick Anderson. This was why everything happened as it did. This was why.

Taking a deep breath, Peter tried to calm his speeding heart. He wanted to chase after Nick Anderson, but it felt as if his boots were nailed to the sidewalk. How? How was he going to tell this man about his past? How was he going to tell Nick Anderson that his destiny had been dramatically changed by one man's selfish choices?

❋Five❋

Giving up on the small shotglass on the table, Nick Anderson leaned back in his chair, grabbed his bottle of whiskey, and guzzled down three mouthfuls—only then did the liquor start to numb his throbbing head. Feeling the growing knot on his face, Nick cursed. The injury was an all too appropriate ending to his rancid Wednesday. With a tired sigh, Nick took another swig from his bottle and mentally reviewed his day—and being fired from his sixth job. Maybe the dismissal was a signal, he told himself. Maybe it was time to leave Willow Ridge. Why not? He had worn out just about everything in town anyway—including his welcome. Nodding, Nick poured more whiskey into his mouth. Yep, the decision was made. He would leave Willow Ridge—and his many unpaid obligations—first thing in the morning.

As he started to take another gulp of whiskey, a shadow passed over him and lingered on the table. Peering upward, Nick blinked his eyes, trying to focus on the man standing next to him. "What do you want?" he asked, finally recognizing the slightly graying, dark-haired stranger who was responsible for his lump. "Come to finish me off?"

"Mr. Anderson, there's something I need to discuss with you," the man returned as he sat on the chair opposite him.

"I didn't say you could join me," Nick growled, pushing himself upright. Then, noticing that the dark-haired man kept looking at him—and his eyes—Nick silently swore. People constantly gawked at his light-blue eyes, and over the years, he had grown weary of the undesired attention. "No, they're not glass. Yes, I can see out of them. Yes, they've always been this color. Any other questions?"

The stranger lowered his gaze and laughed lightly. "I'm sorry…that's not why I was staring…you just look so much like Daven," the man replied as he slowly pulled off his soft felt hat and pushed it onto the table.

"Who's this Daven anyway?" Nick demanded, then he held up his hand. "You know what? I don't really care. Now, pick up your hat and go away Mr...."

"Leighton, Peter Leighton," the man announced, extending his hand.

Ignoring the gesture, Nick leaned forward, and still grasping his bottle, he rested his arms on the table. "Go away, Mr. Leighton, before I make you go away."

"Mr. Anderson, I know you're not going to believe this, but I'm your brother."

Nick rolled his eyes—why did he always attract the lunatics? "Sure you are. I noticed the resemblance right off."

"I mean stepbrother."

Without replying, Nick gulped down another mouthful of whiskey, and as he continued to hold the bottle, he wondered if he could use it to persuade the trouble-some Peter Leighton to leave him alone. After considering the possible outcomes of his offensive, Nick groaned and slid the liquor bottle onto the table instead. The last thing he wanted was to give someone a reason to throw him into jail. Besides, Nick reasoned, it wasn't the lunatic's fault—Leighton didn't know that family was a forbidden subject.

"Look," Nick hissed as he rubbed the two long, vertical scars on his left cheek, "I grew up in an orphanage. I never had no regular folks, let alone stepfolks. It's always been just me," he said, pointing to his chest. "Nikolaus Anderson...no brothers, no sisters, just me. Now...go...away!"

"I know," Peter returned with a nod. "And it wasn't right that you had to grow up alone in Detroit...but you did have regular folks—you were taken away from them and eventually left at that orphanage."

A shiver ran down Nick's back as he listened to Peter's words. He had, long ago, given up the dream of finding his real family—and he wanted to reach across the table and punch Peter Leighton senseless for reminding him of the forgotten desire. But he couldn't get himself to move. How did Peter know that his orphanage was around Detroit? "And what makes you think that I'm this stolen son?"

"Because you look like your father, and you have the same eyes...in fact, your whole family is blessed with those gems."

"If what you say is true—and I doubt it is—why was I taken away from my parents?" Nick replied, trying to keep his voice steady.

Peter exhaled. "It's a very long story, but your father never knew about you...you were taken from your mother by her husband and you were sent away."

Nick laughed out loud, angry with himself for letting Peter's rantings raise his hopes. "You know, Leighton, I've been called many things—includin' an illegitimate piece of garbage—but you're the first one to ever sugarcoat it...get outta here."

"Nikolaus, I know this sounds impossible, and I'm probably not saying it in the right way, but I know how you can get in touch with your family…if you would come back with me to Sandor—"

"Go with you?" Nick cut in. "What're you up to?"

"Nothing…I just want you to know about your family."

Nick grunted. He longed to grab his bottle and get a drink, but he refused to reach for the whiskey and show his shaking hands to Peter Leighton—there was no way he was going to reveal just how unnerving their conversation was for him. He didn't believe what Peter was telling him…he didn't. Then he inwardly cursed…he didn't believe it, but he wanted to.

"There is no proof," Peter continued, "at least no solid proof. I wish there were a way I could let you know that what I'm saying is the—" Suddenly, Peter sat up straight and snapped his fingers. "The chain," he declared, excitedly. "Your father had carved this chain out of wood and gave it to your mother as a gift…when you were taken away, she gave you a piece of it…do you recall ever having a wooden chain?"

Feeling as if a dagger had been plunged into his heart, Nick just stared straight ahead, grateful that his many years of playing poker had taught him how to hide his emotions. There was no way that Peter could know about his chain—none…unless his story was the truth. Nonchalantly, Nick stuffed his right hand into his trouser pocket and fingered the little wooden chain that he had somehow kept ahold of since his days at the orphanage. Did Peter Leighton really know about his parents? Could his dream of having a family possibly come true after so many years?

"I don't remember no chain," Nick lied.

"Oh."

"But, just for fun, let's play this little game of yours for awhile…tell me my father's name."

"Anders Nilsson…you see that's how they work their surnames in Sweden—you're Anders' son."

"Ah."

"But, when he came to this country, he changed his name to Tait Ashby…that's how I knew him. Tait Ashby married my mother."

"Ah ha."

"I know everything I'm saying sounds farfetched, but it's the truth."

"Okay," Nick mumbled, hoping to sound uninterested. Until he knew Peter Leighton's motives, he wasn't about to let the man know that the bit of wooden chain in his pocket had already convinced him that he was being told the truth.

"Even without the chain, I know you're part of my family," Peter went on. "You're Daven…just a little older."

"Who the Sam Hill is this Daven, anyways?"

"He was your half-brother."

"Was?"

"Yeah," Peter answered quietly, "he was murdered a year ago."

"And he looked like me?"

"Yeah, his hair was somewhat darker, and he was an inch or so taller, but…yeah, you both look very much the same."

Nick released a deep exhale and slumped back in his chair. He had a brother… no, he corrected himself, he had a dead brother. Suddenly, as Nick studied Peter's face, anger started to bubble up inside him—Leighton had no right to give him a dead brother. "And where are my so-called parents?"

Peter forced a smile. "I'd rather tell you the whole story, from the beginning, instead of giving you these haphazard pieces."

Nick ran his tongue over his teeth as his wrath toward Peter increased. "This has all been humbug, hasn't it? You have no idea where my parents are, do you?"

"It's no hoax."

"Then where are my parents?"

"They're gone too."

"What do you mean 'gone'? You sayin' they're dead? You tellin' me that I got a family, but they're all six feet under?"

"You still have a family," Peter returned, shaking his head. "You have uncles and aunts and cousins—and me."

Nick glared at Peter with squinted eyes as his rage started to boil. His dream of finding his family was dead—literally…and it was all Peter Leighton's fault. Peter had given him a father, a mother, and a brother, then ripped them out of his grasp. Once again, he had been hurt. Now, he voicelessly proclaimed, it was finally time to return the pain. No longer caring if his trembling hand was seen or not, Nick grabbed the whiskey bottle, lifted it to his lips, and took a long swallow. He wanted Peter to pay for hurting him…but how?

"I'd really like to tell you the whole story, Nick. If you could get away for a few days, I'd be honored if you'd come home with me to Sandorville—that would give me time to tell you everything."

"Well, I'll be honest with ya, Pete. I am between jobs right now, but I got a few debts to take care of first…so I don't think I can."

"I'd be willing to help you out with those, if you'd let me."

Nick smiled inwardly. Money. Yes, that was it. Peter Leighton was going to pay for hurting him…and pay and pay and pay. "I got quite a few debts…you sure about this, Pete?"

"I'm sure, Nick."

Setting his valise on the kitchen table, Peter groaned. Even though he had been gone only a day and a half, it felt like a week. Then, as he looked at his stepbrother, who was surveying the kitchen, it started to feel like a lifetime.

"Just how rich are you?" Nick asked, continuing to examine his surroundings.

Peter dropped his hat on the table and laughed sarcastically. "I'm far from being rich."

"You got all this and don't think you're rich? Your definition of poor is a lot different than mine, that's for sure."

Unbuckling his valise, Peter shook his head. "None of this is mine," he answered as he pulled two books out of the bag.

"Whatd'ya mean, it's not yours?"

"This is my partner's guest house," Peter replied, then, with a grin, he gazed at the bound catalogs in his hands. Willow Ridge had been one adventure after another— and dealing with Kyle Knight was no exception. Tossing the books on the table, Peter chuckled. Knight would probably still be chasing after him if he hadn't agreed to take the catalogs.

Glancing up, Peter started to continue the conversation, but he instantly stopped, realizing that Nick had disappeared. His brow furrowed in confusion, Peter stepped into the short hall that led to his bedroom. Spotting his stepbrother, Peter's frown changed to a smile—then the happiness faded as he watched Nick take a silver dollar off the night table and slip it into his pocket.

Dismayed by the theft, Peter turned and silently moved back into the kitchen. *You're a stranger to him,* he reasoned as he forced his outrage into submission. *You haven't earned Nick's trust yet.* Then his anger resurfaced—only this time it was directed at the circumstances, both known and unknown, that had turned his stepbrother into a scavenger.

As he resumed his unpacking, Peter pulled out the miniature crate that held the glass rose he had bought for Anna. Holding the box up to his ear, he gave it a tender shake to see if the glass bauble had survived the trip home. Pleased that he didn't hear the rattle of broken glass, he smiled and set the wooden box on the table. Starting to dig in the valise again, Peter slid his few items of clothing from side to side. "No," he moaned as he frantically rifled through the contents again…Max's photograph had disappeared.

Standing up straight and cussing quietly, Peter rolled his watch chain between his fingers. *What did you do with it?* he asked himself. *You showed it to Logan MacColl when you ordered the wood, and he put it on the…*

"Man alive," Peter muttered, realizing that the picture was somewhere on MacColl's desk or floor, buried under the catalogs that had tumbled out of Kyle Knight's hands. With a frustrated sigh, Peter ran his fingers through his hair and reprimanded himself for being so careless. Then, as Nick reentered the kitchen, Peter shrugged his shoulders—it was worth losing the photograph for what he had found.

"If this is a guest house, where's Rheinhardt's real house?" Nick questioned.

"Take a look," Peter returned and pointed toward the window.

"I thought you and Rheinhardt was partners," Nick said as he sauntered over to the window.

"We are."

Leaning over the dry sink, Nick gazed through the glass and whistled softly. "That's no house—that's a castle."

Peter nodded in agreement.

"I don't understand," Nick went on, still staring out the window. "If you're partners, how come you ain't rich like Rheinhardt?"

"Because Karl was the sole owner of the old factory—he's had money for as long as I can remember…that's what he brought to our partnership—his design skills and the capital to get the business started again."

"And what did you bring to the partnership, Pete?"

His jaw tensing, Peter eyed Nick, who was now rummaging through the icebox. He usually didn't mind being called 'Pete,' but Nick said the name with so much contempt that it felt like a backhanded slap. "I brought everything else."

"What does that mean?"

"It means that I'm responsible for bringing the factory into a state of…of self-reliance."

"Self-reliance? Ain't that kinda impossible with all the problems you told me about?" Nick asked, shoving the refrigerator door closed.

"It won't be easy, that's for sure."

"Well, what about him and his money?" Nick growled, tilting his head toward the Rheinhardt house. "Won't he help out?"

"Not anymore…the factory's been a leech on Karl's wallet for long enough. It's time to see if the company can survive without his financial support."

"So now it's up to you to make this crippled factory survive on its own?"

"That's about it," Peter murmured.

"And what if you don't?"

"Then I let a lot of people down."

Nick barked out a laugh. "Sounds as if you're gettin' gypped on this whole deal, Pete."

"Maybe."

"It's typical though," Nick muttered under his breath as he started a search of the kitchen cupboards.

"Typical of what?" Peter inquired, removing his clothes from the valise.

When no answer came, Peter grabbed his belongings, walked to the bedroom, and deposited them into the wardrobe.

"Ain't you got anything to eat?" Nick called from the kitchen.

Peter grinned, closing the wardrobe doors. "Not really...I usually have most of my meals at Anna's or out somewhere."

"So what am I supposed to do tonight? Starve?" Nick demanded as he leaned on the bedroom door with his arms crossed.

Peering at his stepbrother, Peter couldn't stop a half-smile from spreading on his face—Daven had used the same stance and tone a thousand times over.

"Whatd'ya starin' at?!"

Peter shook his head. "I just figured you would come with me tonight and have supper at Anna's."

"Oh, sure. Your girl and her family are really gunna 'preciate havin' a complete stranger at their table."

"They'll welcome you...because I welcome you. They've stood by me through everything that's happened this past year...trust me, they will appreciate having you at their table."

Nick grunted. "Sorry, Pete, I don't trust nobody."

With a sad smile, Peter shook his head again. This time his stepbrother's response mimicked someone else's attitude—his own from a year ago. Amazingly, he was face-to-face with the same bitterness and anger that had held him captive for many, many years. "What was typical, Nick?"

"Huh?"

"In the kitchen, when we were discussing the factory, you said 'it's typical though.'"

Shrugging, Nick replied, "The situation...you can work yourself to death, but the rich dandies still got all the advantages."

Peter bit the inside of his lip. Nick's answer mirrored some of the dark thoughts that he had himself—especially when it came to James Wild. "We should get going," he said quietly. "There are a couple of things we need to do before we head out to Anna's."

"Like what? I'm hungry!"

"They won't take long," Peter answered as he followed Nick back into the kitchen. "I want to take a ride out to the factory."

"Why? You said it'd be closed by now."

Peter nodded as he pocketed the little box that held Anna's glass rose. "I know. I just want to make sure..." Peter began, then, laughing at himself, he sheepishly finished with, "that it's still there."

"Seems like a waste of time," Nick mumbled. "Then where?"

"Just to the factory, then Anna's. But first I need to check on the Rheinhardts' house...you can unpack while I'm doing that, if you want," Peter offered, gesturing toward Nick's battered bag sitting on the floor. "You've got your choice of the rooms upstairs."

"Whatd'ya mean, check on their house? I was just lookin' at it—it's still there, just like the factory's gunna be there."

Peter chuckled at Nick's chiding sarcasm. "I just have to make sure all is well with the house and the servants…Karl and his family are in Europe right now."

"A vacation around here isn't good enough for him?" Nick snarled as he picked up his bag.

"Well, it's not exactly a vacation…Karl and his wife are helping their daughter, Lorelei, move over there…they plan on being back here by early September."

"Wait a minute," Nick proclaimed, dropping his valise. "Isn't she the one you were tellin' me about on the train? The one responsible for that whole mess with the old factory?"

"Not the whole mess, but yes, a part of it."

"Shouldn't she be in jail?"

Peter's gaze drifted downward. "Her crime was against Karl, and he didn't pursue any charges."

Nick cursed as he yanked his bag off the floor again. "See? That's what I was talking about—advantages…she should've gone to jail, not Europe."

"Well, Germany's not going to be very enjoyable for her. She'll be staying with relatives, and she won't have access to the kind of money she's been used to—that, for Lorelei, is a jail sentence."

"He still should've made her pay for what she did."

"There was no way Karl was going to put his daughter in jail."

"That's plumb wrong…she was to blame…she should've suffered more."

Once again, Nick voiced some of the thoughts that had passed through Peter's mind—many times. Lorelei Rheinhardt had been the key that wound up the cogs of treachery at the old factory and started them moving. And she was the one, albeit unknowingly, who betrayed Daven into Quentin Fetch's hands. It was true, Lorelei played a definite role in Daven's murder, and all she received for her crime was a stern slap on the wrist. "It wasn't right," Peter sadly agreed.

"And Rheinhardt should've too."

"Rheinhardt should have what?"

"Gone to jail! He was to blame too."

"Well, he was and he wasn't…Karl had no idea what was going on—not until Daven and I exposed Fetch's scheme. When Karl did find out, he made up for all the workers' lost wages," Peter replied. "Because of that, they decided not to prosecute him."

"Why aren't you angry about all of this? Ain't you mad at Rheinhardt for what happened?"

Walking over to the back door, Peter grasped the latch, then glanced over his shoulder and stared at his stepbrother. "I was extremely angry."

"Was?"

"I've forgiven them both."

Nick swore loudly. "Forgave them? That was the easy way out," he hissed, then marched from the kitchen.

As Nick's words vibrated in his head, Peter pulled the kitchen door open and studied the murky clouds congregating overhead. Easy? No, it was far from easy.

He could still remember the day when he found out that Lorelei and Karl were not going to be prosecuted—that was the day a gnawing frustration started to build inside him. And the more he dwelled on the injustice, the more his exasperation transformed into rage. He knew what he needed to do to keep the bitterness from devouring his sanity and his soul—but knowing that he had to forgive—and actually doing it—were two very different matters.

It was only through endless prayer that he had finally been able to gather up his anger and surrender it to the foot of the cross. And it was only the support of his friends that kept him from stealing that wrath back. Every day, for the solace of his spirit, he reminded himself of two things…that whatever is sowed, will surely be reaped…and that, even if she remained unpunished while on the earth, the impenitent Lorelei Rheinhardt would, eventually, have to face God and receive His judgment for her actions.

Suddenly, a drop of water landed on his boot, and the corners of Peter's lips turned upward—thankfully the rain had arrived, which meant the intense pain in his arm would soon subside. Then, as he watched the huge drops splash onto the ground, Peter wished that he could encourage Nick and relieve some of his stepbrother's pain. Maybe he could…maybe all the lessons he had learned could, somehow, help wash away the bitterness in Nick's heart.

❦❦❦❦❦

Arms crossed and making no effort to hide his boredom Nick stood just inside the open doorway of the Spreyers' barn and watched as Peter unhitched the horse from their carriage and led the animal to one of the stalls. Then, turning, Nick gazed through the speeding raindrops and surveyed the large white farmhouse that loomed in front of him. He knew, just from the short time he had spent with Peter, what he would find inside the Spreyers' house—and what he wouldn't find…liquor. At least, Nick told himself, the Spreyers should be able to feed his complaining stomach…that was, of course, if Peter would stop wasting time…

Glancing over his shoulder, Nick frowned. "What the Sam Hill you doin' that for?" he asked as Peter wiped a towel over their rain-soaked buggy. "It ain't your rig."

"That's exactly why I'm doing it," Peter replied with a shrug.

Rolling his eyes, Nick shook his head and returned his attention to the Spreyers' back porch, where a beautiful, golden-haired girl now stood.

"Come on, Pete," Nick called over his shoulder. "Anna's waitin' for ya." As he heard the words come out of his mouth, Nick raised an eyebrow. He was surprised that he recognized Anna from Peter's description—and even more surprised that he had absorbed so much of what his stepbrother had told him on the train.

"Well, I think we'll have to make a run for it," Peter said as he joined Nick at the barn door. "It doesn't look as if the rain's going to let up."

"Of course, if we hadn't wasted time by stopping at a closed factory, we wouldn't have this problem," Nick returned, purposefully trying to jab at Peter's aggravating patience.

"Why don't you go ahead…I'll close up the barn."

Lifting his jacket over his hat, Nick ran toward the house. Then, as he started to bound up the back stoop, he realized that Anna had no idea who he was. Silently cursing Peter for putting him in such a predicament, Nick stopped at the top of the stairs. "Uh, I'm with him," he offered as he slowly walked onto the porch and out of the rain.

Anna said nothing and eyed him closely.

"I'm, uh…I'm…" he stuttered out, not knowing what to say. Then Nick pointed at Peter. "He'll tell ya all about it," he said, pulling his jacket back down to his shoulders.

Instantly, Anna gasped and took a step away from him—then another.

"I ain't gunna hurt ya, Lady," Nick muttered as he noticed the alarm on Anna's face. "I just—"

"No, this can't be," Anna whispered, taking another step back. "Daven?"

Nick growled with annoyance. It was only the second time he had been mistaken for his half-brother, but he was already growing weary of being Daven's ghost. "No, I'm—"

"This is Nikolaus Anderson," Peter announced as he joined them on the porch. "He's Daven's brother…the one Lars told me about."

Looking first at Peter, then at Nick, Anna shook her head. "How?"

"I, uh, sort of ran into him in Willow Ridge," Peter replied with a smirk.

"But…but how?!" Anna stammered, still staring at Nick in disbelief.

Wrapping his arm around Anna's waist, Peter pulled her close. "God sure worked this one out, huh?" he murmured and kissed her on the cheek. "Nick's going to stay with me for a bit."

Pulling away, Anna whipped around and glared at Peter with narrowed eyes. "How could you do this to me, Peter Leighton?" she hissed, then stormed back into the house.

"Anna! What did I—" Peter tried, but he was cut off as the door slammed shut.

"Yeah," Nick commented as he leaned against the porch railing, "I feel real welcome."

"No...no...I'm sure this has nothing to do with you."

Nick grunted and started to move toward the stoop.

"Wait," Peter said, catching Nick's arm. "Please stay. Anna's angry with me, not you."

"I told you this would happen."

"Please stay, Nick. I'll talk to—" Peter began, but he stopped as the kitchen door flew open and a husky, bearded man walked out onto the veranda.

"What's going on out here?" the man demanded.

"I'm sorry, Otto," Peter answered as he tightened his grip on Nick's arm and guided him away from the steps. "I knew Nick would be a surprise, but I didn't think Anna would react like that...Otto, I'd like to introduce you to Nikolaus Anderson— my stepbrother."

"Is this..."

"Yes," Peter announced, grinning proudly. "And, Nick, this is Doctor Otto Spreyer, Anna's father."

Once again, Nick ignored the outstretched hand in front of him, and crossing his arms, he demanded, "Quit starin' at me!"

"Of course," the doctor replied. "That was very rude. I'm sorry," he added, patting Nick's shoulder. "Why, you boys are soaked...come in, come in, before you get chilled."

Reluctantly, Nick followed the doctor into the kitchen, where even more surprised eyes instantly fixed on his face.

"Herr Anderson, this is my wife, Irene Spreyer," the doctor said as he moved to stand behind a frail but regal-looking woman. "And, Irene dearest, this is Nikolaus Anderson—Daven's brother."

Not quite understanding why, Nick tipped his hat and smiled at Irene Spreyer— there was just something about the elderly woman that deserved more than his usual impudence.

"And you've already met Anna," Doctor Spreyer continued, pointing to his daughter, who stood near the stove.

Seeing Anna, now, in the brightly lit kitchen, Nick fully understood why Peter was so captivated with her. Anna's trim figure, golden hair, and soft features combined to create an enticing young lady—very enticing. And yet, because of her earlier outburst, Nick had no desire to speak to her and just offered a nod as a greeting.

"And this is Frau Lynette Chesnay and her son, William," the doctor announced as he gestured toward the sink. "The two of them just joined our family. Frau Chesnay is helping Anna with the household chores."

Growing bored with the introductions, Nick just glanced over his shoulder, but as he caught sight of Lynette, he pivoted on his heel to get a better view of the petite dark-haired woman. He knew many, many beautiful women, but only one of them had made his heart jump—now, Lynette Chesnay was the second.

"Mr. Anderson, it's nice to meet you," Lynette chirped with a gentle smile.

"Ma'am," Nick returned, pulling off his hat.

"Mama, it's him," the young boy at Lynette's side announced, pointing at Nick. "It's the man in the painting."

His grip tightening around the brim of his hat, Nick surveyed the curious yet troubled faces that surrounded him. "Would you all quit starin' at me?"

"Pay-ter," the doctor offered in his pronounced German accent, "why don't you show Herr Anderson the portrait."

Peter nodded in return.

"And," Doctor Spreyer added in a hushed whisper, "we'll stay here, so you can have some time to talk."

With an uneasy smile, Peter nodded again and placed his hat and frock coat on the stand behind the kitchen door. Then, motioning toward the hall leading to the front of the house, he said, "Nick, I need to show you something in the parlor…I think it'll help you understand."

With a sigh of impatience, Nick strolled down the hall, followed by Peter. Reaching the parlor's arched doorway, Nick stopped, and as he examined the room's overly decorated interior, his stomach began to grumble. "You promised me somethin' to eat," he mumbled, glaring at his stepbrother.

"I know," Peter replied, looking into the parlor—not at him.

Releasing an aggravated breath, Nick returned his attention to the parlor, then, as he scanned the walls, he saw it—the subject of Peter's intense stare. Dropping his hat onto one of the chairs, Nick haltingly moved toward the painted portrait above the fireplace mantle. "Is…is this Daven?"

"Yes," Peter answered as he also walked over to the fireplace.

Nick shook his head in disbelief—except for the length and color of the hair, he could have been looking into a mirror. "He's…we…how could…" Nick stammered as he continued to scrutinize his half-brother. From Peter's earlier story about the wooden chain, Nick knew that Daven was his brother, but now, the portrait in front of him erased any trace of doubt. He did have a family…yes, he agreed inwardly—a dead family. "In the saloon," Nick finally said, not being able to pry his eyes from the painting, "you said I was taken from my parents...what happened?"

"Why don't we eat first...then we'll have plenty of time to talk."

Slowly, Nick tore his attention from the portrait and faced Peter. "No. You kept me waitin' for food all day...now, it's your turn. Tell me what happened to me and my parents—now!" he demanded, rubbing the long scars on his cheek.

"Nick, it's complicated. I'd rather tell you...um, slower, rather than just blurting out the facts all at once...it might be easier that way."

"No...tell me—now!"

"All right," Peter surrendered. "All right."

Leaning against the fireplace's mantle, Nick tried to keep an expression of apathy on his face, but as he listened to the tale about his illegitimate conception, his father's ostracism, his uncle's domineering control, and finally, his abandonment, the facade began to crack.

"When Uncle Lars left, he asked me to find you," Peter concluded, "and give you back the family he had stolen from you."

Swallowing hard, Nick blinked away the tears that had formed against his will.

"I thought it would be impossible," Peter added as he grabbed Nick's shoulder. "I had no idea that God already worked everything out."

Peter's brotherly touch sent an unfamiliar warmth through Nick's body, and he yanked away, suddenly craving some whiskey. Why? he wondered. Why had he been given such a wretched life? Then, as he glanced up at his half-brother's cheerful, painted smile, Nick's heart turned cold. And why did Daven get to have such a blessed one?

"Nick," Peter said, breaking the deafening silence, "I know all of this has been a lot for you to accept, but—"

"A lot for me to accept? That's putting it mildly, don't you think? Yesterday, I was just an orphan—now, I'm a piece of garbage that got ripped from my mother's arms and thrown away in another country...a dead rat would have been treated better."

"I'm sorry, Nick, I—"

Cutting Peter off with a wave of his hand, Nick whipped around and marched to the parlor's doorway, snatching his hat from the chair as he passed by. Unsure of what to do next, Nick glanced down the hall and stared at the curious eyes that peered at him from the kitchen. He should have never left Willow Ridge, he reprimanded himself—at least there he wasn't some oddity to be gawked at. Ignoring Peter's pleas, he slapped his hat onto his head, tramped to the front door, and pulled it open.

"Wait," Peter called, grasping Nick's wrist.

Wrenching his arm free, Nick shoved his stepbrother away. "Stop grabbing me," he fumed, then, turning on his heel, he stomped over the threshold. Knowing that he was almost free, Nick headed for the porch steps, but as his boots thudded on the veranda, he reluctantly halted—the rain was coming down so hard and fast that he couldn't even see the road, which he knew was only a few yards in front of him.

"Nick, wait," Peter begged from behind.

With a curse, Nick whacked his hand against one of the large pillars that supported the roof. He had no desire to stay and let Peter continue to bludgeon his ego, but neither did he want to walk out into the biting downpour. Circling to face his stepbrother, Nick hollered to be heard over the deluge of raindrops. "Why should I stay? So you can tell me more stories about my charmed life?"

"No, so you can start to know your family."

"Family?" Nick laughed cynically. "Why would I want to know about a bunch of dead people?"

"But you can also get to know us."

"Stop it!" Nick yelled. "I don't want to know anything else—except where the closest tavern is."

"Tavern?"

"Yeah. You know, Pete, a place to get a drink—and to get away from you."

"You should eat first," Peter said, moving in front of Nick and blocking his escape.

"Sorry, I kinda lost my appetite."

Peter nodded sadly. "I understand…I'll leave the back door open for you at the guest house."

Moistening his lips, Nick shook his head. "Don't bother. I'll probably just stay in town someplace."

"Then take this," Peter offered as he drew a five dollar gold piece from his waistcoat. "That dollar of mine you have in your pocket won't take you very far."

A shiver twitched through Nick as he scrutinized Peter's dark-brown eyes. "What do you mean?" he asked, trying to sound as innocent as he could.

"You can have anything I own, Nick, just ask…don't take."

Grinding his teeth, Nick continued to look into his stepbrother's eyes. He should have been angry at the accusation, but since it was true, he decided to reroute the issue and throw it right back at Peter. "Whatd'ya sayin?" he questioned, his back stiffening. "Am I supposed to sit up and beg for this tidbit you're holdin' out to me?"

"No," Peter returned and pushed the coin into Nick's hand. "This is a gift."

Smirking, Nick slipped the money into his pocket, then, pulling his jacket over his head, he jogged down the porch steps and disappeared into the downpour.

"That went well," Peter mumbled under his breath as he massaged his arm. Bitterness had created a very hard shell around his new stepbrother, and he began to doubt if he had the patience—or the skills—to break through that armor.

Peering into the Spreyers' darkening, rain-blurred front yard, Peter considered the events of the day, regretting that they had led to failure. Suddenly, one moment in particular snapped back into his head—Anna's angry response to Nick's arrival. No, Peter corrected himself, Anna wasn't angry at the unexpected appearance of Nikolaus Anderson—she was mad at you. Walking the few steps back toward the house, Peter ignored the twinge in his arm and grabbed the screen door's handle, determined to find out what he had done to upset Anna so much.

As he neared the kitchen, Peter heard the traces of a conversation between the Spreyers and Lynette, but as he entered the room, the discussion abruptly stopped, causing a ripple of apprehension to run down his back.

"Where is Herr Anderson?" Doctor Spreyer inquired, breaking the awkward stillness.

"He left," Peter snapped as he realized that everyone's eyes—everyone's concerned and condemning eyes—were focused on him. "What's going on?" he loudly asked, directing the question to Anna.

Instantly, a tear rolled down her cheek. "How could you?"

"How could I what?" Peter replied, his voice rising with frustration. "God's just saved me from years and years of searching for my stepbrother, and I get treated as if I had just brought home a plague…I promised Nick he'd be welcome here."

"He is welcome," the doctor put in.

"Well, he didn't feel very welcome—and right now, neither do I!"

"We are just…just worried," Doctor Spreyer added quietly.

"Worried? About what? About Nick?"

"No…about you."

"Me?"

"Yes, you," Anna said with a shaky voice. "You can't replace Daven with this man."

"Replace Daven…" Peter echoed incredulously. "I have no intention of replacing Daven."

No one offered a response to his statement, but the pitying expressions that surrounded him spoke clearer than any words.

"He resembles Daven, I know that," Peter went on through clenched teeth, "but I didn't bring him here because he reminds me of Daven…I brought him here because he reminds me of me."

Still no response.

How could he convince his skeptical audience that he only intended to fulfill his uncle's request and give Nick a family? And what was even more exasperating was the fact that he had to explain his motives in the first place. "Nick's a very bitter man," Peter tried as he swallowed his outrage. "Bitter because his life was changed by other people's choices—something I'm very familiar with. I thought I could help him…no one could ever take Daven's place—not even a look-a-like brother."

Seeing that his speech did little to remove the doubt that permeated the kitchen, Peter headed for the back door, grabbing his hat and frock coat on the way. Jerking the door open, he pivoted and surveyed the sad faces around him. "I miss Daven very much," he said, his voice a low rumble. "And I wish I could change what happened last year—but I'm not so far out of my head that I think I can use Nick to resurrect him."

Then, just as Nick had done minutes before, Peter walked out into the chilly rain, hoping that it would cool his boiling temper.

❦

Nick Anderson leaned back in his chair, stretched out his legs, and refilled his whiskey glass. He definitely liked Sandorville's saloons—they had much more to offer than the little groggeries in Willow Ridge…more liquor…more girls…more anonymity…

Gulping down a mouthful of the biting liquid, Nick raised his drink and smiled as a voluptuous serving girl passed by his table. Although he liked what he saw in the saloon-girl, she could not chase the image of Lynette Chesnay from his head. He was hopelessly smitten with the dark-haired beauty, but he knew he would never be lucky enough to walk down Sandorville's streets with the lovely Lynette on his arm…never. Yet, despite that knowledge, he still found himself thrilled by the idea of being with her—even if she was a widow with a kid. And, as the vision of Lynette lingered in his mind, he wished that she could, somehow, de-throne the other woman who haunted his thoughts.

Why couldn't he forget Lydia Cordell? She had used and betrayed him—and yet he still yearned to hold her in his arms again. Finishing the last of his drink, Nick considered the two women who sent a pulse racing through him. They were so much alike…dark hair, fabulous figures, beautiful faces…they even shared the same initials. Then, as he poured some more whiskey into his glass, Nick laughed cynically. Why was he thinking that there could ever be a future with Lynette? She, like Lydia, probably wanted the things that his meager means could not provide. Besides, he told himself, what would a refined lady like Lynette want with a man who had served a prison sentence?

Laughing again, Nick shook his head and swallowed a gulp of his drink. He had never been very proud of his past, but now, thanks to Peter Leighton, it was appalling. Slamming the glass down on the table, Nick cursed. As much as he relished the idea of milking Peter dry, he just couldn't bear the thought of being around the troublesome do-gooder any longer. Maybe he should just take the money he had and leave town…

Peering into his half-empty glass, Nick sighed. Why wasn't the whiskey working? Why wasn't the liquor completely blurring his thoughts the way it usually did? Why couldn't he stop thinking about Peter...and Lynette...and Lydia...and his horrible past...

Still gazing at the amber liquid, Nick scowled as three men entered the tavern and sat at the table next to him. It wasn't the trio's presence that infuriated him beyond control—it was the topic of their conversation. Leaning his chair backward, Nick eyed the newcomers and offered, "Gentlemen, I'd like to buy you each a drink." Then, before they could react, Nick raised his index finger. "But you gotta promise that you'll stop mentionin' Peter Leighton's name...at least while I'm around."

The threesome looked at each other, grumbling in doubt.

"I'm quite serious."

"What you got against Leighton?" one of the men asked.

Nick studied the thick man who was badly in need of a bath and shave. "I just don't want to talk about him, that's all."

"Yeah?" the man snorted. "Well, we're sorta the 'We Hate Leighton Club.' You oughtta join us...I'm Manning Cole and this is Holden Miller and Jasper Jennings," he offered, gesturing to the men with him.

"We don't hate Leighton," the one called Holden Miller returned, glaring at Manning Cole. "He's been an okay boss—we just like gettin' more money for—"

Giving Miller a sharp jab with his elbow, Jasper Jennings finished with, "We just don't want to work for him anymore."

"I don't remember seein' you at the factory," Manning Cole said between drunken burps. "How you know Leighton?"

Nick sighed in disgust. "He's sort of a long-lost relative—and one I'd really like to forget about...understand?" he replied. Then, pulling himself back to his own table, Nick grabbed his half-filled glass and guzzled down the rest of his whiskey, hoping that it would give him a moment of numbed peace.

"Hey, Mister," Manning Cole continued as he scooted his chair over to Nick's table.

"What do you want?" Nick demanded, now irritated with the grubby man.

Cole swung his head from side to side, scanning the faces in the tavern, then he turned back to Nick and whispered, "You tellin' the truth about not likin' Leighton?"

Almost choking on Cole's foul breath, Nick just nodded.

"Well, there's somebody in town who'd be very interested in talkin' with ya. His name's James Wild and he'll pay ya real good."

"For what?" Nick questioned, mimicking Cole's quiet tone.

"Well, let's just say that he's the pres'dent of the 'We Hate Leighton Club,' and he's always lookin' for new men—especially for somebody like you."

"Whatd'ya mean somebody like me?"

"Somebody who can get real close to Leighton."

"Why?"

"Just go see him," Cole persisted in a hoarse whisper. "He lives in the only brick house on Park Street. It's a real big thing—you can't miss it…and if you see him, tell him it was me that sent ya, so I'll get the credit for it."

"Hey!"

The remark startled Nick and he snapped his head up. Sometime during his clandestine conversation with Cole, both Jennings and Miller had left their table and were now standing opposite him. "What?!" he barked back.

"Where're our drinks? You said you were gunna buy each of us a drink," Jasper Jennings announced as he leaned on the table and pushed his face close to Nick's.

"Yeah, I heard ya say it," Miller added defiantly.

"No, I said I would buy you a drink if you promised to stop mentionin' Peter Leighton's name…but for the last ten minutes, we've been talkin' about nothing else," Nick returned, lacing his words with sarcasm. He knew his condescending tone might ignite Jennings' already sizzling fuse, but after a short deliberation, Nick shrugged off any concern—a little entertainment might be nice after what he had gone through for the past two days.

"We want our drinks," Jennings persisted, edging the table toward Nick.

"I ain't payin' for no drinks—and if you keep pushin' this table at me, I'm gunna break it over your head."

Jasper Jennings feigned alarm, then a sly smile spread on his face, and he shoved the table against Nick's abdomen.

Using his best poker facade, Nick looked up at the two men standing at the opposite side of the table. He was still sober enough to know that his current drunkenness would impede his fighting abilities. But, as he stared at his two challengers, Nick also realized that they were just as inebriated as he was—that fact made the idea of a fight irresistible.

Without warning, Nick thrust the table away and into Jennings' legs, which knocked his opponent off balance. Then, springing to his feet, Nick lunged at Jennings and slammed his fist into the man's cheek.

Jasper Jennings landed hard on the wooden saloon floor, and Nick smiled at being able to get the man down with only one punch—but his gloating ended as Holden Miller slugged him in the jaw. The unexpected blow pushed Nick backward, and he landed on an empty table, then slid to the floor. Shaking his head, Nick gazed up at Manning Cole, who stood over him.

"You okay there…hey, what's your name anyways?" Cole asked as he continued to loom overhead.

"You playin' in this game?" Nick inquired, licking at the blood that was trickling from his lip.

"Sorry…I'd side with ya, but those two are worth ten dollars to me."

"Then get out of my way," Nick said as he pulled himself to his feet, "because they ain't worth nothing to me."

⁓⊶⊷⁂⊶⊷⁓

Pound. Pound. Pound.

Snapping awake, Peter sat upright in bed, trying to catch his breath and calm his racing heart. Although he had finally come to terms with his brother's death, his subconscious mind, obviously, had not—he was still plagued by the same nightmare. And, this time, the dream seemed so real…it was as if he really could hear Daven pounding from inside the coffin…

Pound! Pound! Pound!

Startled by the noise once again, Peter laughed in relief—the hammering was definitely real, but thankfully, it was coming from the front door. Pushing himself from the bed, Peter wrapped his chamber robe over his nightshirt and headed toward the front of the house, feeling his way through the darkness. Grabbing a match from a small metal container on the wall, Peter lit the lamp next to the door, then adjusted the gas lever until the entranceway glowed with a yellowish light.

Pound!! Pound!! Pound!!

Slowly, Peter opened the door and studied the face opposite him. "Patrolman Farrell, is there something wrong?" he asked, his thoughts soaring to the factory.

"I'm sorry to bother you at this hour, Mr. Leighton, but this fellow insists that he belongs here," the policeman said as he pulled Nick into the dim glow of the wall lamp.

"Hey, Pete," Nick mumbled with a tipsy smile and unsteady wave.

As he caught sight of Nick's disheveled appearance, alarm swelled up inside Peter. "What…what happened?"

"Then this man is related to you?" the patrolman inquired.

"Yes…he's my stepbrother."

"Well, your stepbrother, here, and two other men from your factory created quite a disturbance at Conner's Saloon…it was lucky for everyone that I was on my patrol…I was able to put a stop to the brawl before it really got out of hand."

"Is everyone all right?"

"Well, no major injuries, anyway. And, even though your stepbrother, here, started the fight—"

"My name's not 'here,'" Nick cut in as he yanked himself free from the policeman's grip and stepped inside the house.

"As I was saying," the officer continued, "even though your stepbrother, here, started the fight, no one's pressing charges."

"That's good," Peter offered, breathing a sigh of relief.

"Except for…"

Peter's heart sank. "Who?"

"Mr. Conner, the owner of the saloon…however, Mr. Conner said he would forget the whole thing, if I could get a promise that Rheinhardt Furniture would replace all the broken tables and chairs—and pay for the shattered mirror."

Peter nodded. "I'll talk to Mr. Conner tomorrow and take care of the damages."

"Fine," the patrolman replied, "but I will check back with him to make sure that everything's taken care of."

"That won't be necessary," Peter returned with a frown.

"And," the officer added, "if Mr. Conner is not satisfied, I'll be coming back to get your stepbrother, here."

"Quit callin' me 'here,' you—" Nick raged as he lunged toward the policeman.

Thrusting out his arm, Peter grabbed Nick's collar and dragged him away from the officer. "That won't be necessary either, Patrolman Farrell." Then, as Peter eased the door closed, he put in, "Thank you for bringing Nick home."

Turning around, Peter leaned against the door and stared at Nick, who swayed from side to side in an odd, intoxicated dance. He wanted to reprimand his step-brother for drinking the night away and involving Rheinhardt Furniture in another disgraceful skirmish. But, at the same time, he couldn't bare to look at Nick's marred face—it was too much of a tangible reminder of Daven's last days. "Good night," Peter murmured as he twisted the gas lever on the wall lamp.

"That's it? No sermon?" Nick returned, a touch of surprise in his voice.

With his hand still on the light's gas knob, Peter studied his sibling in the glimmering light. If he spoke out now, Peter knew his anger and frustration would muddle his words and only aggravate Nick's mood—he had endlessly made that mistake with Daven. The last thing he wanted was to push his new brother away with some thoughtless statement. "Yes, that's it…but I would like you to come with me to the saloon in the morning, so we both can talk to the owner."

"Why should I?"

Nick's response plunged Peter into a sea of indecision. Should he just walk away and let Nick take full responsibility for the destruction at the saloon? Or should he help take care of things, despite his stepbrother's animosity? And how far should his helping hand extend?

"Because," Peter replied quietly, "I would appreciate it." Then, before Nick could respond, Peter completely cut off the lamp's fuel, allowing the darkness to signal the end of their conversation.

❊Six❊

Pulling the screen door open, Lynette smiled as she watched William climb the back stairs and pass over the threshold, then she and her basket of eggs followed him inside.

"Mama?" William called as the screen door closed with a loud clack. Immediately, the little orange kitten, once again draped around William's shoulders, raised his head to investigate the noise. "It's okay, Bock," William soothed, stroking the animal's paws. "It's okay. It was just the door." Obviously satisfied with the answer, the kitten yawned and laid his head back down on his master's shoulder. "Mama?"

"Yes, Sweetheart," Lynette returned as she placed the egg basket on the counter.

"Can Bock go with us when we sell pies tomorrow?"

"May Bock go…and no he may not."

"But, Mama, he'll get lonely."

"No, William, I don't want Bock to go. We'll be busy and won't be able to watch him—he could get lost…besides, Grandma Irene needs someone to keep her company while we're at the market."

William's eyes widened with excitement. "I forgot! Bock'll take real good care of her…can I go tell Grandma Irene that Bock's staying with her?"

"May I go."

"May I go tell Grandma Irene?"

"Yes. But, if the door's closed, you just play with Bock instead, all right?"

"Okay!" exclaimed William, then, as he bounded toward the hallway, he ran into Anna, who was just entering the kitchen holding a large muslin sack.

"Oh, William, be careful," Lynette scolded, but the boy had already darted around Anna and out of the room.

Laughing at William's enthusiasm, Anna draped the long muslin bundle over the kitchen table.

"I'm sorry, Anna. He has so much energy and just doesn't know what to do with it."

"Oh, I'm fine, Lyn. Don't worry about it," Anna said as she tried to stuff a stray curl into the fine netting that held the rest of her golden locks.

"I can help you with that," Lynette offered. Then, glancing up at Anna's tall frame, she giggled and added, "You'll have to sit down, though."

Slipping onto one of the chairs, Anna sighed. "Thank you...I had to finish the alterations on Mrs. Arthur's dress and just ran out of time this morning."

With an understanding nod, Lynette adjusted a hairpin and gently slid the errant curl into the mesh netting that cascaded down the back of Anna's head. As she checked her handiwork, Lynette studied her young friend—although Anna wore a cheery cotton dress and an even cheerier smile, turmoil still clouded her features. "Is Mrs. Arthur's dress done?" Lynette asked, pointing to the large sack on the table.

"Yes...finally," Anna replied. "Papa's going to drive by her house before we go over to the hospital...I'll be so happy to deliver that dress."

"Why? Has she been difficult?"

"Oh, no," Anna returned with a tired sigh. "It's just with her size, it was like making two dresses."

"And, if she asks you to make another or design a matching hat, you are going to say no...right?"

Anna let out a listless laugh and pushed herself from the chair. "Yes, I will say no...with planning the church bazaar, I won't have time anyway."

"You're working on a bazaar too? Oh, Anna, you should take a respite...what are your plans for today?"

"Working at the hospital, lunch, then helping you...why?"

"I'd like you to do something else this afternoon, instead of helping me."

"Lyn, this is the last day to make anything for the market."

"We have plenty already. And, if nothing else gets done, then nothing else gets done...there's something more important for you to do."

"What?"

"I want you to take the rest of the afternoon and spend it in prayer."

Anna's brow crinkled in bewilderment. "Why?"

"Because I think you could use some time alone to talk with God...just you and Him."

"I talk to God every day," Anna snapped, her look of confusion changing to indignation.

"I'm sure you do. But is it during a time of peace...or when you're running around from one activity to another?" Lynette waited for a response, but Anna's only reply was a harsh stare. Biting at her lower lip, Lynette wondered if she had been too bold. Had she strayed over a boundary that she wasn't supposed to cross? Even though she and Anna had become friends, she needed to remember that she was still an employee of the Spreyers. "Anna, I'm sorry. I didn't mean to criticize you," she tried. "I just know that you've taken on so many responsibilities lately and…and that…well, sometimes our lives get so cluttered with doing things, including things for the Lord, that we forget to just be still and spend some time with Him."

Anna's lips tightened into a thin line and she crossed her arms. "I do spend time with Him."

Lynette took a deep breath and exhaled slowly—she had already treaded on forbidden ground, so what would one more step matter? Besides, she reasoned, keeping her job was not as important as Anna's well-being. "Are you sure that your time with God isn't the same as the time your sisters spend with your mother? You yourself said how busy your sisters are and how they never come over to talk with her, deeply, just one-to-one…"

As Lynette's words faded into silence, Anna relaxed, and the color returned to her lips. "I've told my sisters that Mama misses them, but they say that they're doing all that their time allows," Anna explained, then she lowered her eyes and absently stroked the wrapped dress on the table. "Have I been doing that to God?"

Realizing that she had finally broken through Anna's haze of busyness, Lynette smiled slightly and asked, "Have you?"

Averting her eyes, Anna sank back onto the chair. "You told me, before, to use my words as a mirror and tell my brother and sisters how they've been making me feel."

"Yes…"

"You just did that for me…and the reflection's not very pleasant," Anna continued, her voice breaking. "Yes…I have been taking God for granted."

Lynette's grin widened, and reaching out, she patted Anna's arm. "You're not the first, Anna, and certainly not the last. I've been where you are too. I know how things can sidetrack us…so, please, take the afternoon and go pray."

"That would be nice…thank you."

"No thanks are…oh, my…" Lynette exclaimed, suddenly remembering the popovers that were baking in the oven. Rushing over to the stove, Lynette wrapped her skirt around her hand and pulled the heavy oven door open. "Oh, good, they're baking a bit slower today…they're okay," she sighed as she inspected the golden dough.

"What are you making now?"

"Popovers."

"For the market?"

"No, these are supposed to be for us…if I don't burn them," Lynette replied, latching the oven door. "If you'd like, I can pack a few in your picnic basket…that way you and Peter can have a little treat for lunch."

"Oh…I don't think we'll be having a picnic today," Anna said, her voice breaking again. "I was planning to go over to the factory and tell Peter that I just can't."

"Why? I thought you said that you and Peter always had lunch together on Fridays."

"Usually…but I…I think I'll just have my meal here with you and Mama."

"Why don't you want to meet with Peter?"

"It's not that…I would just rather have my afternoon-meal here," Anna returned as she brushed at a forming tear.

"Anna, why don't you want to see him?"

"I just don't…not right now…not after last night."

"I don't understand…what did he do that was so terrible? Was it bringing Nikolaus home?"

Anna started to answer, then she paused and stood up. "I better put Mrs. Arthur's dress in the wagon," she offered and reached for the garment.

Determined to keep Anna from derailing their conversation, Lynette leaned on the muslin sack. "Are you angry that Peter found his stepbrother so soon?"

"No," Anna snipped, trying to slide the dress from under Lynette's restraining hold.

"Are you sure you're not jealous that Peter has another person to share his time with?"

Anna's delicate, creamy features turned to a stony crimson, and she placed her hands on her hips. "That's ridiculous. I wasn't jealous of Daven, and I'm not jealous of this brother either," she fumed. "It's just…"

"What?"

"I'm worried that Peter won't be able to finish mourning for Daven…that he'll use Nick as a bandage instead of letting the wound of losing Daven heal as it should…now, let go of Mrs. Arthur's dress—you're pressing wrinkles into it," Anna urged as she once again tried to free the covered garment.

Knowing that she was close to the true thorn that was piercing Anna's heart, Lynette increased her stronghold on the muslin wrapper. "That's a valid concern and one you should talk to Peter about, but that's not why you're angry with him…you asked him yesterday 'how could you do this to me?' Why did it hurt you so much when he brought his stepbrother here?"

Anna's eyes began to water, and she released the dress to wipe away the tears. "I don't know why exactly," she whispered, slumping onto the chair once more. "Everything that's hit us this past year has always originated from out there…just like waves in a lake," Anna explained as she motioned with her hand. "They always rushed at us, but they were started far away by lawyers or the factory or busybodies…"

Lynette nodded, recalling one of Anna's statements about her waves…

'I think if one more comes, I'll go down for sure.'

Guessing that Nikolaus Anderson was that last, overpowering wave, Lynette pulled out a chair and sat down next to her friend. "What made this one so different?"

Gazing at Lynette with a somber grimace, Anna murmured, "It just felt as if Peter had produced this wave himself...on purpose...and brought it right to my doorstep."

"You see, that's why it's important that you get your eyes back on God," Lynette soothed, taking Anna's hand. "When you're focused on Him, the waves don't seem so large."

Trying to stifle her tears, Anna looked away.

"Do you remember the story in the Bible where Jesus walked out on the water to the disciples' boat in the midst of a storm? And the apostle Peter stepped out of the boat and started to walk toward Him?"

Anna exhaled with a quivering breath, then, lifting her head, she nodded.

"As long as Peter kept his eyes on the Lord, he also walked on the water, right through all the turmoil around him. But, when he looked around and saw all the waves surrounding him, Peter started to sink."

"Yes, he did," Anna returned with a slight but sad smile.

"And then Peter called out, and the Lord took his hand and helped him back into the boat...you need to do the same thing. Put your eyes back on Christ, and He'll help you over this wave—and show you that your Peter isn't to blame for it."

Anna breathed in deeply and sat up straight. "I don't even remember taking my eyes off God."

Lynette smiled and squeezed Anna's hand reassuringly. "We never do...but the important thing is, you're looking in the Lord's direction once again."

"You must be so tired of ministering to me all the time."

"Not at all," Lynette replied with a sympathetic laugh. "It's difficult to pull yourself out of the mud—until someone lends a hand...I'm sure there'll be a day in the future that I'll need—"

Without warning, Anna jumped up and pointed to the stove—and to the wisps of smoke that were slithering out from around the oven door. "Lyn! The popovers!"

Leaping out of her chair, Lynette hurried to the oven, and using her skirt, she yanked open the door. Immediately, she was hit with a wall of escaping smoke.

"Here," Anna called from behind, handing her a towel.

Using both the towel and her skirt, Lynette pulled the cast-iron pan from the oven and set it on the stove's warming shelf.

"Oh, Lyn, I'm so sorry," Anna volunteered as both women peered at the smoking pastries.

Lynette sighed in exasperation, then, remembering why she had been distracted, her frustration vanished—the talk with Anna was worth a few burnt popovers. "It's all right…you will just have to persuade Peter to eat some pineapple pie at your picnic today."

⸙

"Okay…last one," Peter said as he and Nick lifted a table and shuffled it over toward the showroom door. "This should be good, right here." Slowly, the two men released their grips, and the table quietly thudded onto the wooden floor.

"So we're done, right?" Nick asked, leaning on the table.

Stepping backward a few paces, Peter examined the newly rearranged furniture as he massaged his temple. He disliked the new floor plan, but at least the room didn't look as naked as it did before. "Yeah, I guess we're done."

"It looks fine," Nick put in as he plopped onto a nearby chair.

Peter nodded, yet he still found himself lamenting over the three tables and seven chairs that now sat in Conner's Saloon.

"Oh, that looks good," Del Franz announced from the bottom of the stairs. "You barely notice that anything's missing."

"I suppose," Peter commented with a shrug as he walked over to Del.

"It just looks as if we sold some of our stock," Del added, rocking back and forth on his heels. "Did Mr. Conner like what you took him?"

"Yep. He liked our stuff so much that he said he might order some more pieces to replace the rest of his furniture."

"I guess I done ya some good after all, huh?" Nick called from his chair.

Peter glanced wearily at Nick, then to Del. "I want you to charge those tables and chairs to me," he whispered.

"But they can be—"

"No, I don't want the factory associated with this…complication. Just charge them to me."

Del thrust a stubby finger at Nick. "I should charge them to him."

Peter grunted in response. He agreed, and yet he didn't. In fact, he had so many conflicting thoughts about Nikolaus Anderson that he wondered if he would ever be able to make sense of them. "Please, Del, just let me take care of the tables and chairs," he murmured, rubbing his eyes.

"You have a headache, don't you?"

"Yep, but it's not too bad," Peter said with a grin. Unfortunately, both the statement and his smile were lies. His almost daily afflictions were agonizing enough, but the headaches he woke up with—such as the one he had now—were pure torture. He already knew that his current headache would conquer him before evening.

"So is my sentence up yet, Warden?" Nick hollered.

Peter shook his head. He wanted to be kind to his stepbrother, but the throbbing in his head was draining his composure. "No."

Nick cursed and slumped down in his chair. "My head's not feeling too good after last night," he mumbled just loud enough to be heard.

Ignoring the comment, Peter turned his attention back to Del. "If you need me, I'll be at the factory."

"Oh, I almost forgot!" Del exclaimed as he drew an envelope from his pocket. "I meant to give you this earlier...it came while you were in Willow Ridge."

Opening the letter, Peter scanned the words and smiled. "It's from Frank Hallam...he hasn't written in a long time."

"And this also came."

"Wait a minute," Nick shouted, springing from his chair. "Frank Hallam...isn't he the one who...you mean you write to your brother's killer?!" he demanded, stomping over to Peter.

His jaw tensing, Peter glared into Nick's cool, light-blue eyes. "No, Frank wasn't there when Daven was killed. In fact, Daven was the reason Frank quit working for Quentin Fetch."

"Yeah, but ol' Frank didn't try to warn Daven, did he?"

"No," Peter replied. "And he's paying for that mistake...in prison."

"Doesn't matter...he still didn't try to save Daven...and you write to him?"

"Yes."

Nick cursed. "You are the most peculiar person I ever met! First, you're partners with the man who put Daven in front of a loaded pistol, and then you become friends with the man who didn't stop the trigger from bein' pulled...you're awfully social with the people who murdered your brother."

Peter's jaw clamped down tighter, causing the pulsing in his head to intensify. He didn't like Nick's accusations, but neither did he want to spend the time or energy to explain himself.

"You just be still about Mr. Hallam," Del put in, red-faced. "His change of heart saved Peter's life. And, when the fighting was over, he surrendered to the police. He didn't run away like Mr. Bryce. And," Del added as he stepped forward, closing the gap between himself and Nick, "when Mr. Hallam testified, he told the truth about everything...about Mr. Fetch's secrets...about the crimes he and Mr. Bryce did...and about how Mr. Rheinhardt and Miss Lori didn't know what was going on in the factory."

As he listened to Del, Peter smiled inwardly—he appreciated his bookkeeper's loyalty and protection. Adelbert Franz was often disregarded by society because of his stooped, squat, and stubby appearance, but just like a faithful bulldog, Del could put up a fierce fight when someone trespassed into his territory.

Nick laughed. "Hallam was a fool...he confessed himself right into prison."

"He wanted to make things right."

"He was an idiot, that's what he was."

"Maybe," Del returned, his head bobbing up and down in agreement. "But the Lord spoke to Mr. Hallam's heart, and he did what he did because of that…and that's why he writes to Peter—to learn more about God."

Nick rolled his eyes. "That's all that prison needs is another 'man of God.'"

Peter cleared his throat, trying to break the growing animosity between his stepbrother and bookkeeper. "It's time we get back to work," he announced, placing a thankful hand on Del's shoulder.

"Uh, Peter," Del said as he unsteadily slid another envelope from his frock coat. "Before your stepbrother interrupted us…I was trying to tell you that…that this letter came too."

Confusion flooded Peter's expression until he looked at the familiar handwriting on the envelope. "Ah," he mumbled. Then, taking the letter, he ripped it open and surveyed the terse message. "He's late…it's been at least five weeks since his last note," Peter remarked with as much humor as he could muster.

Del shook his head. "It just isn't right."

"No," Peter agreed and stuffed the two letters into his pocket. "Ready to go, Nick?"

"I was ready to go when I got here."

As both men stepped out onto the wooden sidewalk—and into the bright sunlight—Peter winced and immediately started to dig in his coat for the oblong case that held his dark-lensed glasses. Wrapping his fingers around the box, Peter yanked it from his pocket and, at the same time, caused his mail to flitter to the ground. With an exhausted moan, Peter looked at Nick. "Would you get those for me?"

Muttering a curse under his breath, Nick bent down and snatched up the papers. "What's wrong with you? You been actin' strange all morning."

Slipping the glasses on, Peter replied with a shrug, "Nothing…just a headache."

"And what are those for?" Nick asked, pointing to the spectacles.

Peter drew in a deep breath. He hated talking about his headaches almost as much as he hated getting one, but he figured Nick deserved some words of explanation—and warning. "My, uh, headaches can get pretty bad…light hurts my eyes and I get kind of sensitive to sound…they can even make me sick. Doctor Spreyer thought these glasses might help with the light."

Nick stared at him. "Why do you get the headaches?"

"Nobody knows."

"And the doctor can't do nothing?"

"No. He can only dull the pain so I can sleep…that's all that will get rid of them…most of the time…thanks for picking those up for me," Peter returned, extending his hand for the letters.

Moistening his lips, Nick thrust the letter from Hallam at Peter, but he kept the other one out of reach. "Who…who is…"

"Who is what?" Peter prompted as he repocketed his mail and eyeglass case.

Averting his eyes, Nick grimaced and opened up the second letter. "Who sent you this?" he asked, the page quivering in his shaking hand.

Peter glanced directly at the author's clearly written signature, then back at Nick, who would not meet his gaze. At first, he thought it was the throbbing in his head that made the question seem odd, then, as he considered his stepbrother's actions and background, Peter guessed that reading was not one of Nick's skills. Gently taking the paper, he replied, "This one's from Leland Bryce."

"Bryce?"

"Yep."

"He was Fetch's other henchman, wasn't he? The one that got away?"

"Yep…and unlike Frank Hallam, Bryce was there when Daven was shot," Peter said softly. "He was a man who enjoyed his work—very much."

"And you exchange letters with him?!"

Peter let out a cynical laugh. "No. Bryce just writes to me every month…the same note over and over and over," he explained, his hand tightening around the chronic threat.

"Why…what's he got to say to you?"

As he examined Nick through his dark lenses, Peter's mood lightened—at least he had awakened his stepbrother's interest. Holding the letter in front of him, Peter read the words he knew from memory. "Keep looking over your shoulder, Leighton, because one of these times, I'll be there and you will die. Leland Bryce."

"Why does Bryce want to kill you?"

Peter shrugged. "Fetch allowed Bryce to do what he enjoyed the most—making others miserable…I took all that away when I exposed what was going on…it's a whole lot easier to blame your troubles on someone else, than to deal with them."

"What's that supposed to mean?" Nick snapped.

Peter's brow crinkled as he studied his stepbrother's face. "Nothing…it's just that I used to do the same thing with your father."

Nick grunted and motioned to the horses and wagon waiting in the street. "So where to now?"

"The factory."

"Then can I do what I want?"

"Yes, Nick, then you can do whatever you want to do."

As Nick Anderson entered the Rheinhardt Furniture Factory—and came face-to-face with the whining machines, sawdust-laden air, and stench of hardworking bodies—his senses begged him to flee, but all he could do was gasp for breath and try to cough the choking dust from his lungs. Wiping his sleeve across his eyes, Nick scanned the faces of the others in the factory. No one seemed to be bothered by the hot, heavy air and screaming saws—only him…and Peter. The conditions inside the factory were obviously intensifying his stepbrother's headache, and unfortunately, his own misery kept him from enjoying Peter's suffering.

Shifting his attention upward, Nick watched the heavy power belts swish from the overhead pulleys, down to the machines, and back up again. A typical, dirty factory, Nick thought. Then he noticed something not so typical—most of the employees were smiling and waving their greetings to Peter. Glancing at his stepbrother, Nick smirked with devious delight. He was now quite sure that his status as the boss's long-lost brother would be very, very useful.

"Daven?"

Barely hearing the name over the din, Nick shuddered. When would they stop calling him that? "No, I'm not Daven!" Nick barked, glaring at the small, thin man who stood next to him.

"Hermann," Peter said to the man, "this is Nikolaus, Daven's brother."

Slowly, Hermann reached out and gingerly tapped Nick on the forearm. "You look so much like our Daven."

As he jerked his arm away, Nick realized that many of the factory's men were frozen in place, peering at him as if he were a corpse in a casket. Then, one by one, curiosity touched the rest of the men, and they, too, disconnected their machines from the rotating overhead shafts and joined the gawking group. Overwhelmed by the sudden stillness and army of ogling eyes, Nick's smoldering irritation finally erupted. "Did it ever occur to you…" Nick shouted to Hermann, then, turning to Peter, he added, "to any of you…that maybe Daven looks like me—instead of me lookin' like him?!"

"We're sorry," Hermann returned as he motioned to his fellow coworkers. "It's just that we miss Daven very much."

"Well, that's too bad," Nick curtly replied without a trace of sympathy. "But I ain't your precious Daven…and the next man who says I look like him will eat my fist," he fumed. And, to punctuate his frustration, Nick blurted out several curses and raised his clenched right hand.

"Yes, you are right," Hermann said, shaking his head. "You are definitely not our Daven."

Although Hermann's response sounded innocent enough, Nick clearly heard the hidden insult.

"Hermann," Peter interjected, "with all your brothers, I'm sure you can understand Nick's aggravation about being compared to Daven."

The thin man nodded. "Yes, I do…welcome, Nikolaus," Hermann announced and grasped Nick's hand. "We're sorry for making you uncomfortable…as I said, we all miss Daven's bright spirit—especially Peter. You just helped bring him back to us for a moment."

Twisting his hand out of Hermann's grip, Nick sighed impatiently. "Okay, okay," he muttered, suddenly craving some whiskey or gin or anything that would wash away the thoughts that were dueling inside his head.

He had come to hate being Daven's twin, but something in Hermann's words made him wonder if he was handling the situation all wrong. Silently, Nick repeated the German's declaration…

'We all miss Daven's bright spirit—especially Peter.'

If he did, in a sense, become Daven, would that enable him to also become Peter's puppeteer? He liked the idea of being able to both hurt and control his stepbrother at the same time—or did he? Nick shook his head, trying to forget how pleasant it was to have Peter stand up for him after Hermann's insult.

"Nick?"

"What?" he asked, realizing that Peter was waiting for an answer to an unheard question.

"You ready to go upstairs? Jaxson's working with the assembly men up there… are you all right?"

"I'm just great…let's get this over with, so I can get outta here."

Peter sighed. "You can go now, if you'd rather."

Dumbfounded by the statement, Nick tried to discern his stepbrother's mood, but all he could see was the veil of Peter's tinted glasses. "No…no, I said I'd meet him."

"Good…this way," Peter replied, gesturing toward the staircase.

As he grudgingly followed his stepbrother, Nick noticed that the workers had returned to their duties and were now indifferent to his presence. At first, he sighed in relief, then, unexpectedly, his contentment changed to disappointment. Cursing his own fickleness, Nick trudged up the stairs, grateful to leave the deafening machines and suffocating sawdust behind.

"The assembly men work up here, along with our decorators," Peter explained as they reached the second floor.

Pulling himself up the last step, Nick breathed in deeply, hoping to fill his lungs with clean air—but instead, he found his senses being assaulted once again, this time by the sharp odor of turpentine and paint.

Gesturing to their right, Peter added, "And these are our tables."

Nick grunted. He had no desire to look at the tables, but he figured the sooner Peter finished with their tour, the sooner he could leave. Surveying the round pieces of maple, which were in various stages of being painted, Nick offered, "They're pretty good."

"Most of the credit goes to our decorators," Peter said while motioning toward two identically cute, dark-skinned girls. "Bonnie and Holly Jaye...did I get it right, Holly?" he inquired of the girl closest to him.

The young woman giggled. "No, I'm Bonnie."

"Ah," Peter returned with a shy grin. "I thought I was getting better at telling you two apart—guess not...ladies, I'd like you to meet Nikolaus Anderson—my brother."

Upon hearing the proudly spoken 'my brother,' a warm tingle radiated through Nick's body. When? he inwardly questioned. When was Peter going to stop making himself so impossible to despise?

"Welcome home," Bonnie sweetly announced.

"To both of you," Holly put in.

In response, Nick touched the brim of his hat. And, as he stared at the twin decorators, he couldn't help but wonder if they disliked being mistaken for each other too.

"Did everything go okay while I was gone?" Peter asked.

The two girls eyed each other but said nothing.

"Now what?" Peter groaned as he removed his glasses and slipped them into his breast pocket.

"Jasper Jennings and Holden Miller quit their jobs the day you left."

Holly's statement landed on Peter's shoulders with an almost audible crash. "Where's Jaxson?" he asked.

As Holly grinned and pointed, a deep voice from behind Peter good-naturedly offered, "I'm right here, Partner...question is—where've you been?"

Peter immediately circled and embraced his friend.

"Well, I think we'll let you men talk in peace," Holly stated, then she and her sister returned to their paint brushes.

Moving his head slightly, Nick studied Jaxson Averill, and his eyebrows raised in surprise. During their train trip to Sandorville, Peter had talked endlessly about Jaxson's wisdom, loyalty, support, and friendship—but the man's dark skin was never mentioned. Looking at his stepbrother, Nick grunted quietly. Peter's unbiased outlook was both unexpected and encouraging. And, as much as he tried to fight it, Nick found his hatred waning just a bit.

"Is everything all right?" Jaxson asked. "I expected you early this morning."

"Yeah, well, we had some errands to take care of," Peter answered with a half-smile.

"We?"

"Jax, I have something, uh, rather astonishing to tell you," Peter replied, stepping to one side.

Bracing himself for the inevitable expression of shock, Nick took a deep breath and pivoted to face Jaxson.

"This is Nikolaus Anderson," Peter declared. "Anders' son! And, Nick, this is Jaxson Averill."

As Jaxson beheld Nick's sky-blue eyes, he smiled—it was as if time had rewound itself and he were back in the old factory with Daven. Then, as reality reminded him of Daven's whereabouts, Jaxson's mouth dropped open in disbelief. "What…what's going on?"

"He was in Willow Ridge," Peter responded, grinning broadly. "That's why God kept prodding us toward that town—to find Daven's brother."

At the words 'Daven's brother,' Jaxson's heart plunged into his stomach. How could Peter have found him already?

"You can quit starin' at me anytime, Averill."

Swallowing hard, Jaxson choked out, "I'm sorry…it's just that…that you look so…"

"I know," Nick growled. "I know!"

"I've invited Nick to stay with me for awhile," Peter put in.

"Really?" Jaxson mumbled, not quite knowing why the remark bothered him.

"Excuse me, Mr. Leighton."

The unfamiliar voice shot through Jaxson's muddled thoughts, and turning, he saw a uniformed patrolman standing at the top of the stairs.

"Patrolman Farrell…is there something I can help you with?" Peter called with a touch of apprehension.

"A word with you please."

Peter glanced at Nick, then Jaxson. "Just give me a minute."

Wanting to break the awkward hush that had developed since Peter's departure, Jaxson searched for something to say to the counterfeit Daven that stood next to him, but no words would come. Then his attention was drawn to the private meeting between Peter and the patrolman—and to something that bothered him more than Nick's presence…Peter's constant eye rubbing. "Not another headache," Jaxson moaned.

Nick bobbed his head. "He get them a lot?"

"Yeah. Lately, he's lucky if he doesn't get one."

"He dying or something?"

Jaxson breathed in sharply—it was as if his own thoughts were coming out of Nick's mouth. "I dunno…they keep gettin' worse though."

"Huh…sounds as if the headaches will end up killin' him before Bryce does."

"Bryce?"

"Yeah…don't ya know that Bryce wants him dead?"

"Yes, I know—how do you know?"

"Pete got one of his letters today."

"Oh," Jaxson murmured, moistening his suddenly dry lips. He had thought that, after a year, Leland Bryce would have grown tired of sending the monthly threats—but recalling Bryce's mentality, Jaxson knew that would never happen. Peter would be plagued by the menacing notes until…

"What did he want?" Nick snapped as Peter rejoined them.

"Nothing…he just wanted to let me know that he spoke with Mr. Conner and everything's fine."

"It took him an awful long time to say 'everything's fine.'"

"Don't worry about it, Nick."

"I'm not allowed to go back there—am I?"

Peter shook his head.

Nick laughed. "Don't you worry about it, Pete—it ain't the first time it's happened…so can I go now?"

"Sure…unless you'd like to stay and help out."

Crossing his arms, Nick rolled his eyes. "Is that why you been wantin' me to come here? So you could talk me into workin' in your factory?"

"You know it's not," Peter stated firmly. "I just asked in case you wanted to earn some money."

"I thought all I had to do was ask."

"I thought you didn't want to sit up and beg for your funds."

Nick smiled slyly at Peter's remark. "Huh, I did say that, didn't I? Guess you won this skirmish…so can I—"

"Yes…go."

"What was all that about?" Jaxson asked as Nick strutted down the stairs.

"We, uh, had some trouble last night."

"Trouble?"

"It's been taken care of."

Jaxson's back immediately stiffened—he wasn't comfortable with, nor did he like, Peter's aloofness. Then, as the conversation with Nick repeated itself over and over in his head, Jaxson's dismay deepened. He had become very used to being Peter's confidant…would Nick now replace him? "What kinda trouble?" he tried.

At first, Peter answered with silence, then he exhaled and shook his head. "Nick got into a fight at Conner's Saloon…broke up some furniture…the patrolman brought him home."

"Didn't you just get back last night?"

"Yeah."

His jaw falling open, Jaxson gaped at his friend in disbelief—if Daven had been involved in the same kind of fracas, Peter would have exploded. "What's going on?"

"Nothing…Nick just got a little drunk, but as I said, it's been taken care of…I replaced the furniture that was damaged."

"You can't do this, Peter…it's not right!" Jaxson exclaimed as he attempted to calm the thought that was pulsing through his head—were the headaches now attacking his partner's sanity?

"I'm paying for the tables and chairs myself," Peter returned, his jaw tensing. "You don't have to worry, Rheinhardt Furniture won't be—"

"No, Peter, I'm not talking about the furniture—I'm talking about Nikolaus."

"What about him?"

"You can't let what happened to Daven sway your—"

"Shut up! Just…shut…up!"

The uncommon outburst rang through the second floor, startling everyone—including Jaxson.

"I'm sorry," Peter continued softly. "I got plenty of lectures from the Spreyers last night—I don't need one from you too."

"But—"

"Jax, I'm okay. I know he's not Daven—but he is Anders' son. And I owe that family enough to take Nick in and help him…even if he is slightly, uh, rambunctious."

"Rambunctious?"

Peter shrugged. "It's a better word than the one I was using last night."

Jaxson chuckled, relieved to hear the humor return to his friend's voice. "You gunna try to reach your uncle before he leaves for Sweden and let him know?"

"I was up the rest of last night trying to decide just that," Peter said, running his hand through his hair.

"And?"

"And I think it'd be better if I just let Lars head back to Sweden and then send him a letter…Nick's pretty bitter. I don't think he's ready to face the man who pushed him down the path he's on."

"Yeah, that's prob'ly best," Jaxson agreed—but he would have preferred to see the blue-eyed impostor on a ship headed for Sweden…or anywhere. "I still can't believe you found him."

"I didn't really…it was just perfect timing. I guess our times are in God's hands."

Jaxson smiled—his favorite Bible verse was making quite an impression upon his partner. Then, as Jaxson remembered the news he had to tell Peter, his grin faded. "Listen, I got some bad news…we lost—"

"Miller and Jennings," Peter finished with a nod. "Yeah, Holly told me…what happened?"

"I don't know…they left for a place that pays ten cents more an hour than us. I ain't certain, but I got a hunch that Manning Cole had something to do with it."

"Oh?"

"Yeah, the three of them had quite a few parleys that morning…I think Cole's gunna be more trouble than he's worth."

Peter grunted. "I think so too…but right now, we can't afford to lose anyone else."

"I know…I know. I just wish Hermann's brothers would get here."

"Look, it took both Jennings and Miller, together, to do the job of one man…I'll fill in until we can—"

"No…at least not today. You look as if you're gunna keel over right now."

"I'll be fine…what do you need me to do?"

Jaxson blew out an irritated breath—Peter's stubbornness, at times, was maddening. "Jennings and Miller were working on makin' crates from the scrap wood that…hey, talkin' about wood, what happened with MacColl?"

The corners of Peter's lips slowly turned upward. "A partial shipment by Monday and the rest by Friday," he whispered.

Glancing upward, Jaxson mouthed a prayer of thanks. "That's the best news we've had in a long time…I'll tell the men to—"

"No," Peter cut in sharply. "I don't want anyone to know about the lumber until it arrives."

"Peter…"

"No, Jaxson…I don't want to give Wild even a remote chance of finding out about the shipment."

Although he wanted to melt Peter's granite stance against Wild, Jaxson knew, by his friend's pain-filled eyes, that it was time to end their discussion. Unfortunately, the respite also meant that he would have to wait for the full details about the trip to Willow Ridge, Nick Anderson's drunken brawl, and Bryce's latest letter.

⊰⊱

As she stood on the hospital's front veranda, Anna Spreyer gazed up at the brilliant blue sky and smiled contentedly. The sparkling summer day perfectly matched her emotions—for the first time in a year, she was cloudless too. Grasping the picnic basket sitting at her feet, Anna adjusted the thin blanket covering the meal, then looped the woven handle over her left arm.

Finally, after hours of anticipation, the time had arrived for her lunch with Peter. Shaking her head, Anna laughed at herself. When she had awakened in the morning, she had dreaded the meeting—now, thanks to Lynette's insights, she welcomed it. With blossoming excitement, Anna popped open her parasol and raised it over her head. Yes, she thought as she lifted her skirt a few inches and sprightly bounced down the hospital steps, it was definitely going to be a glorious afternoon.

"Anna!"

Glancing at the passing townspeople, Anna searched for the face behind the beckoning voice, then, as she spotted a familiar carriage, her bright mood dimmed. "James," she called back, her arm tensing around the handles of her basket and parasol.

Flinging the carriage door open, James Wild bolted from his coach and rushed over to Anna. "What won...derful timing," he breathlessly offered as he took her gloved hand and kissed it.

No, Anna returned silently, it was dreadful timing. "James, it's good to see you," she said, trying to control her growing dismay, "but I don't have time to talk, I have a lunch appointment that I want to keep—very, very much."

"Oh...I was hoping I could persuade you to have your afternoon-dinner with me in my restaurant."

"James! You know that wouldn't be proper...I'm an engaged woman," Anna scolded while glaring at Wild through the lace edging of her parasol.

"No, no, of course not. I apologize for my poorly worded invitation...I meant you and your father. I thought you both would enjoy having a special gourmet meal today."

Tilting her parasol backward, Anna stared directly into Wild's eyes. "I am having a special meal today—with my fiancé."

"Ah, yes, that is right. He has returned from his journey."

Anna scowled—she couldn't imagine Peter discussing his plans with James Wild. "How...how did you know about Peter's trip?"

"Oh, I believe I heard it from someone," Wild replied as he dusted his lapels. "I hope his outing to...to...to his destination was successful."

Anna lowered her eyes. Was Peter's trip successful? She didn't know. She had lashed out at him so suddenly the night before that she didn't even know if he had accomplished his goal in Willow Ridge. "We...we didn't have a chance to talk about his journey," she said, blinking back her tears. Then, as a yearning for Peter's forgiveness—and his touch—welled up inside her, Anna added, "I'm sorry, James, but I must be going."

"Dear Anna, you look so troubled...did something go amiss while Peter was in...in...""

"As I said," Anna returned, her voice faltering, "we haven't talked about the trip...he's waiting for me, James. I must leave—now."

"Of course," Wild said, tipping his hat. "Please, remember me to your mother and to her new attendant, Mrs. Chesnay."

As Anna turned to leave, Wild's words echoed in her thoughts and she stopped. "How did you know we hired Mrs. Chesnay?" she asked, her eyes narrowed with confusion.

"When I was visiting the jewelry shop, your sister Marion informed me of the decision…I was simply elated at the news. I was hoping Mrs. Chesnay would meet the qualifications of the position."

"She more than met them."

"Good, good…then I am pleased that I had a part in bringing her to you."

"Yes, I did want to thank you for offering her your carriage that day."

Wild shrugged and plucked an imaginary speck from his coat sleeve. "It was my pleasure—and duty. Such a dainty flower should not have been traveling alone, especially with a child. To have ignored her plight would have been unconscionable."

"Even so, I thank you for your kindness."

Holding up his hand, Wild grinned. "My reward comes from knowing that I aided a lady in need—and that it also benefited you, my sweet Anna."

Grimacing at Wild's affectionate phrase, Anna glanced at the watch pinned to her lapel. She knew Peter was probably standing in the factory's front yard waiting for her, but she couldn't leave yet—not when the door had been opened for her to finally set Mr. James Wild straight. "That reminds me," Anna firmly declared, "Mrs. Chesnay said that you told her to say hello to 'my sweet Anna.'"

"Correct—because you are sweet," Wild cooed, taking her hand again and giving it a light kiss.

"But I'm not yours, James."

"Of course, but I cannot stop wishing that you were," he said with a pout.

"James, please don't…"

"You are right—I apologize. I should not have voiced my heart's desire…but despite how I feel, the message I passed along through Mrs. Chesnay was a simple greeting only."

"Well, she didn't think it was…and what were you trying to say with the pineapples?"

"The pineapples?" Wild replied bewildered. "They were a gift. I thought you and your family would enjoy the treat."

"We did, James. It was a very thoughtful gesture—but it was also a very expensive one."

"Nonsense. Those pineapples were merely extras from a shipment for my restaurant."

"Still, it was inappropriate for you, a single gentleman, to send me, an engaged lady, such an extravagant gift."

"Gracious me! I assure you, the fruit was not sent with any hidden motives. Did they…did they cause friction between you and Peter? I pray they did not."

"He wasn't happy about them."

"Dear me! I had no idea that a few pineapples would trigger that vicious temper of his."

"No, no…it wasn't like that…Peter was just upset that you sent them."

"Oh, Anna, I am so terribly sorry…I knew Peter had a jealous tendency, but I never figured that my gift to your family would propel him into a rampage."

Closing her eyes, Anna shook her head in disgust. Not only did she fail in her attempt to 'finally set Mr. James Wild straight,' but she had caused the situation to worsen. Now—thanks to her—James Wild would, undoubtedly, spread the news that Peter was an uncontrollable lunatic, mad with jealousy.

"My love, are you feeling faint?"

Instantly, Anna's eyes sprang open and she glowered at Wild. "No, James, I'm fine, and Peter has every right to be angry with comments like that!"

"I do not understand."

"You said 'my love.' You must stop calling me 'your' anything."

"As you wish—I do not want to cause you even an iota of distress…and to further ease your pain, I shall immediately send Aaron to your house and have him remove the remaining pineapples."

"No, you don't have to do that…Lynette, um, Mrs. Chesnay made the rest of the pineapples into pies, and we're going to sell them at the market tomorrow."

"Splendid! You must allow me to assist in some way—to make amends for my previous bunglings."

"That won't be necessary. My father is going to help us get the pies to—"

"Your father? What about Peter?"

"He'll be at the factory."

"Say no more," Wild volunteered with a slow and lavish bow. "I will be happy to provide the transportation for the pastries."

"No, James, we need Papa's wagon. We're going to put some boards across the back to create a counter for—"

"Boards? That will never do—you need a proper sales booth."

"There's no time…the market's tomorrow."

"Then I will have my carpenters begin on the booth straightaway."

"No! That will just make Peter—"

"Peter be hanged!" Wild shouted as he pounded the ground with his walking stick. "If he has an issue with my assistance, then inform him that I had the sales booth built for Mrs. Chesnay."

"James, no…"

"It is already settled…whether you utilize it or not, tomorrow morning you will have a new bakery booth for your pastries."

"James…"

"You can continue to resist, dear one, but you will only succeed in making Peter believe that you have forsaken him."

"Oh, my goodness!" Anna cried. "Peter!" Pivoting in the direction of the factory, Anna winced. The discussion with James had caused her to neglect her beloved once again, and knowing that, she ached for him even more.

"Not to worry," Wild announced, gently wrapping her arm around his. "Aaron will drive you to the factory in my coach."

"No, I…" Anna started, but indecision silenced the rest of her answer. She knew Peter would not appreciate seeing her exit James Wild's carriage—yet it was the fastest way to reach the man she longed to hold in her arms. "All right…thank you, James."

"It is my pleasure," Wild returned as he guided her toward the waiting carriage.

"Are you sure this won't inconvenience you?"

"Not one bit. It will give me a reason to visit your father," Wild replied, then, reaching up with his walking stick, he tapped his snoozing driver's right boot. "Aaron!"

"Yes Sir!" the driver answered, snapping out of his sleepy daze.

"I want you to drive Miss Spreyer to the Rheinhardt Factory with as much celerity as you can muster."

"Sir?" Aaron questioned, his face scrunched in puzzlement.

"As quickly as you can!" Wild growled.

"Yes Sir!"

Unlatching the carriage door, Wild lifted the basket from Anna's arm and placed it securely on the floorboards. "Watch your step, Dearest," he murmured as he extended his hand.

Closing her parasol, Anna frowned—even after all her rebukes, James was still labeling her as his property. And, as she grasped Wild's waiting hand and stepped into the coach, she knew she had made a grave mistake—she should have never accepted the carriage ride or the sales booth.

"When would you like Aaron to arrive?" Wild inquired, gently latching the brougham's door.

As Anna discreetly adjusted her bustle and settled onto the forward facing seat, she inwardly repeated Wild's question—then, suddenly, her heart quickened. "I thought…I thought Aaron was going to take me right to the factory."

With a chuckle, Wild leaned on the coach's door and popped his head through the window. "You are a treasure, dear Anna. He will take you to the factory straightaway…I meant, what time would you like him to arrive in the morning?"

"The morning?"

"To transport you, Mrs. Chesnay, and the pastries to the market."

Slamming her parasol down on the seat, Anna's back stiffened with anger and exasperation. "James, I thought I made myself clear that—"

"That you do not want to upset Peter. Yes, you did. But I am quite sure that even he would agree with me…you ladies should not be forced into becoming common laborers. Besides, Peter will have nothing to be troubled about—it will just be my men helping you. I have a meeting tonight in Grand Rapids, and I will not return until early afternoon tomorrow…so what time would you like Aaron to arrive?"

Anna sighed. If she stopped protesting, Wild would win. And, if she persisted, it would further postpone her meeting with Peter. "Six?" she surrendered.

"Six o'clock it is," Wild proclaimed with a broad smile. "I will have the carpenters meet you at the market grounds, and all you will have to do is inform them where to assemble the booth…I will be happy to arrange your return trip as well."

"No, thank you, James. Peter will be done working by then."

"Of course…enjoy your luncheon," Wild replied as he pushed himself away from the carriage.

Leaning toward the window, Anna offered weakly, "Thank you."

"It is a pleasure to come to your assistance, my dear Anna," Wild murmured with another bow. "Now, if you will excuse me, I will make Aaron aware of his duties."

As Wild walked out of view, Anna slumped back in the seat and let out a whimper of defeat. James' incessant buzzing had distracted her better judgment again—and as a result, Peter had gotten stung. *You should have swatted him away when he first called your name*, she silently reprimanded herself.

Gazing out the side window, Anna barely noticed the buildings that raced by. Why did she allow James Wild to be her rudder—steering her according to his wishes? Why? Was she, somehow, attracted to him? As she searched her heart and considered the lanky, long-haired man, Anna shivered, feeling as if a cold hand had suddenly grabbed her neck. *No*, she thought, *there was absolutely no attraction between her and James Wild—at least not on her part.*

"Then why, Lord?" she wondered as her attention slowly moved to the basket on the floor. "Why did I let James distract me?"

Could it be that she really didn't want to see Peter after all? Was she still bothered by the fact that he had brought Nikolaus Anderson into their midst? *No*, Anna replied inwardly, *Lynette had opened her eyes about that matter. Peter Leighton held her heart in his hands, and she wouldn't have it any other way.*

Sitting up straight, Anna sighed and smoothed her dress. *Then why wasn't she able to stand up against James Wild's maneuvers? Was she afraid of saying no?* At that thought Anna laughed—she didn't have any qualms about saying no to James…it was just that she had grown weary of constantly saying it.

Without warning, both the carriage and her thoughts hit a large rut, and as she was tossed from side to side on the seat, Anna found her answers. When her sight had drifted from God, she lost not only her focus but her gumption too—and regrettably, it had become easier to do nothing. Bowing her head, Anna fought to keep her eyes dry. It would only alarm Peter if he saw her in tears—and her apathy had already hurt him enough. It was time, she told herself, to soothe Peter's worries and smother James Wild's advances—for good.

"We're coming up to the Rheinhardt Factory, Ma'am," the driver shouted from above.

Giving her cheeks a slight pinch, Anna slid over on the seat and peered out the window. Peter, who must have given up on her, was on the loading platform, helping Jaxson lift a large crate into a wagon. Even from her poor vantage point, Anna could see her fiancé's well-defined muscles as they strained against his cotton shirt and waistcoat, then her vision moved to his handsome, rugged face and mussed hair. Between Peter's outward appearance and the kind, strong spirit that dwelled within him, Anna knew she was engaged to a remarkable man. And, as she caressed the golden ring on her finger, she scolded herself for delaying their wedding for so long.

Finally, slowing the horses to a walk, the coachman steered the carriage in a wide circle and brought it to a stop near the loading platform. Taking a deep breath, Anna grabbed her parasol and lunch basket and waited for the driver to open the door.

"Thank you, Aaron," Anna said as she stepped out of the coach. Then, as she approached the platform, she offered, "I'm so sorry for my tardiness, Peter...please forgive me."

Although he didn't respond verbally, Peter's tense jaw muscles and squinted eyes told Anna enough—he was annoyed. And, unfortunately, her explanation would only darken his mood.

"We'll see you tomorrow morning, Ma'am...six o'clock," the coachman called, climbing back onto his seat.

Cringing at the comment, Anna waved in return.

"That's Wild's carriage, isn't it?" Peter questioned as he climbed down from the loading platform and peered at the departing brougham.

"Yes...James stopped to talk just as I was leaving the hospital. He knew I was late, so he offered me his coach and driver," she replied, fully aware of her fiancé's mounting anger.

"I see...I guess I should have thanked Mr. Wild for his gallantry."

"Peter, James wasn't in the coach—he stayed at the hospital to talk to Papa."

"Is that right?" he muttered, thick with sarcasm.

Anna glared at Peter. She knew he was upset, but his obvious mistrust pecked away at her patience. "You should know by now that I wouldn't accept an unescorted carriage ride from James Wild—or any man."

"Why did the driver say he'd see you tomorrow morning?" he demanded, ignoring her statement.

"To take me to the open-air market," she snipped, then, as Peter's eyes filled with alarm, she regretted her hasty remark.

"You're going to the market with Wild?" he whispered hoarsely.

"No, no…it's not—"

"What did I do, Anna?" Peter cut in, his voice faltering. "What did I do to turn you away?"

"Nothing," she sobbed as the tears started to flow. She wanted to say more…she wanted to relieve Peter's concern, but at the same time, she was afraid that one more misunderstood sentence would topple their already crumbling romance. Dropping her basket and parasol, Anna reached up on her toes and wrapped her arms around Peter's neck. "I love you, Peter. I love you and no one else," she tried, hugging him tighter.

At first, he remained stiff and unyielding, then Anna felt his arms encircle her and she smiled inwardly—they weren't lost to each other yet. "I need to talk to you," Anna went on. "Can you stop for awhile?"

"No," Peter answered, releasing his hold.

"Please? I want to explain."

Rubbing his forehead, Peter shook his head. "No, we lost two men…I can't leave Jaxson with all the work."

"Yes, you can."

Startled by the additional voice, Anna looked up at the loading platform. She had completely forgotten about Jaxson's presence, and realizing that he had witnessed her passionate embrace, a blush washed over her. "Hello, Jaxson," she offered shyly.

"Miss Anna…you two go and have a good picnic."

"No," Peter said, turning toward Jaxson. "There's too much to—"

"You promised me that you'd rest—remember?"

"Rest? Why? What happened?" Anna worriedly asked.

Peter blew out a long breath. "It's just another headache."

"It ain't just another headache," Jaxson countered, jabbing his finger at Peter, "when it makes you puke."

"I'm okay…stop pushing me, Jax."

"No! I'm gunna hold ya to your promise…now, go and get some rest."

Slipping her hand around Peter's arm, Anna tugged at him gently. "It might help, and if you'd like, I'll try massaging some of your headache away."

Peter growled quietly, then, finally, he nodded. "We'll be down by the river, if you need me," he mumbled to Jaxson.

"I'll send somebody…if I need you."

While she strolled toward the North Pine River, arm in arm with Peter, Anna nervously twirled her parasol as it rested against her shoulder. She wanted, so badly, to explain her recent actions, and yet she hesitated—the last thing she wanted was to plunge into another quarrel. Turning her head to the right, Anna gazed at her fiance. She knew it was time to say something, but she also knew that it would be extremely difficult to interpret Peter's responses through his tinted glasses. "I'm sorry about the carriage ride," Anna started, choosing her words carefully. "Trust me—James was not inside…I thought, by accepting his offer, that I could get here faster, but it wasn't the right thing to do."

"It's not you that I don't trust."

Anna smiled slightly. "And I'm not going to the market with him…James will be in Grand Rapids until tomorrow afternoon."

"Then why did the driver say—"

"Because I agreed to something I shouldn't have," Anna interrupted. "Do you remember the pineapples James sent?"

Only a grunt answered her question, but that—and Peter's stiff jaw muscles—said he definitely recalled the troublesome fruits.

"Well, I gave them to Lynette, and she made them into pies—some very delicious pies—which we're planning to sell at the market…James volunteered to transport the pies and…and to build us a sales booth."

Stopping in mid-stride, Peter jerked away. "I would have done those things for you," he fumed, his face hardened by tension. "All you had to do was ask."

"I know," Anna replied, disheartened by her fiance's hostile remarks. Then Lynette's words flashed back into her thoughts…

'Then you wouldn't mind if another girl in town started giving Peter freshly made fudge or darning his socks? And you wouldn't get the least bit upset if he accepted those gifts with nary a word of caution to the girl?'

At least now, she understood the source of Peter's fury. "I know you would have helped, and I never asked James Wild for anything," Anna continued softly. "He just insisted and insisted and insisted until I agreed…I never should have given him his way—I'm sorry."

Peter started to respond, but instead, he lowered his glasses and peered at her with an expression she couldn't decipher. In fact, his entire visage was unreadable—except for his pain-soaked eyes.

"That headache's really hurting you, isn't it?"

"I'm just tired…I didn't get a lot of sleep last night," he answered, pushing his glasses back into place.

"I apologize if I was the cause of that."

"No…it wasn't you…Nick, uh…"

"Nick what?"

"He had a little too much to drink last night…a patrolman had to bring him back to the house."

"Oh, Peter, are you sure you want to deal with Nick right now?"

"Why won't anyone listen to me?!" he returned through clenched teeth. "I'm fine about Daven. I'm not trying to replace one brother for another, I just—"

"No, Honey…I meant, with the factory and your headaches, do you really want to add Nick to your list of worries?"

"I have to," Peter murmured as he rubbed the back of his neck. "Nick's family…and he's more important than the factory or these stupid headaches."

"You poor dear…why don't we just spread the blanket out here for our picnic?"

"But you like having lunch by the river."

"I like having lunch with you—whether it's by the river, here in the woods, or in the middle of the street."

"The middle of the street, huh?" Peter replied with a tired half-smile. "That might be somewhat messy."

Anna grinned at her fiance's headache-plagued attempt at humor. Then, scanning the area, her smile increased. "Look, there's a small clearing right over there," she said, pointing to a sunlit patch of grass amidst the trees. "See? God wants us to stop." Grasping Peter's hand, Anna tugged and pleaded until he finally yielded and followed her to the clearing. "I don't know why we never saw this spot before," she offered, surveying the sunny opening.

Peter shrugged as he set the picnic basket on a fallen tree and grabbed the cotton blanket. "I guess we never really had a reason to look before," he returned while spreading the coverlet over the grass.

Resting her parasol against a small poplar, Anna gathered her skirt and petticoats to one side and slowly sank onto the blanket. "This is so cozy…I'm so glad you're here."

"I'm glad you're here too," he put in. "I thought that…that after last night…well, that you might not want to have lunch with me."

Flinching at the words, Anna bit the inside of her lip and inwardly thanked Lynette for guiding her away from that very notion. "Come," she said, patting her lap. "Let me see if I can rub some of that headache away."

Peter exhaled deeply and stood motionless with his hand in his coat pocket.

"Honey?"

Still no response.

"Peter? Are you all right?"

"I bought this for you while I was in Willow Ridge," he explained, removing a small wooden crate from his frock coat.

Anna blushed with excitement as Peter placed the gift in her hand—her fiancé's generosity and thoughtfulness always impressed her.

"It's been in my pocket since last night," Peter added as he sat next to her. "I just hope it's still in one piece."

Cradling the little box, Anna leaned over and kissed Peter's cheek. "I'm so sorry for what I said to you yesterday," she said, her voice quivering. "I've been so tired lately, and I lashed out at you for something you didn't do."

"I know Nick was quite a surprise, and I—"

"Yes, he was a surprise," she cut in, "but Nick wasn't the reason I was angry—and neither were you."

His jaw stiffening, Peter pulled off his glasses and scowled at Anna. "You made it very clear that I was the one who hurt you."

"And that's what I'm sorry for…you weren't the one to blame—I was."

"I don't—"

"Somehow, Peter, I've lost touch with God…all the things I've been busy with have caused me to push Him onto the warming shelf."

"But you always attend church and—"

"And I go through all the motions—but with no depth…that's why I reacted so shamefully to Nick's arrival. I saw him only as another problem, instead of the miracle that he is."

"Tell me what I can do to help."

"You can't help me, Honey. It's between me and the Lord…but I do know that I need to spend more time with Him. And, to do that, I need to give up a few things."

"Such as?"

"Well, no more dressmaking—at least for a bit."

"But you love being a seamstress."

"Yes, but I love God more, and right now, I only want to work on one dress…my wedding dress."

Although the corners of Peter's mouth curled upward, he said nothing—much to Anna's dismay. After mentioning the word 'wedding,' she had expected the usual barrage of questions about setting a date, but now, she wondered if her procrastination had crushed Peter's hopes completely. Wearily, Anna looked down, then inwardly gasped—her forgotten gift still sat in her hands, unopened. "How was your trip to Willow Ridge?" she asked as she loosened the top of the miniature crate.

"Good…not only did I find Nick, but MacColl had plenty of maple—and he was actually happy to sell it to us."

"That's wonderful."

"It's a nice little town…rustic but very calm and untroubled," he went on, removing his hat. "And Willow Ridge is the perfect name. It's right on the river, and all you see are willows and poplars behind the buildings…very pretty."

Glancing up from her mysterious present, Anna studied Peter's suddenly relaxed countenance. "You really liked it there, didn't you?"

"Yeah, I guess I did."

"So what happened to the Peter Leighton who enjoys being surrounded by a bustling city?"

"I don't know," he replied with a shrug. "Maybe he's learned to appreciate—and prefer—peace and quiet."

With a wink of understanding, Anna smiled, then, refocusing on her gift, she pulled a wad of pink fabric from the wooden box. Slowly, she unrolled the material until the treasure—a small glass rosebud—lay in her hand. "Oh, Peter, it's lovely… thank you!" Anna exclaimed as she examined the delicate bauble. "Does the artist live there in Willow Ridge?"

Hearing only the chirping birds, Anna looked at Peter, who now sat with his elbows on his knees, rubbing his temples. Quickly, Anna rewrapped the rose and placed it back into the crate. "Peter, Honey, let me do that…come, lie down," she said. And, as Peter wordlessly stretched out and laid his head in her lap, Anna realized just how much pain he was in—rarely did he comply so easily. "This is a bad one, isn't it?" she asked softly as she caressed his face.

Peter closed his eyes and murmured a quiet, "Uh huh."

"I really like the glass rose…I wish I had been able to go to Willow Ridge with you."

"Uh huh."

"Maybe we could plan a trip there real soon."

"Uh huh."

"Or maybe we could go there on our wedding tour."

Immediately, Peter's eyelids fluttered open. "What?"

Anna beamed uncontrollably as she gazed down at Peter's brown eyes and sturdy features. "Since you liked Willow Ridge so much, I thought it would be a nice place for our honeymoon."

"But what about Niagara Falls?"

"It's too…too far away."

Peter frowned and sat upright. "You mean too expensive," he mumbled, keeping his back toward Anna.

"No, I mean far. We should stay closer to home…in case something happens at the factory or with Mama."

"Wild could give you Niagara Falls," Peter returned as he ran his fingers through his hair. "He could give you Europe."

Anna's expression clouded. Her procrastination had indeed damaged Peter's hopes of marriage—and it had also sent him a message that wasn't true. "Peter," she soothed, stroking his back, "I'm not interested in James Wild, the third—or his money…even if he had the wealth of a king, I still wouldn't be interested."

Silence.

"And, if you were penniless, my heart would still yearn for you."

Peter turned toward her, but his head remained bowed. "If Wild's tables don't get done, that could happen by September first."

"It wouldn't change my feelings about you."

"Wild can give you so much more than I can," he replied, barely audible.

Holding Peter's chin, Anna gently lifted his face up. "Peter," she whispered, waiting to continue until he met her gaze, "James Wild could never give me the joy that you've already given me…I love you and it's you I want to marry."

"I love you too."

"Then what do you think about August twenty-seventh?" she asked, her features twinkling with glee.

"For what?"

"For our wedding date."

"Our what?"

"Our wedding date."

"What about Hans? That wouldn't give him enough time to come."

"My brother has already had a year to make arrangements…it's time we planned our nuptials."

Peter smiled wide, then, slowly, his grin weakened. "August? What about September instead?"

"We don't have to wait for Hans anymore."

"It's not that."

"Then why?"

"I just think we shouldn't do anything until after the first of September."

Anna studied Peter's pain-saturated expression. What was on September first? she asked herself. Then, recalling her fiancé's earlier statement, she sighed. "No matter what happens with the factory—and James Wild's tables—I want to be Mrs. Peter Leighton."

Peter half-smiled. "I still want to wait…we've lost two more men. I'll practically be living at the factory until those tables are finished."

"All right…late September."

"Early October."

"Peter…"

"The leaves will have turned by then—they'll make Willow Ridge even nicer for our trip…and that'll give Hans enough time to come…if he wants to."

Placing her hands on the sides of his face, Anna pulled Peter toward her and kissed him on the forehead, on the eyes, then, finally, on the lips. "I can't wait to tell Mama and Papa," she announced as they parted.

Peter nodded. "I'm looking forward to telling a few people myself."

Nick Anderson surveyed the newly built mansion in front of him and grumbled in exasperation. Why did the rich always have to flaunt their money? he wondered. Already knowing the answer, Nick growled under his breath and grudgingly meandered toward the long-haired man who was blurting out instructions to the carpenters that stood around him.

"Are you James Wild?" Nick questioned as he approached the group.

Wild examined him from hat to boot—twice—but said nothing.

"My name's Nick Anderson," he put in. "Manning Cole told me that you might be int'rested in talkin' to me."

Finishing his orders, Wild dismissed his workmen with a flip of his hand, then he jabbed a thin, pale finger at Nick. "Do not interrupt me."

Bristling at the rebuke, Nick glared at his accuser. "Sorry," he offered without sincerity. "Then you are James Wild?"

"Yes."

"I've been tryin' to find you all morning."

"And why, exactly, have you been trying to find me?"

"I told you, Manning Cole said that you might pay for what I know—I'm kin to Peter Leighton."

Wild's face lit up with mirth and he smiled slyly. "Ah, yes, I do recall Mr. Cole's comments about you."

"Why do you want to know what's goin' on with ol' Pete?" Nick asked, crossing his arms.

Wild chuckled and pulled a small golden cylinder from his waistcoat pocket. "It is very simple, Mr.…forgive me, I was rather preoccupied when you introduced yourself…what is your name again?"

"Nick Anderson."

"Well, Mr. Anderson," Wild returned, fondling the bevel cuts on the outside of the cylinder, "it is quite simple…Karl Rheinhardt has asked me to send him reports about the factory—and Peter's activities."

"Why?"

"Karl is rather skittish after the incident last year, and he wants to guarantee that Peter does not abuse his position in the company as Quentin Fetch did."

"But wasn't it Pete who stopped Fetch?"

"Yes, it was," Wild replied as he twisted the decorated tube, causing a gold toothpick to emerge from one end. "However, with Karl in Germany, Peter has the perfect opportunity to form his own dictatorship—that is why Karl requested my assistance."

"So what do you want from me?"

Eyeing his horde of busy workmen, Wild motioned with his arm. "Come, I will give you a tour of my property, which will also enable us to speak in private...what do you think of my soon-to-be new home?" Wild inquired, motioning toward the structure with the golden toothpick.

"Kinda big," Nick answered as he followed Wild to the back of the house.

"Big? My dear fellow, this is a cottage compared to my Grand Rapid's estate."

Nick sneered at the obvious boasting. "Grand Rapids? You have another house there?"

"I have many, many houses," Wild said with an amused smirk. "But do not misunderstand, when the carpenters complete the interior, this home will rival any chateau in Europe."

"Then you'll be payin' me real good for my information, won't ya?"

Wild paused, and scraping his teeth with the golden pick, he eyed Nick. "If you supply me with some useful tidbits, I will be extremely generous."

"How generous?"

"Before we discuss those details, please, enlighten me...why are you so willing to divulge Peter's secrets? He is family, is he not?"

"Yeah, sorta...but he's still a stranger to me—just like you. So I'll go where I can get the best hand dealt to me."

"I see," Wild murmured as he twisted the toothpick closed and slipped it into his pocket. "Then you are prepared to become my ally?"

"If you pay enough."

Wild roared with laughter, then turned and strolled into a manicured garden behind them. As he watched the finely dressed Wild amble through the precisely trimmed plants, Nick shook his head. He didn't like James Wild—he didn't like the man's snobbish attitude...or his immaculate appearance...or his half-finished mansion. Then why, Nick asked himself, do you want to work for him? And why do you want to betray the only person who's treated you with any amount of respect?

"Mr. Anderson...if you please."

Reluctantly, Nick walked over and joined Wild under a large arbor covered with climbing roses. "Yeah?"

"Peter Leighton departed Sandorville on Wednesday—what was his destination?" Wild asked, holding a sizable coin between his thumb and index finger.

Moistening his lips, Nick stared at the twenty-dollar gold piece. "Willow Ridge," he blurted out before he could stop himself.

"Ah, so he chose Willow Ridge…and did he succeed in obtaining his lumber?" Wild pressed.

Nick blew out a long, deep breath. He wanted to remain silent, but he wanted the money even more. Besides, he inwardly argued, with two simple words, he had already branded himself as a snitch. "Yes," he replied quietly.

"From whom did Peter buy the lumber?"

"A man named Logan MacColl."

"And when will the shipment arrive?"

"Monday."

Wild exploded with a high-pitched belly-laugh and thrust the coin out. "Take it," he said gleefully. "You have more than earned it."

With a frown Nick plucked the money from Wild's hand.

"Why are you troubled, Mr. Anderson?"

Peering into Wild's eyes, Nick wondered the same thing. Why was he having so much uncertainty about being one of Wild's confederates? And why did the double-eagle in his hand feel so cold? It just didn't make sense. "I'm not troubled," he lied.

"Then you are satisfied with your payment?"

"Sure."

"May I also assume that you are interested in providing me with daily reports for the same amount?"

Nick's mouth fell open. "Twenty dollars a day?"

"As long as you continue to provide me with such pertinent information, yes, I am willing to pay you twenty dollars a day."

"Yeah," Nick muttered with a smirk. "I'm interested."

"Excellent! Starting Sunday night, I will expect you at my interim home on Park Street at eleven o'clock, every evening."

"Eleven?!"

"Yes. That diminishes your chances of being seen."

"And what about tomorrow?"

"Come to the open-air market when you have completed your work at the factory. I will meet you there."

"Whatd'ya mean when I complete my work? I don't have a job there."

"Well, I suggest that you apply for one. I want you as close to Peter Leighton and the factory as possible."

"All right," Nick mumbled, feeling as if he had just hammered a nail into Peter's coffin. "Where am I supposed to meet ya at the market?"

"I will find you when I am ready."

"I'm just supposed to wait around 'til you get there?"

"If you want your money—yes," Wild answered as he adjusted his diamond-studded sleeve buttons.

Nick sighed deeply but said nothing. Twenty dollars a day was worth the aggravation, he reasoned.

"Do you have a complaint, Mr. Anderson?"

"No, none at all."

"Very good...oh, yes, I almost forgot—do not share our financial arrangements with Mr. Cole."

"Why?"

"Because I asked you not to," Wild replied brusquely. Then, relaxing somewhat, he added, "Mr. Cole may become jealous of the fact that you are receiving more compensation than he is."

"What does he do for you anyways?" Nick asked, his eyes narrowing.

"That, my dear Mr. Anderson, is my business."

"Does he snitch for you too?"

Wild's lips curled up mischievously. "Among other things."

"Then why do you need me?"

"Because you will be able to supply me with Peter Leighton's thoughts—Cole cannot...Cole can barely supply me with his own thoughts."

Nick exhaled, and gazing downward, he studied the gold coin in his palm. You owe Peter nothing, he said silently as his hand closed around the bribe. You are the only one you have to be loyal to.

Seven

As Jaxson inspected the factory's frighteningly low stock of lumber, he shook his head and scribbled on the piece of paper in his hand. "Praise God we only have a half day tomorrow," he moaned, counting the wood again.

"I agree."

His eyes opening wide, Jaxson gazed upward, waiting for God to continue. Then, finally recognizing the voice—and realizing that it came from behind, not above—Jaxson sheepishly turned around and faced Peter. "Make a little noise when you enter a room, will ya?" he teased with a grin.

"Sorry...I thought I did," came the faint reply.

Instantly, the humor drained from Jaxson's face. "Takin' a break didn't help ya, did it?" he asked, already knowing the answer.

"Not the headache," Peter returned, rubbing his temples. "But something good did happen."

"What?"

"Anna and I made definite plans for the wedding...it's going to be in early October."

"Peter, that's great!" Jaxson exclaimed and jostled his friend's arm.

"Yeah, we talked things through...I can't really explain it, but everything's better between us. It's almost as if our engagement has been revived...Anna too."

"God's been moving."

"Yes, He has," Peter said, then, suddenly, he clutched at his stomach and sank onto a stack of lumber.

"You want me to take ya to see Doc Spreyer?" Jaxson worriedly offered as he sat next to his friend.

Peter smiled weakly. "Right now, I don't think anything's going to help...I'm sorry, Jax, I know you need my help, but I think I should go home."

"I've been tellin' you to do that all morning," Jaxson chided good-naturedly.

"I know…I know."

"I'll bring one of the wagons around and drive—"

"No, I'll be fine…they need you here."

Sighing resignedly, Jaxson nodded—he knew it was both cruel and pointless to argue with one of Peter's headaches. "All right," he finally replied, "and if you need tomorrow too, take it."

"Nope, I'll be here tomorrow, regardless…I want to make sure I get to the open-air market. Anna and Lynette are going to be there selling pies—pineapple pies."

"Oh, yeah?" Jaxson commented quietly.

"Yeah…Wild's having his carpenters build them a sales booth…he's even providing the transportation for the pies."

"Huh, seems as though ol' Wild's been helpin' out a lot lately," Jaxson returned, wondering how Peter was staying so calm.

"Yes, he has…but this will be the last time," Peter declared, more to the absent Wild, than to Jaxson. "With us ready to announce a wedding date, Wild cannot—and will not—ignore that ring on Anna's finger anymore."

Jaxson inwardly cheered Peter's determined statement—Anna wasn't the only one experiencing a revival.

"You do know," Peter added, smiling slyly, "that the open-air market is a good place to start a courtship."

Trying to hide his surprise and embarrassment, Jaxson folded the paper he was holding and stuffed it into his pocket. Of course, he knew. The same thought had occurred to him—for months—but he always lost his voice and courage when he approached Holly. "Whatd'ya mean?" he murmured with mock bewilderment.

Peter shrugged. "Anna and I met at the market."

"I know."

"The Jayes usually go there after the factory shuts down, don't they?"

"Yeah…I mean, I guess…I've seen them there…sometimes."

"Why don't you bring them by and introduce them to Lynette."

Jaxson sighed loudly. He resented Peter's meddling, but at the same time, he appreciated the innocent strategy. "I guess I could…it'd be good for Lynette to know more people in town."

"Exactly."

"Maybe I'll even get one of those pies for the Jayes and me…you know, to help Anna and Lynette out."

"I'm sure they'd appreciate that."

"Unless you don't want me to buy a pie."

"Why wouldn't I?"

"You know…the pineapples," Jaxson said in a whisper.

"Hey, the sooner those things are gone, the better…I plan on stopping at the marketplace in the morning to help the girls set up…I'll tell them to put a pie aside for you," Peter offered with a slight grin.

Shaking his head, Jaxson moved sideward and studied Peter. For the first time, he completely understood the remark Daven had once made about his older brother…

'With the caring, there always comes a bit of shepherding.'

Then, as Jaxson continued searching Peter's tormented features, he shook his head again—this time with sympathy. "Why don't ya just go home?"

"I will…but I want to ask you something first."

Jaxson's heart quickened—the last time Peter used such a serious tone was when he talked about his crippling headaches. "Whatd'ya wanna know?"

"Would you be my best man?"

"Your…your what?" Jaxson stuttered, reeling from the unexpected question.

"My best man…at the wedding."

As the request—and the compliment—finally broke through his befuddlement, Jaxson smiled broadly. "I'd…I'd be honored," he said as he and Peter exchanged a firm handshake.

"Thanks…you've stood by me through everything this past year, and I can't think of anyone I'd rather have at my side."

Jaxson beamed at his friend's warm words, but he knew they weren't entirely true…there was one person Peter would rather have at his side—Daven.

"Hey, Pete."

Glancing up, Jaxson scowled. He didn't know which annoyed him more—the interruption or the interrupter.

"Nick!" Peter exclaimed, unsteadily rising. "What's wrong?"

"Nothing," Nick muttered as he sauntered toward his stepbrother. "I just got to thinkin' about what you said earlier. I do wanna earn some money—you still got a place for me?"

"Yes, absolutely," Peter replied, giving Nick a brotherly slap on the shoulder.

As he watched the gesture, a pang of dread and suspicion rippled through Jaxson's gut. "We can sure use the help," he said, trying to suppress the foreboding that had welled up inside him. "And," he added, standing up, "it'd be great if you could start right now, 'cause Peter's goin' home."

Nick frowned. "It's gotten that bad, huh?"

"Yeah, it didn't take long…would you do me a small favor, Nick?"

"What?" he demanded, crossing his arms.

"After you're done here, would you go to Anna's and let her know that I won't be coming for supper tonight? At our picnic, I told her I'd try, but it's just not going to happen."

Letting out a deep breath, Nick smirked and nodded.

"I can go to Anna's," Jaxson put in, fiercely eyeing Nick.

"No," Peter countered, "you need to talk to Benjamin Jaye."

"Ben? Why?"

"To make plans for tomorrow."

Jaxson started to answer, but as he looked at Peter and Nick, he bit the inside of his lip instead. He agreed—it was better to extend an early invitation to the Jaye family, rather than waiting until the day of the open-air market—but Peter's statement still gnawed at him. Or did it?

Was it his friend's persistence that irked him? Or was it just Nick?

❧❧❧❧

Pounding on the Spreyers' front door for a second time, Nick sighed. Why was he doing this? Why didn't he just forget about Peter's request and go back to his newfound saloon? Beating on the door again, Nick peered into the house through the screen, and immediately, an uneasiness grabbed at his neck. Why? he inwardly moaned. Of all the people in the house, why did it have to be Anna coming to answer his knock?

"Nick, I'm so glad to see you," she said, pushing the door open.

"Pete just wanted me to tell ya that he won't be comin' for supper," he blurted out, then, turning on his heel, he headed for the porch steps, hoping to escape before Anna flew into another tirade.

"Don't go, Nick…please."

Cursing under his breath, Nick stopped and circled. "Why? So you can welcome me the way you did last night?"

"No, so I can apologize for the way I treated you," she returned as she walked over to him. "I was upset over something else, and you and Peter got caught in the middle…I am so sorry."

"Yeah, okay…can I go now?"

"Won't you stay for supper? We have plenty."

"No…I…I gotta…no."

"Please, Nick. I'd like to make up for yesterday. Despite what you may think, I really am very happy that Peter found you and brought you to Sandorville."

Nick inhaled deeply. He wanted to refuse and force Anna to keep begging for forgiveness, but her sweet face and remorseful tone melted his resolve. "I guess I can."

"Oh, good!" Anna exclaimed, beaming. "Is Peter working late?"

"No, he went home."

"Home? Why? Is he all right?"

"I suppose…his headache got real bad."

"Did he go see Papa and get some medicine?"

"I dunno," Nick replied with a grimace, tiring of Anna's inquisition. "He went home and I took his place at the factory. I don't know nothin' else."

Anna smiled brightly. "It's very kind of you to help Peter like that."

As he struggled with a twinge of guilt, Nick shrugged and offered, "I suppose."

"I appreciate your coming here to tell me. I would have worried myself sick if he had never shown up tonight…did you have any difficulty finding the house again?"

"Naw, I found it okay," Nick muttered, neglecting to add that he had also found a very accommodating tavern along the way.

"Oh, here comes Papa now," Anna announced as she gestured to a small black buggy in the distance. "I want to talk with him about Peter…you can go right on inside—Lynette's just finishing up with the supper preparations."

Yanking the screen door open, Nick stepped inside the house and started down the hall. Then, as he passed the parlor, he paused and angrily eyed the portrait of his half-brother. Why? he wondered. Why did everything turn out as it did? And, as he continued to study the picture, he began to loathe the friendly-faced boy who lived the life he should have had.

"Guten Abend."

Startled by the quiet greeting, Nick scanned the parlor's interior and spotted Irene Spreyer sitting on one of the overstuffed chairs by the windows. "Ma'am…I'm sorry if I disturbed you…Anna, uh, your daughter said I could come in," he said as he pulled off his hat.

Closing the tattered book in her hands, Mrs. Spreyer smiled. "You are part of our family…you may come and go as you wish."

Nick forced a grin and backed away from Irene Spreyer's line of vision. "Family…sure," he whispered under his breath. When were Peter and the Spreyers going to realize that they would never fill that void?

Slowly, Nick continued his trek toward the kitchen, glancing into both the library and the dining room as he went by. Although it was rurally decorated, the big farmhouse still exuded a richness that confused and, at the same time, comforted him. And, without quite knowing why, Nick ventured into the kitchen with a relaxed smile on his face. "It smells real good in here," he commented, inhaling the cinnamon-scented air.

Turning from her tubful of dishes, Lynette's eyes lit up with delight. "Mr. Anderson…what a pleasant surprise!"

"Call me Nick," he returned. "I never did like Anderson, and now, I downright hate it."

"All right, Nick. Please, have a seat," Lynette said as she motioned to the table with a sudsy hand. "Supper will be ready soon."

Taking a few steps forward, Nick nonchalantly flung his bowler toward the hat stand. Then, as it landed on one of the rungs, he glanced at Lynette, hoping that she had noticed the successful toss—but unfortunately, she had returned to her dish washing. With a disappointed grunt, Nick strolled to the table and sank onto a chair. Why are you trying to show off? he asked himself as he studied the back of Lynette's shapely figure—she's too good for you and you know it. Yes, he silently agreed, but he still longed to slide his arms around Lynette's tiny waist and caress her radiant features.

"I don't mean to be rude," she offered, looking at Nick over her shoulder, "but I'm very behind with my chores…if I don't finish these dishes, we won't have anything to eat with."

"It's okay," Nick replied as he elbowed a large ceramic bowl away from the edge of the table.

"Oh, I'm sorry. I haven't been able to clear the table yet."

"It's okay."

"No, you shouldn't have to stare at all those dirty dishes."

"It's fine—really."

With her hands still dripping wet, Lynette darted to the table and piled a stack of soiled utensils into the huge mixing bowl. "Anna and I are going to sell some baked goods at the market tomorrow," she explained, grabbing the heavy dish. "It seems as if all I've been doing is…oh, no!"

Even before her shout of alarm, Nick saw the clay bowl slip from Lynette's wet hands, and thrusting out his arms, he caught the dish just inches from the floor.

"Oh, Nick…thank you," Lynette breathlessly whispered.

Proudly, Nick stood up, holding the bowl. "Aw, it was nothing."

As Lynette reached out to take the elusive container, her fingers brushed against Nick's hands, and instantly, a spark rippled through him. Unnerved by the fiery sensation, he jerked away, almost causing the dish to fall once again. No one's touch—not even Lydia's—had ever made him feel so alive…so hopeful…so happy…

"I'm…I'm just glad that I was here…you know, to help."

"And so am I," Lynette said, tightly cradling the clay bowl in her arms. "I love that Jesus cares about even the smallest detail of our lives, don't you? He not only brought you into the kitchen at the perfect time, but He also saved me from having to explain my carelessness to the Spreyers."

Immediately, Nick frowned—his luck never changed…why did his pretty little Lynette have to be a God-fearing Bible-peddler? "It wasn't Jesus—it was just a good catch…I'm livin' proof that God don't care about 'details.'"

"But the Lord does—"

"Mama, are we going to eat soon? Bock's really hungry."

Spinning around, Nick's scowl deepened. That's right, he reminded himself, Lynette also had a child.

"Yes, Sweetheart…William, do you remember Mr. Anderson? We met him last night."

William nodded. "He's Peter's brother—but not the one in the painting."

"That's right…and, Nick, this is my son, William."

"Uh huh."

"This is Bock," William declared, approaching Nick. "He's my best friend."

As he looked at the tiny puff of orange fur, lying like a baby in William's arms, Nick cringed and blew out a lengthy breath. Only he could be attracted to a woman who laid claim to three of the things he despised the most—God, children, and cats.

"Yeah, he's real nice," Nick returned as he patted William on the head.

Suddenly, William backed away. "You smell like my papa does."

His brow wrinkled in confusion, Nick glanced at Lynette, but her sad, apologetic simper provided no explanation.

"Why don't you and Bock go play for awhile," Lynette put in quietly. "I'll call you when everything's ready."

Giving Nick a final pout, William tenderly hugged his kitten and ran out of the kitchen.

"I smell like his papa does?"

"He didn't mean to insult you," Lynette answered as she slowly returned to the sink. "It's just that the odor of liquor reminds him of his father."

"But why did he say 'does'? He meant to say 'did,' right?"

"No."

"Aren't you a widow?"

Depositing the bowl into the washtub, Lynette shook her head. "No, Mr. Chesnay is quite alive."

"Oh," Nick murmured, "I thought it was just you and your son."

"It is…I divorced my husband."

Instantly, Nick's face lit up. "Really?"

"Yes."

"Why?" As soon as the question came out of his mouth, Nick flinched. He knew, deep inside, that regret for his brashness was the proper response, but since he had never worried about propriety before, he decided to continue digging. "Mr. Chesnay drank a lot, huh?"

"Yes," she softly replied, swishing the sudsy dish water.

"And, I take it, he wasn't a very pleasant drunk."

"No."

"Was he violent toward you?" Nick asked, moving next to her.

"Yes," she said with a quiver in her voice. "Almost always when he drank…I tried to cope, but between his temper and constant womanizing, things just kept getting worse."

Nick nodded. He didn't know what pleased him more—Lynette's bravery or the fact that she was sufficiently spouseless. "Hey, you did what you had to," he returned. "Sometimes, you don't have any other choice—it's either leave or be destroyed."

Lynette sighed and tilted her head to look at Nick. "Why does that remark sound as if it comes from experience?"

With a shrug, Nick picked up the towel lying on the counter next to him. Although he had no desire to share his sordid past with anyone, he still found himself wanting to continue. "It does…I was adopted when I was eight and ended up in the same kinda situation," he said, plunging his hand into the rinse tub and lifting out a plate. "Old man Dengler and his wife just wanted another farmhand that they didn't have to pay…that man treated his animals better than me…so I had to do the same as you…leave or let Dengler destroy me."

"Did he give you those?" Lynette inquired, motioning toward his face.

"These?" Nick muttered as he put the plate down and fingered the two scars on his left cheek. "No, these were a gift from someone else."

"I'm sorry, Nick…I shouldn't have asked that. It's none of my business."

He agreed, but then again, he was just as guilty of prying as she was. "Dengler gave me plenty of other scars, though…I stayed with them for about six years, then the beatings got so bad that I had to leave."

Her eyes swimming with tears, Lynette gazed at him and smiled. "It looks as though the Lord escorted us both to safety."

Nick laughed vehemently and threw the towel down. "God's the reason I got into the mess in the first place."

"What do you mean?"

"I asked God for a caring family, and I got the Denglers instead…that was the last time I trusted Him for anything…He didn't get me to safety—I did."

"But the Lord did give you a loving family…Peter and the Spreyers."

"Yeah, right…it's a little late, don't ya think?" he mumbled as he meandered to the back door and absently stared out the screened window.

"It's never too late to be loved."

"I don't need a brother now—I needed him when I was growing up."

Wiping her hands on her apron, Lynette joined Nick at the door. "But it just wasn't the right time."

"Wasn't the right time? Every minute is the right time when you're an orphan…I waited and waited for a good family…I was ready, but God never sent them."

"But they might not have been ready for you."

"Whatd'ya mean?"

"Sometimes our blessings are dependent upon other people's actions…Anna told me that Peter used to be a very different person than he is now and—"

"Are you sayin' it's Pete's fault that I never got my family back then?" Nick loudly cut in as his grudge against his stepbrother ballooned.

"No, Nick," Lynette soothed, "it's not anyone's fault…it's just that Peter might have had to do something or maybe certain things had to happen in his life before he could meet you…and accept you…and love you."

"That's real nice," Nick returned, crossing his arms. "Because Pete didn't do whatever he was supposed to do, I didn't get my family."

"If anyone's actions have harmed you or caused a delay in your blessings, the Lord knows all about them, and He'll make everything right—in His time."

Nick grunted. "You really believe that?"

Lowering her eyes, Lynette circled and slowly moved back to the sink. "When I petitioned for a divorce, it was my desire to get myself and my son away from Mr. Chesnay's philandering and cruel temper," she explained, resuming her dish washing. "I had gathered plenty of evidence against him, but he used his unending charm to convince everyone—his family…my family…my witnesses…even the judge—that I was the adulterer and the one hurting William. Because of those horrible lies, there was no possibility of getting custody of my son—and that was what Mr. Chesnay wanted…he knew I wouldn't leave without William…from my point of view, I had lost the battle." Dabbing her eyes with the back of her hand, Lynette took a few deep, fluttering breaths, then continued, "That was when my Aunt Noelle, my only ally during that time, told me what I just told you. I believed her, but I couldn't see how God could fix the harm Mr. Chesnay had done."

With a grunt, Nick shuffled back to the sink. He did not plan on giving Lynette his full attention, especially since she was preaching the usual 'Christ is on your side' sermon. But he had been drawn into her story, and he wanted to know the outcome—even if that meant hearing more about the God he despised. "So what happened?" he questioned as he picked up the dish towel once again and dried a handful of forks.

"The day came for the judge to make everything final…and when Mr. Chesnay showed up, he came in filthy drunk…that was when I knew the Lord was with me. Mr. Chesnay tended to lose his charm when he drank, and on that day, he lost it completely. He insulted the judge, his lawyer, and my aunt, and he struck me…as a result, I received my divorce—and my son."

Nick laughed. "So God fixed everything by getting your husband drunk?"

Lynette grinned with a wide, patient smile. "Well, I don't know about that, but normally, Mr. Chesnay would never have been that careless so close to a victory."

Pulling another plate from the rinse tub, Nick frowned. "That's all wonderful for you," he scoffed, "you got what you asked for while it was still useful to ya…what good is a family gunna do me now, after all these years?"

"I'm sure the Lord will make that clear, very soon."

❦

Standing motionless, Jaxson Averill gulped and studied the walkway leading to the home of Benjamin Jaye. Stop being stupid, he shouted voicelessly. Just move your legs and go up to the house. But still, he hesitated. How could such a simple task be so difficult? he wondered. Then, as he stared at the wooden planks, the answer crystallized in his head—this one gesture could change his life.

Drawing in a deep breath, Jaxson marched up the walkway and rapped on the jamb. At first, all he could hear was his heart beating, then the latch clicked and the door swung open.

"Jaxson, how nice of you to stop by."

"Uh, hello, Miss Holly," he stammered, sliding his hat from his head. "Is uh, Benj…I mean your father home?"

"Sure," Holly returned with a sparkling smile. "Come on inside."

"Uh, no, thanks. I just came to ask your pa something."

"Well you can still ask him from in here," she reasoned, tugging on his arm.

Reluctantly, Jaxson stepped over the threshold, and as he did, his eyes were greeted by a multitude of creative wonders. Brushstroked ornaments appeared everywhere he looked—even the walls were adorned with hand-painted vines. And standing in front of him was the most delightful sight of all—his beautiful Holly, whose smile out-dazzled the sun. "You look mighty pretty tonight, Miss Holly," he offered. Then, as he heard his own words, a shiver shook through him—he had never meant to voice his thought out loud.

"Why, thank you," Holly squealed, her smile widening. "I'll tell Pa that you're here."

Swallowing hard, Jaxson nodded. There's no turning back now, he told himself. You've just kicked a very big boulder down a steep hill…you just better hope that it doesn't end up rolling over you.

"Jaxson!" Benjamin Jaye exclaimed as he emerged from the kitchen. "Do you need us back at the factory?"

"No…no," Jaxson replied, wringing the brim of his hat, "I'm here 'cause of the open-air market, not the factory."

"The market?"

Scrunching his derby further out of shape, Jaxson glanced toward the kitchen, where he saw Holly, Bonnie, and their younger sister, Aimee, peeking back at him.

You've just made the worst blunder of your life, he inwardly declared. What if Benjamin says no to the invite? How will you ever face him or Holly again? Forcing his eyes from the giggling trio, Jaxson shook his head. His innocent boulder was surely going to squash him—somehow, he had to stop it...

"I'm sorry, Benjamin. I'm prob'ly interruptin' your supper...I can come back."

"You're not interrupting...why don't you stay? The girls are tryin' something new."

"Uh, no...that's...I should go."

"Wait...you wanted to say somethin' about the open-air market."

"It ain't important."

Immediately, the corners of Benjamin Jaye's mouth started to curl upward. "We're plannin' on going tomorrow...you want to join us?"

His hat dropping from his hands, Jaxson examined Benjamin's jovial expression. "You...you mean it?" he asked as he squatted to pick up his anxiety-battered cap.

"Yes, I mean it," Ben laughed.

"Well...that's kinda why I came tonight. Anna Spreyer and her friend are gunna be sellin' pastries at the market. I wanted to treat you and your family to one of their pineapple pies."

"Pineapples? How in Sam Hill did they get pineapples?"

"James Wild gave 'em to Miss Spreyer."

Benjamin Jaye grunted. "I bet that made Peter a bit wrathy."

"To say the least," Jaxson replied, suddenly realizing that his nervousness had melted away. "That's why I thought we should eat up one of the pies—you know, to help Peter out."

Ben barked out another deep laugh. "Well, we can't let Peter down, can we? My girls and me would be mighty pleased to share one of those pies with you."

Curbing his desire to holler in delight, Jaxson beamed at Benjamin's warm and humorous response. Not only did his boulder miss crushing him, but it ended up rolling down the perfect path. "Great. I look forward to it."

"Me too," Benjamin returned as he clasped his hand over Jaxson's shoulder. "It'll be nice to have another man around—I'm usually the only one in a whole sea of women...so you ready to try the girls' new concoction?"

His smile widening, Jaxson nodded. Yes, he inwardly cheered, his life was definitely changing.

❦

"Good evening, Mr. Wild...welcome home."

"Crandall."

"How was your train trip, Sir?"

"Fine, just fine."

"Excellent…I trust everything is going well with the new house," Crandall offered as he gently grasped the collar of Wild's frock coat.

"Yes," James Wild returned, shrugging his arms out of the coat, "everything is going splendidly. It should be livable by winter."

"How fortunate, Sir."

"And, soon, I will need your decision."

"Decision, Sir?" Crandall asked, hanging the frock coat on a rack near the front door.

"Yes…you will need to decide which home you wish to attend."

"I do not understand, Sir…I thought you were going to sell the Park Street house when you move into the new one."

"I am."

"What about Robert? I thought he would move with you."

"Robert's skills are fine for that minuscule shack on Park Street, but my new chateau needs a more experienced servant."

"Ah, I see," Crandall said as he removed a quilted lounging jacket from the coat rack. "I am your butler, Sir. I'll go wherever you need me…however, I do prefer to stay here in Grand Rapids."

"As do I, Crandall," Wild laughed. "Sandorville is quite dull."

"I'm grateful that you have Miss Spreyer to help you through the monotony," Crandall replied, helping Wild into the quilted garment.

"Yes, she—and a few other amusements—make Sandorville quite tolerable."

"I assume Miss Spreyer is looking forward to decorating her new house."

"When Anna and I are married, this will be our home."

"Oh? I thought she would want to live in Sandorville, near her family."

"My wife will live where I say she will live."

"Of course…your brandy, Sir," the butler announced as he picked up a silver tray and held it out to his employer. "And the calling cards you received while you've been away."

Grabbing the snifter, Wild studied the stack of cards on the tray and sighed. "Hold the cards until morning."

"Yes Sir…also, there is a Mr. Wit Dearborn in the library. He insisted on seeing you…I tried to explain that you would be tired after your trip from Sandorville, but he—"

"It is fine, Crandall," Wild cut in, swishing the amber liquid in his glass. "I sent for him."

"Oh…he never mentioned that."

"I know Mr. Dearborn is somewhat uncouth, but he is performing a critical mission for me. Always welcome him—at any hour."

"Yes Sir!"

As he headed toward the library, James Wild grinned and took a sip of his brandy—the game, finally, could continue.

"Mr. Dearborn, I am so pleased that you could come on such short notice," Wild proclaimed, entering the library.

"Well, I'm pleased that you're pleased," Wit Dearborn replied as he reclined on a satin-covered bench built into the third bay window. "But I'd be more pleased if I got my money."

"You will be paid, Dearborn, and quite well, I might add," Wild returned, strutting over to the window.

"I assume you were also pleased with the job I did for you."

Wild laughed and extended his brandy glass to Dearborn. "Burning that lumber while en route to the depot was absolute genius."

"Then Leighton was, uh, surprised?" Dearborn asked as he took the glass and downed the liquor in one swallow.

"Quite. He did conceal his dismay behind a brave facade though—he looked me directly in the eyes and told me that everything was proceeding on schedule."

Dearborn grunted and sat up straight. "Yeah, he always was a good liar...so whatd'ya want me to do now?"

"Leighton has located another source for his lumber—a sawmill in Willow Ridge," Wild answered, settling himself next to Dearborn. "I would like you to visit that mill and cancel the order on Peter's behalf."

"I can do more than that."

"Yes, Dearborn, I am well aware that you can—and want—to do more, but I would like you to do as I ask."

"I don't understand you," Wit Dearborn offered as he scratched his bald head. "I thought your goal was to destroy Leighton. All you're doin' is just tossin' dirt in his face."

"Are you a chess player, Mr. Dearborn?"

"A what?"

"A chess player."

"I've played a few games...but what's chess got to do with Leighton?"

As he peered into Dearborn's cold, sinister eyes, Wild doubted that the man even knew what a chessboard looked like, but shrugging away his skepticism, he continued with his explanation. "When most people compete in a game of chess, they attempt to capture their challenger's king as quickly as possible."

"Yeah," Dearborn snorted, "it's called killin' the king and winnin' the game."

"Ah, but there are different ways of winning…I prefer to attack my opponent's kingdom first—taking each playing piece away, one at a time. Eventually, my rival becomes so disillusioned that he concedes, and I get what I want."

Tilting his head, Dearborn glared at Wild through his gold-rimmed spectacles. "What you got against Leighton, anyways?"

"Nothing. He merely has a couple of items that I want."

"What items?"

"That is none of your concern…what should be your concern is doing what I ask—and I am asking you to go to Willow Ridge and inform the sawmill that Peter has changed his mind and does not want the lumber."

Dearborn grunted in return. "I think it would hit Leighton harder if I destroyed the wood like before."

"Enough!" Wild exclaimed, rising to his feet. "I do not pay you to think—I pay you to carry out my wishes."

"Yeah?" Dearborn seethed, also standing. "Well, maybe I'll just start carryin' out my own wishes."

"No, you will not…I know you are accustomed to receiving your assignments and then having the freedom to choose your own method of execution, but as long as · you are in my employ, you will follow my directions—exactly."

"And how do you know what I'm used to?" Dearborn demanded.

"Because, my dear Sir, I know who you are."

"Yeah, I'm Wit Dearborn," the bald man replied, his eyes transforming to ice.

Wild laughed. "You can shave your head, grow a mustache and beard, don spectacles, and change your name—but those things do not alter the fact that you are Leland Bryce."

Suddenly, Dearborn's features turned to granite. "I think you're mistaken about that," he said as he inched his right hand toward his inside coat pocket.

"No need to reach for your derringer, Bryce…I have known your true identity from our very first encounter."

"Is that so," Leland Bryce replied, his arm still tense.

"Yes. In fact, when you stepped into my office and inquired about a position, I knew I had to hire you."

"Why?"

"Well, I assumed that you might enjoy the chance to torment Peter Leighton," Wild returned as he strolled to his desk and pulled out a drawer, "considering that it was dear Peter who terminated your previous career."

"You guessed right."

Removing a bulging velvet sack from the drawer, Wild chuckled. "I also figured that your association with Quentin Fetch left you, well, let us say, unafraid to be unscrupulous."

Bryce smirked. "If that means 'willing to do anything'—you guessed right again."

"So you see, Bryce, those qualities made you the perfect candidate to aid me with my plans for Leighton."

Leland Bryce laughed and relaxed his arm. "Why didn't you tell me you knew who I was?" he questioned as he rubbed his bald head. "I could've let my hair grow back."

"Up to this point, it has not been necessary for me to reveal my knowledge about your identity."

"But now it is?"

"Correct."

"Why?" Bryce demanded, marching over to the desk.

"Well, dear Bryce, this leads us to the final reason that I decided to retain your services."

"And what's that?"

"Your unique position in life."

"Whatd'ya mean my 'unique position'?"

"Well, let me put it this way…if you betray me—and that includes disobeying my orders—I will inform the authorities that you are a fugitive."

With a sharp curse, Bryce propped himself on the edge of the desk. "And whatd'ya gunna do when I tell those same authorities that you hired me to torture Leighton?"

"I will simply tell them that I had no idea that Wit Dearborn and Leland Bryce were one in the same…who do you think they will believe—a wanted criminal or a man who is able to buy them anything they desire?"

Bryce growled out another curse and crossed his arms.

"Stop whining…you may not have the freedom you had under Fetch, but you will find, I assure you, that my rewards are much more substantial," Wild smugly put in as he held up the velvet sack.

❧❧❧

Rubbing the persistent twinge in his forearm, Peter grimaced and looked upward. Rain was positively coming—the swarming clouds and the pangs in his arm were proof of that. But he hoped, for Anna and Lynette's sake, that the afternoon showers would wait until nightfall—even if it meant suffering through more spasms.

"Looks as if the girls are doin' real good," Jaxson commented, pointing to the line of people wrapping around the sales booth.

"Yeah, it does. It also looks as if we'll be waiting quite awhile to get anything ourselves," Peter returned. "And, Nick," he added with a glance to his left, "I know Anna put something aside for you, but if you don't want to wait for—"

"Naw, it's fine. I can wait."

As the three continued their walk to the bakery stand, Peter scrutinized his brother. Nick's amicable answer completely confounded him—until he noticed the subject of his stepbrother's intense stare…Lynette Chesnay. Grinning, Peter nodded—the more that kept his brother in Sandorville, the better.

Signaling his arrival, Peter waved at Anna, who responded with a frantic gesture, beckoning him to come over. "Something's wrong," Peter announced and ran toward the booth with Jaxson and Nick at his heels. Then, as he neared, he heard exactly what the problem was…

"Please, ladies, just a few questions," the man at the front of the line urged. "My newspaper has quite a large readership and everyone is looking forward to my story…'The Rheinhardt Factory—A Year After the Fire.'"

Instantly, Peter's hand curled into a fist, and he pulled his arm back, determined to answer the reporter's request with a solid blow to the jaw, but a dark-skinned hand on his forearm interrupted the plan.

"I know you hate newspaper men," Jaxson whispered, "but you're just gunna make it worse by sluggin' him here in front of everybody."

With a reluctant nod, Peter relaxed his hand and massaged his aching arm. "Sir, if you're not going to buy anything from the ladies, why don't you step aside," he reasoned, trying to calm his outrage. "That way they can take care of the people behind you."

The man eyed Peter, shrugged off the suggestion, and refocused on Anna. "Please, Miss Spreyer, my readers are very curious about—"

His jaw clamping shut, Peter grabbed the newspaper man's collar and yanked him from the line.

"What is the meaning of this?!" the reporter demanded.

Without a word, Peter gestured toward a stand of birch trees a few yards away.

"What do you want?" the man asked, his eyes darting from Peter, to Jaxson, to Nick, and finally, back to Peter.

"If you want to know about the Rheinhardt Factory, I'll talk to you—but only over there," Peter replied between gritted teeth.

"And who, pray tell, are you?"

"Peter Leighton."

Immediately, the reporter's eyes widened and he moistened his lips. "Peter Leighton? As in the man who burned the corruption out of the old Rheinhardt Factory?"

Growling at the man's grandiose phrasing, Peter motioned again to the birches. "Over there."

"Yes, yes, right…Peter Leighton—I just can't believe my luck," the newspaper man rambled as he ushered Peter toward the trees. "So, tell me, now that it's approaching the one-year mark, how do you—"

"No," Peter interrupted sharply, "not today."

"But you said—"

"I will answer all your questions—on Monday."

"But—"

"Look, Mr.…."

"Russell," the reporter finished, holding out his hand.

Staring at the man's extended arm, Peter remained still—he knew, from Nick's expert teaching, that he could inflict the perfect insult by refusing the handshake. "Look, Mr. Russell," Peter raged, "I don't like newspaper men. For the past year, you story-hunters have done everything to get at me, my workers, and my family—everything from hiding in the shrubs to posing as customers…one man even broke his own arm, so he could question my future father-in-law…if it weren't for my friend, you'd be going to the hospital right now with a busted jaw."

"But I'm not like those other reporters."

"No, of course you aren't, that's why I caught you badgering my fiancee."

"It was not my intention to harass Miss Spreyer, I only wanted to write a story based on the facts."

"Well, if that's true, you're the first."

"It is true…that's why I wanted to talk to someone who actually lived through the ordeal…you, Mr. Leighton, would be the ideal person for me to interview."

"I agree. And I told you I would speak with you—on Monday."

"But—"

"Mr. Russell," Peter fumed, seizing the reporter by the lapels of his coat, "come Monday I will answer any and all of your questions. I'll even escort you around the factory, if you'd like…but if you bother my fiancee, or her family, or my employees, or me before that time, I will escort you to the hospital instead…do I make myself clear?"

The newspaper man swallowed hard and nodded. "Yes Sir, you do."

"Good!" Peter snapped as he released his grip. "Now, go away."

"Yes, yes, of course," Russell said, his voice fluttering. "I'll uh, I'll see you Monday." Then, tipping his hat, the reporter whipped around and hurried away.

Trying to calm his pounding heart, Peter closed his eyes and took a long, deep breath. He never regretted bringing Quentin Fetch's crimes into the light—not even once. But, as every day passed, he wished he had done it anonymously.

"Why'd you tell him to come back?" Nick's voice boomed.

Startled, Peter turned to find his brother and Jaxson standing directly behind him. "How long have you two been here?"

"The whole time," Jaxson replied with a smirk. "If you ended up sluggin' him, you would have needed somebody to help ya carry him to the hospital."

Peter chuckled at the lighthearted but very truthful remark.

"Yeah," Nick put in, "you're fairly wicked when you're mad."

"Well, unfortunately, I've had a lot of practice at being angry…and I had to tell Russell to come back…otherwise, he would have never given us a minute of peace this weekend," Peter explained as he protectively scanned the area around the bakery booth. Then, seeing a familiar face approaching the line of customers, Peter's gray mood instantly lifted. "Emerson," he hollered cheerfully, "over here."

Emerson Brant burst into a smile and jogged toward the birch trees. "I looked for you in your usual picnicking spot, but this is probably why I couldn't find you there, huh," Emerson joked as he reached Peter.

Giving his young salesman a brief, brotherly hug, Peter asked, "When did you get back?"

"About an hour ago. I just stopped to get a snack before my base ball game starts…what are you doing way over here?"

Peter laughed and pointed. "Anna and her friend are selling pastries today…you were standing in line to buy your snack from them."

"Wow, really? What a marvelous coincidence," Emerson returned, glancing in the direction of Peter's gesture.

"So how was your trip?"

When no reply came, Peter scrutinized his salesman, whose attention was glued to the bakery booth.

"Em?"

No response.

"Emerson?" Jaxson chimed in, also attempting to break the salesman's trance.

Still oblivious, the young man just stood motionless, staring at Lynette and Anna.

"Em!"

Finally, Emerson blinked a few times and murmured, "Hey, Peter? Who's that beautiful woman with Anna?"

"That's Lynette Chesnay," Peter replied with a chuckle—Nick wasn't the only one smitten with Lynette.

"She's gorgeous! Is she visiting Anna? How long is she going to be in town?"

"I hope she'll be here for awhile…she came in answer to the advertisement that the Spreyers placed in the newspaper."

"Really? Will you introduce me when the crowd lessens?" Emerson almost squealed as he adjusted his flat-topped base ball cap and straightened his striped shirt.

"I thought you had a base ball game to go to," Nick mumbled under his breath.

Instantly, Peter's eyebrows raised—not only was Nick's statement unanticipated, but its edges were scorched with jealousy. "Hey, that's right," he interjected, trying to apply some polish to his brother's surly comment. "You two haven't met…Em, this is my brother Nikolaus Anderson. And, Nick, this is Emerson Brant, our salesman."

"Your brother?" Emerson questioned. "I thought he was…I thought…"

"A lot happened while you've been out of town…I found out I had another brother."

"Wow, that's great," Em returned, smiling so wide that deep dimples formed in his cheeks. "It's good to meet you, Mr. Anderson," he offered and extended his arm.

Peter assumed Nick would ignore the gesture as usual, but surprisingly, his step-brother reached out and clasped Emerson's hand. Then Peter understood why—his brother's grip tightened and tightened and tightened until Emerson winced.

"Kinda young for a salesman, ain't ya, Kid?" Nick asked, finally releasing his white-knuckled hold.

Massaging his crushed hand, Emerson stared at Nick in bewilderment and replied, "Well, Peter was generous enough to overlook that fact and give me a chance."

"And we're lucky to have him," Peter put in. "Em's a great salesman…he's been able to bring in order after order despite the factory's reputation."

Emerson grinned and kicked at the dirt with the toe of his shoe. "You taught me everything I know, Peter," he said. And, with a sparkle in his eye, he added, "The men's club finally decided to give us their order."

Peter's mouth dropped open. "The men's club in Grand Rapids?"

"Uh huh."

"That's great, Em," Jaxson shouted. "I thought they had their hearts set on carved furniture."

"They did."

"So how'd you get them to change their minds?"

"It wasn't me…it was the samples of Bonnie and Holly's painting that I took with me. The councilmen saw those wonderful brushstrokes and everything changed. Now, they want their tables made of oak, and they want them decorated—with painted oak branches—and…they want twenty of them."

"Twenty?!" both Peter and Jaxson exclaimed.

"Uh huh…and eighty chairs and ten bookcases…all in oak and all painted."

As the order's magnitude struck him, Peter pasted a wide smile on his face, hoping that it would disguise the doubt and fear swelling within him. The job was fantastic, he admitted that, but could they get the resources they needed to fill it? "You certainly have a knack for sales, Em," Peter sincerely offered as he patted his salesman on the shoulder. "I'm proud of you."

"Proud enough to introduce me to Lynette?" Emerson returned, pointing to the now customer-free bakery booth.

Ignoring his stepbrother's stone-faced glare, Peter nodded. "Absolutely."

With a yelp of glee, Emerson grasped Peter's arm and trotted toward Lynette.

"Slow down, Em, she's not going anywhere."

"But I want to ask if she'd like to watch my base ball game."

"You know she's divorced and has a kid," Nick commented as he followed.

Glancing over his shoulder, Emerson studied Nick from hat to boot, then grinned. "That's great. I adore children. And now, I know she's available to court… thanks, Mr. Anderson."

Trying to alter the course of the conversation and cool the brewing rivalry, Peter called to Anna, "Looks as if your pastries were a success."

"We're almost sold out," she happily replied as the men arrived at the sales counter. "But don't you worry, Jaxson, I saved a pineapple pie for you."

"I'm obliged, Miss Anna," he returned with a tip of his hat. "That was real nice."

"And thank you," she said, squeezing Peter's hand. "That newspaper man was dreadful."

"No matter what we said," Lynette added, "he kept asking questions."

Peter nodded. "I'm just sorry it happened at all," he murmured. Then, as Emerson coughed out a reminder of his presence, Peter smiled and announced, "Lynette, I'd like to introduce Mr. Emerson Brant. He's our salesman at the factory, and he's just returned from a very successful sales trip…Em, this is Mrs. Lynette Chesnay and her son, William."

Removing his base ball cap, Emerson gently held Lynette's hand and kissed it. "Your beauty makes this day shine even brighter," he stated with a dimpled smile.

Lynette beamed and a pink glow saturated her features. "Thank you, Mr. Brant, but today has been far from shiny," she responded, pointing a finger toward the congregating rain clouds.

"From my perspective, it's very shiny," he declared.

As Lynette's blush intensified, Peter glanced at his stepbrother, whose face was also crimson—but obviously, for very different reasons.

"Hey," Jaxson exclaimed, elbowing Peter, "you're bein' paged."

"What? I didn't hear any—" Then the call rang through his ears.

"Paging Mr. Peter Leighton…paging Mr. Peter Leighton…"

"Here," he called, signaling the messenger.

Seeing the gesture, the delivery boy held up a piece of paper and ran over to the booth. "I took a chance that you'd be somewhere in the marketplace, Sir," the boy panted. "An urgent telegram just came for you."

As he exchanged a tip for the unwanted news, Peter's heart began to hammer against his chest. What calamity, he wondered, had fallen on them now? Then, as he scanned the scribbles on the page, he felt as if a thousand laughing demons had landed on his shoulders. How? he silently moaned. How did it happen? He had been so careful. Glancing up at the worried faces surrounding him, Peter tried to speak, but the words caught in his throat.

"Peter, what's wrong?" Anna asked. "What does the telegram say?"

Once again he couldn't find his voice, and shaking his head, he shuffled away from his concerned entourage.

"Peter, what's going on?" Jaxson urged as he followed after him.

Stopping under the wind-swept birch trees, Peter circled and looked at his friend. "I don't know how much more of this I can take, Jax," he said, his eyes moistening.

With a frown, Jaxson plucked the message from Peter's hand and read it aloud. "Mr. Leighton. Gentleman arrived this morning to cancel maple on your behalf. Is this your desire? MacColl."

"Every time I start making some progress, God allows something like this to happen...why?" Peter questioned, leaning against one of the birches.

"But God didn't let it happen...MacColl could have just canceled, but the Lord had him telegraph you instead."

Peering into Jaxson's encouraging eyes, Peter half-smiled. Although it could be bothersome, he did, at times, appreciate his friend's optimistic perspective. Then, suddenly, another thought wriggled its way into his beleaguered head...

"MacColl talked to this man," Peter said. "He could tell us if the guy had long light-brown hair."

"You still think it's Wild?"

"More than ever...Anna told me that Wild was going to Grand Rapids last night and wouldn't be back until this afternoon. That gave him plenty of time to get to Willow Ridge."

"Yeah, I guess...but no matter who it was, this proves you were right—somebody's causin' all our troubles on purpose."

"Are you all right, Honey?" Anna inquired as she approached the cluster of birch trees. "Papa's still at the hospital, if you want to see him."

Peter sighed and grinned slightly. "No, for once it's not a headache...I just have to send an answer to this telegram...MacColl had a question about our lumber order."

"Is it something serious?"

"No, no," Peter lied, "he just needs the answer before he can ship, that's why he made it urgent."

"You want me to send it for ya?" Jaxson asked.

"No, you're having dessert with a certain family—remember?"

"Yeah, I remember…I suppose I better get goin' before they think I did forget about them."

"Guard your pie well," Anna added with a wink. "The people are in a frenzy over them."

"Yes, Ma'am, I will, and thank you for savin' it for me," Jaxson returned. Then, to Peter, he murmured, "I'll stop by later to see if you got everything cleared up with MacColl."

Nodding, Peter mouthed a silent 'thank you' to his friend—the solid staff that always helped him to stand straight, even in the worst storm.

"I'll walk with you," Anna offered as she slipped her hand around Peter's arm.

"Hmm?" he wordlessly questioned.

"To the telegraph office…I'll walk with you."

"But that'll leave Lynette alone to watch the—"

"No, Nick said he'd stay and help her."

"Yeah?" Peter replied, chuckling at his brother's obvious scheme to be alone with Lynette. "Still…"

"Don't fret, Honey. As I said, we're almost sold out. By the time we get back from the telegraph office, the pastries should be gone. Then we can pack up the booth and pans and enjoy the festivities ourselves…besides, I think Nick prefers it this way."

Peter laughed. "I prefer it this way too," he said as he slid his arm around Anna's waist and gave her a quick kiss.

<hr />

"Oh, Mrs. Chesnay, this is delicious," Emerson Brant said as he stuffed another piece of molasses fruit cake into his mouth. "Truly delicious."

Rolling his eyes, Nick grumbled and leaned on the sales booth.

"Would you like some, Nick? Anna and I saved a big piece just for you."

"No, I don't want nothin'."

"I'll take it," Emerson announced, slapping a coin onto the counter.

"That's very kind, Mr. Brant, but I'm sure we'll sell it."

"I'd love to say I'm just being generous, but I can't—this cake is fabulous."

"Well, then, Mr. Brant, it's all yours," Lynette returned as she placed a hunk of molasses cake onto a cloth napkin and slid it toward Emerson.

"Please, my friends call me Em…and I'd be honored if you'd allow me to call you Lynette."

"That would be very nice…Em," Lynette replied with a glowing smile. She knew Emerson Brant was infatuated with her—his dreamy gaze and bemused expression made that fact very clear. And she also knew that she should stop being flattered and squelch his naive advances, but his sweet, boyish enthusiasm triumphed, and she chose to remain silent.

"Don't you have a base ball game to go to?" Nick barked, crossing his arms.

Gulping down a mouthful, Emerson glanced at Nick and smirked slyly. "Thanks for reminding me...I almost forgot to ask," he said. Then his attention fixed on Lynette again—and a wide, dimpled smile spread across his face. "Would you and your son like to come and watch our base ball game? We're playing Crestfield today—it should be quite exciting."

"Oh, Em, that's such a splendid offer, but I have to remain here at the booth."

"What about when you finish? Don't worry, I'll make sure you both get home safely."

Lynette started to refuse again, but as she glanced down at the small, pleading face at her side, her resistance faded. "We'll try, Em, but I can't promise."

"Fair enough...the weather may decide to wash us out anyway. If that does happen, I'll come back to help you pack up," he offered, gathering up the last morsels of his cake. "And, if I do miss you today, I look forward to seeing you tomorrow."

"Tomorrow?!" Nick exclaimed.

Giving Nick an innocent simper, Emerson bobbed his head. "Yes, tomorrow...I have a weekly invitation to Sunday dinner at the Spreyers. And," he put in as he leaned over the counter and eyed William, "I'll bring a bat and ball with me...would you like to play base ball tomorrow, William?"

"But I don't know how," the boy quietly murmured.

"Well, I'll teach you...just you and me...what do you say?"

William's features lit up with excitement. "Is that okay, Mama?" he questioned, tugging at her skirt.

As she studied William's hopeful countenance, Lynette smiled. For so long, Redmund Chesnay's treachery had tainted her son's trust in men—now, after only a short time with Peter and Doctor Spreyer, he seemed to yearn for masculine company. It was a wonderful transformation, and inwardly, she thanked God for placing William in the midst of such kind and patient gentlemen. "Yes, Sweetheart, that'll be okay," she replied. "Thank you, Em, that's very generous of you."

"I look forward to it and to seeing you again," Emerson said as he raised her hand and gently kissed it. "Now, as much as I hate to, I better go, before my team gives up on me."

With a farewell wave and a quivering sigh, Lynette watched her youthful admirer until he was out of sight. Should she have said no to his advances? she wondered. Should she have told the cute, brown-haired Emerson that she had much too much experience—both good and bad—for such a young man? As she searched her heart, Lynette's eyes drifted to Nick, who had been in a sour mood ever since he arrived at the booth and who was now staring at her with an expression of anger, hurt, and surprise. "Are you all right, Nick?"

"He's just a kid...whatd'ya doin' settin' your cap for him?"

"Setting my...Nick, I agreed to watch Emerson play base ball, not to marry him."

"Still...I don't think you should go," he muttered.

"Why?"

"Because I...because I wanted to...you just shouldn't, that's all."

"Why is this bothering you so much?" Then, as she said the words, the reason for Nick's gruff, quarrelsome manner crystallized in her head—he was drawn to her also, and Emerson's romantic overtures were evidently interfering with his plans.

"Good afternoon, Mrs. Chesnay. How are the pastries selling?"

The voice dragged Lynette from her speculation, and circling, she looked up at her unnoticed customer. "Well, good afternoon, Mr. Wild...we've done excellent, thank you."

"Good. I am very happy to hear that."

"The booth has been a big help also."

Touching the brim of his hat with his walking stick, James Wild shrugged nonchalantly. "I am just pleased that I could be of assistance...I thought, perhaps, that my sweet Anna would be here."

"She's with her fiancé," Lynette retorted, irked at Wild's audacity.

"Of course, it was quite improper of me to inquire—forgive me."

Even though he sounded sincere, Lynette sensed that James Wild was not the least bit sorry about his inquiry. "Would you like to have a piece of molasses fruit cake, Mr. Wild?" she asked, forcing herself to be civil. "I'm afraid it's all we have left, but it's still very good."

"I am quite sure it is, but alas, I cannot," Wild returned as he brushed an imaginary spot from his lapel. "I must rendezvous with a business associate on the west side of the brass band's gazebo."

"I see," Lynette murmured, puzzled by the overly detailed answer.

"Perhaps I will have the opportunity to partake of your baked goods another time, Mrs. Chesnay," he concluded, tipping his hat. "Good day."

As Wild strutted away, Lynette blew out a deep breath. Why did she always feel like washing her hands after dealing with James Wild?

"Who was that, Mama?"

"That was Mr. Wild, Sweetheart. He was the gentleman who let us use his carriage when we arrived in Sandorville, remember?"

William nodded. "I remember...can we go watch the base ball game now?"

With a patient smile, Lynette tousled her son's hair. "May we go...and no, not right now. We have to finish here first."

"Can I...May I play with my kite until then?"

"Oh, William, I think the wind's getting too strong for your little kite."

Patting Lynette's skirt, William whispered, "Maybe Nick can help me."

Amazed by the remark, Lynette nodded and said in a hushed voice, "Maybe...why don't you ask him." Then, as her son skipped around the booth, Lynette's smile increased. It seemed, at least for the moment, that William had overcome his aversion to Nick.

"Can you help me with my kite?" William asked as he tapped Nick's fingers.

"Huh?"

"My kite...can you help me fly my kite?"

"I...I...I don't..." Nick stuttered, averting his eyes, "I don't know how, Kid."

"Oh," the boy replied, "well, maybe Em can show you how on Sunday."

Bending down so that he was nose-to-nose with William, Nick hissed, "I don't need Emerson Brant to show me nothing!"

Jarred by the scolding, William backed up a step, then two, then three. "Now, you sound like my papa too."

Biting her lower lip, Lynette shook her head. As much as she agreed with her son's accusation, she also understood the reason for Nick's pride-filled outburst. And, not quite knowing what to say, she offered, "William, Sweetheart, why don't you play with your blocks instead...the wind is getting too strong to play with your kite."

Without even a glimpse toward Nick, William leaned his toy against the bakery booth and wandered over to his pile of brightly painted blocks.

"Please don't let his comment bother you, Nick. He didn't realize what he was saying."

"Yeah? Well...I still don't need Brant to show me nothing."

"I know you don't...may I sweeten our apology with some molasses cake? I still have two pieces left."

Nick sighed and caressed the long scars on his cheek. "No, I gotta...I gotta go do something."

"If you're leaving because of what William said, I—"

"No, it's just somethin' I gotta do...um, when James Wild was here, did he ask to see his 'sweet Anna'?"

"Yes, he did...do you know Mr. Wild?"

"I, uh, I know of him...doesn't he realize that Peter and Anna are supposed to get married?"

"Yes—but he's choosing to ignore that fact and pursue her anyway."

Slamming his fist on the sales booth, Nick bellowed out a curse. "They think, just 'cause they got money, they can take whatever they want!"

Now, it was Lynette's turn to be frightened by Nick's harsh words, and she backed away from the sales counter. Although she knew he wasn't really lashing out at her, she still couldn't fight the fear that hung from her shoulders like a cloak.

Suddenly, Nick's expression mellowed. "I…I didn't mean to scare you, Lynette… I…I just don't like Wild's tactics."

Smiling in both relief and embarrassment, Lynette slowly returned to the counter. "I'm sorry…sometimes the memories come back to haunt me."

"Lynette, I would never hurt you."

The gentleness of Nick's statement washed over Lynette like a warm summer mist, and lifting her head, she gazed into his vivid eyes. "I'm glad to hear that."

Gingerly, Nick reached out and fingered Lynette's hand, then he yanked his arm back and announced, "I…I better go." And, without another word, he wandered off and disappeared through the stand of birch trees.

As she absently twisted her ruby ring, Lynette gulped in a deep breath. Yes, Nick was, without a doubt, attracted to her—but why was she flushed? Was it Nick's temper that was making her feel so strange? Or was it his touch? And why, she wondered, couldn't she decipher her own emotions?

"Excuse me, do you have any pineapple pie left?"

Her brow furrowed, Lynette blankly eyed the young girl on the other side of the counter, then, finally, she awakened from her daydream. "I'm sorry, Miss, what did you need?"

"Do you have any more pineapple pie?"

"No, Dear, they're all gone…I have just two pieces of molasses fruit cake left."

"Okay, I'll take them instead," the girl said as she placed a coin on the counter.

"Both pieces?"

"Yes, please."

"Do you want some help carrying the cakes?" she asked, peering at the youngster.

"No, thank you."

"All right, Dear," Lynette replied with a worried smile. And, as she placed a small napkin and a piece of cake onto each of the girl's outstretched hands, she prayed that both her customer and the cakes would make it to their destination without falling. "Be careful," Lynette called as the little girl headed into the crowded marketplace.

"I will…thank you," came the faint reply.

With a light laugh, Lynette picked up the girl's payment and dropped it into the bulging sack tied to her waist. What a day, she silently exclaimed. In only a few hours, every crumb of her baking had been gobbled up—God had truly showered her with His favor.

Then, as she draped three heavy towels over the booth's counter, her thoughts, curiously, drifted back to Nick Anderson. Why are you thinking about him? she asked herself.

You have been in Sandorville for less than a week—how can you even think of starting a romance…especially with a man whose actions so closely mirror Red Chesnay's?

Suddenly, Lynette shivered as if she were standing in the middle of a snowstorm. Redmund Chesnay—just the man's name made her quake with dread. What if Red finds you? she silently questioned. What if he, somehow, persuades the Spreyers to oust you from their lives? How will you cope with losing this wonderful new home?

As she pondered her concerns—and predicament—a violent gust of wind ripped through the market grounds, hurling her towels and empty baking tins to the ground. Gazing at the wind-blown goods, Lynette's eyes filled with tears. Just as easily, Red Chesnay could throw all her blessings into exile…

"Mama! Mama! My kite!" William screamed as his toy tumbled away with the wind.

"Stay right here, Sweetheart, I'll get it."

───────

"Where have you been?" Wild demanded, tapping his foot.

"Whatd'ya mean?" Nick snipped.

"You are late."

"Well, I couldn't just follow you here, you know."

"I realize that, Mr. Anderson, but I calculated the time it should have taken you to arrive, and you are eleven minutes overdue."

"Look, if I had hurried right over, somebody might have gotten suspicious, so I talked to Mrs. Chesnay for a few minutes, then came around the back way."

"I do not wish to hear your excuses. From now on," Wild countered as he jabbed his finger into Nick's chest, "I expect you to be more timely, or I will be forced to reduce your compensation…do you understand?"

Nick reluctantly nodded and tried to calm his pounding heart. Why did he suddenly feel as if he were back in prison?

"Now," Wild went on, "how is everything at the factory?"

"Okay."

"Well, I do hope Peter enjoys the peace while he has it."

"Whatd'ya mean?"

A shrug was his only answer.

"Whatd'ya mean?!"

"Well, come Monday," Wild replied, trying to stifle a laugh, "our poor Peter is going to be waiting for a shipment of lumber—that will never arrive."

Nick's eyes narrowed. "Why?"

Wild just snickered and grabbed the brim of his hat as a strong gust of wind pushed against them.

"Why?!" Nick urged.

"The order was canceled."

"How…how do you know that?"

"I arranged it."

"You what?!" Nick exclaimed as a shiver ran down the back of his neck. "Why would you do that?"

"My dear, naive Mr. Anderson, what did you think I was going to do with the information that you provided?"

"Send it to Rheinhardt, like you said."

"Excuse me?"

"You told me you wanted the information 'cause Rheinhardt wanted to know what Peter was doing."

"Did I?" Wild smirked.

"Yeah, ya did," Nick seethed. How could he have been so stupid…how could he have forgotten the lesson he had learned long ago? Never—never—trust a rich dandy.

"When Peter realizes that his lumber is not going to arrive," Wild continued, "I want you to memorize his expression."

"Why?"

"Because I want you to share it with me."

Disgusted with himself—and the part he was playing in Wild's scheme—Nick gritted his teeth and silently cursed. "I think Pete already knows it ain't coming," he muttered.

"Oh? And what makes you believe that?"

"He got a telegram just a few minutes ago…I don't know what it said, but it was definitely bad news."

"Hmm, I was not made aware that he received a message today. I knew having only one associate at the telegraph office could eventually cause me difficulties…so, tell me, why is it that you do not know what the telegram said?"

"Because Pete talked to Jaxson about it, not me."

"You seem to be missing the point, Mr. Anderson…I am paying you to advise me of Peter's strategies, and the only way to accomplish that task is for you to become his main confidant…I expect a full report on this issue the next time I see you."

"Why are ya doin' this to him?"

"That is my business."

"No, it ain't. I should know what you're tryin' to do."

"I disagree," Wild replied as he polished the gold knob of his walking stick with his glove. "However, if you supply me with some tantalizing morsels about Emerson Brant's sales trip, I may reconsider."

Nick opened his mouth to answer, then hesitated. He had dug himself into a hole—he knew that—but maybe, if he refused to answer, he could, somehow, pull himself out. "I can't do that."

"Hmm…either you have developed an unfortunate sense of brotherhood or you are an extremely shrewd businessman," Wild returned, leaning on his walking stick. "I am going to assume that it is the latter."

"Huh?"

"You are trying to negotiate a larger salary for yourself, correct?"

"Uh…"

"I thought as much. All right, this is my final offer. If you abandon this annoying sense of loyalty that you have developed and supply me with the information that I desire, without hesitation—I will, in return, answer all of your questions and reward you with the sum of thirty dollars a day. Are those terms agreeable with you, Mr. Anderson?" Wild asked as he extended his arm.

Nick swallowed hard—he didn't like the idea that he could be bought so easily. And, trying to console himself, he inwardly offered, yeah, you can be bought real easy, but at least you're expensive.

"Yeah, they're agreeable," he replied aloud, shaking Wild's wet rag of a hand.

"Splendid!" Wild exclaimed as he dug in his coat pocket. "And, to show you how much I trust you," he continued, holding out a palmful of coins and notes, "I will allow you to take your fee in advance."

As he studied Wild's skinny, pallid hand and the pile of money, Nick voicelessly cursed—only James Wild could make him feel like a horse being offered a treat. Then, with a growl, he snatched up his thirty dollars. "So why are ya doin' this to Pete?" he asked again.

"Because he has something that I want," Wild returned, pocketing the remainder of his cash. "What kind of orders did Emerson Brant bring home?"

"Tables, chairs, and bookshelves for a men's club," Nick answered, and as he heard himself say the words, he also heard himself pound another nail into Peter's coffin. "What does Pete have that you want so bad?"

"His factory, for one…what is the name of the men's club, and where is it located?"

"I don't know the name, but it's in Grand Rapids…why do you want his factory? You got enough money to start your own."

"I want it because Peter has told me that I cannot have it…what other orders did Brant bring in?"

"I dunno…why are you chasin' after Anna Spreyer?"

"Same reason as the factory—because I want her."

"But she's engaged to Pete."

"For the time being—yes."

Nick's hand angrily clenched around his money. "So you're just usin' your funds to take what you want?"

"No. Taking is simple…but forcing Peter Leighton to surrender, ah, that, my dear Mr. Anderson, is a game of skill."

Nick grunted in response, trying to hide his escalating outrage. Not only was he digging himself into an ever-deepening hole, but now, he was dragging Peter and Anna into it as well. "Pete's not gunna give up so easy."

"Quite true. In fact, he has proven to be an extremely challenging opponent. But, I assure you, I will conquer him…are you through with your questions?"

"Yeah…for now."

"Good. Now, Mr. Anderson, when you arrive at my home tomorrow night, I want to know about this mysterious telegram, and I want the name of the men's club and the exact quantity and description of what they ordered. In addition, I expect to hear similar details about the other orders that Mr. Brant acquired."

"And what if I can't get Pete to tell me all that?"

"You appear to be a resourceful man, Mr. Anderson. I am confident that you will find out—one way or another."

Nick grunted. As much as he wanted to pivot away from Wild's arrogant grin and be loyal to his brother, he still couldn't resist the allure of the thirty dollars pressing against his palm.

⁕⟋⟍⟍⟋⟍⟋⟍⟍⟋⟍⟍⟍⟍⟋⟍⟋⟍⟋⟍⟋⟍⟍⟋⟍⟋⟍⟍⟋⟍⟍⟋⟍⟍⟋⟍⟍⟋⟍⟋⟍⟍⟋⟍⟍⟋⟍⟍⟋⟍⟋⟍⟋⟍⟋⟍⟍⟋⟍⟋⟍⟍⟋⟍⟍⟋⟍⟋⟍⟋⟍⟋⟍⟍⟋⟍⟍⟋⟍⟍⟋⟍⟋⟍⟍⟋⟍⟍⟋⟍⟋⟍⟋⟍⟋⟍⟍⟋⟍⟍⟋⟍⟋⟍⟋⟍⟋⟍⟍⟋⟍⟍⟋⟍⟍⟋⟍⟋⟍⟍⟋⟍⟋⟍⟍⟋⟍⟍⟋⟍

Breathlessly, Lynette chased after the escaping kite, dashing this way and that through a tree-filled section of the market grounds. Worried that she would lose William's newest plaything, Lynette increased her speed, but the erratic toy still evaded capture. "Lord, I…I can't run…much farther…please…help," she panted and lunged for the kite one last time. Feeling the string brush against her fingers, Lynette's hand clamped shut and she abruptly stopped. "Ah ha…I have you…now," she proclaimed, reeling in the wayward toy.

Tightly holding onto the fluttering kite, Lynette scanned her surroundings, trying to get her bearings. "All right, Mr. Kite…you got us this…far. How do we…get back?" As soon as she asked the question, fear ran its cold fingers down her spine. She didn't know the marketplace very well—how was she going to find William again? Then, as she stood motionless amidst the trees, a cheerful melody floated over to her and she sighed. The brass band's gazebo was nearby, she knew her way to the bakery booth from there.

As she rushed closer and closer to the spirited tune, Lynette caught sight of two familiar faces, and immediately, her gait slowed. She couldn't explain it, but seeing James Wild and Nick Anderson, together, in earnest conversation, worried her to the bone. And, as Wild's remark about 'rendezvousing with a business associate' jumped back into her head, she shuddered in apprehension. No, she told herself, James' appointment wasn't with Nick…this was just a chance meeting…

Then, as if answering her denial, the brass band finished their song and a portion of Wild's words wafted over to her on a strong breeze…

"…is my final offer. If you abandon this annoying sense of loyalty that you have developed and supply me with the information that I desire, without hesitation—I will, in return, answer all of your questions and reward you with the sum of thirty dollars a day. Are those terms agreeable with you, Mr. Anderson?"

Disheartened, Lynette slipped behind a tree and waited for Nick's response. Maybe, he would squash her concerns and walk away from the slimy Wild…

"Yeah," she heard Nick reply, "they're agreeable."

Shaking her head sadly, Lynette pushed herself from the tree. "Oh, dear Lord," she whispered as she continued her hurried trek toward William and the sales booth, "please open Nick's eyes and guide him away from James Wild."

⌒⌯⌲⌯⌒

Stepping through the parlor doorway, Peter gazed at the painted portrait of Daven, then at his new stepbrother, who stood next to the fireplace, smoking a cigar. Looking up at the picture again, Peter shook his head. The physical resemblance between his two stepbrothers was uncanny, and for the first time, he began to wonder if the likeness was, indeed, blinding him to certain truths.

"Would you stop starin' at us like that?"

Raising his eyebrows at the word 'us,' Peter peered directly into Nick's sky-blue eyes. "Sorry, but it's going to happen for awhile, Nick. Until people, including me, get used to having you around, they'll still see a little bit of Daven when they look at you."

"Great," Nick snidely muttered. "That's just great."

"Tomorrow's dinner would give us all a chance to get to know you better."

Nick sucked at his cigar, then exhaled long and deep. "I told you I don't wanna come—there's gunna be too many people."

"It's only Anna's family and our friends…and Anna and I are planning to announce our wedding date. It'd be nice to have you there."

"I dunno."

"Just come to eat—a Spreyer Sunday dinner can keep you full through Tuesday."

"Everybody's just gunna stare at the fake Daven."

"No, they won't. Anna's sisters and their families never met Daven—they'll have no one to compare you to."

"I dunno…I still think it'll be better if I just go to a tavern instead."

As he rolled his watch chain between his fingers, Peter sighed slightly. He knew he had to choose his next words carefully, or they would surely set off Nick's volatile temper. "While we're on the subject of taverns," he said, sauntering over to the fireplace, "I would appreciate it, very much, if you would not come to the Spreyers' house after you've been drinking."

Removing his cigar, Nick glared at Peter. "You runnin' a temperance meeting, Pete? Tryin' to get me on that narrow path of yours?"

His jaw clenching tight, Peter growled under his breath—just once he wanted to have a conversation with his stepbrother that didn't erupt into a feud. "This is not a request for you to stop drinking, Nick," he sharply returned.

"No?"

"No...you two are enough alike," Peter snapped as he waved his finger back and forth between Daven's portrait and Nick, "that I know, if I ever asked you to stop, you'd just drink all the more...I'm asking you not to come here after you've visited a saloon—like last night. Lynette and William don't need that kind of aggravation—and neither do the Spreyers...just go home instead, all right?"

"Home?"

"Yes, to the guest house."

With a weak grin, Nick nodded. "I guess that'd be okay," he offered. Then, after a few puffs, he put in, "You, uh, you seem a lot better than you were this afternoon—you know, after you got that telegram."

Dumbfounded by his brother's caring tone, Peter smiled. "Yeah, I am."

"So...uh, what...what was it about?"

"A man went to see MacColl and told him that I wanted to cancel my maple order," Peter explained.

"Huh...so whatd'ya gunna do?"

"Nothing. It's all taken care of."

"Whatd'ya mean?"

"I telegraphed MacColl and told him that someone was trying to hamper our progress on the tables—and that I positively wanted the wood."

"Did he answer back?"

"Yeah, he said he thought something was wrong...that's why he wanted to contact me first."

"So MacColl's still sendin' the wood?"

"Yeah. And he's going to warn his men that there might be trouble...I can't believe he's willing to deal with the overflow of our problems."

"Me neither," Nick grunted.

"I think it helped, though, when I also told him that we would be ordering more lumber."

Nick frowned. "More?"

"For the men's club."

"Oh, yeah," he returned, averting his eyes. "You're really lucky that your sales-man got that order."

"You don't know how right you are…the club's council kept insisting that they wanted carved furniture—which we couldn't do without a talent like Daven's. I'm just grateful that Emerson was tenacious enough to keep trying."

"You said that club's in Grand Rapids."

"Yeah, with so many furniture factories there, we're very fortunate to get the order."

"So what's the…what's the name of…so Daven was a pretty good carver, huh?"

Tilting his head, Peter studied his stepbrother's downcast expression and fidgety mannerisms—it was a Nick he had never seen before. And, even though he wanted to comment on his brother's suddenly sullen mood, he refrained—he didn't want anything to lead them into another argument. "Daven was a marvel to watch and so was your father," Peter replied as he ambled over to the sofa and laid his hand on the long, narrow table behind it. "This is some of Daven's work…he also did that bookcase, those shelves, and that table," he continued, pointing to the other three pieces as he called them out.

Moving over to the couch, Nick fingered the finely etched pattern on the table's edge. "Daven was good." Then, glancing to the floor, Nick quietly asked, "Do you… do you have anything that my fath…father carved?"

With a long sigh, Peter shook his head. "No, nothing's left," he returned as the memories gushed into his head. How could he ever tell Nick that debt and revenge had goaded him into selling all but one of Anders' remarkable carvings? "Daven had a piece that he kept with his tools, but it was lost in the fire last year…the rest of your father's work was…well, it was our sustenance for awhile, I'm sorry to say." As he surveyed the room, trying to overcome the nagging guilt that had grabbed him around the neck, Peter spotted the wooden box on the mantle and smiled. "I do have, however, a keepsake that belonged to your father," he announced, guiding Nick back to the fireplace.

"I don't want nothin'…I was just asking."

Ignoring the remark, Peter opened the box and grasped Anders' timepiece. "This was your father's watch…he kept it with him—always—and Daven did the same. I want you to have it…to carry on with the tradition."

"No…no, I don't want it," Nick said without much conviction.

"Unfortunately, it doesn't keep very good time," Peter went on as he held the pock-etwatch by its thin, silver chain, "but it's the only inheritance I have to give you."

At first, Nick just stared at the pendulating heirloom, then, slowly, he reached out and wrapped his fingers around the watch. "You…you're wrong, Pete," he choked out.

"About what?"

"About my father's carvings."

"I don't understand."

Switching the pocketwatch to his left hand, Nick dug in his right trouser pocket and pulled out a weathered chain made of wood. "They're not all gone."

As he beheld the handcrafted chain, Peter instantly recognized it, even though he had never seen it before. "That's the chain, isn't it? The one your father carved for Nilla."

Nick shrugged his shoulders. "I guess…it was definitely made by a master carver, and I've had it for as long as I can remember."

His brow crinkled in confusion, Peter stretched out his arm and touched the wooden legacy. "In Willow Ridge, when I told you about that chain, you said you didn't remember it."

"Yeah, well, at the time I thought you were a lunatic."

Peter chuckled and massaged the dwindling pain in his forearm. "I'm sure if a complete stranger told me that he was my brother, I'd think he was a loon too."

Nick just nodded and gazed at the priceless treasures in his hands.

"Your father's carving would make a nice watch chain."

"Uh huh," Nick replied, then, looking at Peter, he asked, "Would you…would you tell me about my father?"

Peering into Nick's tear-flooded, powdery-blue gems, Peter beamed. He never doubted that Nick was Anders' son—and now, neither did Nick.

❋Eight❋

Ding. Ding. Ding.

The chimes resounded through the Spreyers' backyard, but they did little to quiet the multitude of conversations.

Ding. Ding. Ding.

Tapping a fork against his lemonade glass for a second time, Peter stood and waited for silence. Finally, the clamor faded and the faces of his friends and family turned toward him.

"I know everyone is ready for dessert, and I don't want to waste this wonderful Sunday afternoon by talking," Peter declared as he took off his tinted glasses and set them on the table, "but I do have a couple of announcements to make, if there are no objections."

"As long as you don't speak for two hours as the Mayor did last month," one of his soon to be brothers-in-law called out.

Peter laughed, remembering the bombastic speech. "You mean you don't want me to take five minutes worth of news and extend it into two hours of drivel?"

"Nope," his future brother-in-law returned, "unless you're talking about me—of course, then it wouldn't be drivel."

Chuckling at the joke, Peter shook his head. "I promise this will only take a few minutes…I know you all met Nick when you arrived, but I just wanted to formally introduce my brother, Nikolaus Anderson, to everyone," he said, saluting his step-brother with his lemonade glass. "Welcome to our family, Nick."

"Speech! Speech!" one of the men yelled as a round of applause broke out. "Speech!"

Noticing his brother's sudden shyness, Peter kidded, "I thought you wanted this to be short."

"All right. Short speech! Short speech!" came the reply.

"Come on, Nick, say a few words," another shouted.

"Yes," a third yelled, "it's all part of becoming a member of this family."

Reluctantly, Nick rose to his feet. "I ain't real good with words," he offered, nervously stroking his pocketwatch. "And I'm even worse with names...it's gunna be a long time before I know everybody, but I 'preciate the welcome."

"Don't you worry, Nick," Doctor Spreyer bellowed, "you'll get used to every-one—eventually."

"It's true," Peter agreed, surveying Anna's four sisters and their families sitting at the many tables set up in the yard. "I think I finally remember everyone's name now." As he waited for the guffaws to come to an end, Peter glanced at Nick, who was still trying to hide his awkwardness by fiddling with his watch—and who, because of that new habit, looked precisely—and eerily—like Daven. "And, while we're on the subject of names," Peter continued as the others quieted down, "everyone is going to have to get used to yet another name in this family...on October eighth, Anna will finally become Anna Leighton."

Upon hearing the news, everyone cheered and applauded.

"Finally, a date!" someone hollered.

"It's about time, you two," another said.

"What a wonderful month for a wedding," one of Anna's sisters added.

Standing up, Anna looped her arm around Peter's. "I hope everyone can make that date," she commented as the shouts of glee hushed, "because we won't, God-willing, be postponing it again."

"What about Hans?" her sister Marion cried out in a shrill voice.

"We don't have to worry about him—Papa's going to send a telegram and straighten everything out."

"Well, that's all for the announcements," Peter went on, "so let's have dessert."

"Yes, let's do that!" the doctor agreed. "What have you baked for us today, Lynette?"

"A snow cake with golden frosting...I'll clear these dishes and bring it right out," she replied as she stacked the empty plates near her.

"Here, let me help you with that," Emerson Brant volunteered, gathering together some of the flatware.

"I'll help her," Nick called from his table. "You promised to teach William how to play base ball, remember?"

As he watched the rivals vie for Lynette's attention, Peter smiled in amusement. The poor woman had two entirely different men pursuing her—different in every aspect, except one...stubbornness.

"It looks as though Lynette has a couple of suitors to contend with," Anna whispered.

"Uh huh…she's definitely going to have her hands full," he murmured as he squeezed Anna around the waist. Then, seeing a movement out of the corner of his eye, Peter glanced to his right. "Hey, Jax."

"Can I talk to ya for a minute, Peter?"

"Yeah, sure."

"I'm sorry, Miss Anna," Jaxson put in, "I didn't mean to be rude."

"You're never rude," Anna returned. "I should check on Mama anyway and see if she wants to move her chair into the shade."

"This sounds kind of serious," Peter remarked as he and Jaxson meandered toward the barn.

"No…no…it's not. I, uh, I ended up stayin' with the Jayes through supper yesterday and—"

"That's two suppers in a row, isn't it?"

"Yeah, I guess it is," Jaxson replied, leaning against the barn. "That's why I didn't get a chance to stop by…did MacColl answer your telegram?"

"Yep, it wasn't Wild—it was a bald-headed man with glasses and a beard who called himself Dearborn…I should have known that Wild wouldn't get his own hands dirty."

"Peter, we don't know for sure that it's Wild…it could be somebody else."

"Wild's the only one who would gain from us not finishing the tables."

"Gain what?"

"A partnership."

"But it ain't gunna happen…Rheinhardt doesn't want Wild any more than we do. And, even if he does break down and agree to make Wild a partner, you and me, together, outvote him."

Peter sighed and grabbed a twig lying near his boot. "Okay, you have a point," he offered as he snapped the stick into inch-size pieces, "but it still doesn't change the fact that Dearborn, whether working on his own or for someone else, tried to cancel our order."

"You're right about that…so what about the wood? Is the first shipment still gunna reach us by Monday?"

"Yeah, MacColl seemed very understanding…I'm not sure why."

"Maybe the Lord was talkin' to him."

"Maybe He was…and I'm glad MacColl listened."

"Me too."

"So," Peter prompted, "how was supper with the Jayes last night…and the night before?"

"Fine…why does Nick have Daven's watch?!"

Stunned by the abrupt—and angry—detour, Peter dropped the twig and studied his friend. "Because I gave it to him."

"Why? Daven gave it to you."

"I know, but Nick and I got to talking about Anders, and…well, it seemed the right thing to do."

"He's just gunna sell it for drinkin' money."

"I don't think so," Peter replied, not fully understanding Jaxson's animosity. "Do you remember that chain I told you about? The one that Anders carved and gave to Nilla, who sent part of it with Nick when he was taken away?"

"Yeah."

"Nick still has it…after all this time. If he never gave up that chain—which came from an unknown parent…I don't think he'll sell the watch—which comes from a father he now knows."

Jaxson kicked at the grass and crossed his arms. "But that watch is your reminder of Daven."

"No, it's not…I've got the portrait and all the furniture in the parlor…and I've got Daven," Peter returned as he tapped his chest, "right here."

Finally, the sternness drained from Jaxson's features. "I don't think Nick deserves it, but if you want him to have it…" he murmured, drifting into silence.

"I think it's what Daven and Anders would have wanted."

"Do you want Nick to be your best man, instead of me?"

Although he was thrown, once again, by Jaxson's sudden change of subject—it was the question itself that knocked Peter completely off balance. "No, why do you think that I—"

"Because, if ya do, I'd—"

"No, Jax, I asked you because I want you at my side…you're the first person I thought of…you're the only person I thought of."

"What about Nick? He's your brother."

"Jaxson," Peter continued, clutching his friend's shoulder, "Nick and I are brothers in name only—but you and I, we're brothers without being related…that's why I asked you, not Nick."

Jaxson's expression glowed with embarrassment and pride—and he smiled a toothy grin. "I'm sorry…I keep forgettin' that he's not Daven."

Swallowing a lump in his throat, Peter nodded but said nothing. As much as he wanted to, he couldn't bring himself to tell his friend that, lately, he was having a difficult time remembering that fact too—especially when Nick caressed Anders' pocketwatch…just like Daven…

"So," Peter said, this time derailing the conversation himself, "are you going to be my best man?"

"Yeah," Jaxson chuckled. "And, if I start doubtin' ya again, you can row me up Salt River."

Peter laughed and wrapped a brotherly arm around Jaxson's shoulders. "I'll keep that in mind, Friend."

❦

As Nick piled the dirty dishes together, he inwardly laughed at himself—he still couldn't believe that he had volunteered to clear the tables just to be near a woman.

"That's a very interesting watch chain you have there."

Looking up, Nick gazed into the eyes of…of…

With a silent curse, Nick sighed—he was lucky that he remembered his own name after all the introductions he had been forced to endure. "Yeah," he returned, "my father carved it."

"Really? May I see it?" the chubby, curly-haired man asked, reaching his arm across the table.

With a bit of hesitation, Nick loosened his watch and chain from his waistcoat and handed it to…to…

"Who are you again?"

The man smiled sympathetically. "I know, from experience, that the names do come easier after awhile…I'm Michael Nealy—Marion's husband. I own the jewelry store in town," he explained as he examined the weathered chain and silver watch.

"Jewelry store, huh," Nick murmured with a smirk.

"Yes. You know, Nick, I could offer you a marvelous deal on a new chain."

"Uh, no…no, that's okay," he replied, taking his keepsake from Michael. "I like this one…but do…do you have any broken watches?"

Michael snorted. "My friend, all I have is broken watches."

Nick's brow furrowed as he reattached the wooden chain to his waistcoat and tucked the timepiece into his pocket. "Whatd'ya mean?"

"I mean, I lost my local repairman when James Wild bought the clockmaker's shop…the poor craftsman thought he was getting a partner, and instead, he lost his livelihood."

"Can I have one of those broken watches?"

"Have? For what purpose?"

"For parts…to fix mine. It don't keep good time."

"You have the skills to do something like that?"

Nick shrugged. "Yeah."

"Well, well," Michael whooped, "after dessert, I'll take you over to my store. You can go through my stock of broken watches and take whatever you want…and I'll even loan you the small number of tools that I have."

"Great," Nick returned, picking up his stack of dishes.

"As long as…"

Bristling at the added requirement, Nick glared at Michael. "As long as what?!"

"As long as you fix another timepiece for me…I promised the Mayor that I would have his pocketwatch repaired by Tuesday."

"So all I gotta do to get my watch parts is to fix this other one for ya?"

"Well, yes, that's all, but it might not be quite that easy…the Mayor's piece keeps stopping for no reason. Do you think you will be able to determine what's wrong with it and fix it by Tuesday?"

"I ain't been stumped yet," Nick replied, and as he carried an armload of plates, forks, and knives to the back door, he couldn't stop a wide smile from spreading across his face. It had been years since he tinkered with a watch, and he relished the challenge. Climbing the porch steps, Nick lightly knocked on the screen door with his boot. "I got some more dishes for ya," he announced.

Lynette swung the door open and pointed to the counter. "Please, put them next to mine…thank you for your help, Nikolaus, I appreciate it."

Immediately, Nick's back stiffened. "Nikolaus?" he questioned, setting his plates down. "What happened to Nick?"

"I don't know…what happened to him?"

His eyes narrowing, Nick studied Lynette's delicate face, trying to find a reason for her disapproving tone. "Whatd'ya mean?" he finally asked.

"Nothing."

"No, it's not nothing…I wanna know why you're mad at me."

"I'm not mad at you, Nikolaus—I'm disappointed in you."

Suddenly, a bead of perspiration trickled down Nick's temple. "Why? What did I do?" he inquired, not quite knowing why Lynette's opinion mattered so much to him.

"You…you…" she stammered, then, shaking her head, she moved toward the door. "There are still some dishes out there."

Realizing that Lynette was trying to dodge him and his questions, Nick rushed to the door and blocked her escape. "Tell me why you're disappointed…please?"

With a long, audible sigh, Lynette looked up at him and frowned. "You agreed to become partners with James Wild," she returned in a harsh whisper. "First, you blast him about his pursuit of Anna, then you become his partner…why?"

"What…what are you talkin' about?" he choked out.

"I saw you both at the gazebo on Saturday."

His heart racing, Nick wiped at the sweat drenching his brow. "Oh, that," he said as calmly as he could, "I just got turned around and asked him for directions."

Instantly, Lynette's lips tightened into a thin, angry line, and turning on her heel, she stomped toward the front of the house.

Unnerved by the furious departure, Nick trotted down the hall and gently clasped his hand around Lynette's tiny wrist. "Wait, Lyn, wait," he urged, stopping her in the library's doorway. "What's wrong?"

"You're a liar, Nikolaus Anderson," she seethed. "I heard you at the gazebo too… what information are you giving James Wild for thirty dollars a day?"

Quickly, Nick crossed his arms, hoping to conceal the trembling that pulsed through them all the way to his fingertips. Lynette had definitely overheard some of his conversation with Wild, but obviously, not all. Now, he wondered, how much truth and how many lies would it take to get Lynette to stop hating him? "He asked if I'd snitch to him about the goings-on in the factory."

"Nick! How could you agree to do that?"

"I…I didn't."

"Stop lying!" she hollered. Then she covered her mouth with her fingers and continued in a muted tone, "James Wild asked if his terms were agreeable and you said yes."

"But, later, I told him no," Nick tried as another drop of sweat rolled down his face. "I wouldn't…I wouldn't do that to Pete."

Lynette scrutinized him with doubt-filled eyes. "I hope you're finally telling me the truth."

"I am," he lied.

"Good," she offered with a warm smile. "You've been given a great gift in Peter. He's been so good to you…giving you trust and encouragement and protection and—"

"I know…I know."

"Then why do you treat him so badly?"

"I don't!"

"Yes, you do, Nick…I've watched you. Take this afternoon for example."

"What?"

"You're kind one minute, then you lash out at Peter for no reason."

"There're reasons."

Lynette moaned softly. "I'm sorry to hear that…but to betray Peter's secrets to James Wild…that's downright vicious—no matter what the reason."

"I told you—I'm not gunna do it," he snapped, feeling as if Lynette had just stabbed him in the heart with his own appalling deed.

"Maybe this is why it took so long for you to get the family that you prayed for."

"Whatd'ya mean?"

"When we were talking on Friday, you told me that you waited and waited for a good family and that you were ready, but God never sent them."

"Yeah, that's right."

"I don't think that you were ready for a family back then—and I don't think that you are even ready for one now."

"What?!"

"Look how horrible you've been to your only brother. Is that how you would have treated your loving family?"

Nick swallowed hard, not being able to answer. Unfortunately, Lynette had a point. He did, finally, have a brother…a caring and generous brother. And, instead of embracing Peter, all he wanted to do was punish him. Suddenly, Nick's thoughts soared to his father and Daven. Would his animosity and selfishness have corrupted his relationship with them too? "Are…are you going to tell Pete or Anna about…about Wild's offer?"

"No, that's your responsibility."

Taking a deep breath, Nick shook his head. "Pete will never forgive me."

"He might get angry that you considered Mr. Wild's proposition, but I'm sure Peter will appreciate your loyalty—especially when he finds out that you turned down thirty dollars a day to stay on his side."

"Yeah," Nick murmured, not being able to look Lynette in the eyes.

"Promise me that you'll be careful with Mr. Wild—and with Peter."

"With Wild?"

"Yes, he has the same spirit as Redmund Chesnay—heartless and manipulative…please be wary of him."

"And why should I be careful with Pete?"

"Because he's a gift, Nick…if we don't take care of the gifts God gives us, He might choose to remove them."

Propping himself against the library's doorjamb, Nick leaned his head back. After prison, he thought nothing could ever scare him again—but he was wrong. Losing Peter, the only friend he ever had, frightened him to the core. Then, closing his eyes, Nick realized that he had already lost his brother—he had sold him to James B. Wild, the third, for thirty dollars a day.

Sitting on the edge of a red velvet-upholstered chair, Nick clicked his watch open and gazed at the time in the dim lamplight. Three ten. With a chuckle, he snapped the cover shut—his timepiece truly needed some adjusting. Although he knew it wasn't after three, he did know that it was long past eleven. "I have to be on time," he mumbled, "but it's okay for him to be late."

"Is there a problem?" Wild asked, entering the solarium with a drink in his left hand and three gold eagle coins in his right.

"I was here on time," Nick said, annoyance ringing through his voice.

"I know," Wild replied as he sank onto a large, overstuffed chair and put his feet up on a matching ottoman.

"So it's okay for you to keep me waiting, but I can't make you wait?"

Wild grinned and jiggled the coins in his hand. "Precisely."

Gritting his teeth, Nick exhaled in exasperation and tugged at the top button of his shirt. Wild's carefully placed restraining collar was growing extremely tight, and he yearned to make his jailer just as uncomfortable. Then, suddenly, an idea crept into his thoughts and he smiled—the news of Peter and Anna's wedding date would surely cripple Wild's smugness. "You'll have to give up pursuing Anna Spreyer," he said with an inward snicker.

"And why is that?"

"She and Pete announced the date of their nuptials today—October eighth… you lost that part of your game."

James Wild took a sip of his drink and swished the liquid around in his mouth before swallowing it with a grin. "October eighth, you say."

"Yep."

"Thank you, Nikolaus."

Instantly, the smile slid off Nick's face. "Thanks for what?"

"For the warning. If I am to accomplish my goals, I will need to change the rules of the game."

"But they set a date."

Wild laughed. "That is not a concern…you did well, Nikolaus," he said, dropping a ten-dollar coin onto the table next to his chair. "You have just earned that gold eagle."

Wiping his hand over his face, Nick slumped back in his seat—Wild had even found a way to use Peter's wedding against him.

"Now, what about that telegram Peter received?"

Taking a few deep breaths, Nick pushed himself upright again. "It was from MacColl…the wood's still coming."

"Excuse me?"

Nick shrugged. "MacColl figured somethin' was wrong, that's why he tele-graphed Pete…and Pete told 'im that he still wanted the lumber."

"Ah ha," Wild returned as he slid another gold coin onto the glass-topped table. "What an interesting turn of events—I will certainly need to alter my play-ing strategies now."

"Why don't ya just leave Pete alone?"

Picking a fleck off his brocaded chamber robe, Wild bobbed his head. "I will— when he concedes…all right, what about the order for the men's club?"

"Um…um…" Nick stuttered. How could he tell Wild that he had failed—no, that he didn't even attempt—to pry Peter open. "They, uh, they want twenty tables," he finally announced, recalling Emerson Brant's enthusiastic declaration, "and eighty chairs and ten bookcases in oak and painted with oak branches."

"Oak, you say."

"Yeah."

"Hmm…and from whom does Peter anticipate purchasing the lumber needed for the project?"

"MacColl."

"Perfect," Wild announced as he rolled his last ten-dollar coin toward the other two.

"Why is it perfect?"

"My carpenters are using oak for the interior of my new home, and their inventory is diminishing…I believe I will direct them to Willow Ridge to acquire—"

"No," Nick cut in with a shiver.

"No?"

Surprised by his own brother-like outburst, Nick moistened his lips and forced a smile. "Uh, I mean that, uh, Pete already told MacColl that he needed the wood, so he prob'ly won't sell it to you."

"Oh, do not worry. MacColl will allow me to buy the lumber—no businessman will refrain from taking double the selling price."

Caressing the vertical scars on his cheek, Nick cursed Wild under his breath. "You think your money can get you everything, don't you?"

Wild chuckled and swallowed another mouthful of his drink. "It always has… now, what is the name of the men's club?"

"I dunno."

"Mr. Anderson," Wild hissed, "I thought we resolved this hesitancy issue yesterday."

"Yeah, we did," Nick murmured. "I just don't know."

"Would you please repeat that with a little more clarity?"

"I'm not keepin' anything from ya—I just don't know…I never got Pete to tell me."

"I see," Wild said as he plucked one of the coins off the table and slid it into the breast pocket of his robe.

"Hey! Whatd'ya doing? That's mine," Nick hollered, rising to his feet.

"No, it is not…our contract states that you will provide me with the information that I desire…my desire was to know the name of the men's club, and you did not provide it."

"But—"

"Do you have the other information that I requested?"

"Um…I, um…"

"Then you do not have the particulars on the additional orders from Mr. Brant's sales trip?"

Nick reluctantly shook his head and watched another of his golden eagles disappear into Wild's pocket.

"I am very dissatisfied with you, Nikolaus."

"But I told you some good stuff," he said, walking over to Wild's chair and the glass-topped table.

"Yes, you have. And that is the only reason I am allowing you to keep this," Wild replied as he pointed to the ten dollars remaining on the table.

Reaching out, Nick snatched up the single gold coin, but before he could pull his arm away, Wild grabbed him around the wrist and whispered, "In order to receive your full compensation tomorrow evening, you must have the name of the men's club and the details about Brant's other orders—do you understand?"

⬦

"Are you sure you don't want something to eat?" Anna asked. "It's no trouble… we only finished a little bit ago—even the bread's still warm."

"No, I'm all right," Peter murmured, surveying the plateful of hard-boiled eggs and freshly sliced bread sitting on the kitchen table. Although his growling stomach disagreed with his statement, he still didn't want anything to interfere with the massage Anna was giving his shoulders.

"I can pack something for you to take home," she offered. "I'm sure Nick's hungry too."

Peter chuckled and leaned forward in his chair so Anna could reach farther down his back. "He probably is—he unloaded half of the lumber shipment today."

"I'm so glad that your wood arrived safely."

"So am I—and it's some of the finest maple I've ever…ah ha," Peter interjected as Anna reached a knot near his shoulder blade.

"By the sound of that," she said, carefully rubbing the tender area, "you were probably the one who helped Nick unload the lumber."

Peter nodded as the delicious pain caused by Anna's massage tingled down his arms. "Yeah, it arrived right before closing time—that's why I'm so late getting here."

"It sounds as if you had a pretty busy day."

"Uh huh…it started out rotten, but getting the wood made up for it."

"Why? What happened to make it rotten?"

"That nuisance of a reporter showed up for his interview at seven o'clock this morning…at least, he has his story now. He won't bother you anymore."

Sliding her hands onto Peter's chest, Anna hugged him tightly. "It's you I wish the newspapers would stop bothering."

"Someday they will—I hope."

"Hello, Peter," Lynette greeted as she entered the kitchen. "We missed you and Nick at supper."

"Yeah. We had to unload a lumber shipment…Nick was so exhausted that he went straight home—and probably straight to his room."

"I didn't mean to interrupt," Lynette added, heading over to the stove, "but I need to check on the turnovers."

As he sniffed the warm air, Peter smiled. "And are they the kind of turnovers that I think they are?"

Anna laughed. "Yes, Honey, they're blueberry turnovers," she said with another hug. "We wanted to surprise you…things were quiet at the hospital, so Papa said I could leave early. That's when Lynette, William, and I decided to go berry picking."

"Mmm," Peter returned, inhaling the delicious aroma, "that sounds like fun—a lot more than unloading lumber."

"It was," Lynette agreed, "but we ended up spending so much time picking that we fell behind with everything else…that's why your surprise is still in the oven."

"That's okay with me…as long as I get a taste."

Anna giggled and resumed her massaging. "You'll have many chances for tasting…Lyn's going to teach me all her blueberry recipes."

"Oh, yeah?" Peter replied, his eyes lighting up. "I look forward to trying each and every one."

"You'll have to make sure that William doesn't beat you to them," Lynette put in with a laugh as she pulled the oven door open and peered inside. "He loves blueberries too."

"I think that boy put more berries into his mouth than into his pail," Anna remarked with a grin.

Closing the oven, Lynette nodded. "He usually does…the turnovers need a little more baking time, but they'll be ready soon. I'll even pack some up, Peter, so you can take them home with you—it'll be a nice treat for Nick too."

"Yeah, that sounds great…Nick deserves some kind of reward. He did a lot today…I don't want to judge the man, but I don't think he ever worked that hard in his whole life."

"How are…how are you and he getting along?" Lynette asked quietly.

"Okay…actually, quite good. He's even becoming interested in the factory's activities."

"Oh?" Lynette prompted, slipping onto the chair opposite Peter. "What do you think piqued this new interest of his?"

"I don't know, but he's been asking all kinds of questions about our new orders and work methods and—"

"Oh, dear," Lynette groaned.

"What's wrong?"

"Oh, Peter, I was hoping I wouldn't have to tell you this…and maybe I'm wrong. Maybe Nick is just curious about the factory…but I still feel I should warn you about…about…"

"About what?" he questioned, disturbed by Lynette's tone.

"Well, on Saturday, at the mar—"

Suddenly, Doctor Spreyer's voice boomed from the hallway, filling the house with an angry mix of German and English roars.

"That's Papa!" Anna exclaimed.

Springing to his feet, Peter bolted down the hall with Anna and Lynette close behind him. Then, as he neared the foyer, Peter caught sight of a familiar face, and a chill raced through him—it was the first time James Wild had invaded his sanctuary at the Spreyers'.

"For the last time, Herr Wild," Doctor Spreyer bellowed, "get out of my house!"

"What do you want, James?!" Peter demanded.

"I do not understand, Sir," Wild went on, ignoring both Peter and his question, "I thought you would be overjoyed to have Anna courted by a gentleman who is financially capable of giving her the world."

As he listened to Wild's speech and noticed the bouquet of roses in the man's thin hand, Peter's eyes grew wide with fury. "Leave! Now!" he raged. "Or those flowers are going to be decorating your tombstone."

"Ah, there you are, my sweet," Wild said as he moved toward Anna and extended the flowers to her as if Peter were invisible. "These roses reminded me of you—beautiful, pure, and—"

With a loud cuss, Peter knocked the flowers to the floor, then clasped his hands around Wild's neck. "This twisted game is going to stop—you hear me?!" he yelled, pushing Wild backward and slamming him into the wall next to the front door. "It's going to stop—now!"

"Remove your hands this instant," Wild hissed.

Tightening his grip, Peter stared into Wild's beady eyes, and in them, he saw a horrible image…his precious Anna—and his enemy—embracing. Just snap the man's scrawny neck, he inwardly told himself, and you'll never have to worry about him again…

Then, just as the thought flashed into his head, Peter slackened his hold. Killing Wild wasn't the answer, he silently reasoned. He would be rid of the man, yes, but he would also end up losing everything he cared about.

"Let go, Peter…let go…" Doctor Spreyer hollered as he tried to pry Peter away from Wild.

"Please, Peter," Anna begged from behind.

Finally, he yielded and released his rival. "You're lucky I didn't break your neck, Wild," Peter seethed. "Now, get out—and I don't ever want to see you around Anna again."

"Consider yourself the fortunate one, Leighton," James Wild fumed. "Normally, I would have you arrested for assault, but for Anna's sake, I will not—this time."

"Me?!" Peter shouted, taking a step forward. "You're the one who should be arrested!"

"Herr Wild," Doctor Spreyer barked as he grabbed Peter's arms and pulled him back. "Leave this house at once!"

"As you wish," James Wild said, smoothing the wrinkles from his lapels. Then, to Anna, he offered, "Why would you ever consider marrying such a foul-tempered failure, when I could give you so much more?"

Feeling the sting of Wild's words, Peter yanked himself from the doctor's hold and balled his right hand into a fist.

"And, as for you, Leighton," Wild continued, "you had better curb your savage jealousy—or I may be compelled to cancel my tables and chairs."

Instantly, Peter froze in place. Wild, obviously, had been waiting for the perfect opportunity to trap him into submission with the table order. Although his nemesis would pay penalties for the cancellation, Peter knew that the factory would still feel the revocation more. Now, if he fought for Anna, the factory would suffer—and if he protected the factory's interests, he would lose Anna…

Picking up the fallen bouquet of flowers, Anna shoved them at Wild and pointed toward the door. "You heard my father and my future husband," she announced, breaking the chilly silence. "Please leave."

With a slight bow, James Wild tipped his hat and smiled victoriously. "Yes, sweet Anna, I shall go—but soon, you will realize that I am the better choice."

As his rival exited the house, Peter reached for the staircase railing and sank onto the first step.

"Peter? Honey, are you all right?" Anna asked as she sat next to him.

Forcing himself to grin, Peter nodded. "I apologize, Otto," he said, looking up at the doctor. "I always bring so much trouble into your home."

"Nein, Peter," Doctor Spreyer replied, "this isn't your fault. It's Herr Wild who is in the wrong."

"I can't believe he did this," Anna put in.

Peter sighed. "I can…he's proving to be a very clever adversary…and maybe, he's right."

"No, he isn't," Anna whispered as she caressed Peter's face. "I want to be your wife—I've known that from the first time I saw you…and more important, God wants us together."

Gazing into Anna's caring and concerned eyes, Peter half-smiled but said nothing.

"And," Anna added, "if God wants us together—nothing, not even James Wild or his money, can keep that from happening."

"Uh huh," Peter returned softly. Deep down, he knew Anna was right, but he was still having a difficult time believing it.

⚜

Setting the jeweler's eyeglass and a small, toothed wheel on the table, Nick yawned and stretched his arms upward. He knew it was foolish to continue working on the pocketwatch so long after sunset, but he just couldn't bring himself to stop. And, as he examined the dissected timepiece in the lamplight, he sighed. Why? he wondered. Why couldn't his life be more like one of the wheels in a watch? At least then he could be himself and, yet, be a part of something else…

Slam!

Jumping at the noise, Nick sat bolt upright. Obviously, his brother was home—or was he? From the violent door slam and the cusses emanating from the front hall, Nick wasn't sure if it was Peter who had entered the guest house or a very angry burglar. Then, as his brother stomped into the kitchen, he knew that it was definitely not a thief—and he also knew that something was terribly wrong. Not only was Peter's face etched with rage, but his usual quiet and restrained demeanor had completely vanished.

"Hi!" Peter growled as he threw his frock coat and vest on one of the chairs.

"Hi," Nick returned, studying his brother's fierce actions. "Lemme guess, you're angry about something, right?"

Immediately, Peter stopped and stared at him with a wide-eyed expression.

Nick smirked—he was getting very used to that look. "I sound like Daven too, don't I?"

Peter nodded. "Right then you did," he replied with a cooler tone.

"Well, it's like the looks—I can't help it."

"I know," Peter said, holding out a towel-covered pie tin. "Anna and Lynette made some blueberry turnovers."

"Great!" Nick exclaimed as he rose, grabbed the baking dish, and settled back onto his chair, cradling the treat.

"I figured you'd be in bed already."

"Why?" Nick asked, unwrapping the turnovers. "It's only nine o'clock."

"Well…because you worked quite hard today…and because it's actually five minutes past ten."

"Really? I've been workin' with the watches…guess the minutes just got away from me—so to speak." Again, Peter gawked at him, but this time, Nick understood why—even he was surprised by his own jovial mood. "I thought you were only goin' to Anna's for a few minutes."

"That was my intent…but they wouldn't let me leave until I 'calmed down.'"

"Why? What happened?"

Grasping the back of a chair, Peter sighed and bowed his head. "I don't know," he moaned.

Biting into one of the turnovers, Nick scrutinized his brother—he had never seen Peter look so...so hopeless. "What's goin' on?" he questioned between chews.

"Quentin Fetch was a vicious, domination-hungry louse," Peter answered as he straightened up and combed his fingers through his hair, "but at least that made him predictable and beatable...I just can't..."

"You just can't what?" Nick prompted, unsettled by his brother's rambling.

"I just can't figure Wild out. He is a whole different kind of enemy...one I'm not sure how to deal with."

Almost choking on his mouthful of turnover, Nick swallowed hard and looked up at his brother. "What...what're you talkin' about?"

"James Wild came to the Spreyers' tonight—to court Anna."

His jaw falling open, Nick placed his half-eaten pastry on top of the other turnovers and set the baking tin on the chair next to him. "He did what?"

"He came with flowers and asked Doctor Spreyer for permission to court Anna."

Gritting his teeth, Nick cursed under his breath. "You slugged him, I hope."

"No," Peter returned, meandering toward the kitchen door. "He slugged me first."

"Wild punched you?!" Nick sputtered and leaped to his feet.

"Yep...and he knew right where to hit me...he told me that I had better curb my 'savage jealousy' or he'd cancel his furniture order."

Shaking his head, Nick walked over and joined Peter at the door—Wild had definitely changed the rules of the game. And, as guilt stabbed at his conscience, Nick reached out and placed his hand on Peter's shoulder, then, quickly, he pulled it back. "Just don't...don't let him trick you into doin' something stupid," he offered.

Turning to face his brother, Peter frowned, "What do you mean?"

With a shrug, Nick replied, "I knew somebody like Wild...his name was Cass Phillips, and he snagged me into makin' the biggest mistake of my life."

Propping himself against the counter, Peter crossed his arms. "You mentioned something about the rich dandies getting all the advantages—was that remark about Cass Phillips?"

Nick took a deep breath and nodded. The last thing he wanted was to delve into his past, but then, as he searched his brother's face, he reconsidered—maybe it was time to put Peter's loyalty to the test...

"Yeah. Cass' father made carriages—and a lot of money—which Cass liked to spend...and we both had our eye on a pretty gal by the name of Lydia Cordell."

Peter grunted. "Sounds rather familiar."

"Uh huh, but unlike Anna, Lydia wanted everything to be gilt-edged...I know she liked me, and she liked me courtin' her, but she also liked Cass' money. And he knew it. So he'd buy her all kinds of costly stuff…stuff I couldn't afford even if I saved for a year."

Bowing his head, Peter rubbed the back of his neck. "That sounds familiar too."

"Then, one day, Cass tells me that he's havin' a special necklace made for Lydia—a real expensive one. And, when it was ready, he was gunna give it to her and ask her to stop seein' me…I told him she wouldn't agree to that, and he said, unless I could prove that I was his equal—dollarwise—she'd give me the mitten without a second thought…" Drifting into silence, Nick shuffled back to the table and sank onto his chair. He knew churning up the memories would be unpleasant, but he never expected them to hurt so much…

"So what'd you do?"

"I stupidly took the challenge—which was exactly what he wanted me to do…I saw this real nice hair comb at the jeweler's—it was black with emeralds all around the edge, and I knew Lydia would love it. So that's what I planned on gettin' for her, you know, to show her that I was better than ol' Cass and his necklace."

"But how'd…how'd you, uh…"

"Afford it?"

"Yeah."

"I couldn't…so I stole it," Nick said, and in the flickering, yellowish glow of the lamp, he watched his brother for the smallest reflex to his revelation.

"But…but wasn't the theft reported?" Peter asked as he also moved to the table and sat next to his brother. "Didn't Lydia wonder where you got such an extravagant gift?"

Slouching down in his chair, Nick glanced at the watch pieces scattered on the table. "It was my plan to give her the comb, but it didn't work out that way…I got caught…and I got sent to prison." As he finished speaking, Nick lifted his head and waited for his brother's response. *Why do you care what Peter thinks?* he asked himself. *His opinion doesn't mean anything.* Then, as the silence mounted, Nick realized that his brother's approval meant everything to him.

"Prison?" Peter murmured. "For how long?"

"Two years."

"Two years? For a lousy comb?"

"Yeah," Nick answered and absently fingered the scars on his left cheek. "Do…do you care?"

"Yes, I care," Peter replied.

Instantly, Nick's heart plunged into his gut. "I suppose you want me outta here."

"Nick," Peter said, knocking on the table to get his brother's attention, "I care that you had to go through that bleak time without your family being there to support you…how old were you?"

"Twenty-one."

"Twenty-one," Peter echoed. "That ended up being a very costly comb."

"Yeah…so you want me to vamoose?"

"No—those two years don't change the fact that you're my brother."

Nick half-smiled and rubbed his moistening eyes. "So this is what it's like to have a family, huh?" he mused. Then, realizing that he had said the words aloud, Nick searched his mind for something he could say to change the subject. "That's why…why I want you to watch yourself around Wild. Him and Cass are just the same—and I know Cass told me about gettin' that necklace for Lydia because he knew I'd try somethin' desperate to win her back…and I did."

"Do you know whatever happened to them?"

Nick grunted, and pushing himself from his chair, he stepped to the cupboards behind him. "Before they carted me off, I gave Lydia my wooden chain and asked her to wait for me. When I finally got out and went back to see her…she was gone. She gave my chain to her brother to give back to me…she married Cass and they moved to…uh…I think her brother said Port Huron…I ain't sure, I kinda stopped listenin' after I heard she went off with him," he explained as he reached up and grabbed a glass from the shelf. "She left a letter for me, but I can't read, and I didn't want anybody else to know what she said, so I just burned it." Taking a deep breath, Nick meandered to the sink and pumped some water into his glass. Why did you tell him that? he inwardly reprimanded himself. Don't you know the more you reveal, the more he can use against you?

"Did Cass have anything to do with you getting caught?"

As he stood at the sink and gulped down his glass of water, Nick repeated the question in his head…

'Did Cass have anything to do with you getting caught?'

Did he? Nick wondered. In all the years since that luckless night, he had never considered that possibility…

"I dunno," Nick said as he refilled the glass and gazed at his reflection in the darkened window. "Cass did know that I spent an awful lot of time in the jewelry store lookin' at stuff for Lydia, but I don't think he had any idea what I was planning…it was just bad timin' on my part…the jeweler lived above the store, and I think he just heard me."

"He…he wh…what?" Peter stammered.

"Yeah," Nick returned, still staring at the darkness. "The jeweler and his wife lived upstairs, and I broke in after they were asleep…the guy had to have heard me, 'cause he came down and caught me with the comb in my hand." Suddenly, a ghostly stillness filled the kitchen, and as Nick slowly turned around, he saw a tear fall from Peter's eye. "What?!" he demanded, alarmed by his brother's odd response.

"I, uh, I really don't want to talk…to talk about this any longer," Peter choked out, looking half like a boy who had done something wrong and half like a man who had been handed a black-edged envelope.

"Huh…so my prison stay does matter to ya, doesn't it?"

"No, it doesn't! I just don't want to discuss this with you anymore!" Peter shouted as he rushed past Nick and headed toward his bedroom.

With a curse, Nick slammed his water glass down on the counter. You idiot, he silently screamed at himself. Haven't you learned by now that you can't trust anyone? Especially a lying brother who says he cares, then turns his back on you?

"Well, Pete," Nick quietly whispered to the empty, glimmering kitchen, "if that's the way you feel, that's fine with me…I'll take my shameful face and get outta your precious, polished life…that is, of course, after I tell James Wild everythin' I know about you…and your stupid furniture orders."

❀

"Seems as if we're always runnin' outta something," Jaxson said as he patted one of the horses and checked its harness.

"Uh huh."

"At least we don't have no problems buyin' painting supplies."

"Yeah…I just wish we could buy them somewhere closer than Grand Rapids," Peter returned. "I hate leaving you shorthanded."

Jaxson's mouth fell open in disbelief. How could Peter have forgotten his own strategy to conquer two jobs at once? "Peter…remember the bookcase that's in the wagon? You or me would still have to drive to Grand Rapids and deliver it."

"Right…right."

"Headache?"

"No, I'm fine," Peter offered, brushing his hand through his hair. "I'll try to get back as soon as I can…I really hate taking Benjamin away from you too, but it's just not proper for Bonnie and me to ride around without some kind of chaperon."

"I know," Jaxson replied with a nod. "You already told me that—three times… and I told ya it's okay. You need his help to unload the bookcase anyways."

"That's right," Peter absently remarked as he leaned against the bed of the wagon.

Taking a frazzled breath, Jaxson peered at Peter's spectacles, wishing that he could see through the dark barriers and into his friend's eyes. "What's going on?" he tried.

"Nothing…I just didn't get any sleep last night."

"Why? For once, things are workin' for us, instead of against us."

Peter's only reply was a sarcastic laugh.

"Well, I can drive to Grand Rapids, if you wanna stay put."

"No, I need someone coherent to be in charge here—and that wouldn't be me right now."

Jaxson shook his head. Somewhere, between Monday's twilight and Tuesday's dawn, Peter's entire morale had changed—and not for the better. "What's gnawin' at you?"

"Nothing important."

"We got enough cash for the painting stuff, don't we?"

"Yeah…yeah, that's no problem."

Moving to stand in front of Peter, Jaxson reached out and clutched his friend's shoulder. "Sakes alive, would you take off those spectacles and talk to me?"

"Not right now," Peter answered. And, twisting his arm free, he marched away from the wagon—and Jaxson.

"What'd Nick do now?"

Suddenly, Peter stiffened as if he had been splashed with a bucket of cold water. "What makes you think this is about him?" he asked as he slowly turned around and slid his glasses off.

Alarmed by Peter's bloodshot eyes, Jaxson winced and walked over to his friend. "Because, lately, everything's been about him."

"Well, you're wrong."

"Oh?"

"Yeah…it's only half about Nick," Peter returned, rubbing his eyes.

Completely puzzled, Jaxson loudly sighed. "Talk to me, will ya?"

"Okay," Bonnie announced as she bounded down the loading platform steps, followed by her father, "I've got the list of what we need."

"We'll talk when I get back," Peter murmured.

"No, we won't," Jaxson whispered. He was all too familiar with his friend's escape tactics—if they didn't speak now, Peter would avoid the issue until it was forgotten or replaced by another dilemma. "Benjamin, you and Bonnie can get aboard," Jaxson called to his approaching coworkers. "Me and Peter gotta discuss somethin' first."

"Jax, I want to get going while it's still early. It's going to be a long ride."

"Yeah, I know," Jaxson replied, then, with a firm grip on Peter's arm, he dragged his friend farther away from the wagon.

"Jaxson, would you st—"

"You remember what happened in the dryin' room the other day?" Jaxson cut in, stopping under a poplar tree in the factory's front yard. "Well, the same thing's gunna happen now—I ain't gunna let you leave 'til you tell me what happened last night."

Peter's jaw muscles tensed, and he responded with a low grumble.

"I can be just as stubborn as you can," Jaxson added.

Still no reply.

"All right, let's try it another way…if Nick's only half of the problem—then what's the other half?"

"You mean who's the other half," Peter finally muttered.

"Okay, who?"

"Who else?"

A grimace enveloped Jaxson's face as he struggled to decipher the meaning of Peter's question. Then, as he stared into his friend's crimson-streaked eyes, the haze in his head evaporated, and he clearly saw the answer. "Wild."

"He came to court Anna last night," Peter declared in a simmering whisper.

"What?!"

"Uh huh," Peter went on, his jaw tightening even more. "Of course, he did follow a degree of etiquette and asked the doctor's permission first."

"Man alive! What'd you do?"

"I tried to snap his neck!"

"Did you?" Although he was sure the answer was no, a fragment of doubt still lingered in Jaxson's head—Daven's murder had showed him just how focused—and intense—his friend could become.

Peter let out a caustic laugh. "No, his puny little neck is still in one piece," he continued bitterly. "And, after I let him go, he told me if I didn't behave myself, he'd cancel his table order."

His own anger mounting, Jaxson inwardly cursed James Wild. When would the man stop tormenting Peter?

"He's got us in a noose, Jax. You know we can't afford to lose those tables and chairs…we've just got too much invested in them."

Jaxson nodded—the statement was, unfortunately, completely true. "Maybe you should have cracked his neck just a little."

A grunt answered him.

"But what does Nick have to do with all of this?"

"Oh, Jax, I messed up so badly with him," Peter replied as he yanked a twig off one of the poplar's low-hanging branches.

"How so?"

"I ended up telling Nick about Wild's little prank last night, and as we were talking, he told me something that happened to him…for the first time, he opened up and started unveiling his past, and I…I…" Peter stammered, segmenting his stick into tiny pieces, "I turned him against me."

"Peter, all ya have to do is look sideways at Nick, and he'll turn against you."

"No, Jax, this was serious…he told me about a time when he was fighting against a wealthy man for a girl's affections…he stole a hair comb to try and impress her—and spent two years in prison because of it."

"Prison?!" Jaxson exclaimed. "I figured he had a crooked past, but I never counted on somethin' like that."

"Yeah, it was a surprise for me too…I told him it didn't matter—and it really doesn't. I mean, the man's been beaten down enough, he didn't need me condemning him all over again—especially when he's already paid for that mistake with two years of his life."

Jaxson crossed his arms and sighed. He knew Peter's heart had greatly expanded in the past year, but with Nick, maybe it was a little too big. "If that kind of charity turned him against you, then he doesn't deserve—"

"No," Peter cut in and tossed the end of his twig into the air, "the problem didn't start until he told me how he went about stealing the comb…the jeweler…the jeweler and his wife…they lived above the store…and…and Nick broke in at night…the man heard him and came downstairs…that's…that's when he…he caught Nick."

As he listened to Peter's faltering speech, a tremor of bewilderment fluttered through Jaxson, and he scrutinized his friend's face, which was engraved with distress. "What aren't you tellin' me?" Jaxson gently prompted.

"That's…that's…" Peter mumbled, wiping at his water-filled eyes.

"What?" Jaxson urged, his confusion switching to concern. It was clear that Peter's anguish extended far beyond Nick…or even Wild.

"That's…that's how…how my dad died," Peter choked out, his voice breaking. "Only when my father heard a noise one night and went downstairs in our store, he didn't run into a lovesick kid stealing a comb for a girl—he ran into two thieves…who didn't hesitate to use the pistols they were carrying."

"So that's how it happened, huh?" Jaxson whispered.

"Nick's story wasn't long…but it brought back all the memories…I wanted to tell him…tell him what was going on inside my head, but I couldn't—I just walked away…now, Nick thinks I rejected him because of his stint behind bars."

"When you tell him what you just told me, he'll understand."

Pulling another twig from the tree, Peter shook his head. "I don't think that's going to happen…I heard him leave the house at twenty to eleven last night—and he never came back. His clothes were still there this morning, but I know he's going to move on."

"Did he say that?"

"No, but I've become very familiar with his temperament, and I just know it."

"Well, he never did appreciate anything ya did for him."

"But I think he was finally starting to trust…" Peter replied, drifting into silence.

Trying to remedy his friend's sorrow, Jaxson offered, "Maybe Nick'll surprise ya and stay around so you can explain it to him."

Doubt clouded Peter's features. "Maybe," he said, his voice filled with uncertainty. Then, with a sigh and a weary smile, he added, "So have I talked enough? May I go get our painting supplies now?"

Jaxson grinned, amazed at Peter's resilience. "Yeah, I guess so."

"Good," Peter returned, dropping what was left of his second stick.

"You know, this whole thing is kinda strange."

"How so?"

"Well, you and Nick have had the same things happen to ya…well, not exactly the same, but between the rich dandies and the downstairs thieves, it's almost as if God has your lives goin' parallel to each other."

"You think so?" Peter questioned.

"Uh huh."

"For what purpose though?"

"I dunno," Jaxson answered with a shrug, "but I'm sure the Lord will make it clear in His time…do ya want me to keep the factory open 'til you get back?"

"Naw, just close up as usual…I'm sure Benjamin will lend a hand if I need any help."

"All right," Jaxson said and headed toward the wagon. Then, after a few steps, he paused and glanced at Peter. "You know you can trust me—to tell me stuff…I won't go spreadin' it around."

"I know that, Jax, and I do trust you—with my life…I just don't like sharing my failures—with anyone."

"But this ain't your failure—it's Nick's."

Even though his friend nodded, Jaxson knew, if Nick left, Peter would eternally blame himself for the loss.

❦

"Why do I have to do it?"

"Because, Manning, I'm your boss and I told you to."

"But bein' a lugger is a kid's job."

Jaxson exhaled and propped himself against the drying room's counter—his daily confrontations with Manning Cole were becoming extremely annoying. "Look, with Peter and Benjamin gone, I need to move you men around—and that means I want Billy on one of the saws."

"Well, put me on a saw," Cole snarled, "and keep Billy lugging the wood around—'cause that's what a kid's s'pposed to do."

"Cole, I've seen your work on the saws," Jaxson said in exasperation. "You're gunna be the lugger or nothing."

"Where's Pete?"

Grateful for the interruption, Jaxson sighed in relief and glanced over his shoulder, then, immediately, his cheered mood dimmed. Although he disliked Manning Cole, he still preferred the stout, unwashed man over the person standing in the drying room doorway. "I'll be right with ya, Nick," he called.

"I wanna talk to Pete—not you," came the reply.

As he bit the inside of his lip, Jaxson pasted an artificial smile onto his face. "Peter's on his way to buy paint, and he won't be back 'til late—I'm all ya got."

"Fine. I'll wait out in the yard…when you're done here, come and get me. That way I can tell ya what I need to tell ya and get outta here," Nick hollered from the door.

Despising the idea of chasing after Nick Anderson, Jaxson immediately returned, "No need to go—Cole and me are more than done." At least, Jaxson silently reasoned, he could get Manning Cole's gamy body out of the cramped drying room. "Well?" he offered to Cole. "Are ya my lugger?"

"There's gotta be somethin' else I can do," Manning whined, his hands on his hips.

"Cole, everyone in this company does what they can to help out—that's why one of the owners is out makin' a delivery—and right now, I need ya to get the wood to the men so they can do their jobs."

Manning Cole opened his mouth to respond, but all that exited was an agitated snort.

"Does that mean you'll be a lugger?"

"I s'ppose," Cole muttered.

"Then would you mind goin' downstairs and gettin' to work?" Jaxson asked.

With an angry growl, Manning Cole strutted toward the doorway, giving Jaxson a poison-eyed glare as he passed. And, upon reaching Nick, Cole whispered under his breath. Although Jaxson couldn't decipher all of the muffles, he heard enough to know that he and the color of his skin were being fiercely insulted. "Cole…downstairs…now!" Jaxson shouted, wishing that he had listened to Peter and never hired the lazy bigot.

Laughing, Manning Cole circled, flashed Jaxson a mock salute, and swaggered out of the room.

"And what can I help you with, Nick?" Jaxson inquired.

"How come you're not askin' me why I'm late for work?" Nick snapped as he marched into the room. "Is it because I don't have a job no more?"

"What're you talkin' about? You still have a job."

"Well, that comes as a surprise…Pete didn't want me dirtying up his spotless life—I figured he didn't want me here, neither."

"Nick," Jaxson sighed, "he doesn't care about what happened before."

"So he told ya about my little prison stay, huh?"

"Yes, he told me—and it doesn't matter to him."

"Uh huh," Nick sneered, "he keeps sayin' that—but he don't mean it...that's why I'm leaving town."

"Leaving?" Jaxson echoed, realizing that Peter's prediction about Nick's departure had been more than a guess.

"Yeah, I'm tired of Pete's lies," Nick growled, and as he extended his arm and held his pocketwatch out in the palm of his hand, he added, "and give this to him."

Swallowing hard, Jaxson gazed first at the watch, then at Nick. Had it really been a whole year since he had heard Daven's faint voice choke out almost the same words? Why? Jaxson wondered. Why couldn't it be that sweet kid in front of him, instead of a bitter and vengeful ingrate?

"Sure, I'll give it to him," Jaxson replied. "You don't want it?"

"Yeah, I want it, but I don't want ol' Pete sayin' I stole it."

"Put the watch away, Nick. Peter gave it to you—he'd never say that."

"No? Well, I think he would...he said that my bein' in prison didn't change nothin'—then he runs away from me as if I had typhoid or something."

How easy it would be, Jaxson thought. How incredibly easy. He could just say a simple 'well, so long, Nick,' and all concerned would be able to continue their life's waltz without the fear of stepping on Nikolaus Anderson's precious toes. And, more important, Peter would finally be free from his stepbrother's shenanigans.

No, Jaxson countered, recalling Peter's expression as they talked that morning. If Nick left now, anguish would forever hound his friend. Sponging his face with the cuff of his shirt, Jaxson puffed out a resigned breath. Even though his head told him to remain mute, he knew, in his heart, he had to intercede...

"You know, Nick, it's not always about you."

"What?"

"When people say stuff—and do stuff—it's not always gunna be because of you."

"Whatd'ya mean?"

"Peter didn't walk away from you last night because you spent time in jail."

"No?"

"No. You ended up reminding him of somethin' he didn't wanna remember."

"Right," Nick returned with an unbelieving nip.

"Sometimes, I just can't figure you out," Jaxson fumed as he wiped his brow. "You've kept certain things from your past a secret—but when Peter does the same thing, you blast him for it."

"Can we finish this out in the assembly room?" Nick simmered, poking his thumb toward the door. "It's too hot in here to talk."

Although he fully agreed, Jaxson chose to ignore the perspiration trickling down his back. Between the box stove and the heated conversation, he was sweltering too—

but the last thing he wanted was to make Nick comfortable. "No," Jaxson retorted, "nobody needs to hear this, but you."

"Fine," Nick snapped. "Just make it quick."

Immediately, Jaxson's hands curled into fists. If only Peter didn't care so much for Nick's welfare…if only…

"Peter's lost a lot of people in his life," Jaxson began, curbing his desire to punch Nick in the face and toss him out the window. "Daven…your father…his mother… and his own father. He's never been very talkative about his father, but this morning, Peter finally told me how he died."

"What's this got to do with—"

"Shut up and I'll tell ya," Jaxson cut in sharply as he brushed his sleeve across his sweat-drenched features. "Peter's father owned a general store in Bradlee, and one night, two men broke into it…well, his father was upstairs and heard a noise, so he came down—and they shot him. Sound familiar?"

"I didn't shoot nobody!"

"Man alive, Nick! I told ya that not everything's about you! Your story about how you broke into that jewelry shop just brought back all the memories for Peter and ended up rubbin' salt in a gash that had never healed. He didn't desert you last night…he just went off to tend his wound—that you opened up."

"Why…why didn't Pete say something?"

"Hmm, maybe because you never gave him the chance," Jaxson answered, placing an intentional sting on his words. "So, if you're gunna leave…leave—but don't you dare do it before Peter can talk to ya about this himself…you owe him at least that much, Nick."

⚜

Slowly, Peter shuffled into the guest house, and closing his eyes, he leaned back against the door, causing it to shut with a loud clack. Why had he insisted on nudging his wedding into October? If he had accepted Anna's suggestion of August twenty-seventh, he'd only have five more weeks of waiting…just five more and he could remain with his beloved—even into the night. Now, because of his own worries, he had over two months to wait…two months of entering a lonely guest house that didn't belong to him…months that would have been bearable, if he hadn't chased his brother away.

His eyes fluttering open, Peter gazed upward. "I'm sorry, Lord," he whispered. "I didn't do a very good job of restoring Nick's faith in mankind—or in You."

Elbowing himself from the door, Peter slipped out of his frock coat and hung it on the rack in the entranceway. Then, as he pulled off his hat, he glimpsed his reflection in the hat stand's mirror—and in the twilight, he saw the likeness of his father staring back at him. Shocked and amazed by the image, Peter slowly shook his head. He knew many of his father's traits had been bestowed upon him, such as his already graying hair, but obviously, the concerns of the past year had accelerated the favoring process. Now—just like Daven's painted portrait—every time he peered into a mirror, he'd be reminded of a loved family member who died because of a poor decision on his part…

Glancing away from his reflection—and the bittersweet memories—Peter noticed a shimmer of golden sunlight radiating from the kitchen. But, as he continued to observe the persistent shaft of light, a sudden realization slapped at him…you walked home as the sun was setting…

"I know I turned the gas off," Peter murmured as he rushed through the parlor and into the kitchen—which, he envisioned, was being consumed by a smoldering fire.

Instantly, relief and surprise engulfed him, and he slid to a halt just inside the kitchen doorway. Not only was the room flameless, but his brother, once again, sat at the table, puttering with an assortment of watch pieces. "Nick!" Peter exclaimed, wondering if he was, somehow, reliving the previous evening in a dream. "I…I didn't expect you to be here."

"Where'd you expect me to be—breakin' up another tavern?"

Rubbing his eyes, Peter silently cussed. He did it again—with a simple comment he ended up igniting his brother's mercurial temper. "No, I merely meant—" Peter began, then, as he eyed his brother's features, he abruptly stopped—Nick was actually smiling.

"You merely meant what?" Nick asked, his grin widening.

Inspired by his brother's unusually light-hearted mood, Peter decided to try the raw truth. "I thought you had left town, Nick."

"And why is that?"

"Because I know I made you angry last night, and I heard you leave…I really didn't think I'd ever see you again."

"But why?"

"I don't know—I just did…I'm glad I was wrong."

"Lemme understand this," Nick said as he placed his elbows on the table and rested his chin on his intertwined hands. "You knew I was mad, and you really thought I was gunna leave town 'cause of it?"

Peter sighed. Was his brother just stating the facts? Or growing angry? "Yeah, I did."

"Huh…you wanna know something? That's exactly what I had planned to do."

Boggled by Nick's honesty, Peter stepped over to the table and sank onto the chair opposite his brother. "What made you decide to stay?"

"Two things," Nick replied. "First, I had to finish the Mayor's watch so I could give it to Michael."

"And did you?"

"Yep…I went to the factory for awhile, but then I came back here and worked on the watch…his was pretty easy to fix, since it was still in ticking order."

Although he was disappointed that his brother didn't help out at the factory, Peter decided to keep his mouth shut on the matter—he wanted nothing to interfere with their current conversation. "Ticking order?" he inquired.

"Yeah, that means it runs, just not very good. I cleaned the inside and replaced a few worn wheels…I just got back from takin' it to Michael. That's why I didn't have a chance to clear this up yet," he said, pointing to the medley of watch fragments. "Michael seemed pretty impressed that I got the watch fixed in time for him to still get it to the Mayor tonight."

"Where'd you learn to repair watches like that?"

Nick shrugged and slouched down in his seat. "Here and there…sometimes, when I needed money, I'd go through the garbage and pick up stuff, then fix it and sell it. Clocks and watches were my favorite—they were easy for me to fix, and I liked workin' on them."

"You are definitely your father's son," Peter said as he admired the tools and parts spread out on the table.

"Whatd'ya mean?"

"Your father and Daven had the same kind of God-given knack when it came to their carving. They just knew how to carve…and they were in their glory when they were doing it."

"Carving's a lot different than what I do."

"True, but your talent is just as remarkable…and quite sought after. You could get a job anywhere."

"Yeah," Nick laughed, "Michael was so happy with the Mayor's watch, he offered to hire me to fix all the other watches he has."

"That's great, Nick," Peter returned with an approving nod. "Are you going to take the job?"

"I dunno…I'll think about it. I really wanna start workin' on my watch and get it back to working order, before I do anythin' else."

Grabbing one of the tiny wheels off the table, Peter held it up between his thumb and index finger, and as he studied the little gear, he exhaled deeply. "I wish I had been blessed with some kind of creative skill."

"What about what you do at the factory?" Nick questioned as he simultaneously crossed his arms and lifted his feet onto the chair next to him. "It takes a lot of skill to run that place."

"Well, that's not really the kind of ability I was talking about…besides, all I've done lately is prove just how bad I am at taking care of the factory—or anything," Peter replied, setting the small wheel down. "And, while I'm on the subject of my blunders, I want to apologize for…for abruptly ending our discussion last night…it didn't have anything to do with you or your time in prison…you see, your story… well, it reminded me of…"

"Your father—I know."

"How?"

"I talked to Jaxson this mornin' and he told me—that's the second reason why I didn't leave town…after talkin' with him, I realized that…that it wasn't about me."

"No, it wasn't," Peter agreed as he pushed himself from his chair and ambled toward the open kitchen door. "I meant what I said…the fact that you were in prison doesn't change anything between us…I guess I should also apologize for blurting everything out to Jaxson the way I did."

"Nah…it's the same as him tellin' me about your father. It…it just needed to be said—you know, to straighten everything out."

"I also confided in Anna…but in my defense, it was after I thought you had left town."

"It's okay. You can tell your family—they'll find out eventually, anyway."

"Nick, they're your family too." Getting no response, Peter shook his head and propped his shoulder against the doorjamb. You just went a little too far down that road, he told himself. Then, thinking of a safer route, he put in, "I should…I should have told you about my dad last night."

"Well, I don't like talkin' about people who've made me miserable, either."

"Oh, no…no," Peter countered, standing up straight. "My dad was a wonderful person, and I worked with him in his store whenever I could. He was the best example of a businessman that I ever knew…I wish, now, that I had listened to him more…maybe then I could figure out how to resuscitate the factory."

"Then why don't ya like talkin' about him?"

"I do like talking about him," Peter returned as a gentle, evening breeze wafted through the open door and embraced him, "but it always leads to how he died."

"So it's death you don't like talkin' about?"

"Not when I'm the cause of it," Peter murmured and slowly circled to face the indigo sky.

"Whatd'ya mean?" Nick called from his chair.

Although he heard his brother's question, Peter remained speechless—hoping to delay—or even prevent—the exploration of his most dreaded secret. And, as he considered the mountainous confrontation that loomed before him, Peter's thoughts wandered back to Jaxson's earlier comment…

'It's almost as if God has your lives goin' parallel to each other.'

Did the Lord really have a reason for allowing him and Nick to live kindred lives? Of course, He did, Peter told himself. You know Nick's jewelry store catastrophe is the only reason you're even thinking about…about…

"Whatd'ya mean you caused it?" Nick tried again. "I thought your father was killed by those robbers."

"He was," Peter said, stepping through the kitchen door and onto the guest house's wide, wooden veranda. "They both shot at him—and one of the bullets caught my dad square in the heart."

Nick's forehead creased in bewilderment, and pushing himself from his chair, he followed his brother outside. "So why do you keep sayin' you caused it?"

"Because my father wasn't supposed to die that night…I was," Peter whispered as he blankly gazed at the first few stars peeking through the darkening overhead veil. "I've never confessed that to another living soul—not even God."

Nick perched himself on the veranda's railing and shook his head. "I don't understand."

"I should have gotten shot, not my father," Peter offered. Then, as his words met the evening air, a wave of memories flooded his thoughts—and suddenly, as if a theater had opened its curtains, the entire ghastly scene appeared in the sky.

"My dad and I were both upstairs that night working on the bookkeeping," Peter continued, describing the tragic play unfolding before his eyes. "And he heard a noise and asked me to go down and see what it was. I told him that it was probably the Walters' cat…they were our neighbors, and they had an old tomcat that kept finding its way into our store…and my father said, 'cat or no cat, would you please go down and see if everything's all right.' But I didn't budge—I just sat there with my nose in the books. Well, he finally got tired of waiting for me, and he went down to investigate…and…and…"

His voice breaking, Peter fell silent as his past repeated itself amidst the emerging stars. Don't let him go down those steps, he inwardly screamed at his younger self, who was still stubbornly refusing to move…get up and stop him…come on you lazy, disrespectful, rotten son—get up and do what you were asked to do. But, despite all his voiceless pleas, his young, pigheaded essence just stayed seated…until the shots rang out…

"Why didn't you go downstairs? Why didn't you do what you were supposed to?" Peter yelled aloud as the curtain lowered and the ghostly figures faded from the sky.

"Just 'cause you stayed upstairs, doesn't mean you caused your father's death."

Wiping his eyes with his shirt cuff, Peter turned his face away from Nick. "Yes, it does," he replied. "I cut my father's life short because I wouldn't honor a simple request…I…I tried to make it up to him by keeping the store going…that's why I hated your father so much when he put us into debt, and I had to close my dad's dream forever…" As his voice gave out once again, Peter glanced upward, hoping that a sign of forgiveness would manifest itself among the glittering spots of light—but his message of absolution failed to appear.

"The one time I chose to disobey my father—I get him killed," Peter mumbled, more to continue his self-condemnation, than to finish his explanation. Then, the moment he finished speaking, a horrible thought hit him like a fist…could all his failures be his punishment for disregarding God's commandment to honor his father?

"Whatd'ya mean the only time?" Nick asked, walking over to Peter. "You tellin' me that you never disobeyed your father before that?"

As they stood in the faint glow from the kitchen's lamplight, Peter glanced into his brother's vivid eyes for a moment, then bowed his head. "No."

"Man alive, Pete, your thinkin' is all wrong…your pa knew ya were a good kid. That one time of not doin' what he asked wouldn't stop him from lovin' ya—not if he was a decent father…besides, if he had really wanted you to go down there, he would have made you go."

Peter nodded but said nothing.

"And," Nick went on, "ain't fathers supposed to love their kids—even give things up for them?"

Peter bobbed his head again.

"Well, what do you reckon your pa was thinkin' when he got downstairs and saw those pistols aimed at him?"

"Nick," Peter countered, "it was dark…I'm sure he didn't see—"

"It don't matter," Nick cut in, "whatd'ya think went through your pa's head? Do ya think he said…'I'm gunna get shot. Why didn't Pete come down? At least then it would be him, instead of me'…or do you think he said…'thank goodness I came downstairs instead of Pete. I'd rather it be me who gets shot, than my son.'"

Slowly, Peter looked up, and blinking his eyes clear, he studied Nick in the dim light.

"Well?" Nick persisted. "You knew your father—what went through his head?"

Peter swallowed hard. He knew Nick's latter scenario was the correct answer, but he had spent so many years submerged in guilt that it was still difficult to see the truth.

"Maybe it was supposed to happen the way it did," Nick continued. "Maybe your father, somehow, knew that…that somethin' was gunna happen and that he had to go downstairs instead of you…to save you from it."

His jaw falling open in amazement, Peter scrutinized his brother. He knew Nick was smarter than he pretended to be, but Peter never expected to find such wisdom hiding behind the crystal-blue gems. "That's quite prophetic," he said in a whisper.

Nick scowled. "What's that mean?"

"It just sounds as though God's giving me a message through your words."

"Huh…that ain't too likely—Him and me ain't speakin' to each other these days."

"Well, either way, I'm obliged to you, Nick."

"For what?"

"For extending an open hand—instead of a fist."

"Ain't that what a brother's supposed to do?"

Peter smiled and wordlessly cheered. His father's death had always been a steep and sharp obstacle for him, but now, thanks to his brother's outstretched arm, it seemed easier to climb. And, even though his head pounded as if it were being used as a battlefield, he would scale the same emotional mountain again and again if he had to…as long as it led to the identical outcome—Nick's acceptance of their kinship.

"I have an idea," Peter announced, feeling as though he had just been given permission to relinquish his hold on a hundred-pound burden. "Why don't we go inside and finish off those blueberry turnovers?"

"Sure," Nick returned with a half-grin. "I got some time before I gotta go see Wi—"

"Where?"

"Uh…to, uh…see a man about some whiskey."

"You know, I think Karl has some over at his house…I can go get that so you don't have to—"

"No…no, I have to go, uh, I mean, I wanna…I wanna go to the tavern."

Sensing his brother's growing resentment toward his parental remark, Peter sighed. There were, obviously, many tall hills that he and Nick had yet to conquer. "All right…just be careful going out so late. I hate to say it, but there are some very unscrupulous people in this city."

"Yeah," Nick murmured, averting his gaze, "I know."

❦Nine❦

Once again, Nick settled onto what was now his customary spot—the red velvet seat opposite Wild's overstuffed chair. And, as he continued to wait…and wait…and wait for his host, he became increasingly disgusted with himself. This has to end, he inwardly declared. He had to get out of his self-made predicament. But was it even possible anymore? He had dug so deep…was he entangled beyond hope?

"And what news do you have for me tonight, Anderson?" Wild announced as he entered the solarium, clutching his usual nighttime drink and three gold coins. "I do hope it is as exciting as what you disclosed yesterday."

"I ain't got nothing," Nick returned, rising from his chair. "I didn't work at the factory today."

"That is not completely accurate—you were there for a short time."

Nick scowled. "How'd you know that?"

"What was the purpose of Peter's journey today?"

"What?"

"Peter's journey…what was the purpose of it?"

Shaking his head, Nick gritted his teeth. He was definitely trapped inside his ever-deepening hole. "To buy paint."

"Hmm," Wild murmured and took a sip of his nightcap.

"How'd you know I was at the factory today?"

"Oh, I know a great deal about you, Anderson," Wild smirked. "And, I will inform you now, you will be emptying your pockets before you depart tonight."

"Emptyin' my…why?"

"So I can be assured that all my gold and silver are where they should be," Wild replied, then, with a snicker, he added, "and, of course, my jewelry…since that is your specialty, is it not?"

Nick swallowed a knot in his throat and choked out, "My specialty? How…how do you know about that?"

"I told you previously—you are not my only informant in that factory."

"Manning Cole," Nick snarled as a wave of anger swelled within him—he was used to being a snitch, but not the one being snitched upon.

"Yes, Mr. Cole explained that he overheard a conversation between you and Jaxson Averill—and he advised me of your incarceration."

"He didn't overhear nothing," Nick fumed. "He stood outside the door and eavesdropped."

"Nonetheless, he still provided me with some very pertinent information—that you failed to mention."

"The time I spent in prison is my business."

"On the contrary, Anderson, it is now everyone's business."

"Whatd'ya mean?"

"I believe Mr. Cole has become the town crier on the issue."

With a loud curse, Nick stomped his boot heel on the floor. "I quit."

"Excuse me?"

"You heard me—I quit. I ain't comin' here no more…no matter what you offer me."

"I see…then you will no longer need these," Wild returned, ceremoniously dropping the ten-dollar coins, one by one, into his chamber robe pocket. "I must tell you though, it does distress me that you desire to terminate our contract at this point in time."

"Why?"

"Because you are one of my finest playing pieces. The information you divulged yesterday absolutely thrilled me…and it also enabled me to water the seeds of surrender that I have planted in Peter."

"Why? Whatd'ya do?"

Strolling over to the glass-topped table, Wild set his drink down and dusted off his overstuffed chair. "I wish I could share that with you, Anderson," Wild responded as he fanned out his robe and settled upon his upholstered seat as if it were a throne, "but you have severed our contract, and I am no longer obligated to answer your questions."

"What did ya do?!" Nick demanded, ignoring Wild's excuse.

Grabbing his glass from the table, Wild took a long drink of his hot toddy, then a bemused smirk spread on his face. "Sit—and I will enlighten you."

With a weary sigh, Nick sank back down on his chair.

"No," Wild put in and motioned to the ottoman at his feet. "Here."

Immediately, Nick's simmering indignation started to boil. "You want me to sit…or kneel?" he snipped.

Wild laughed, then his features instantly turned to granite. "Tread carefully, Anderson, my patience with you is quite thin…now, sit, before I change my mind about replying to your queries."

As he tried to calm his rampant breathing, Nick glared at Wild. He wanted, so badly, to slug the pompous dictator and walk out of the solarium, but he knew he had to comply—it was the only way he could learn about the blockades Wild had created for his brother. "So what've you done to Pete now?" Nick asked as he reluctantly moved to the ottoman.

"I have put many things into motion…for example, Peter will soon lose the furniture order that Mr. Brant acquired from the men's club in Grand Rapids."

"Why? You already said you were gunna buy up all the oak in Willow Ridge— that'll interfere with the order enough."

"That is correct. However, I have discovered that Peter has an annoying streak of good fortune—and that has forced me to develop a multifarious offensive."

"Huh?"

Wild chuckled. "I am attacking the problem from all sides."

"And is courtin' Anna Spreyer one of those 'sides'?"

"If that incident disturbed you, Anderson, why did you not inquire about it when we spoke yesterday?"

Nick moistened his suddenly dry lips. "Why're ya tryin' to court Anna?" he questioned, once again ignoring Wild.

Swishing the last swallow of his drink around in the glass, Wild caressed his chin. "Anderson, I know you are a convict, but—"

"I ain't a convict no more."

"As I was saying, I know you are a convict, but you still seem to be a fairly intelligent man—so…speak…like…one."

Nick's features instantly reddened with outrage. He had faced humiliation at the hands of many people, but James Wild was proving to be the worst of them all—and every fiber within him wanted to rip out the man's tiny, manipulative heart. Yet, despite the urge, he remained motionless. That act would bring only one result…his return to prison. "Why are you courting Anna Spreyer?" he tried, stifling what was left of his pride. "You're never going to win her over that way."

"My Monday night visit was not for Anna's benefit—it was for Peter's."

"Peter's?"

"Correct…an angry opponent makes mistakes."

Nick swore and sprang up from his tufted stool. "Leave him alone, will ya?"

"You are quite an enigma, Anderson. Last night you sold me every secret that Peter had, without any hesitation—but tonight…tonight, you have terminated our agreement and have shown immense concern for his well-being. Why?"

"I just don't like what you're doing to my brother."

"Your brother?" Wild replied as he fingered the rim of his glass. "I see the knowl-edge of Peter's father—and how the poor man expired—has altered your beliefs."

"How do you know about Pete's father?" Nick asked, then he realized how—Manning Cole must have listened to every word that he and Jaxson had said to each other. "I just don't wanna cause Pete no more grief."

"Again, if you please…in English," Wild teased.

Nick growled and gritted his teeth. "I don't want to hurt my brother anymore."

"I see," Wild sighed woefully. "Well, I am incredibly sorry to lose your services, Anderson—and I wish I could find a way to convince you to reconsider…so tell me," he went on, his features hardening, "where do you plan on living after Peter applies the tar and feathers?"

"What?"

James Wild poured the last of his drink into his mouth, then smacked his lips together as he set the glass on the table. "Hmm, I thought my meaning was quite clear…where do you plan to go after Peter throws you out of his life and, as the knav-ish say, 'rides you out of town on a rail'?"

Nick shook his head, unsure of why he suddenly felt ill. "What…what are you talking about…he's not going to—"

"Are you daft? Do you honestly believe that Peter will continue to stand by your side when he learns about the treacherous acts that you have already committed against him?"

"But he's not going to learn about them."

A wide, devilish smile emerged on Wild's face. "Yes…he…will. I intend to make sure that he becomes aware of everything you have ever told me."

Shaking his head again, Nick recalled his valiant thoughts about ripping Wild's heart out. You should have done it, he reprimanded himself—because now, he's doing it to you. If Peter finds out that you betrayed him…he'll never forgive you…he'll never forgive you… "No," Nick murmured, not even realizing that he voiced his plea aloud.

"Yes," Wild countered, pushing himself from his throne and staring Nick in the eyes. "I will reveal every treasonous word you have ever spoken—and maybe, even embellish upon them—unless, of course, you agree to a new arrangement."

"Whatd'ya mean, embellish?"

"Embellish…exaggerate…distort…lie. Even you should be able to understand that last one."

"You filthy piece of—"

"Now, now. A gentleman does not use such vulgar language," Wild cut in with a chuckle.

Squelching the remainder of his curse, Nick pulled in a deep breath and rasped, "What do you want from me?"

"Your continued cooperation. However, there will be a slight change in our agreement…you will provide me with information about Peter's activities, just as you have been—and in return, instead of paying you thirty dollars, I will refrain from informing your brother that you have betrayed his trust."

"I oughtta beat you senseless, Wild."

"Place even one finger upon me and you will find yourself back in the penitentiary—for the remainder of your life."

As his guts churned, Nick rubbed the long scars on his cheek and lowered his eyes. He cringed at the idea of having Peter slip away from him, but nothing alarmed him more than the thought of being shut up in prison again.

"Ah, I believe we finally understand each other," Wild declared. "Do you agree?"

Nick nodded.

"Oh, yes, there is one last item to discuss," Wild said as he gestured to the solarium door that led to the backyard. "I believe it is proper etiquette for thieves to utilize the back door, instead of the front."

❦

"What do you mean you don't have any more pineapple pies?"

"Marion," Anna returned as she continued to slice the skin off the cucumbers lying on the counter in front of her, "for the hundredth time, we sold all those pies at the market on Saturday."

"So make more."

"It's a little hard to make pineapple pies without any pineapples."

"Then ask Mr. Wild to get you some."

Anna's expression stiffened and her careful paring turned into reckless hacking. "No," she firmly announced. "Mr. Wild is not welcome in this house any longer—and neither are his gifts."

"Why?"

"Because they're not."

"Why?" Marion pressed.

"Mr. Wild disgraced himself and our family Monday night—when he came to court me."

"How exciting—they say he's one of the richest men in these parts."

"Marion!" Anna exclaimed, glaring at her sister over her shoulder. "That doesn't matter—I'm engaged to Peter…it was a scandalous thing for him to do."

"Well, James is quite taken with you—perhaps you should reconsider your choices."

"How dare you!" Anna shouted as she turned to face Marion. "You have been against me marrying Peter from the very beginning, and I'm tired of your jaded remarks about him."

"I'm just thinking of you, Dear," Marion said, perching herself on the edge of the kitchen table. "James Wild could provide you with your every desire and take you to a social level that most women would die for—but you choose a man who cannot even buy you a decent engagement ring and who forces us all to associate with…with undesirables."

Still holding onto a half-peeled cucumber and the paring knife, Anna stepped over to the table and peered into her sister's steely-blue eyes. "First of all, Peter Leighton is my every desire," she countered, and to emphasize her declaration, she punctuated every word with a slap of her knife against the cucumber. "Secondly, it would be me who would die if I had to be with James Wild…thirdly, I'd still love Peter if he could only afford to put a braided string on my finger…and lastly, what do you mean Peter's forced us all 'to associate with undesirables'?"

"I mean precisely that…for example, his friend Jaxson. He's always bringing that man to our family gatherings…it's absolutely disgraceful."

Anna's jaw instantly dropped open, and she stared at Marion in disbelief. When did her sister become so biased? "Marion, Jaxson is a part of our family."

"Are you blind? He's a little dark to be part of our family."

"I don't see him as anything but a brother."

"Of course not—that's because Peter has infected you with his distorted notions."

"What's that supposed to mean?"

"Answer this for me first…do you plan on having Lynette join our luncheon again this week?"

"Yes, why wouldn't I?"

Marion rolled her eyes. "You see? Distorted notions. She is a servant…our Wednesday luncheons are for the women of this family—and only the women of this family."

Shaking her head, Anna once again beat the cucumber with her paring knife. If eating with 'undesirables' bothered her sister so much, what, Anna wondered, would Marion do if she ever learned of Lynette's divorce or Nick's jewelry theft and imprisonment? "Marion, Lynette is a part of this family—those are Papa and Mama's words as well as my own…and I plan on asking her to be my matron of honor."

"You do?" Lynette softly called from the other side of the screen door, her arms loaded with firewood.

Anna smiled with a touch of disappointment—she had wanted to ask Lynette in a much more formal—and friendly—manner. "Yes, I do…Marion, would you please open the door for her?"

"No!" Marion snapped as she stood up and crossed her arms. "I'm not the servant—she is."

"Go open the door!" Anna shouted, gesturing with her arm—and as she did, the tip of her knife caught on her sister's dress, cutting into the embroidered trim on the sleeve. "Oh, my goodness!" Anna exclaimed as she witnessed the knife's destruction. "I'm so sorry, Marion. Are you hurt?"

"You did that on purpose, Anna Helene!"

"No, I didn't, Marion," Anna replied, but her sister had already soared out of the room and down the hall, loudly shrieking about her ruined dress. "I'm definitely never going to hear the end of this one," Anna murmured. Then, tossing the knife and cucumber onto the table, she hurried over and opened the screen door for Lynette. "I'm sorry, Lyn…how…how much of that did you hear?"

Stepping over the threshold with her armload of cut wood, Lynette smiled. "Quite a bit, I'm afraid," she answered, then she headed toward the woodbox next to the stove. "Your sister has some very…rigid opinions."

"And, lately, they've become even more so," Anna put in as she grabbed some of the firewood from Lynette's stack and followed her friend to the box. "I think Marion has spent so much time with her society friends on their self-exalted plateau that she thinks she can look down on everyone else."

"If you don't want me to attend the luncheon today, I would understand," Lynette offered, dumping the lumber into the box.

Throwing her pieces of wood onto Lynette's heap, Anna grasped her friend's arm. "I want you there, Lyn—Marion's the one who shouldn't attend…I know you've been here only a short time, but in that time, you've become closer to me than my own sisters…that's why I would like you to be my matron of honor."

"Oh, Anna, that would indeed be an honor, but I'm sure that your sisters wouldn't think—"

"I don't care…I'm doing what makes me smile and makes the Lord smile—and if that makes other people frown, that's their worry, not mine."

"Even if those other people include your family?"

"Yes, even then," Doctor Spreyer proclaimed from the back door.

"Papa?" Anna questioned, surprised to see her father. Usually, it was his goal to stay far away from their weekly all-female luncheons. "Are you joining us today?"

"Just for a little while, Liebchen," the doctor responded, stepping into the room. "I was at the hospital and received this telegram."

Confused by the cryptic answer, Anna hesitantly walked toward her father and took the crinkled piece of paper from his outstretched hand. "Is it from Hans?"

"Unfortunately, no," he sighed.

Fighting back a surge of concern, Anna skimmed the words of the lengthy telegram addressed to her father. At first, the letter slandered Lynette's character, questioned her adequacy as a wife, and challenged her competency as a mother. Then it went on to discredit Lynette's trustworthiness as an employee, as a tenant, and finally, as a human being.

Horrified by the corrosive words that she knew were lies, Anna glanced at the sender's name—Redmund Chesnay. How? she inwardly asked. How could a man be so cruel to a woman that he had once promised to cherish? "Oh, my goodness," she moaned aloud.

"What's wrong?" Lynette asked. "Is it bad news?"

"No…well, yes…it's…it's from Mr. Chesnay," Anna replied, and as she said the name, her friend slumped under the weight of the news. "Do you…do you want to read it?"

With slow and labored steps, Lynette approached Anna and the menacing telegram. "I…I wrote to my family, to tell them that I had found a new home," she said, taking the paper. "I begged them to keep my whereabouts from him…how could they do this to me?"

Wiping away her tears of sympathy, Anna glanced at her father, then, reaching out, she brushed a stray wisp of Lynette's dark hair back into place. "Don't worry, it'll be all right."

"What he says isn't true," Lynette offered, her voice quivering. "But, if you want me to leave, Doctor Spreyer, I will…I'll just need time to pack and—"

"You are not going anywhere," the doctor returned in a firm, strong voice. "I know Mr. Chesnay's lying…my wife has been blessed with the gift of discernment, and I have learned to trust her intuition. She told me how good your spirit is—and how wicked his is," he continued as he motioned to the telegram. "God brought you into our family—and I would not be honoring Him if I let you leave because of that letter."

Again Anna dabbed at her tears, but this time, they were tears of admiration and relief. She knew her father was a godly man, but she had never realized how deep his devotion flowed.

"I…I could be an embarrassment to you and your family," Lynette whispered.

"Nein. Running through the street without your clothes, now that would be an embarrassment—but until you do that, we will be proud to have you in our family," Doctor Spreyer replied with a wink. "Now, I'll take my leave and say good afternoon to my other girls…then we will eat, ja?"

Anna chuckled at her father's unquenchable appetite. "I was just getting ready to dress the cucumbers, then everything will be all set."

"Wonderful," the doctor declared and departed into the hallway.

"Your father is a good man," Lynette said as she slid the malevolent letter onto the table. "But Mr. Chesnay isn't...what if he comes here?"

"He won't, Lyn."

"But you don't know Red," Lynette countered, moving to the sink to gaze out the window. "He told me that I would, someday, be his again, and now, he knows where I'm living...what if he comes and...and..."

Joining Lynette at the sink, Anna hugged her friend. "You're not alone anymore, Lyn...he would have to fight all of us first."

"That's what I'm afraid of."

"Well, Anna," Marion announced as she reentered the kitchen, examining the trim on her sleeve, "Mama was able to fix the results of your little carving accident, so you're forgiven, unless, of course, it wasn't an acci—what's wrong with the hired hand?"

Her lips tightening in anger, Anna glanced over her shoulder. Her sister's timing—and manners—were becoming thoroughly unpleasant. "Marion, just go back with the others...we're almost finished preparing the meal."

"I wish I could," Marion sighed, gliding onto the chair near the stove, "but Papa told me to come and help you finish up."

"Lyn, why don't you go out back for a bit and talk things over with God," Anna suggested. "Maybe then you'll feel—"

"She's divorced from her husband?!"

As the words crawled up her back, Anna whipped around and saw a sight that was more alarming than a hungry wolf devouring a helpless rabbit—Marion with Red Chesnay's letter in her hand. "You had no right to read—"

"I hope she's crying because Papa just dismissed her," Marion screeched and hopped up from her seat so quickly that her chair fell backward, hitting the floor with a loud clatter.

"No...and you had no right to read that telegram."

"What do you mean—no?"

"Just what I said, Mama and Papa already knew that she was divorced when they hired—"

"I see that Peter has also poisoned them with his notions!"

"Peter has nothing to do with this!"

"No? Then why else would our parents—and you—ignore the fact that this... this...this woman committed adultery and stole her son away from his father?"

"That letter is a fabrication—created by Redmund Chesnay to soil Lynette's name."

"That's the truth," Lynette put in. "I have the papers to prove—"

"You shut up, you harlot!" Marion shrieked, flinging the telegram at Lynette. "Anna, I will not allow this woman to stay in this house one moment long—"

"Marion!" Doctor Spreyer bellowed as he marched back into the kitchen. "I will decide who stays or who does not stay in this house."

"Father! You want this kind of woman to take care of Mama?"

"Yes, she is exactly the kind of woman that I want for Mama."

"What has happened to you both?" Marion hollered, her eyes darting back and forth between the doctor and Anna. "You used to know how to live respectable and proper lives."

"Please…please," Lynette begged, stepping into the middle of the feud, "I don't want to cause your family any more strife."

"So who is going to leave?" Marion demanded. "The strumpet or me?"

"Lynette is not leaving," Anna returned sharply.

"You choose a woman of…of her background over your own sister?"

"Lynette is my sister too—my sister in Christ."

"Fine!" Marion blared. "Then you can just be a family of two, because none of the other girls are going to stand for this either—I assure you!"

"Please, everyone," Lynette pleaded, "I'm not worth all this."

"Well, at least the harlot knows she's trash…why don't you, dear Sister?"

"That is quite enough!" the doctor roared.

Taking a deep breath, Marion raised her chin and glared at Anna. "If you insist on having that strumpet at your wedding—the Nealys will not be in attendance," she hissed, then, flipping her hand as if to rid herself of an insect, Marion spun around and stormed out of the kitchen.

"Oh…oh, I'm so sorry," Lynette cried.

"It's going to be all right," Anna soothed, moving over to hug her friend once again.

"No, it's not, Anna…this is only the beginning of the battle. It's just going to get worse."

Holding Lynette's hand, Anna gazed at her father, who nodded and winked in return. Both knew the forthcoming war would end much quicker than Lynette believed. Marion was a strong and determined warrior, but she was no match for the general that she was about to encounter…Irene Spreyer.

<hr />

"Move!"

Arms crossed, Nick stood in front of Manning Cole's cartload of cut lumber pieces and glared at his enemy. "I want to talk to you, Cole!" he yelled, trying to project his voice over the squealing machines.

"Well, I don't wanna talk to you," Cole snapped. "Now, move! Or I'll ram this wagon int'ya so hard it'll bust both your legs."

His eyes narrowing, Nick stepped to the side, and sweeping his hand in a large arc, he feigned submission. "Go right ahead, your majesty."

"Yeah. And don't you forget it," Cole returned smugly and leaned on the handle of his pushcart, but before he could get the load rolling, Nick kicked out his foot and shoved the cart away. "Whatd'ya think you're doing?" Cole shouted.

Now, with nothing between them but dusty air, Nick lunged at Cole and grabbed him by the collar. "What kinda stories are you spreadin' about me?"

Cole smiled wickedly, revealing a mouthful of stained, crooked teeth. "I dunno what ya mean," he offered with mock innocence.

"Yes, you do! You been tellin' everybody something because they're all afraid to come near me."

"Well, maybe it's the way ya smell," Cole sneered. "Now, lemme go, or I'll start hollerin' about your meetings with you know who."

Swallowing his escalating outrage and frustration, Nick exhaled and swore under his breath. He had shoveled himself so deeply into his dilemma that, now, even Manning Cole could blackmail him. "What have you been tellin' people?" Nick demanded, releasing his grip.

Chuckling in triumph, Cole straightened the collar of his filth-stiffened shirt. "That's better," he barked over the wailing saws.

"What've you been tellin' them?"

Cole shrugged. "Only what I heard you and Averill talkin' about yesterday."

"What we said in that dryin' room was our business—you got no right spreadin' it to…to you know who—or anybody else."

With another shrug, Cole snickered. "I ain't doin' nothin' that you ain't doing… 'cept, maybe, I'm havin' a little more fun."

Nick frowned and balled his hands into fists. "Whatd'ya mean 'fun'?"

Only a yellow-toothed grin answered him.

"Whatd'ya mean 'fun'?!" Nick raged. "What've ya been tellin' people about me?"

Obviously enjoying his reign of domination, Cole licked his lips and straightened his shoulders. "Oh, lots of stuff."

"Like what?"

"Stuff like…how, ever since you got into town, people've been missin' some of their jewels…and how, a month after you got outta prison, that jeweler you robbed turned up dead…stuff like that."

Nick blurted out a curse and raised his fist. "You blackguard! That's nothin' but humbug!"

Shrugging once again, Cole stepped closer to Nick and said in a loud, rancid-smelling whisper, "Maybe so, but folks love listenin' to it…just wait 'til I start tellin' them about how, one night a long while back, you and another fella broke into a general store in Bradlee, and when the owner heard ya and came downstairs, ya shot at him."

Nick's heart plunged into his gut and he lowered his fist. The walls of his self-made pit were crumbling down around him—and to make matters worse, the dirt was also falling upon his brother's innocent head. "You leave Pete outta this," Nick warned.

"Me? You're the one sellin' his secrets to Wild."

As soon as Cole's statement reached his ears, Nick shivered, and he quickly scanned the faces of his nearby coworkers to see if they had heard it also. But, by the men's solemn expressions, he guessed that the screech of the machines had drowned their words. "Shut up!" he hollered at Cole. "Just shut up about him!"

"What's the matter?" Cole taunted, his voice growing steadily louder. "Don't ya want ever'body to know that you're partners with James Wi—"

Immediately, Nick swung his fist at Cole's mouth, cutting off his opponent's badgering and sending him to the floor.

As he propped himself on his elbow, Manning Cole wiped at the blood streaming from the corner of his mouth. "You wanna fight, Anderson? I'll give ya one, that's for sure!" Cole snorted, then, in one motion, he scrambled up from the floor and rushed at Nick.

Leaping aside, Nick, once again, thrust out his leg. Although he saw the maneuver, Cole couldn't slow his momentum, and tripping over the obstacle, he returned to the factory's wooden floor with a thud.

"All...right!" Cole breathlessly called as he seized a handful of sawdust and pushed himself up. "I've...had...enough!"

Noticing that the other workers had stepped away from their saws and formed a curious but alarmed audience, Nick blew out a long breath—the fight was only confirming the image Cole had painted of him. "Okay," Nick yelled to Cole, then, to his fellow laborers, he offered, "just a misunderstanding...everything's fine now."

After a few unsure moments, the men slowly headed back to their machines. And, with a relieved sigh, Nick scanned his surroundings and finally located his enemy, who was now standing near one of the saws.

"Look, I don't wanna fight ya," Nick said as he approached Cole, "I just—"

Without warning, Manning Cole charged toward him and whipped a handful of sawdust at his face. Completely blinded by the minute missiles, Nick felt a hard fist hit him in the gut, then the jaw, then the gut again. As he struggled to block the continuing unseen punches, Nick violently wiped at his eyes, trying to brush away the excruciating particles. Then, after what seemed like hours, the blows to his body subsided and his sight finally cleared—just in time to see a piece of lumber sweeping toward his chest. Darting to the left, Nick ducked, but unfortunately, not low enough, and the board grazed the side of his head, forcing him to the ground.

Looking up at the twirling ceiling and overhead lights that swam around and around, Nick groaned and clutched his throbbing skull. "Nobody hits me!" Cole's face echoed as it hovered over him. "Nobody!" Suddenly, a kick came to his kidneys…and another…and another. As Nick and his body cried out in pain, the jabs abruptly ceased, and he was yanked to his feet and thrown against a counter, landing hard on his bruised back.

"I'm gunna make sure ya don't hit nobody ever again!" Cole seethed, pressing his elbow into Nick's throat. "You hear me?"

Twisting from side to side, Nick wrestled against his captor, but between his injured head and compressed windpipe, he had no strength, and Cole's grimy body kept him pinned to the counter. Barely able to breathe, Nick glanced to his right, and instantly, his dazed mind realized an awful truth…

He wasn't leaning against a counter…he was leaning against a saw. And, even though the sawyer had disengaged the machine's leather belt from the overhead power shaft, the extreme nearness of the slumbering blade sent a twitch through him.

"I said, did ya hear me?" Cole insisted as he reached up and shoved a lever to the side, immediately waking the sleeping saw. "You ain't gunna hit nobody again…'cept, maybe, with a stump."

His eyes widening in terror, Nick fought to escape from his tormentor's hold, but Cole just jabbed his elbow in deeper, making it impossible for Nick to draw in a breath. Please, Peter, help me, Nick silently wailed—but his brother didn't come— and all he could do was watch Manning Cole shove his upper right arm closer and closer to the spinning blade…

Then flesh and metal met.

Nick tried to scream out, but he couldn't even get a whimper past Cole's vise-like grip on his neck. And, as tears of agony and anguish filled his eyes, Nick turned his face away from the imminent amputation. How? he wondered as his air-starved thoughts started to blur. How could he work on his watches without his hand?

Abruptly, as if a huge eagle had descended from above, he felt Cole being lifted up and off him. Gasping and coughing, Nick pulled what he hoped was his whole right arm to his chest and slid to the floor. Air, he inwardly cheered, finally, some air. Slowly, his choking eased, and propping himself against the leg of the saw, Nick hesitantly glanced down at his damaged limb. Although covered with blood and sawdust, it was still intact—the blade had not even reached the bone. Smiling in relief, he leaned his head back. Thankfully, all he'd have to live with was another scar.

As his thoughts continued to clear, Nick drew in some deep breaths and surveyed the area around him—and for the first time since he had been freed, he realized that another battle had erupted. Peter, obviously the 'huge eagle from above,' was pummeling Manning Cole's face and body while Jaxson and some other factory workers struggled to pull him away.

"I'll see you hang if you hurt him!" Peter roared as he was dragged from Cole.

Spitting out a mouthful of blood, Cole hung onto one of the machines for support. "He started it! Ask anybody—Anderson hit me for no reason."

"But you're the one who tried to cut off his arm!" Peter raged, fighting against the men holding him. "And I'm going to make sure you pay for it…somebody go find a patrolman, so we can get this piece of sludge behind bars!"

Although he appreciated his brother's protection and concern, Nick still flinched at the idea of having a herd of patrolmen tramping through the factory…asking questions…and hearing what Manning Cole had to say…

"No, Pete," Nick called out hoarsely as he leaned forward. "I'm okay."

Glancing over his shoulder, Peter stared at Nick as if he had spoken in a foreign language. "Nick, he tried to—"

"I know," Nick rasped, "but I'm okay…no police…please?"

Peter sighed in exasperation, then nodded. "Pack up your stuff, Cole…you're fired."

"Fired? I told ya, he started the whole thing."

"I don't care…I want you out of my factory—now!"

"I bet things would be diff'rent if he weren't your brother," Cole muttered.

With a sudden, glacial calmness, Peter twisted away from the men restraining him and walked over to Cole. "I would fire any employee—even my brother—if he held another man's arm against a running saw blade. Now…get…out!"

"What about my pay?"

Clenching his teeth, Peter peered into Cole's crusted eyes. "You just donated your wages to get his arm fixed," he growled. Then, without waiting for a retort, Peter spun around, ran over to Nick, and knelt in front of him. "Are you sure you're all right?"

"Yeah."

"Nick, please let me get a patrolman. Cole shouldn't get away with—"

"No," Nick coughed, "no, patrolmen…not with my background."

With an expression of frustration and understanding, Peter nodded again. "All right…now let me see what he did to you," he returned as he tried to examine the injury.

At first, Nick fought to keep his wound hidden, but as he studied his brother's careworn features, he surrendered and uncovered his arm—he was truly beginning to enjoy the nurturing.

"It's better than I thought it'd be, but you're still gnawed up pretty badly," Peter offered, removing his waistcoat. "I better get you to the doctor right away."

"I can go by myself," Nick replied, surprised by his own heroism.

Peter laughed with a touch of skepticism and ripped the waistcoat's lining out. "You're not leaving here without help," he said, then he bandaged Nick's arm with the lining material.

"But they need you here."

Peter shook his head. "Nothing—not even this factory—is more important than making sure you're okay."

Swallowing hard, Nick averted his gaze before Peter could see the tears welling up in his eyes. "Let Billy walk me to the hospital," he murmured, "then you don't have to leave."

"You're as stubborn as Daven and your father," Peter chuckled as he rose to his feet and pulled Nick up with him.

"So are you," Nick chided in reply.

Peter grinned and suddenly hugged him—briefly but firmly. "Thank God you're okay," he whispered in Nick's ear before he let go.

Confused by the first real hug he had ever experienced, Nick just stood motionless. Even though the gesture hurt his injuries, he still found himself warmed by it—and by his brother's loyalty. Now, all he had to do was keep Peter from ever learning about his betrayal.

If only he hadn't allowed his bitterness to push Peter away when they first met in Willow Ridge…if only he hadn't allowed his greed to listen to the clink of James Wild's gold coins…if only he hadn't allowed his selfishness to dig such a deep chasm that was burying him alive…if only…

Seated on the third step of the porch stairs, Lynette absently gazed into the Spreyers' backyard. Then, wiping her tear-swollen face, she examined, for the countless time, the harsh scribbles on the worn piece of paper in her hand. Why? she asked herself. Why did her family betray her trust and tell Red where she was? Did they really want her to return to a man who had constantly beat her down—both physically and emotionally? Suddenly, the tears began to flow again, and Lynette hugged her waist and bowed her head. She truly cherished her new home, and the thought of leaving hurt as much as Red Chesnay's piercing words.

"Lyn?"

Snapping alert, Lynette peered up—and immediately, her eyes widened in alarm. "Nick! Oh, my goodness!" she exclaimed as she surveyed his chafed neck, battered body, and blood-stained clothes.

"It looks worse than it is," he said hoarsely, easing himself down next to her.

"I'll get the doctor," she offered as she grabbed the railing to pull herself up.

"Not yet."

"But you need help," Lynette countered, rising to her feet.

"First, tell me why you were crying."

With a long sigh, Lynette slowly settled back on the stoop. "Doctor Spreyer received this today," she replied and held out the wrinkled telegram.

As Nick leaned over and hesitantly plucked the paper from her grasp with his left hand, he winced and tried to stifle a moan.

"Oh, you poor dear! I better get the doctor for you."

Drawing his bloody arm to his chest, Nick shook his head. "In a minute," he rasped.

"How did you get hurt?"

"I, uh, I had a…a disagreement with one of the men at the factory."

"It must have been a terrible disagreement."

"Yeah."

"You're very lucky that the doctor came home for lunch today. He's not usually here on Wednesdays."

Nick chuckled wryly. "If there's anything I'm not, it's lucky…they told us at the hospital that the doc went home for his noontime-dinner."

"Us? Is Peter with you?"

"He tried to be," Nick returned, his voice low and pained, "but I told him to stay at the factory…so he made one of the luggers usher me around instead."

"That's because he cares about you."

"Yeah, I guess he does," Nick murmured and bowed his head.

"You may not think that you're a lucky person, Nick," Lynette put in, dabbing her eyes with a handkerchief, "but you are…you're very lucky to have a family that is so concerned about your welfare."

"Family?" Nick echoed as he tilted his head to look at her. "I have a…a…a half-stepbrother—that ain't a family."

Lynette sniffled in a deep, quivering breath. "Sure it is…and believe me, it's better to have one loyal 'half-stepbrother,' than a whole brood that betrays you."

"What…whatd'ya mean?"

"I sent a letter to my family—just to let them know where I was and how William and I were doing…my family and I haven't been on the best of terms since my divorce, and I wanted to mend the rift between us…I ended my letter as I always do…'please don't reveal my whereabouts to anyone—especially Mr. Chesnay'…that," she stated, gesturing toward the telegram, "is their response to my request."

Nick studied the paper for what seemed like an eternity, then his hand started to tremble, and unwillingly, he looked up and gazed at Lynette with an expression of worry and shame.

As she observed Nick's reaction to the telegram's message, Lynette's hope unraveled. Of all the people in her life, she was sure that Nick would disregard Red Chesnay's brackish words and remain her ally. If only he knew that she had done the same for him…that she had chosen to overlook his background after Anna secretly told her about his imprisonment…if he knew that, then, maybe, he would be more forgiving…

"None of it's true, Nick…please don't believe what he says," she moaned and covered her face with her hands.

"I don't believe nothin' that's written here," Nick replied, barely audible.

Cautiously, Lynette lowered her arms and stared into his azure eyes, which were now clouded over with…with…no, she had to be wrong, she inwardly told herself. Why would Nick be embarrassed?

"I can't read," he choked out as if answering her thought.

Lynette smiled wide and her spirit began to knit back together. "What a relief."

"It's a relief I can't read?"

"Yes—I thought you read the letter and believed what it said about me."

"What does it say…what'd your family do?"

"They told Mr. Chesnay of my whereabouts, which, I realize now, they've done every time I've written to them…and he, in turn, sent that telegram to Doctor Spreyer—just as he has to all my other employers and landlords."

Scanning the text again, Nick scowled and shook the page as though trying to force the words to speak. "But what does it say?!"

"It says that I'm an evil person…and promiscuous…and irresponsible…and that I kidnapped my son," Lynette returned, and as she finished, she closed her eyes, trying to hold back the tears. "Why did they tell Mr. Chesnay?" As she silently pondered her question, Lynette felt Nick stroke her hair. And, after a moment of enjoying his gentle touch, her eyes fluttered open, and she searched his kind, wounded features.

"I'd never believe those things—no matter who said them—because I know they ain't true," he whispered.

Lynette nodded gratefully. Nick was proving to be the friend she needed him to be. "Other people have believed them, though—Anna's sisters, for example…a feud's been going on here this afternoon…and it's my fault."

"I don't understand."

"There's now a hedge between Anna and her sisters—namely me and my reputation."

"You're not to blame," Nick countered in a gritty voice. "It's Chesnay's fault for spreadin' lies and your family's for tellin' him where you were."

Lynette grinned sadly as Nick reached over and brushed a freshly fallen tear from her cheek with his thumb.

"Do you see now," she questioned softly, "why I would prefer to have one brother like Peter, than a whole family like mine?"

"Yeah," Nick murmured, and leaning in close, he tilted his head and kissed her on the lips.

At first, Lynette didn't move, surprised by the unexpected gesture. But, as Nick's caress continued, a tingle spread through her body—one she had never experienced before—and she lightly touched the side of his face and returned the kiss. Then, as Lynette found herself sliding into Nick's embrace, the events of the day tapped her on the shoulder and she jerked away.

"I…I'm sorry," Nick offered quietly, pulling back. "I shouldn't have done that—not without askin' you first."

As the heat of a blush engulfed her, Lynette looked, once again, into Nick's bright-blue eyes. "I…I didn't mind," she returned, stunned by her own boldness. "I just…I just can't right now."

"Why?"

"Because Red knows where I am."

"What's he got to do with it—you ain't his anymore."

"But he thinks I am. I know him…he's writing those letters to exhaust me—so I'll return to him. And, if that tactic doesn't work—which it won't—he may come after me."

"He won't come near you…not while I'm around."

"Oh, Nick," she said with a warm smile, "you can't stand guard over me every minute of every day."

"Sure I can."

"No…that's what Mr. Chesnay used to do, and I just couldn't live in that kind of prison again."

With a long sigh, Nick nodded and massaged the scars on his cheek. "I can understand that…you must really hate your family for tellin' him about you."

Glancing at Nick's now hardened expression, Lynette shook her head. "I'm disappointed that they failed me again, but I don't hate them—I gave up that grudge long ago, when I forgave them all for abandoning me when I filed for a divorce."

"Whatd'ya mean you forgave them?"

"I mean just that—I forgave them."

"But…but they've done such rotten things to ya…and you still forgive them?"

"Yes—even Mr. Chesnay. I had to release the hate I was keeping inside me—it was corrupting my soul, curdling my thoughts, and clogging my heart."

"But they hurt you."

"Jesus forgives all those who hurt Him…if I'm going to be a follower of His, I need to do the same."

"So...so it's really possible to pardon somebody who betrayed ya?" Nick asked, scratching his head.

"Sure...why don't you think so? Haven't you ever forgiven anyone?"

Nick glanced away and said nothing.

Saddened by his response, Lynette cradled Nick's left hand between hers and squeezed it tight. His spirit was gorged with bitterness, and she knew it would continue to eat away at him, unless she could show him a more blessed path. "It can sometimes be a difficult thing to do, but forgiveness is always possible," she tried.

"What about Pete? You think he could show mercy to a traitor?"

"Anna told me that he's already forgiven a great many people who have hurt him."

Jerking away from Lynette's grasp, he whispered, "Ya think he has room for one more name on that list?"

Her eyes narrowing, Lynette shifted her position on the stoop so she could study Nick's features. "Who?"

"Me."

"Why? What have you done?" she inquired as her pulse quickened. Was her unvoiced fear from Monday night truly justified?

"I lied to ya the other day...you remember when I told ya that I didn't take Wild's offer to snitch on Pete?"

Lynette gasped—yes, the fear was justified. "I remember."

"I lied—I did agree...actually, what ya heard was him offerin' me more money... I've been workin' for Wild all along."

"Oh, Nick," Lynette groaned.

"I don't wanna do it no more, but Wild's threatenin' to tell Pete if I stop."

Once again, Lynette grabbed Nick's hand, and bringing it to her lips, she gave it a light kiss. Although she was frustrated with his incessant lies, she was still thankful that the Lord had heard her prayer—Nick's eyes had been opened, and he had been guided away from James Wild. "On Monday, when I heard Peter say that you were asking all kinds of questions about the factory," she told him, "I was afraid that you were helping Mr. Wild—and I almost warned Peter about it."

"Almost? Then you didn't?"

"No...that was when Mr. Wild came to call on Anna."

"Oh."

"But now, I understand why God allowed me to be interrupted...He wants me to stand by my words from Sunday—it's your responsibility to talk to Peter and let him know what's happened."

"I...I can't..."

"Nick, if you did, it would break the tether that Mr. Wild has around you... maybe that's why the Lord wants you to face your brother."

Nick gritted his teeth. "Pete would never forgive me for what I've done…and I don't blame him—I wouldn't forgive me."

"It can sometimes be a difficult thing to do, but forgiveness is always possible," she offered, hoping that her repeated words would finally penetrate Nick's stubborn resolve. "It'll take time for Peter to heal, and he may lose confidence in you for a little while, but it would help if you confessed…it would be so much harder if he heard it from Mr. Wild."

"I dunno," he mumbled and twisted his hand out of her embrace.

Maybe it was the pain of his injuries or maybe she had crammed too many details into his head—either way, Lynette sensed that she was losing Nick's attention. Knowing that he might shut his ears to her words at any time, she tried one last attempt to minister to him. "It might help," she added, "if you forgave someone who hurt you…then you would know it was possible."

"Whatd'ya mean?"

"Well, you don't believe that Peter can pardon you because you've never released any of your grudges. If you did, it might help you realize that it is possible…try forgiving the Denglers for not being the family you needed them to be…or try forgiving Lydia and that man Cass for their treatment of you…or try forgiving yourself for stealing that comb…"

"How…how do you know about those things?"

Covering her mouth with her fingers, Lynette's eyes opened wide. In her impatience to turn Nick onto a different path, she had forgotten to check her words before speaking them…

"And, maybe," she continued softly, "you could try forgiving Anna and me for chattering about things that should have been kept to ourselves."

"Then you…you know 'bout me bein' in prison?"

Although she heard a slight jingling behind her, Lynette focused all her attention on Nick's anxious and troubled features. "Yes. I'm sorry, Nick…I apologize for Anna and for myself. We really weren't gossiping about you, we were just talking—it's just our way of learning how to accept news that we aren't always prepared to hear."

"You know about it all? Cass and Lydia and the jewelry store?"

Biting her lower lip, Lynette nodded, worried that her slip of the tongue had just shattered any good their discussion had accomplished.

"And you still let me kiss you?"

Lynette gazed at Nick in disbelief—it was amazing how differently their thoughts had journeyed. "Nick, you were a foolish young man, and you made a terrible mistake that you, unfortunately, had to go to prison for…why would that make me reject your kiss?"

"Because, when most people hear that I'm a thief, they grab their handbags and wallets and run the other way."

"When most people hear that I'm divorced, they lift their noses into the air and run the other way."

Nick chuckled cynically. "I guess we got a lot in common, huh?" he remarked as he absently fingered the scars on his left cheek.

"That's where you got those, isn't it? While you were in jail."

Nick nodded. "One of the inmates—he called himself Hannibal the Bear—liked fighting, and I…I don't even know what I did, but he smashed up a stool durin' a meal and came after me with the splintered end of one of the legs."

"I'm sorry, Nick."

"I'll tell ya somethin'…all I ever wanted to do was please Lydia—but if I knew that breakin' into that jewelry shop and stealin' that fancy hair comb was gunna cause me so much grief, I would've never—"

"I think I have heard quite enough from you two!"

Instantly, Lynette's back stiffened—she was becoming very familiar with the shrill voice that squawked at her from behind. Glancing over her shoulder, Lynette groaned. "Marion." Only now did she realize that she should have paid more attention to the jingling that she had heard before.

"Mama orders me to be civil and apologize—and I come out here and find the two of you bragging about all your crimes and lustful behavior!"

Quickly, Lynette stood up and faced her steaming accuser. "Marion, we were—"

"Address me as any servant should—I am Mrs. Nealy, you…you harlot."

"Don't talk to her like that!" Nick growled as he unsteadily rose to his feet.

"Keep your distance!" Marion hollered, pointing her finger at Nick. "Now, it all makes sense…all your talk about fixing our watches was just a ploy, so you could break into our store and steal our jewels away!"

"I don't care nothin' about—"

"Just forget about that job my husband offered you. And I want the tools he loaned you returned at once!"

"But I ain't finished with—"

"At once! But don't you dare set foot into our store—leave them here."

"What's all the yelling about?!" Doctor Spreyer bellowed as he and Anna walked out onto the back porch.

"Oh, Nick, what happened?!" Anna exclaimed. "Come in, right away, and Papa will take a look at—"

"And you!" Marion screeched, turning toward Anna. "You knew that he was a convict, didn't you?"

"Marion, now is not the time—Nick's hurt. He needs—"

"You have an awful habit of bringing strays into this family!" Marion cut in and gestured toward Nick and Lynette.

"Strays?"

"Strays!" Marion blared. "First it was Peter, he's brought—"

"Peter?!"

"Yes, Peter! He's brought nothing but scandal and danger to our family…then it was Jaxson and all those foreigners at that disgraceful factory…now, it's these two! A divorced strumpet and a convicted thief! You have allowed this family to be disgraced, Anna Helene!"

"That is quite enough, Marion Bertha!" Doctor Spreyer hollered as he glared at his daughter. "You are the one disgracing this family! I raised my children to behave with Christian charity and love—and you are displaying neither of them right now."

"But Papa, he's a crim—"

"He's a man who is obviously hurt and in need of my help…and he is also a member of our family. I suggest you start treating Nick—and Lynette—as you wish to be treated." Pausing for a moment, the doctor sighed heavily and added another few lines of sternly spoken German. Then, stepping toward Nick, he extended his hand. "Come, Nikolaus, and I'll see to your wounds."

Wearily, Nick climbed up the few steps to the veranda, but before shuffling over the threshold, he circled and glanced at Lynette. "Is she," he muttered, tilting his head toward Marion, "an example of when it can sometimes be a difficult thing to do?"

With a surprised grin, Lynette nodded in return. Maybe her words about forgiveness had permeated deeper into Nick's soul than she had thought.

⁕⁂⁕

"You look dreadful," James Wild offered with a sarcastic lilt. "And I do find it interesting that Manning Cole was the victor in your encounter."

"Yeah, well," Nick returned, shifting positions on his velvet chair, "it's amazin' how the odds change when you get a face full of sawdust and hit on the head with a hunk of wood."

"I understand that Cole's position at the factory was terminated because of the skirmish."

"No, Pete fired him 'cause he tried to saw my arm in two!" Nick rasped out.

"Do not take your frustrations out on me," Wild reprimanded, then swallowed a mouthful of his nightcap. "Now, I want you to arrange for Cole to be rehired."

"What?"

"Inform Peter that it was your fault—that you antagonized Cole to the point that he defended himself the only way his meager brain knew how."

"Pete's not gunna believe that."

"Excuse me?"

"He's not gunna believe that."

"Try that one more time—in English."

Nick sighed and gritted his teeth. Between the banging in his head and the throbbing stitches in his arm, he had no desire to play Wild's game. "Pete won't believe a story like that."

"Well, you had better hope that he does."

"Why?"

"Because, if Peter does not rehire Cole, you will be required to perform his duties."

"And what, exactly, were Cole's duties?"

"We shall discuss that when, and if, the need arises."

"Fine," Nick murmured resignedly, too exhausted to argue. "Can I go now?"

"Go? We have not even begun to discuss the events of the day."

"The events of the day? Let's see...Cole almost cut off my arm, then I spent the rest of my time at the doctor's house until Pete came for supper and drove me home—those are the events of the day."

Wild downed the rest of his drink and set the empty glass on the table next to him. "Ah ha...well, tomorrow I want you to be more vigilant."

"I can't work with this!" Nick snarled, motioning to his right arm, which now hung in a sling.

"Your excuses are becoming tiresome, Anderson—just be at Peter's side tomorrow. He will receive some very disturbing news, and I want a full description of how he reacts to both messages."

Nick's heart sank. "News? Who from?"

"At my recommendation, the Oak Park Men's Club in Grand Rapids has positively decided to cancel their furniture order."

Moaning, Nick lowered his eyes. Lynette was wrong—it would never be possible for Peter to forgive him. Then, suddenly, Wild's words sprang back into his thoughts, and Nick's head snapped upright. "Whatd'ya mean 'both messages'?"

"The correct pronunciation is 'what do you mean.' I am growing extremely weary of your plebeian utterances. You will eliminate this horrible method of communicating that you have adopted—or you will start compensating me for having to listen to it."

"I'll what?"

"Every time you 'don't talk good,' you will pay me...let us make it...a dollar. Perhaps that will be the incentive you need to speak like a gentleman."

Nick swallowed hard and rubbed his aching neck—even Hannibal the Bear had been easier to deal with than Wild. "I ain't got...I don't have...I did not have the schooling you had. I don't...do not know how to talk like you."

"Then I suggest you learn…now, what was your question?"

With a scowl, Nick shook his head—he had completely forgotten what he had wanted to know, then the words, once again, came crashing back. "Whatd'ya…what did you mean when you said 'both messages'?"

Wild snickered and intertwined his fingers. "You are such an entertaining pawn…I want a full description of how Peter reacts to—one, the news of the men's club cancellation, and two, the news that every board foot of oak in Willow Ridge has been purchased by someone else."

"So you went ahead and did that too, huh."

"No, I did not…my associate, Mr. Dearborn, made those arrangements. Tomorrow should be quite a stimulating day for Peter."

Massaging the scars on his face, Nick exhaled in exasperation. His pit just kept getting deeper and deeper and…

"Now, Anderson, is there anything else that you wish to discuss before you empty your pockets and depart for the evening?"

"Yes," Nick croaked out as fatigue started to blur his thoughts. "Can we change the time of this meeting to something earlier? Pete's startin' to ask, uh, Pete is starting to ask all kinds of questions. I keep telling him that I'm…that I am going to the tavern, but…"

"But?"

"But that lie's gettin' too hard to tell…I don't wanna go to the tavern no more, but I have to 'cause Pete's gotta smell the liquor on me, or he'll really start to wonder where I go every night."

"Hmm," Wild returned, moistening his lips, "within that explanation, you have just accumulated nine dollars worth of errors."

Nick rubbed his hand over his face in defeat. "I don't…do not have that much with me."

"Then I will expect payment tomorrow evening when you deliver your report at eleven-thirty."

As Jaxson reached the top of the showroom stairs, he heard the sounds of a debate emanating from Peter's office—complete with arguments, rebuttals, cheers, and grumblings. Knocking on the doorjamb, Jaxson waited for a moment, then, still unnoticed, he stepped into the room and surveyed the faces of the five men responsible for the commotion. Peter, perched on the edge of his desk, rubbed his neck and 'uh huhed' as Del and Josef, their dual bookkeepers, and Hermann, their prized band sawyer, argued about an issue that was still undiscernible. And, finally, standing by the window—occasionally anteing up his opinion—was Nick.

Or was it Daven, Jaxson wondered for a few eerie and timeless seconds. Nick's resemblance to Daven was already uncanny, but now…now, it was practically impossible to distinguish between the two half-brothers. The bruises from Nick's beating were so similar to the injuries Daven had received during his last days that Jaxson wondered if God had a plan for it all. And he also wondered if Nick's evolving appearance was producing the same thoughts in Peter's head.

"What's goin' on?" Jaxson inquired, but the flood of voices drowned his query in mid-air. "What's going on?!" he barked out again, getting the same result. Finally, Jaxson waved his arms until Peter met his gaze. 'What's going on?' he soundlessly mouthed to his friend.

This time an answer came—Peter held up a sheet of paper and shook his head.

'What is it?' Jaxson returned, letting only his lips ask the question.

"A telegram from Emerson," Peter announced, and suddenly, the din began to fade. "The men's club canceled."

"Oh, no," Jaxson murmured in the now quiet office.

"But Emerson is trying to get the order back," Del Franz explained.

"And you know Em," Josef put in. "He can talk anybody into anything."

"That much is true," Jaxson offered as he stepped over to Peter. Then, taking the telegram, he perused the terse message.

"Those men have changed their minds as often as a woman does when she's choosing a hat," Del said.

"And they'll change it back again," Josef added, finishing his father's thought.

"I suppose," Peter replied with a nod. "But the last time I telegraphed MacColl, I told him to send some oak along with the rest of our maple—so we could start on the club's furniture…now, we're buying wood we don't need."

Although Jaxson's shoulders sagged with the same oppressing worry that plagued Peter, he knew he had to buoy his friend's outlook or they'd both sink. "Peter, look how God's converted every bad turn we've had into a good one…He knows about this, and He'll make it right too."

"That's correct," Hermann chimed in. "And things are getting better every day."

Trying to hide his brimming joy, Jaxson wiped at his face and tilted his head toward Hermann. "Did you tell him yet?"

"Tell me what?" Peter asked apprehensively.

"Nein," the wiry German returned, looking at Jaxson. "Emerson's note arrived before I did, and I haven't had the chance."

"What're you two talking about?" Peter persisted.

"I asked Jaxson," Hermann went on as a small grin crept onto his face, "if I could be excused from my station, so I could tell you face-to-face."

"Tell me what?!"

"My brothers and their families are arriving on Saturday's train!" the small, spry German proclaimed, his grin exploding into a wide, toothy smile. "They can start work on Monday."

Peter's jaw dropped and his eyes darted from Hermann, to Jaxson, and back again. "Really?"

Hermann yelped out a chuckle. "I would never joke about such a thing."

"But do they really want to start working so soon? Don't they want to settle in first?"

"Nein, nein…they want to help right away—and they're very sorry that their journey took so long."

Laughing, Peter reached out and shook Hermann's hand. "You, my friend, definitely know how to cheer a person up!"

"That's why I wanted to tell you myself," Hermann replied as he motioned to Peter's mirthful expression. "It's been a long time since I've seen such delight in your eyes."

Peter half-smiled and pulled in a deep breath. "Yeah, I guess it has."

"That's wonderful news!" Del put in, rocking back on his heels. "See, Peter? God is definitely watching over us."

"Yes, He is," Jaxson agreed, crumpling their note of bad news into a ball. "And He's watchin' over the factory too. Everything's gunna be different now that Manning Cole's gone…I just found out that he was causin' some of our troubles."

"What?! How?!" Peter questioned, his eyes narrowing.

Tossing the scrunched up telegram onto the desk, Jaxson answered, "The Jaye girls just told me that Cole was talkin' to them and Benjamin yesterday mornin'—right before his fight with Nick. He kept tryin' to get them to leave our factory and go work for the Sullivan and Smith Furniture Company in Grand Rapids—for a lot more money…I think that's what happened to Miller and Jennings. They let it slip that they were going some place that paid more."

"Grand Rapids, huh?" Peter returned as his jaw clamped down tight. "Now, I really regret sending Cole over to you that day."

"Don't go blamin' yourself for this—I'm the one who hired him," Jaxson said with a shake of his head, "and kept him on too."

"You know," Peter continued, "we also told everyone—including Cole—that we were going to be starting on the men's club order."

"Are you sayin' Cole had somethin' to do with them canceling?

"Uh huh. You read the telegram, Jax…'we regret to inform you that, after speaking with another furniture maker, we have chosen to place our order elsewhere.'"

Jaxson chuckled at the apparent joke, then, realizing that his friend was utterly serious, he frowned. "You think they talked to Cole? Our thick-headed, sour-smelling Manning Cole?"

"No, I think they talked to the person who hired him to ruin us."

"Who?"

Silence.

"Sakes alive, you think it's Wild—don't ya?" Jaxson asked, although he already knew the answer.

Peter nodded. "It would be just like him to do something like this. Cole probably told Wild about every move we made, and little Jimmy, in turn, starts throwing his money around, causing all kinds of trouble for us. Then I bet Wild figured he could just swoop in and offer to relieve our financial woes—as a partner, of course."

Jaxson sighed and leaned on the desk. Either he was tired of fighting Peter on the issue or his friend's accusations were becoming more convincing—because he, too, was beginning to believe in Wild's guilt. "God just keeps turnin' things around for us," Jaxson remarked, feeling his own anxiety melt away. "The Lord got Cole outta the factory before he could do any real damage."

"Not quite," Nick interjected from his place at the window, raising his bandaged arm. "I call this 'real damage.'"

"I didn't mean it like that," Jaxson moaned, weary of Nick's sensitive tendencies. "I meant that the Lord got Cole outta our lives before he got the chance to do alotta damage—I know he hurt your arm real bad…I'm sorry."

Nick walked over to the desk. "It's okay," he offered with a shrug.

Jaxson stared at Nick and considered the good-natured reaction. Was the man's attitude really mellowing? Or was his relaxed demeanor only a ploy?

"You're right about Cole bein' a snitch, though," Nick put in as he rubbed the scars on his cheek.

"Why?" both Jaxson and Peter queried in unison.

"He listened at the door when Jaxson and me were talkin' in the drying room the other day—he heard everything."

"How do you know that?" Jaxson questioned, his brow furrowing with suspicion.

"Uh, because he, uh, he told me he did…Cole was braggin' about it, uh, at the saloon Tuesday night. He's been tellin' people about me bein' in prison. And he's been addin' stuff to the story…he's sayin' that I went back and killed that jeweler after I got out and that I'm stealin' from everybody here in town."

"It's true," Hermann said, casting a cautious eye toward Nick.

"None of it's true!"

Instantly, the little German took a step back. "I meant it's true that he's spreading those stories."

"Oh," Nick murmured, then, bowing his head, he added, "that's what our fight was about yesterday—I told him to stop tellin' his tales."

Peter shook his head. "I'm glad that man's out of our midst…Hermann, I'd appreciate it if you'd let the other workers know that Cole's rumors were just fabrications."

Hermann nodded but said nothing.

"The prison part is true," Nick offered to the wary German. "I served two years for tryin' to steal a fancy hair comb for a girl. But I didn't kill that jeweler—you can go talk to the man, if you want to…and I'd never do anything that would put me back in prison."

At first, Hermann just stood still, peering into Nick's pale eyes, then he smiled. "Manning Cole constantly spoke out against us immigrants and against Jaxson and the Jayes. Everything that came out of his mouth was a foul and vicious lie…knowing all of that, I don't know why we believed what he said about you—but we did…forgive us, Nikolaus."

Nick gritted his teeth and laughed as if an angel had whispered a joke in his ear. "Yeah, sure," he choked out, "you're…you're forgiven."

Hermann's smile swelled. "Good! I'll tell everyone at the factory that we were wrong—that you are someone who can be trusted."

Nick adjusted his sling and looked away. "Thanks," he mumbled in return.

"Well," the wiry German announced, "I should get back to my station."

"And so should we," Del Franz said, motioning to his son. "We have plenty of—"

"Excuse me," came a call from the door.

Instantly, all six men turned their attention toward the uniformed boy in the doorway.

"I have a telegram for Peter Leighton," the delivery boy went on, wiggling the message back and forth.

"I'm beginning to hate those words," Peter whispered as he pushed himself from the desk and reluctantly ambled over to the youngster.

As Jaxson watched Peter slowly peel open the note, he held his breath and prayed. Please Lord, he inwardly begged, please let this be good news for a change. Then, just as Jaxson finished his voiceless plea, Peter looked up, his expression a mix of dread and amazement.

"What's wrong?" Del asked.

Peter opened his mouth to speak, but nothing emerged.

Jaxson's shoulders instantly slumped. "It's not good—is it?"

"I don't know," Peter sighed. "It's from Logan MacColl…he says that Wit Dearborn, the same bald man who tried to cancel my order, came to buy every piece of oak in his lumberyard—for double the asking price."

A multivoiced grumble echoed throughout the room.

"But he refused to sell it," Peter replied, laughing in disbelief.

"What?!" Nick exclaimed.

"Yeah...MacColl says that he was leery of Dearborn and told him to vamoose."

"Why would anybody give up all that money?" Nick murmured incredulously.

The corners of Peter's mouth turned upward. "Because, when you follow God's will, you sometimes have to sacrifice things like that. The world may think you're crazy as a loon—but knowing that the Lord's smiling at you makes it all worth it."

"Does MacColl say anything about the rest of the maple we ordered?" Jaxson questioned as he offered up a silent 'hallelujah' for their glorious fortune.

"Yep. It—and the oak—should arrive late tomorrow."

"Now, do you believe that God's watching over us?" Del put in, shaking his finger at Peter.

"Yeah, I do."

❦ ❧ ❦

It was amazing, Nick thought. He had spent just a few evening suppers with Peter, the Spreyers, William, and of course, Lynette—yet he had grown to enjoy the nightly meals and lively conversation. He even found himself laughing and joining in. It was all so different than anything he had ever experienced...different and warm and wonderful...and he knew he wanted to become a permanent part of the devoted group that surrounded him. It was absolutely amazing, he inwardly repeated, shaking his head.

Then, as he picked at his precut food with an awkward, left-handed hold on his fork, Nick realized that this supper was unlike the others. Tension and dismay hovered over the kitchen table, stifling everyone's voice—even William's. This was the kind of gathering he was used to...silent and strained...where only the clink of flatware could be heard. It was also the kind of gathering he now wanted no part of.

"It's so quiet tonight," Irene Spreyer announced as if she had sensed Nick's thoughts. "The food is delicious, but that usually doesn't stop this family from talking."

Everyone nodded, but the stillness continued.

"This bread is very good, Lynette," the doctor put in. "Will you be making some to sell at the market?"

"No," Lynette murmured. "I won't be...we're going to be—"

"Lyn's decided to leave on Saturday," Anna cut in, her voice drenched with sadness.

"Leave?!" Nick exclaimed. Only he could have this kind of luck, he moaned to himself.

"Why, dear Lynette?" Mrs. Spreyer asked.

"It's just best that we move on...I don't want Mr. Chesnay to come here and cause any trouble for you."

"He's not the reason and you know it," Anna countered. Then, to the others, she explained, "It's because of Marion. She came by today and started hollering at Lyn again—and right in front of William."

"When?" Irene questioned, her voice unusually agitated. "I never heard her come in."

Anna placed her fork on her plate, then pushed the dish away. "She came when you and Papa went for your walk."

"She made Mama cry," William added, patting Lynette's arm. "She's mean."

"I know Marion waited until she was sure that you and Papa were gone…then she came in and went right for Lyn's throat."

"I'll talk to her again," both the doctor and his wife declared in unison.

"Please don't," Lynette begged. "I've caused this split in your family—if we leave, the gap will mend itself and then—"

"No," Irene said softly. "Marion is in the wrong, and your leaving will not change her attitude. We need to give the problem to the Lord. He—" Suddenly, a bout of coughing chopped Irene's statement in half, and she turned from the table, hacking into her napkin.

Instantly, Anna jumped up from the table. "Do you need some water, Mama?"

"No…no…I'm…all right."

With a relieved but watchful visage, Anna settled back onto her chair.

"Mama's right," the doctor offered. "God's the only one who can deal with Marion's disposition."

"We can't…let her actions…cause us to walk away from His will," Irene rasped to Lynette. "You joined our family for a reason…to leave now would be going against the Master's plan."

"But Marion shouldn't be able to come here and talk to Lyn like that," Anna persisted.

"She won't do that anymore," the doctor returned firmly.

Nick shoved his plate toward the center of the table and slumped down in his chair. "When Marion left Wednesday, she said she'd never come back here as long as me and Lyn were going to be around—why'd she come anyways?"

Anna looked at Lynette, then down at the table, then, finally, at Nick. "She wanted me to remind you to return the tools that Michael loaned you or she'd… she'd…"

Nick swallowed a curse and shook his head—he knew the rest of the statement all too well… "Or she'd send a patrolman over to get them—and me…right?"

A sad, slow nod answered him.

"Wait a minute," Peter interjected. "Nick, you never told me that Marion wanted the tools back."

Staring at his brother, Nick grimaced. There's a lot, he said silently, that I never told you about. "Yeah," he replied. "And she also said I should just forget about the job Michael offered."

"Why didn't you tell me any of this?"

"Because, Pete, my arm had you troubled enough—besides, it was just between Marion and me."

"No, it isn't, Nick…whether you like it or not—what concerns you, concerns me."

Nick grunted and eyed Peter. He still wasn't sure if brothers were a blessing or a bother…maybe they were both…

"Well, don't worry," Peter continued. "We'll get you some tools. You're good enough to start your own watch repair business."

"Pete, I don't want—"

"For now, you could work out of the guest house."

"Pete, I said I—"

"But, eventually, we could get a small place in town and—"

"Quit pushin' me, Pete!" Nick yelled, slamming his fist on the table.

Immediately, a chilly hush enveloped the room.

"You're absolutely right," Peter murmured, his voice resounding in the deafening quiet, then, rising, he dropped his napkin onto the table. "Please excuse me," he mumbled. And, stepping to the back door, Peter disappeared into the last remnants of daylight.

"Mama, can I go too?" William whispered. "Bock's scared."

With a scowl of confusion, Nick leaned to the side and peeked at the tiny, orange ball of fur soundly sleeping on a blanket near the sink, then he gazed at William, who stared back at him wide-eyed. Great, Nick thought, with one outburst he repulsed both his brother and his girl's kid. When was he going to stop scaring William? And when was he going to stop taking his frustrations out on Peter? He wished he could tell his brother that he relished the idea of fixing watches for his livelihood, but James Wild would never allow that to happen.

"You can stay, Kid," Nick said quietly. "I'll go so your kitten won't be scared no more."

Walking onto the back porch, Nick searched the yard, but Peter was nowhere in sight. With a grunt of disappointment and relief, Nick circled to go back inside the house. It was probably best, he inwardly reasoned. He had no idea what to say anyway…

Then he heard it—a strange, faint murmuring coming from behind the large pine tree in the yard. Meandering down the stairs, Nick headed toward the voice, which, with each step, sounded more and more like Peter's. Finally, as he reached the tree, Nick froze in place. It was definitely his brother making the utterances—but he wasn't speaking to anyone, just the cloud-saturated sky.

"…to remember," he heard Peter say, "that You're my brother's shepherd, not me. I just can't seem to stop—"

"Who you talkin' to?" Nick announced, scanning the area for the recipient of Peter's statement.

Startled by the unexpected interruption, Peter let out a short laugh. "You frightened me, Nick."

"Yeah, I do that to a lot of people…who were you talkin' to?"

"I was just talking things through with God."

"Oh…I can leave if you—"

"No, no," Peter returned and rubbed his right arm. "I'm glad you came out—I wanted to apol—"

"What's the matter with your arm?"

"Huh? Oh…it was broken last year in my fight with Quentin Fetch. It starts aching when we're about to get—" Cutting himself off, Peter peered at his own arm, then at Nick's bandaged limb. "It's happened again."

"What?"

"We keep paralleling each other—just as Jaxson said."

"What're you talkin' about?"

"Jaxson pointed out that we keep having the same things happen to us…meddling, rich dandies…robberies that changed both our lives…now this," he said as he waved his finger between their damaged arms.

"It's just bad luck, Pete."

"Maybe…or maybe, God really does have a reason for it."

Nick smirked—why did everyone around him have to be an all-fired crusader? "Look, Pete, I just came out here to say I'm…to say I didn't mean to flare up at ya the way I did. I just didn't like—"

"No, Nick, you were right," Peter countered, shaking his head. "I do push too hard. I did with Daven and I'm doing the same to you…I can't seem to allow my brothers to make their own decisions."

"But I bet perfect little Daven never yelled at ya for it."

Peter stared into Nick's eyes and frowned. "Daven yelled at me all the time—I, unfortunately, just never listened to what he was saying."

"I knew you'd end up seein' it that way."

"What do you mean?"

Nick exhaled. He was treading on sacred ground, he realized that, but he had become weary of his half-brother's luminous shadow following him everywhere.

"Daven gave ya a tongue-lashing, yet you take the blame…even when Daven was wrong, he was still perfect."

"Why do you keep saying that he was perfect?"

"Because you—and everybody else—have never had a bad thing to say about him. All I ever hear is how wonderful Daven was…and how talented…and kind and giving and bright-spirited. I'm sick of it—and him."

Peter laughed wryly. "Daven was far from perfect."

"Sure."

"Nick, I loved my…our brother very much, but he was not perfect…he was impulsive, undisciplined, and unruly."

Unconvinced, Nick grunted. "Okay, so he had a few faults…but I'll still never be as good as him."

"No one is expecting you to be like Daven."

Nick rolled his eyes. "Everybody's expectin' it—'specially you."

Peter backed up a step at the comment. "No, I'm not."

"Yes, you are…you only brought me here so I could—"

"I'm getting so blasted tired of everybody telling me why I brought you to Sandorville," Peter fumed. "You look like Daven—I'll be the first to admit that. And, right now, with all your injuries, you look like his twin. But I didn't ask you to come here to be a living statue of him."

"No?"

"No. On the outside, you look like Daven, but on the inside, I recognize someone else—someone I know very well."

"Huh?"

Peter bowed his head and massaged his eyes. "You, Nick Anderson, hate the fact that other people have forced your life to go in directions that you didn't want it to go in…and you're angry with God for allowing it to happen…and you can still list every wrong that anybody has ever done to you."

Nick's mouth dropped open and he scrutinized his brother's features. "How… how…"

"Because that was me. Parallel lives—remember? I know what's going on inside your head—I've lived with the same bitterness…I asked you to come to Sandorville because your uncle wanted me to find you…and because I know how awful it is to lose your family—again and again…and because I wanted to show you that life's a lot sweeter when you're not dragging around a chain of grudges…and…and because I thought we could be friends."

Without a word, Nick turned away and ambled toward the empty lot next to the Spreyers' yard. He never expected to have the truth spread out so carefully in front of him—or for it to astound him. Peter was not his enemy, but his ally…his advocate, who would come to his aid at a moment's notice…his friend, who looked at him as an equal…his brother, who saw him as an individual and not as Daven's replacement.

"I'm sorry," Peter offered as he jogged up to Nick. "I never seem to know when to keep my mouth shut."

"It's okay, Peter," Nick choked out, still trying to flee the unfamiliar emotions that swarmed around him. "I just need to…to think."

✳Ten✳

Standing in the open solarium doorway, Nick gazed out into the darkness. He dreaded what he was about to do, but he was still determined to carry out his decision—losing Peter was better than continuing to hurt him. Laughing at himself, Nick backed inside the room as a light rain began to tap at his boots. Just a week ago, he had vowed to milk Peter Leighton dry—now…now, he would do anything to help and protect the man. Somehow, during the past seven days, his heart had been transformed…he never saw the turnabout take place—but it did.

"Close that door at once, Anderson," Wild demanded from behind him. "That damp night air will send me to an early grave."

Not early enough, Nick voicelessly returned as he latched the door. Then, circling to face the long-haired dictator, Nick reminded himself to harness his temper and check his tongue. Just one more parley to get through, he reasoned—just one more, and you'll never have to kneel in front of Wild again.

"I see you have already removed your sling," Wild offered. "Cole must not have injured you as badly as you pretended."

Gritting his teeth, Nick sneered at the comment. "I just got tired of it—that's all…it was too confining."

"Your aversion to confinement is quite understandable."

Nick rolled his eyes but said nothing.

"Well?" Wild prompted as he removed his toothpick from his chamber robe pocket. "Were you successful in procuring another position for Cole at the factory?"

"No."

"No? I am not pleased with that answer. Tomorrow you will—"

"Cole can't ever come back…Peter already figured out that he was put there as a spy," Nick explained, neglecting to mention that he had confirmed his brother's theory and contributed to Cole's blacklisting.

Wild sighed loudly and rotated the golden pick out of its hiding place within the cylinder. "And who, pray tell, does Peter believe placed Cole into the factory?"

Nick paused, not quite sure if he should offer up a fib or honesty.

"So Peter suspects me, does he?"

"Yeah," Nick returned. Obviously, his hesitation spoke louder than any words— and unfortunately, it uttered the truth.

Shaking his head, Wild scraped at his front teeth with the pick. "Cole's altercation with you has completely upset my playing strategy…he is useless to me now…as of this moment, you will assume his duties."

"No," Nick replied and shoved his left hand into his jacket pocket.

"Excuse me?"

"Here is what I owe you from yesterday's speech lesson," he went on as he dropped a handful of paper notes and coins onto the narrow table sitting by the back door. "Now, I don't owe ya nothin' anymore—and I quit."

"Quit?" Wild echoed, absently twisting the toothpick in and out of the little tube. "Do I need to remind you of the ramifications of that action?"

Nick cradled his aching right arm and stood firm. "You'll tell Peter I was helpin' ya—well, go ahead."

"Your brother will discard you like an old shoe—do you wish for that to happen?" Wild questioned as he sauntered toward the door.

With a hard swallow, Nick shook his head. The last thing he wanted was to be shunned by his brother. "No, Wild, I don't wish for that to happen, but I won't help ya destroy Peter anymore—no matter what you do."

James Wild twirled the toothpick closed and stroked his chin with the bevel-cut tube. "So it is Peter now, is it? Hmm…it seems you have developed a misguided respect for your dear brother."

Drawing his arms closer to his chest, Nick inhaled deeply, hoping to hide the trembling that rippled through his limbs. Wild was proving to be a very perceptive and intimidating opponent. "Yeah, I guess I have."

"And you would actually prefer to have Peter disown you than to stay in my employ?"

"Yeah," Nick mumbled as his confidence wavered. After hours of wandering through the streets of Sandorville and rehashing Peter's latest revelations, he knew he had to end his partnership with Wild—even if it meant saying good-bye to his brother. But, as Nick stood alone in the midst of evil, his resolve slowly waned.

"Well, well. It appears that you are the victor," Wild pouted, moving directly in front of Nick.

"Whatd'ya mean?"

"I mean, simply, that you have triumphed. You have, as you gamblers so eloquently say, 'called my bluff,'" the lanky Wild returned as he straightened the collar on Nick's jacket. "You are free to go to your brother's side."

"Your bluff?"

"Yes."

Nick's eyes narrowed and he pulled away from Wild, who was fingering the pockets of his jacket. "You mean ya never planned to tell Peter that I was workin' for ya?"

Wild laughed and propped his shoulder against the door. "Think, Anderson…if I explained to Peter that you have been my informant, I would be exposed, and the game would cease immediately."

Nick bowed his head, disgusted with himself. Why hadn't he thought of that?

"I trust," Wild continued, "that you will remain mute about my agenda for your brother."

"Remain mute? You want me to just stand there and let ya ruin him?"

"Yes."

"Sorry—that ain't likely to happen."

"Is that carved in marble?"

A sudden chill cascaded down Nick's spine. "Yeah."

"Very well," Wild said, elbowing himself from the door. "You are free to go…just remember—every decision has consequences."

"What's that supposed to mean?"

Snapping his fingers, Wild smirked and pointed at Nick. "I almost forgot! You need to empty your pockets before you depart."

Nick glared at his adversary—he despised the degrading, nightly ritual. "I emptied my pockets when I gave ya your nine dollars…there ain't nothin' in them now but lint."

"Humor me."

Grumbling under his breath, Nick gingerly slipped his aching, stitched arm into his jacket pocket and pulled up the lining. "See?"

No response.

With another growl, Nick shoved his other hand into the left pocket—and instantly, panic shot through him as his hand brushed against a small, bevel-cut metal tube.

"Is there a problem, Anderson? You look as if you were just informed that you would be returning to the penitentiary."

Cursing, Nick wrapped his fingers around the little cylinder and pulled his hand from his jacket.

"My toothpick!" Wild exclaimed with mock alarm. "You attempted to steal my toothpick!"

"No, I didn't!"

"The proof is right there in your hand."

His heart pounding against his chest, Nick tried to suck in a much-needed breath. Now, he fully understood Wild's obsession with his jacket. "I…I didn't take it…you…you put it in there!"

"Preposterous."

"You did! And you know it!"

"I know nothing of the sort—however, I do know that the police will not be amused about this unpleasant event."

"No," Nick groaned, his hand and the pick twitching uncontrollably.

"And, I assure you, the judge will not be lenient with your sentence."

"No…no," Nick begged, not being able to conceal the terror that pulsed through him. "I didn't do it! You slipped it into my pocket when you were fiddlin' with my jacket!"

"Ah, but whom will the judge believe?" Wild whispered as he yanked the toothpick from Nick's grip.

Nick cursed again.

"Of course," Wild went on, "I may be persuaded to overlook this incident."

"How?"

A devious smile crawled onto Wild's face, and he slid the golden cylinder into his robe. "Continue as my informant and convince Peter that I am not responsible for his tribulations."

Running a quivering hand through his hair, Nick swallowed hard. "Okay," he gulped, regretting the word. Even as he, himself, was being buried, he was still hammering nails into Peter's coffin.

"Excellent!" Wild declared and clapped his hands together as if he were a child who had just been given a pony. "I told you that every decision had consequences."

"I reckon you did."

"So come, sit, and enlighten me about the events at the factory today."

His shoulders drooping, Nick shuffled over to his chair.

"But, first, we should discuss my compensation for your verbal atrocities."

Nick pointed to the pile of money lying on the narrow table. "I paid you."

"Yes, for the faux pas from yesterday…however, by my calculations, you have accumulated thirty-two errors so far tonight."

Immediately, Nick's legs turned to jelly, and he slumped onto the velvet chair. Peter, please help me, he silently called out again. But his brother couldn't rescue him this time—no one could. He was trapped at the bottom of his self-dug pit, and with great skill, Wild was refilling the hole, covering him with shovelfuls of dirt and deception. There was no chance of escape…no hope…he was lost. And only one soul knew where he was interred—his enemy, James B. Wild, the third.

⸙

Lying on the sofa in his darkened office, Peter sighed and massaged his pulsing temple. Why today? he wondered. Why did he have a headache today? And, more so, why did he have them at all?

He had wanted to accomplish so much before the weekend, but it would be impossible now—he couldn't even think without it hurting. His dear Anna would have to contend with another headache-stricken picnic—if he could persevere until lunchtime…and Jaxson would have to struggle in the factory without his help—again…and worst of all, he would have to postpone his talk with God regarding his most recent fortunes and failures.

Without warning, another surge of nausea crashed against him, and turning on his side, Peter clutched his stomach, hoping that, this time, he wouldn't vomit. Then, almost as if it were jealous for his attention, a cramp rippled down his right arm. Groaning, Peter pulled his aching limb to his chest and closed his eyes. Lord, he silently begged, please…please take away some of this pain.

"Peter?"

The whispered name roared inside his ears, and his eyes slowly fluttered open. "Yeah?"

"I'm so sorry to bother you," Del murmured, entering the room and tiptoeing over to the sofa. "Did you get any rest?"

"Yeah…some," Peter lied as he pushed himself to a seated position. "Is…is something wrong?"

"Mr. Wild is here…I explained to him that you were ill, but he insists that he must see you."

Brushing his hand through his hair, Peter cussed—the last thing he wanted was to battle James Wild along with his headache. "I…I don't think I can, Del."

"You're right," the bookkeeper said. "I shouldn't have bothered you. I'll tell Mr. Wild that—"

"Peter, it grieves me so to hear that you have been afflicted with an ailment."

"Mr. Wild!" Del exclaimed, whipping around. "I asked you to wait downstairs."

"True," Wild replied as he stepped into the office. "However, I thought I could be of assistance."

"We're quite capable of taking care of Peter, thank you."

Holding his head in his hands, Peter moaned. He appreciated Del's devotion, but the bookkeeper's verbal contest with Wild only magnified the hammering in his skull. "It's...it's all right," Peter returned, his own voice adding to his misery. "What do you want, James?"

"No, Peter," the bookkeeper persisted, "you're not—"

"It's okay, Del."

"Are you sure?"

"Yeah, I'm sure," Peter offered. Then, after faltering twice, he rose to his feet—and immediately grabbed onto his bookkeeper's sleeve to keep his balance. "Do me a favor?"

"Anything," Del replied softly.

"Have Josef go to the hospital and get Doctor Spreyer...or at least some laudanum...I...I need something."

"Will you be okay until then?"

Squeezing Del's shoulder, Peter forced himself to grin. "Right now," he whispered in his bookkeeper's ear, "I wish I would collapse."

As Del Franz hurried out of the office, Peter tottered toward his desk. "What do you want, James?" he repeated as he sifted through the papers trying to find his tinted glasses.

"Would you please open the curtains? I would prefer to conduct our business in some degree of light."

"I'm working on it, James!" Peter growled, finally locating the spectacles. "Now, what do you want?!"

"I see that you are unable to conceal your true essence when you are plagued by one of these headaches."

Too miserable to dispute the insult, Peter clenched his jaw and slipped his glasses on. "Well?!" he demanded as he turned and staggered toward the window.

"You may not believe this," Wild replied, "but I regret that you have these afflictions as much as, I am sure, you do."

"And why is that?" Peter inquired. Then, with a sweeping motion, he shoved the heavy curtains aside—and gasped. Even with the protection of his dark-lensed spectacles, the hazy daylight stabbed him in both eyes, causing a wave of dizziness to well up inside him. Covering his face, Peter circled and blindly staggered to his desk, where he gratefully sat and caressed his aching head.

"Because they give you an unfair advantage."

With reluctance—and a touch of worry—Peter looked up. He knew Wild had answered him, but all he heard was the buzz of bees. "What?"

"You inquired as to why I regret that you have these headaches...and I said, because they give you an unfair advantage," Wild restated impatiently.

"They give me what?" Peter mumbled, barely able to comprehend the words.

Wild rolled his eyes and lowered himself onto the chair opposite Peter's desk. "An...un...fair...ad...van...tage," he enunciated as if trying to make a dog understand.

"How?"

"Anna's altruistic nature is attracted to your helpless condition. Her mind is so pre-occupied with your ailment that she has very little time to...to consider other options."

Peter breathed out a heavy sigh. "Is that what you came here to talk about? Because, if it is, you can just get out of my office!"

"I came to offer my assistance," Wild said, pulling his golden toothpick from his waistcoat pocket.

"For what?"

"I heard a rumor that you were unable to retain a rather large furniture order, and I wanted to make myself available for any financial—"

"You heard a rumor?"

"Yes."

"From whom? Your spies?"

Wild tittered out an artificial laugh. "My what?" he questioned as he scraped the pick against his teeth.

"Spies!"

"Dear, dear Peter, I do believe these headaches are affecting your sanity. I said it was a simple rumor."

Rubbing his temple, Peter released a quiet growl. He knew he'd only accomplish one thing with his accusations—making himself sicker. "Whatever you heard and however you heard it, Wild, the information is incorrect...so we don't need any assistance from you."

"Is that the truth...or is your pride speaking instead?"

"I told you everything is fine!"

"And my tables?"

"Are right on schedule."

As he twisted the toothpick back into its holder, Wild rose to his feet. "Superb!" he exclaimed, returning the pick to his waistcoat. "I do hope you receive some relief from your malady...conquering an ailing rival is not very challenging."

Peter cussed, and pushing himself up, he leaned on the desk and glared into Wild's amused eyes. "We are not rivals, Wild. Anna and I are going to be married. That's what God wants—and His will is greater than yours...now, get out of this office, because, if you don't—headache or no headache—I'll throw you out."

"Do I need to remind you," Wild countered as he, too, propped himself on the desk, "about the consequences your poor attitude may bring?"

Tightening his jaw, Peter hoped he could hide the dread that suddenly blanketed him—in the midst of his pain, he had indeed forgotten about Wild's threat.

"I realize," James Wild went on, his face stiffening, "that the imminent arrivals of your remaining lumber and new German employees have you rejoicing—but please keep in mind, they will become liabilities if I cancel my order."

With a hard swallow, Peter stared at his enemy's stony features. There was something so wrong with Wild's statement, but his massive headache wouldn't allow his mind to concentrate. Think, Peter yelled within himself. Think! Then, slowly, the fog cleared for a moment, and the answer came into view. Cole had been fired on Wednesday…but Wild was referring to things that had happened after that day… things that he shouldn't know about…

Obviously, just like rats in a garbage pile, Wild had his spies everywhere. And, as he studied the rodent-keeper in front of him, Peter's anger boiled over. "You had better lose some of your arrogance, Wild, because you're not just fighting against me—you're fighting against my Father."

His face contorting into a confused grimace, James Wild straightened up and adjusted the satin cuffs on his frock coat. "That headache has definitely shattered your sanity…your father is dead—remember? Shot by a thief in the late hours of the evening."

Peter's eyes narrowed in fury. Cole and the other snoops were keeping Wild well informed. "John Leighton is dead, yes—but it's my Father in Heaven that you need to be wary of."

Wild chuckled and rolled his eyes again. "Well, the both of you have been interesting opponents, but not very formidable…I am not concerned."

Peter stood firm. "Our times are in His hands—and your power will ebb."

An expression of mock horror washed over Wild's face, then he laughed. "Maybe it will, someday—but not before I crush you…which, by your appearance, would not require more than a twist of my heel."

⌖

With an elbow on the table, Jaxson rested his chin on his hand and absently poked at his food. No matter how much he tried to erase the memory, Peter's tormented features were still engraved in his thoughts. It was the first time a headache had ever forced his friend to beg for someone—anyone—to remove the pain.

"Are you all right?"

Dragging himself from his daze, Jaxson looked up—and into the eyes of his precious Holly. "Yeah…sorry…I'm just…just not very hungry."

"You're still worried about Peter, aren't you?"

"Yeah. I never saw him that bad before," Jaxson returned as the day's events, once again, flashed through his mind…

Joe Franz running breathlessly into the factory, explaining that Doctor Spreyer was on his way to take care of Peter at the showroom...helping Nick and the doctor move Peter into a wagon to transport him to the Spreyer house...watching his friend plead for laudanum, which seemed powerless to halt the agony.

"You shouldn't worry so much," Bonnie put in. "The doctor, Anna, and Nick are all there helping him."

Jaxson guffawed and stabbed his fork into a hunk of meat. "I'm the one who should be there—not Nick...he's partly to blame for Peter's misery."

"Why?"

"Because he's been nothin' but trouble...he complains, and whines, and says rotten things about Peter—sometimes right in front of the man!"

"Nick seemed really concerned today," Holly offered. "I think he was the first person out the door after Joe told us what was happening."

"No, he wasn't," Jaxson snapped, bristling at Holly's high praise of his foe. "The only reason he cares is 'cause Peter takes care of all the bills...Nick should just leave—that would make everything better."

Holly glanced at her father and two sisters, then refocused on Jaxson. "Or would Nick's leaving just make you feel better?"

Jaxson scowled at the comment, not believing that it emerged from the woman he adored. Why was he suddenly the villain? "I ain't jealous of Nick," he growled. "This ain't about him—it's about what's best for Peter."

"Are you certain?" Benjamin chimed in.

"Yes! Peter's got enough to worry about," Jaxson fumed as he continually jabbed at the meat. "James Wild...Manning Cole...spies...lumber...the payroll...Peter doesn't need to have Nick's name on the tally."

"Why is Peter worried about the payroll?" Bonnie asked.

As he heard the question, Jaxson's fork immediately toppled out of his grasp and clattered to the floor. No, he silently moaned as he stared, wide-eyed, at Bonnie Jaye. How could he have said that? How could he have let his aggravation loosen his tongue so much? "Uh...uh, no, he's not...I...uh...I meant...you know with his headache," Jaxson stammered, searching his brain for the words that would repair his momentous blunder, "Peter was worried...worried that he couldn't be there when everybody gets paid tomorrow."

Benjamin Jaye shook his head. "You're a poor liar, Son...what's wrong?"

Jaxson surveyed the four faces seated at the table with him—three of which worked for him. Even though they were becoming his friends, they were still, first and foremost, his employees. "Really, everything's okay."

Pushing his plate away, Benjamin reclined in his chair. "Jaxson, we trust Jesus for our keep—and nobody else...even if you said there was no money, this family wouldn't fear…when we came north our funds were dry, yet somehow, we ate every night…now, what's wrong?"

Jaxson sighed. He had no choice—the more denials he made the more Benjamin and the girls would know that there was a problem. "Well," he began softly, "after payin' for the lumber shipment today and the payroll tomorrow, our cash is gunna be kinda scarce…Peter and me were talkin' about it early this mornin'…I think that's what triggered today's headache."

Benjamin Jaye peered into Jaxson's eyes and smiled. "That's easy for God to fix."

With a deep exhale, Jaxson nodded. He fully agreed—he had said the exact same words to Peter during their discussion. But now, after the clock had ticked most of the day away, his spirit and stamina were quickly fading.

"Christ didn't bring us to this point just to desert us," Holly volunteered. "It's going to all work out, I just feel it."

"I pray you're right, Miss Holly," Jaxson returned, his head bowed. "I don't think Peter can take much more."

"Then that's exactly what we're gunna do tonight—pray," Benjamin announced. "It's time to put Peter, his worries, and all our concerns at the Lord's feet…God knows what's happening, and He'll make some good come of it."

⁂

Poking at the burning embers, James Wild sighed wearily. His current contest with Peter Leighton was one of the toughest games he had ever played—and for the first time, he wondered if he should just withdraw from the match.

"You're crazy as a loon, you know that?"

Jabbing the fire again, Wild glanced at his visitor, who was guzzling down a third glass of brandy. "And why do you say that?"

"Because you're the only man in Sandorville who'd build a fire in the middle of summer."

"It is not due to insanity, my dear Bryce. I merely prefer a heated room over a damp one…the rain may have stopped, but the moisture it has left behind is unbearable."

"Ya mind not callin' me Bryce? The name's Wit Dearborn, remember?"

"Of course, how indiscreet of me," Wild said as he leaned the poker against the stone fireplace wall. "However, I warn you, if you continue to botch your assignments, you will be called 'unemployed' instead."

"Hey, it ain't my fault that Logan MacColl is an idiot."

"You should have been more persuasive."

"What'd you want me to do? Hold a gun to his head? He wasn't gunna sell that wood to me for five times his price. He said he was followin' God's desires or some such rubbish."

Wild stroked his chin and sauntered to the tall window next to the fireplace. "This game has developed into quite a quandary," he mused, more to himself than to Bryce. "If I am to continue, I will need to create a new battle plan. One with polish and finesse—and the capability to pulverize Leighton…quickly."

"Yeah, well," Bryce put in, setting his empty brandy glass on the elaborately carved mantel, "you're gunna have to do it without me."

"Excuse me?" Wild replied as he turned to face his key playing piece.

"I'm leavin'…things are just gettin' too risky for me around here."

James Wild exhaled with a loud, audible rumble. Although he disliked Leland Bryce, his army would surely suffer if he lost such a brash, unprincipled player. "So how much do you want?" he offered.

Bryce answered with a wide, yellow smile. "You have been an interestin' person to work for—most of the time—and a lot more generous than Fetch ever was…but I can't stay. I've been watchin' the patrolmen—here and in Grand Rapids—and I don't like the fact that they've been watchin' me in return…I just need to meet with somebody on Monday and finish a business deal, then I'm headin' west."

With a nod, Wild moved to the chaise longue near the window and sank onto the cushioned seat. He knew if Bryce was in danger of being identified, the man definitely had to go—but he was still perturbed by the complication. Who would be his knight now? Who could he lure into such a crucial role? Then a sly grin wriggled its way onto Wild's face, brightening his somber expression.

Anderson. Yes, Anderson, he whooped inwardly as he leaned back, his hands folded behind his head. The new strategy was brilliant and cunning—and would, unquestionably, inject his game with a very unique kind of thrill and satisfaction. "Of course, Bryce…pardon me, Dearborn…I would not want you to jeopardize your freedom…perhaps, when my holdings expand into the frontier, you can be of—"

Suddenly, the door to the parlor burst open, and Manning Cole charged into the room, followed by the butler, who was frantically grabbing at the intruder's jacket.

"Let me alone!" Cole raged as he shoved the butler away. "I said I was gunna see 'im and I'm gunna see 'im."

"But you do not have an appointment!" the butler declared, still trying to halt Cole's advancement.

Leaping to his feet, Wild held up his hand. "Stop this lunacy! Both of you!"

"I apologize, Mr. Wild," the butler offered. "Mr. Cole stormed into the house wanting to see you. I tried to explain that he was no longer in your employ, but—"

"That is all right, Robert," Wild cut in. "I will handle things from here."

"What does he mean 'no longer in your employ'?" Cole shouted as he jabbed his thumb at the departing servant.

"He means that you have been terminated."

"Huh?"

"You have been discharged."

Cole scowled and silently mouthed the word—obviously, it, too, was beyond his grasp.

"Dismissed," Wild uttered with an impatient sigh.

Again, the word hit Cole's granite intellect and fell to the floor unrecognized.

"You have been fired, Cole!"

"Why?"

Rolling his eyes, Wild exhaled, thankful that he had finally succeeded in penetrating Manning Cole's gravel-filled mind. "Because you are no good to me now. You compromised your position at the factory when you attacked Anderson."

"But he started it!"

"Cole, listen to me…you were hired to supply me with information about the factory and to persuade your fellow workers to desert—the only way to accomplish that was from inside the factory."

"But Anderson hit me first!"

"That is irrelevant! Leighton let you go—permanently. And, as a result, you are now useless."

"You mean you ain't gunna pay me no more?"

Wild shook his head in amazement—the log burning in his fireplace had more intelligence. "Yes, that is precisely what I mean."

His body shaking with rage, Manning Cole pointed at Bryce, who was trying to muffle a snicker. "Is he gunna take my place?"

"No. Mr. Dearborn was just paying his respects—he is departing Sandorville very soon."

Cole continued to glare at Bryce, then he turned his attention back to Wild. "Ya know, I could go to Leighton and let him know what you're doing."

"You could…but you will not."

"No?"

"No."

"And why not?"

"Because, Cole, you do not want to cross me…besides, if you sever your ties with me now, you will never be able to work for me again."

"Then I can still do stuff for ya?"

"Yes—when the need arises, I will call for you."

"What's that mean?"

"It means, you idiot," Bryce hollered from the fireplace, "that he wants you to go away until he whistles for ya."

Cole's face immediately reddened, and he gestured an obscenity to Bryce. "Don't call me an idiot!"

Crossing his arms, Wild nodded with approval. Even though it altered his game completely, he was extremely happy with the current situation. No longer would he have to govern the unpredictable and crude Bryce or the malodorous and feeble-minded Cole. Yes, it was much better this way, he told himself. Anderson was so much easier—and enjoyable—to manipulate.

⁂

Seated on the Spreyers' front porch swing, Peter leaned forward, his elbows on his knees, and blankly studied the wooden planks beneath his boots. Not only did it feel as if someone were still beating his skull with a shovel, but after an entire day of swallowing laudanum and taking unrestful naps, an odd sort of disorientation now enveloped him, making it even more difficult to keep a coherent thought in his brain. Why was this headache so much worse than the others? he wondered. What wrong turn did he take that led him to such a painful realm? Then, in the midst of his pondering, he felt a gentle hand stroke his hair.

"You're still hurting?"

Slowly, Peter forced himself upright and gazed at the source of the question. "Yes, Ma'am…a little," he answered as Irene Spreyer's face blurred, then pendulumed back to clarity.

"My poor dear," she returned, sitting next to him on the swing. "What worries are fighting inside of you, causing you so much pain?"

Although he understood the question, Peter's sluggish mind couldn't form a response. "I don't know," was all he could offer.

"I know James Wild is one of them."

Peter nodded.

"You shouldn't worry so…Anna's heart belongs to you, as does the factory."

With a grunt, Peter massaged his burning eyes. "But Wild has spies every-where…the telegraph office, the factory, the streets…James Wild has no idea who Hermann Winkel is, but he knows Hermann's brothers are due in town soon…how can I win against all of that?"

"There's only one way," she replied and patted his hand. "God's angels outnum-ber Mr. Wild's snoops a hundred to one."

"But when are they going to stop him? Every time something good happens, Wild does something to subvert it…when is God going to act?"

"That question has been asked by many people for many years…and the answer is always the same—when it's the right time."

Peter sighed deeply. "I'm just worried that it's…that it's too late for me."

"God is never late."

Peter wanted to reply, but instead, he just nodded—the discussion was depleting what little strength and lucidity he had left.

With a determined glint in her eye, Irene Spreyer grabbed Peter's hand and stroked it gently. "God's timing is perfect, Pay-ter—even when we think it's too late…Lazarus' sisters thought it was too late—four days too late—but Jesus showed them that they were wrong, didn't he?"

A bolstered smile parted Peter's lips. "I guess so."

"What may look like delay or denial is just the Lord's wisdom—He has a schedule that we can't—"

"Now," Doctor Spreyer announced as he burst through the front doorway, followed by Nick and Anna, "I want you to give him all of this in a glass of water—the moment you get home," he explained, handing Nick a small brown bottle.

"I know," Nick said, "ya told me a dozen times already."

"Well, I'm telling you again."

"Yes Sir."

Circling, the doctor studied Peter with a father's concern. "I still wish you'd stay here in my office for the night."

Peter shook his head. "You already have a patient to take care of."

"I am quite capable of treating more than one patient."

"I know, Otto," Peter returned, using the swing to help pull himself to his feet. "I just need…I need it to be more quiet. Ol' Alec's broken leg sure hasn't stopped his mouth from functioning…he just talks and talks and—"

"All right," Doctor Spreyer surrendered. Then, turning back, he peered into Nick's eyes and poked his finger at the brown bottle. "The entire contents—"

"In a glass of water—I know," Nick cut in, half amused, half irritated. "I'll take him home and give him the medicine—all of it in a glass of water—then I'll bring the wagon back and help the girls load up for tomorrow."

"Tomorrow?" Peter questioned as he staggered to the porch railing.

"For the market," Anna put in, moving toward him. "Tomorrow's Saturday."

Peter wiped at his stinging eyes—he had completely forgotten about the girl's outing to the open-air market. "I'm sorry…I…I'll come by in the morning, like last week, to help you set—"

Placing her fingers over Peter's mouth, Anna stopped him in mid-sentence. "You will not. Papa and Nick have volunteered to help…you just need to concentrate on getting a good night's rest."

"I'm really sorry, Anna."

"Stop fretting, Honey," she said as she brushed her hand along the side of his face. "You have nothing to apologize for."

Peter nodded and remarked that his fiancee was right—but in his heart, he thoroughly disagreed with her statement. There was a great deal he needed to apologize for...

He was sorry that he had dragged his terrible headaches into their relationship... and he was sorry that the factory's woes were dominating all his resources...and he was sorry that he couldn't afford a honeymoon or even a wedding gift...he was sorry for so much. And he hoped that Anna would accept the only recompense he could give—the pledge of his undying love.

Extending his arms, Peter caressed his fiancee's shoulders, and pulling her close, he kissed her on the forehead. "I love you," he whispered.

"And I love you," she replied, giving him a firm kiss on the lips.

Grinning at Anna's boldness, Peter leaned in for a second, deeper kiss—and promptly lost his balance. Immediately, he reached out and braced himself against one of the porch's pillars, then he massaged the back of his neck, trying to suppress the wave of nausea that swirled inside him.

"I think it's time to go," Nick announced as he stuffed the medicine into his pocket.

"I believe you're right," the doctor added.

Walking over to Peter, Nick smiled at Anna and grasped his brother's arm. "Come on, Peter...let's go home."

With a reluctant nod, Peter yielded and allowed himself to be pulled away from Anna's concerned grip.

"If you have any trouble, come and get me," Doctor Spreyer called as Nick helped Peter down the porch steps. "And, remember, the entire contents in a glass of water."

Nick acknowledged the repeated command with a wave and continued his trek toward the wagon waiting in the street. "Peter, you wanna lay down in the back or sit up front?"

"Up front."

Nick chuckled to himself—he had guessed the answer before it had even been spoken. Then, with a pensive grimace, he guided his determined sibling to the front of the vehicle. Climbing onto the seat, Nick leaned over the side, extended his left hand, and hauled Peter up next to him. "You sure ya don't wanna lay down?" Nick asked, grabbing the reins.

"No...I'm...I'm fine."

Shaking his head, Nick urged the horse to a walk—he had never known anyone so stubborn. "All right," he put in, "but if you fall off, I'm not stopping."

Peter grunted at the comment as if he doubted its validity, causing Nick to grin—his brother trusted him far too much.

As the wagon crept along the rutted dirt of Highview street, Nick kept his eyes on the road but shifted all his thoughts to the man sitting next to him. He had been so confident, so sure, when the doctor asked if he could take care of Peter for the night. But now, seeing how much his brother really needed him, Nick's certainty began to deteriorate. He had never cared for anything in his life—not even a pet. What made him think he could look after another human being?

Grateful to see the Rheinhardt mansion looming in front of him, Nick expelled a breath of relief. His troubled journey was finally finished, and steering the horse in a wide turn, he brought the wagon to a careful stop at the back of the guest house.

"How…how far away are we?" Peter questioned, wiping his sleeve across his sweaty face.

His brow creasing with apprehension, Nick turned sideward, and in the fading light, he focused on his brother's pallid features. "We're…we're here."

Peter gazed at the house with squinted eyes, then, without warning, he slid off the wagon and rushed for the bushes near the back door. Scrambling down from the seat, Nick hurried to Peter's side, arriving just in time to see him throw up the few morsels he had choked down for supper.

"Please…please," Peter groaned, "just cut off my head."

Nick chuckled once again—although Peter's words sounded serious, they were softened by a light-hearted lilt. "Nah," Nick replied as he wrapped his good arm around his brother and pulled him up. "Let's try the doctor's medicine instead."

"Not more laudanum…I don't like what that stuff does to me."

"You're gunna take it," Nick returned, ushering Peter to the house. "I ain't gunna have Doc Spreyer yellin' at me 'cause I didn't follow orders."

As they reached the stairs, Peter twisted out of Nick's hold and grabbed the railing. "I'm okay," he mumbled as he dragged himself up the first step.

Shaking his head, Nick watched Peter stumble up the next two steps. "Sure you are," he muttered. Then, marching onto the stoop, he once again clasped his arm around his brother.

"I said, I'm all right," Peter whispered, trying to wrestle himself free.

"Stop fightin' me or I'll pick ya up and carry you in," Nick declared. And, without waiting for any kind of response, he tightened his grip and tugged Peter onto the veranda and into the house. "You're worse than a mule when it comes to bein' willful, ya know that?"

Peter offered a weak laugh in response as Nick lowered him onto one of the kitchen chairs. "I…I guess I'm just used to…to doing things myself."

Returning to close the door, Nick smirked and took a match from the metal box attached to the wall. "Well, even so, ya gotta let people help ya once in awhile," he said as he scraped the match on the box.

As the flickering flame illuminated the shadowy kitchen, Peter covered his eyes.

Instantly, Nick doused the bright glimmer. "Sorry, I forgot…why don't I take ya to your room, instead. Then I can make your medicine."

Peter held up his hand and pushed himself from the chair. "No, just get the laudanum ready…I can…I can make it to my room myself."

Gritting his teeth, Nick stepped over to Peter, blocking his way. "I don't care if you are used to doin' things yourself," he said, and even though he knew his blaring words were stabbing his weakened sibling like little daggers, he decided to finish his reprimand anyway. "Ya gotta stop bein' so pigheaded and let somebody help ya."

Suddenly, Peter started to laugh, then, wincing, he stifled his mirth. "Okay," he retorted, staring at Nick with agony-filled eyes. "Just remember those words the next time I try to help you."

His mouth falling open, Nick studied Peter. It was as if he were looking into a strange yet enlightening mirror. Then, as Peter continued to scrutinize him in return, Nick pivoted away, fearing that, somehow, his brother might see through his eyes and into his disloyal soul.

⚜

Sipping his nightcap, James Wild glanced at the large standing clock in the parlor as it began its chiming ritual for midnight. Although he had to rise earlier than his customary ten in the morning, he still couldn't resist having Nick Anderson continue to wait—the delay irked his puppet to no end and made the man utterly uneasy. Plus, the teasing was just plain fun.

With a contented sigh, Wild sauntered into the solarium. Surprisingly, his pawn was seated on the fireplace's stone hearth instead of the velvet chair, and as he considered the lowly position, Wild half-smiled. It appeared as if Nick were groveling—and that suited him very well.

"I see that I am not the only one who enjoys a few burning embers in July."

Scrambling to his feet, Nick gritted his teeth and glared at Wild. "It's…it is twelve midnight!"

"So?"

"So…Peter is sick and I'm…I am supposed to be watching him, and I can't… cannot do that sitting here."

"True, but neither can you watch him while sitting in a penitentiary."

Nick's shoulders instantly sagged, and Wild grinned—his employee's misery and fear warmed him as much as the fire.

"Can we…may we just get this meeting over, so I can get back home?" Nick asked as he stepped toward his usual seat.

"Of course," Wild said, sweeping his arm in a downward arc. "Please, return to the hearth."

"No, I'm...I am okay now—I just had a chill when I came in."

"No, no, no," Wild replied with a wide smirk. It was amazing how often Nick, himself, opened the door and allowed the harassment to enter. "I was not being kind, Anderson. I was dictating an order—return to the hearth."

A spark of fury illuminated Nick Anderson's bright-blue eyes. "It is already too hot."

"Well, I suggest you become accustomed to the heat, since you will, most likely, end up in Hades."

Nick sneered, grinding his teeth. "And I will greet you when you get there."

"What a clever answer," Wild snickered. "Now," he continued, his features stiffening, "I believe you have a debt to rectify."

As he gestured toward the glass-topped table, Nick nodded. "It's...it is right there—all of it."

Taking a drink of his hot toddy, Wild meandered over to the table and fingered the coins and notes lying on the glass. "Thirty-two—perfect," he said. Then, turning back toward Nick, Wild glowered. "I told you to sit!"

At first, Nick stood firm, casting a venomous scowl, but eventually, he obeyed and lowered himself onto the hearth.

"So," Wild went on, beaming with delight, "how is your arm?"

"Why do you care?"

"I am just curious."

"It is okay, I reckon...Doctor Spreyer says everything is healing real good."

"Then you will be resuming your work at the factory."

"No, not yet—the doctor said I shouldn't...should not try—"

"No, Anderson, you are in error once again. I was stating a fact, not asking a question...you will be resuming your work at the factory...I require your presence there."

"But I—"

"Stop whining, Anderson! I have already had a mutiny from my best playing piece—I am not in the mood for more excuses from you."

"Cole was your best playing piece?"

"No, not that imbecile. Bry...Dearborn resigned today."

"Huh."

Although it was a simple grunt, the reply infuriated Wild to the bone—Nick was definitely gratified by the setback. "Wipe that triumphant simper from your countenance," Wild seethed as he moved back to the fireplace and stared down at Nick. "The loss will be heartily felt, yes, but this game is far from being concluded—you will be assuming Dearborn's duties, as well as Cole's."

Abruptly, the grin fell from Nick's face and found its way onto Wild's.

"I can't," Nick whispered.

Wild breathed out in annoyance. Nick Anderson's loyalty was proving to be a difficult bond to break. "That is not the answer I was hoping to hear."

"Okay—I cannot."

Chuckling, Wild flipped his long hair behind his shoulders. He had trained Nick well concerning his language skills—now, he just had to dissolve the man's allegiance to Peter Leighton. "You can—and you will…business calls me to Grand Rapids this weekend, but during my absence, you will do as much damage to Peter's factory as humanly possible."

"Damage?"

"Yes, damage…persuade the new employees to retreat…impair the equipment…incinerate the lumber…and—"

"I won't!" Nick declared, jumping to his feet.

"You 'won't'?"

"No, I won't…you can put a hundred gold toothpicks in my pocket, but I still ain't gunna do any of that!"

Wild rubbed his chin with the rim of his glass. Nick's resurfacing courage was admirable—and aggravating. He had to shatter his pawn's conviction, or the man would be as useless as Manning Cole. "There is a possibility," Wild replied with a sly smile, "that it will not be a toothpick next time—it may be a watch or a ring or a—"

"It doesn't matter…it's just you pointin' a finger and me denyin' it—your word against mine…it won't prove that I'm stealin' from ya…it won't prove nothing."

"That is true—however, I am sure the city officials will be quite interested if there are multiple fingers pointing in your direction."

"Whatd'ya mean?"

Finishing the remainder of his drink, Wild smacked his lips together. Even though Nick displayed a facade of defiance, his eyes expressed the opposite. Now was the time to throw his strongest punch. "Whom do you believe Mr. and Mrs. Nealy would accuse if their jewelry shop was suddenly burglarized?"

"That'd…that'd never happen."

"I think even Peter would doubt your innocence."

"You…you're bluffing, you rotten—"

"I assure you, Anderson, I am not 'bluffing'…the task can easily be arranged."

"Nobody's gunna rob a jewelry store just 'cause you paid them to or told them to do it."

"No? You betrayed your brother at my request."

Suddenly, Nick's entire visage turned ashen, and he slowly sank back onto the stony hearth.

"So have my words made an impression upon you?"

Nick nodded.

"I want a reply!"

"Yes, they have," came the barely audible answer.

"Then may I assume that your report on Sunday evening will contain the details of some dreadful events that happened at the Rheinhardt Factory this weekend?"

Wrapping his arms around his legs, Nick bowed his head. "Yes."

"Very good," Wild announced, then, not being able to resist casting one final blow, he tapped Nick's foot with his shoe. "Anderson?"

Wearily, Nick looked up, his powdery-blue eyes drowning in a sea of moisture. "Yes?"

"You do realize that you uttered out twenty-one verbal improprieties during your tirade, do you not?"

"Twenty-one? How did you count—"

"I want your mutilation of our language to stop—immediately."

"I…I am trying!"

"Perhaps this will motivate you to try even harder…as of this moment, the cost of each atrocity has just doubled."

"Doubled?"

"Yes, your debt to me is now forty-two dollars."

Nick swore loudly in return.

"That curse raises it to forty-four…do you wish to increase it to forty-six?"

Nick swallowed hard. "No."

"Good…I expect to be paid—in full—on Sunday."

"I…I do not think I have that much."

Wild shrugged. "You are a resourceful man, I am sure you will find a way to acquire the funds…the sale of your pocketwatch, alone, should substantially increase your capital."

<hr />

Standing behind the makeshift counter, Peter glanced at Jaxson and Del Franz, both of whom were busily reviewing and updating the time book. He knew for a fact that his company had enough funds for the current payroll, but consternation still lunged at him with a sharp saber. Unless he received his much-needed miracle, he would soon have to say good-bye to everything he had worked so hard to achieve—and worse than that, he would have to say good-bye to the people who relied on him for their sustenance.

With a sigh of trepidation, Peter eyed his brother, who stood motionless next to him—and immediately, his concern mounted. Nick had only spoken seven words since the previous night, and now…now, his brother wouldn't even meet his gaze. "Nick? You all right?" he whispered.

"Yeah, I'm…yes, I am fine, thank you," Nick replied, his eyes downcast.

His mind ablaze, Peter turned and faced his brother. The answer was…was so unNickish—and thoroughly puzzling. It was as if someone else had uttered the cool and precisely worded answer. "Nick, did I…did I say something last night that offended you? I know my headaches can make me, well, rather ornery," Peter offered, combing his fingers through his hair. "I don't remember saying anything, but then again, most of yesterday is a blur."

Reluctantly, Nick looked up, then quickly averted his eyes. "No, you didn't…did not do anything wrong, Peter…you have not done anything at all."

His brow crinkling in alarm, Peter grabbed his brother's sleeve. "Nick, what's wrong? Why are you speaking like—"

"We're ready," Jaxson announced as he laid the time book on the counter. "Everybody line up."

Aggravated by his partner's timing, Peter exhaled in disappointment—discovering the reason for Nick's odd behavior would have to wait. Then, forcing himself to smile, Peter returned his attention to the payroll and to the first person in line to be paid. "Hi, Bonnie. How are you?"

"I'm okay—how are you?"

"Better," he lied. Although his headache had partially subsided, it was still looming, ready to pounce on him again.

"You must be feeling better," she teased. "You knew it was me right off."

Peter grinned. "I reckon." Then, looking at Jaxson, he nodded. "Let's get started."

"All right," Jaxson said, glancing at the time book. "Bonnie Jaye—nine-eighteen, this week."

Suddenly, Bonnie's features glowed as if she were holding a candle under her chin. "You can keep my wages 'til next week," she brightly declared.

Simultaneously, Peter, Jaxson, Del, and Nick exchanged puzzled glances and scanned the faces around them, trying to find an explanation for Bonnie's statement.

"What?" Peter finally blurted out.

Bonnie giggled. "You can keep my wages until next week."

"But…but…" Jaxson stammered as he stared at Bonnie.

"What's going on?" Peter asked, looking directly at Jaxson—the gracious sacrifice was reminiscent of something his friend would arrange.

Jaxson shrugged. "I ain't got a clue."

"You can keep mine until next week too," Holly chimed in as she peeked around her sister.

"And mine," Hermann called from behind her.

"What's...what's going on?!" Peter exclaimed, scanning his workers' cheerful yet foxy expressions. "Would somebody please tell me what's going on?"

"Those of us who can wait to be paid have decided to do just that," Bonnie explained.

Then, stepping from the line, Hermann added, "We know that...that the factory is going through some rough seas right now, so we—"

"How do you know?" Peter questioned, peering first at Hermann, then at Bonnie, then, finally, at Jaxson.

His partner's only response was another shrug.

"God let us know," Hermann said as he winked at Bonnie. "And we will do everything we can to help the factory, until our prayers are answered and a miracle comes."

"But you earned this money—it's yours!"

Hermann straightened his back and stood up as tall as his small frame would allow. "I know—I'm loaning it back to the factory."

"I can't let any of you do this," Peter persisted, completely overwhelmed by his employees' compassion and charity. "I appreciate the gesture, but you all deserve to take what you have earned...you and your families need—"

"Peter," Hermann cut in, his voice strong and unwavering, "we work for you, yes, but we also love and respect you—and we think of you as part of our families...please, let us help."

"But—"

"Hermann's right," Benjamin Jaye added, now standing behind his daughters. "We care about what happens to this factory—and to you."

Speechless, Peter studied the smiling faces of his workers—never before had he felt so blessed, so thankful, and so indebted. And now, more than before, he knew he had to defeat the evil that was trying to raze the factory—and him. "I...I don't know what to say."

"How about 'hallelujah'?" came a shout from the factory door.

As all eyes focused on Emerson Brant's ecstatic face, Peter felt a wonderful warmth surround him as if he had been hugged by an angel.

"I got the men's club to reconsider...and this time, they signed the contract and gave us a deposit!" Emerson hollered as he trotted over to the group, holding up a piece of paper.

Peter's mouth fell open as he marveled at his salesman. Irene Spreyer was right again. Although it seemed too late to save Lazarus—or the factory—the Lord knew the precise and perfect time to act. "Em you're...you're amazing," Peter proclaimed, walking over to his salesman.

The young man smiled, causing his cheeks to instantly dimple, then, slowly, the grin faded. "I'm not that amazing...the order is smaller than it used to be. They couldn't decide what to do, so they went with half of their furniture painted and the other half carved."

Peter nodded in approval and gave his salesman a brief but firm hug. "Being able to salvage any of that order is amazing," he replied, barely able to hold back his tears of relief and joy. Then, surveying his team of dedicated workers and friends, Peter smiled and offered up a silent 'thank you.' He had prayed so hard for a miracle—and within five minutes, he had witnessed two.

❦

As two more women hiked up their skirts and scurried themselves and their children past the bakery booth, Anna's aggravation inwardly exploded. The market-goers were usually filled with such charity and warmth—how could they have become so cruel and judgmental in three days? Lynette was a wonderful, godly woman, and she had not done anything to warrant such treatment—except remove herself and William from a torturous man.

"It seems the news of my divorce has spread like a plague."

Anna gazed into her friend's dark-blue eyes and grinned weakly. "My sisters can put the telegraph system to shame, I'm sorry to say."

"This was a mistake," Lynette replied, twisting her ruby ring around her finger.

"It was not a mistake—we've sold a few things."

"A few."

"I know it doesn't compare to last week, but at least we know there are unbiased people in Sandorville—even if they are just a few."

"Or maybe those people were just really hungry," Lynette put in with a jesting lilt.

Chuckling, Anna clutched her friend's hand. "Don't worry. The others will come back after they get to know you and forget about my sisters' gossip...or when they get hungry enough."

Lynette nodded in agreement, but the gesture was engraved with skepticism.

"It's going to be all right," Anna offered. Then, as she squeezed Lynette's hand, she added, "I'm so glad that you decided to stay...I would miss you so much if you left us."

"Well, your mother can be very persuasive—and I would miss you too...I just hope Mr. Chesnay doesn't—"

"He won't, Lyn," Anna cut in. "Not with us praying about it every day."

"But, he's—"

"And," she went on, ignoring her friend's protests, "if Mr. Chesnay does come, do you really think Emerson and Nick are going to let him near you?"

Lynette's cheeks instantly reddened, and she pulled away from Anna's grasp. "What...what do you mean?"

Anna smiled broadly and winked. "Lyn, it's more than obvious that they've both taken a fancy to you."

Creases of worry carved themselves into Lynette's face, and she bit at her lip—then, slowly, her features eased and she laughed. "I…I didn't set my cap for either of them, but…"

"But you ended up with two beaus anyway."

Nodding again, Lynette glanced at William, who was searching for a four-leafed clover in the grass. "Yes, I did," she returned, her cheerfulness fading, "but I'm going to have to give them both the mitten."

Pouting at the proclamation, Anna searched her friend's face. "Why?"

"Because, Anna, neither of them are…are what I need right now—and I'm not what they need either…especially Emerson. He is such a sweet young man, and I…I just don't want to taint that innocence with the horrors of my past."

"Lyn, your past is what's made you such a strong Christian—and that could never taint Emerson."

Lynette half-grinned and absently brushed at some cake crumbs lying on the booth's counter. "He is still a child…with a clean, fresh slate for a future. He doesn't need to muddy that up with a used wife and a four-year-old."

Anna exhaled, saddened and frustrated by Lynette's downtrodden tone. What could she say that would dissolve the dusky cloud that hovered overhead—as her friend had done so many times for her? "You are an extraordinary gem, Lyn," she tried. "You may not think so, but you glimmer with a precious light. And, one day, God'll bring a man into your life who will cherish that light—instead of trying to control it or extinguish it…in fact, he might already be in our midst."

Looking up with watery, suspicious eyes, Lynette smirked. "You mean Nick, don't you?"

Anna sheepishly tilted her head to the side—her comment had been as subtle as a sledgehammer. "Yes…Nick's somber expression always vanishes when he's around you…and lately, you sparkle in return when you're around him."

As she averted her gaze, Lynette, once again, dusted off the now crumbless counter. "I am beginning to really like Nick—a lot—but I don't ever see us being together."

"Why not?"

"Because his actions resemble Mr. Chesnay's…and although I've seen glimpses of a kind and gentle spirit hiding inside Nick's thick, angry shell, I don't know if I'm capable of breaking through that barrier…or if I even want to try," Lynette said as she dabbed at her falling tears with a handkerchief. "I might end up finding out that he's just another Red Chesnay."

"Or you might find a wonderful treasure."

"I've considered that," Lynette murmured. "I've even entertained the notion, but God hasn't given—"

"Hello there, Anna!"

Startled by the call, Anna's pulse quickened until she saw the thin but far from frail woman approaching the bakery booth. "Mrs. Warrington…hello," she replied, raising her arm and waving.

"I was hoping I'd find you," the woman said as she reached the counter. "I've needed to speak to you for days."

"Oh? Is something wrong?"

"No, no, I had some dress orders come…"

It was then, in the middle of Mary Warrington's explanation, that Anna noticed it—the woman's eyes never wandered from staring straight ahead…she didn't even glance in Lynette's direction. Instantly, Anna's maternal dander flared up. Lynette deserved some kind of acknowledgement, even if it was just a nod. "Forgive me, Mrs. Warrington," Anna declared as the woman completed her request, "I've been terribly rude. I've forgotten to introduce you to my baking partner…this is Lynette Chesnay."

"Very nice to meet you," Lynette offered, holding out her hand.

Looking down her nose, Mary Warrington scanned Lynette's petite frame, glanced at her outstretched hand, and then turned back toward Anna. "So, dear Anna, are you interested in making the dresses?"

Fiddling with her ring, Lynette choked out a sad laugh. "If you both will excuse me, I need to check on my son."

As her friend limped away from the snubbing, Anna's lips tightened into a thin line, and she glared at Mary Warrington—a woman she had always admired for standing up to the society snobs and rejecting their biased rules. Then a marvelous idea crept into Anna's head…

"I am so glad that you came to our booth," Anna happily announced. "The other townswomen have shunned us completely."

"Well, I'm sure you can understand why, Dear," Mary whispered.

"No, I can't…I just can't understand why so many people want to listen to the gossip instead of trying to find out the truth."

Straightening up, Mary Warrington blinked repeatedly as if trying to clear the cobwebs from her thoughts. "The truth? You mean she's not div—"

"No, Lynette is divorced," Anna cut in, her hands on her hips. "That's not what I meant…they are judging her just on that one fact, rather than trying to get to know her…Lynette's a caring, Christian woman, but no one seems to care about that."

"Well, Dear, this is a rather serious sin to—"

"It reminds me," Anna interrupted again, staring directly into Mary's green eyes, "how everyone treated you."

"Me? When?"

"When Mr. Warrington passed away, and you decided to keep the store open and run it yourself…I remember so clearly all the snubbing and grief you received."

Mary sighed and placed her hand on her chest. "Oh, my, I haven't thought about that in years."

"And I recall how the men insisted that no female could ever run a dry goods store…and how the women said that no refined lady would even try."

Mary bowed her head and adjusted her gloves. "Yes, and sometimes, I thought they were right…if it hadn't been for people like you and your parents, who supported me with their finances and prayers, I would have lost my will to go on."

Anna silently cheered. She had hoped to hold up a verbal mirror and bring Mary Warrington face-to-face with her own hypocrisy. Now, Mary's reminiscing was casting the perfect reflection. "That's why I'm grateful that you came to see us," Anna continued. "You are one of the few people in Sandorville who knows, firsthand, how Lynette feels and how much she needs tolerant and dauntless advocates—such as yourself."

A full smile edged its way onto Mary's face. "Ah, I suppose I do," she replied with a wink. "Why don't you wrap up one of your spice cakes for me."

Relief and victory welled up within Anna, and she glowed with renewed vigor. "Of course…and thank you, Mrs. Warrington."

"I'm just happy that I could help…now, what do you say about helping me fill some of those dress orders?"

As she lifted a spice cake loaf onto the counter, Anna glanced at Mary, realizing that she had ignored the woman's earlier remarks about the dresses. "Oh, Mrs. Warrington, I wish I could, but with my wedding so close, I just don't think I can," she offered with a touch of liberty…and a touch of sorrow. "Lynette is a marvelous seamstress, though."

"Really?"

"Yes, I'm sure you'd be pleased with her work," Anna returned and watched Mary Warrington's face contort as the woman obviously considered the rewards and repercussions of embracing Lynette's skills—and status. "You said her name was Lynette Chesnay, right?"

"Yes…yes, that's right," Anna answered, her soul dancing with delight. And, as Mary turned from the counter and headed toward Lynette, Anna's spirit soared. Maybe now, her friend would receive smiles from the townspeople—instead of scowls.

As he slammed his whiskey bottle down, Manning Cole plopped onto a chair at a vacant corner table. It wasn't fair, he grumbled to himself as he surveyed the interior of the saloon. It just wasn't fair. He wasn't rich like James Wild…or sure and strong like Peter Leighton…or blessed with a protective brother like Nick Anderson. He wasn't any of those things, but he still deserved better than what he had received in the past two weeks. He deserved a lot more—and he would make every one of his enemies suffer for controlling him…and beating him…and treating him like sludge. They would all be sorry—someday.

"Do you know how many taverns I've been to lookin' for you?"

Peering upward, Cole sneered. He had forgotten the man's name, but he remembered everything else…the bald head, the gold-rimmed glasses, the beard, the cold black eyes—and the fact that the stranger was a friend of James Wild. "Whatd'ya want?" Cole demanded.

"The name's Wit Dearborn," the stranger replied as he seated himself at the table. "We met yesterday at James Wild's house…you recall?"

Cole snorted. "Yeah, I do…ya called me an idiot."

"Well, I think I can make up for that."

"How?" Cole asked, pulling the bottle of whiskey toward him—the last thing he wanted was for Dearborn to think that he was generous.

"I have an important job to do on Monday, and I figure I could use a couple of strong hands to help me out…I'll pay ya a hundred dollars."

His body quivering with astonishment, Cole started to take a drink, but his grip faltered, and the bottle toppled over onto the table. Cursing loudly, Cole snatched up the fallen container and wiped the spilled alcohol off the table's edge. "A hundred?" he echoed quietly. "What…what do I gotta do?"

"Well," Dearborn returned, "I have a debt to collect, and the man ain't gunna like seein' me coming for him…so I wanna have somebody around to help me, uh, keep him in place while I get what's due me."

"You wanna pay me a hundred dollars just to keep this guy 'in place'?"

"Yep…of course, it may get," Dearborn began, then, after scanning the faces of the others in the room, he leaned forward and continued in a murmur, "bloody—real bloody."

"Oh?"

"Yeah, this guy owes me a lot…you, uh, have any concerns about that?"

Cole took a long swig of his whiskey, then swished the biting liquid around in his mouth before swallowing. "For half of that hundred right now, I ain't got any concerns at all."

Dearborn eyed him with a hard, icy stare. "All right."

As he smiled in triumph, Cole shoved the bottle across the table toward Dearborn—for that much money, he figured he could be a little generous.

"Just don't cross me, Cole," Dearborn hissed, "or I'll put a bullet in your chest too."

Cole grunted out a curse. "Don't worry—I ain't gunna mess up the chance to get the rest of my money."

"Good," Dearborn muttered, then he grabbed the liquor and downed a mouthful.

"So who's this bummer I gotta keep 'in place,' anyways?"

Dearborn's eyes glazed and his grip tightened into a stranglehold around the neck of the bottle. "Peter Leighton."

❊Eleven❊

Leaning against the Spreyers' twin-trunked pine tree, Nick studied the small, subdued groups scattered around the backyard. Although Anna's sisters and their families wore happy smiles and talked politely, it was quite evident that the gathering had broken into two factions—those that were not bothered by his and Lynette's presence…and those that were. Maybe, he reasoned, it was just the sullen sky and impending rain that had soured the Sunday feast…or maybe, it was the girls' lackluster outing at the open-air market the day before…or maybe, it was just him.

"Would you like some dessert?"

Anna's soft voice halted his musing, and tilting his head, Nick gazed into her pretty hazel eyes. "No, thanks."

"You hardly ate any dinner either. Are you feeling ill?" she asked, placing her fingers on his forehead.

Nick shrugged and pulled away from Anna's touch. "I…I just have a bit of a headache."

"You can go inside and lie down, if you'd like."

"No, I…I think I'll…I will just go," he replied, purposefully leaving out the destination—he still hadn't decided if it should be the guest house or another town.

"Are you sure? Ol' Alec went home yesterday, so Papa's office is empty."

"No…no…that is okay…thanks."

"All right," Anna sighed resignedly. Then she reached out and gently grasped his hand. "I'm so glad that you're here—especially now."

Nick's brow crinkled with bewilderment. "What do you mean?"

"Peter really needs you close by, right now."

"I still have no idea what you are talking about," he returned, shaking his head.

"Tomorrow is the first anniversary of when Daven was shot."

"What? I thought he died on July thirtieth."

Anna lowered her gaze. "Yes, he did."

Confused, Nick remained silent, allowing Anna to continue and, hopefully, to make more sense.

"Daven was shot on the night of the twenty-ninth…but he didn't die until very early Monday morning…that's why tomorrow is going to be so difficult for Peter—in his eyes, that was the beginning of the end."

"Oh."

"Peter says he's okay, but I know his heart is aching for Daven."

"Well, if that's true, then the last thing he needs is to have me and my face as a reminder."

"No, Nick, he does need you…he needs someone to confide in…someone who understands what he's going through…he needs a brother."

Breathing out long and hard, Nick forced himself to grin. He had fooled Anna, Peter, and so many others into believing that he was trustworthy and kind—and it sickened him. "I…I better go," he said, and tapping the brim of his hat, he left Anna behind, along with her tender thoughts about him.

Trying to ignore the many loathsome glares from Anna's sisters, Nick sauntered over to Peter, who, along with Doctor Spreyer, was listening to Michael drone on about his jewelry store.

"Nick!" Peter exclaimed, obviously grateful for the interruption.

"I am sorry to bother you, but—"

"No, no, it's fine," the doctor quickly chimed in.

"I'm gunna…I am going to go back to the house…I am kinda…kind of tired."

Immediately, the doctor moved in front of Nick and scrutinized his countenance. "Your arm was healing very nicely, but you better let me look at those stitches again."

"No, my arm is fine," Nick protested, backing up. He knew he should just run out of the yard and leave as he had planned, but his family's warmth and compassion were slowly erasing that resolve.

"Nick," Peter added, his face brooding and troubled, "if you don't feel—"

"I am just tired!"

"Go into my office and lie down," Doctor Spreyer ordered. "Both beds have clean linens. I want to—"

"No, I—"

"Not another word, Nikolaus," the doctor interjected. "I want to examine that arm and the rest of your injuries…just to make sure that nothing has turned septic."

With a low moan, Nick surrendered. Although he knew he could save himself and the doctor a great deal of bother, he remained silent. How could he explain that guilt, not injury, was the source of his condition?

"I'll be in soon to check on you," Doctor Spreyer said as he gave Nick a fatherly pat on the shoulder.

"And, after Otto finishes with you," Michael announced, crossing his arms, "I want to have a word with you."

"Why?" both Peter and Nick asked in unison.

"To discuss the Mayor's watch and the—"

"I returned your stupid tools already!" Nick shouted. "I brought them here days ago, just as Marion wanted."

"I know," Michael returned and touched his lips with his index finger. "There's no reason to yell."

"Michael, Nick's not feeling well," Peter put in angrily. "You can pester him another time about the—"

"But I don't want to discuss the tools," Michael barked out. "I want to talk to him about the job I offered him."

A sudden hush encircled the four men, and as a gust of wind wafted around them, they looked at each other with leery expressions.

"So what about it?" Nick asked, finally breaking the stillness.

"I just wanted to tell you that the Mayor is overjoyed at having his watch fixed and that I would like to hire you as my repairman."

Nick's mouth fell open in surprise. Michael Nealy? A broad-minded employer who wasn't afraid to hire a social outcast? He would have never believed it. "You really want me to work for you?"

"Yes," Michael returned. "Your expertise is unquestionable, and I want that kind of excellence for my customers…of course, you do understand, that with your background, I could never allow you into the shop. You would have to pick up the broken watches and your supplies and work elsewhere."

As Peter and the doctor instantly reprimanded Michael for his insulting offer, Nick's rage boiled inside him. He was so tired of being disregarded as if he were a pebble in the road…and tired of being spurned…and rejected…and manipulated…

"Look, you no-account, sniveling snob," Nick finally exploded, jabbing his finger into Michael's chest, "if you're gunna offer me a job, then you're gunna offer me the respect that comes with it…I don't have to work for you to repair watches…I could open up my own shop, then everybody could just come to me, instead of goin' to you."

His eyes widening with fury, Michael glowered at Peter. "Are you going to just stand there and let this guttersnipe speak to me like that?"

Peter nodded. "Yep. And consider yourself lucky—he said it a lot nicer than I would have."

"My wife was right!" Michael announced, red-faced. "The strays have corrupted this family! We're going home—and we won't return until we receive a proper apology."

"Fine!" Nick hollered as Michael strutted toward Marion. "But, 'til I get an apology from you, I ain't fixin' your watches." Then, as his outburst drifted away on a brisk breeze, Nick realized what he had said and nervously brushed his hand through his hair. Although Michael deserved the chastisement, it probably shouldn't have been said quite so loudly or while the doctor was standing next to him. "Doctor Spreyer, I...I didn't mean to...to..." he tried, stumbling over his words.

"Don't worry, Son, your rebuke was more than justified...now, go inside and rest—and I'll be in as soon as I do a little rebuking myself."

Gritting his teeth in trepidation, Nick glanced at his brother. "I didn't mean to cause you more trouble."

"It's okay," Peter replied with a nod, then, smiling, he tilted his head toward the house. "Go on inside."

With a sigh of relief, Nick turned and meandered toward the kitchen door, all the while trying to steady his thoughts—but none of them would comply. They all just kept jostling each other out of the way, vying for his attention. Yet, in the midst of the jumble, he did know two very crucial points—he knew he wanted to stay in Sandorville...and he knew he never could...

Leaving was the only way to unfasten the collar Wild had around his neck...and it was the only way to protect his brother from further scandals...and unfortunately, it would be his only choice—once Peter learned the truth about...

"What's wrong, Nick?"

"Huh?" he grunted, stepping over the threshold and into the kitchen.

"You looked so distracted just standing there in the doorway," Lynette said as she stood at the sink, her arms immersed in a tubful of sudsy water.

He shrugged and walked over to the table. "It's nothing."

"Did you tell Peter what you needed to tell him?"

"Not yet."

"How come?"

Nick shook his head. "Are you always so bossy?"

"Yes—and when someone is supposed to do something that he won't do, I'm even more bossy."

Lowering his gaze, Nick stroked the scars on his cheek. "I can't tell him."

"Oh, Nikolaus, why?! Is the money really that important to you?"

"I don't get money anymore," he mumbled as he sank onto a chair. "Now, I pay Wild."

"What are you talking about?"

Exhaling in frustration, Nick cradled his head in his hands. He had every intention to remain speechless, but he soon found himself babbling on to Lynette about Wild's threats to send him back to prison…and his forced speech lessons…and his desire to stay in town. "I have to meet with Wild tonight," Nick finished in a low tone, "but I haven't got his money, and I didn't wreck any of the stuff he told me to…I don't know what he'll do now."

Without a word, Lynette dried her hands, and walking over to Nick, she knelt on the floor next to his chair. "Then don't go see him," she said softly, caressing his forearm.

"I have to," he replied, looking her in the eyes. "If I don't show up, he might start scheming to ship me off to jail."

"Then confess everything tonight—that way you won't have to go."

His hopelessness mounting, Nick pushed Lynette's hand away and sprang to his feet. "Didn't you hear what I said? All Wild has to do is toss some of his magical money around, and I'm back in prison."

"So you're just going to continue divulging Peter's secrets to him?"

Circling, Nick studied Lynette, who was now sitting on his vacated chair. Every fiber inside him yearned to wipe the disappointment from her delicate features…and to caress her dark tresses…and to kiss her…

"No, I'm not gunna betray my brother anymore."

"But you just—"

"The only choice I have is to leave Sandorville."

"Leave?" she moaned, her shoulders slumping.

"Yeah, that way Wild can't do nothin' to me, and I'd be able to stop hurtin' Peter…leaving's the only answer, but it's not what I want to do…I want…"

"What?"

As he blinked back the moisture in his eyes, Nick lowered himself to the floor in front of Lynette. "I want to say good-bye to Wild and not go back to prison…I want to tell Peter what I've done and not have him hate me…I want to stay in town and…" he returned, not being able to voice his last wish of wanting to stay in town and court her.

"That's all possible, Nick…ask and it shall be given to you."

Nick rolled his eyes—he needed help, not useless phrases. "No, it's not."

"If you'll remember, it wasn't possible for me to get custody of my son…and it wasn't possible for Logan MacColl to refuse double the asking price for his lumber…and it wasn't possible for Peter to find you as quickly as he did…none of that was possible for us, but it was so easy for God to do…I know you don't trust the Lord, Nick, but it's only through Him that your desires are ever going to come into fruition."

"I've done some fairly rotten stuff…what do I do if God won't listen to me?" Nick asked as a sudden fear jumped into his heart.

"He isn't like us…He doesn't hold grudges…He likes to have people return to Him," Lynette replied, gently stroking Nick's scarred cheek. "Tell Him your desires, then listen for His answer."

Gritting his teeth, Nick glanced upward, then back at Lynette. Her words made it sound so simple, so doable. And, for the first time since he was a child, he considered giving God another chance.

<hr>

"Explain yourself, Anderson."

"There is nothing to explain—I don't…do not have your forty-four dollars," Nick replied, shifting his position on the cold fireplace hearth.

"Then render what you do have."

Nick swallowed hard and dropped all the cash he had on the stones next to him.

James Wild's eyes contracted and his hand tightened around his customary nighttime drink. "That amount is not satisfactory."

"It is all I have."

"Are you positive that is all? What about your wages from the factory?"

"We did not get paid on Saturday…well, we got paid, but most of us gave it back."

"Excuse me?"

Looking up from his place on the hearth, Nick expelled a tense breath. He wanted so badly to invent a story that would satisfy his long-haired warden, but a sinister glint in Wild's eyes suggested that he should offer the truth instead. "Everyone wanted to do something for Peter and the factory, so we told him to keep our wages until next week."

Wild chuckled and started to roam throughout the solarium. "And why, pray tell, did you participate in this act of insanity?"

"I…I wanted to help too."

"Help?"

"Yes."

"Did you forget that our purpose is to ruin Peter, not to help him?" Wild questioned, returning to the fireplace.

"At that moment, yes, I forgot…and I forgot that I owed you money—that's… that is why I refused to take my pay along with most everybody else."

"And what about my instructions to persuade the new employees to retreat and to impair the equipment?" Wild asked as he hovered over him. "Did you forget about them also?"

Studying the fine embroidery on Wild's satin chamber robe, Nick began to shiver as a familiar brick of oppression landed on him. And, even though it was a warm summer evening, he wished there were a few burning embers in the fireplace to comfort him. "I just…I just couldn't…could not do those things."

Without warning, Wild threw his half-filled glass at the stone wall behind Nick, causing everything in the vicinity to be showered with glass shards and drops of liquor. "I will not tolerate this insubordination any longer! Stand up!"

Unsteadily, Nick rose to his feet and stared into Wild's fierce, blue eyes.

"Now, because of your disobedience, I will be forced to reevaluate my strategies for dealing with Peter—again!"

"I…I am sorry, Mr. Wild."

"Sorry? Yes, you will be…you do realize that you must be punished for your defiance, do you not?"

Nick just held his breath, waiting for the guillotine blade to drop.

"Give me your pocketwatch."

His jaw dropping open in shock, Nick just shook his head. Wild already possessed so much of his spirit, but to give the man his precious timepiece would be like giving him the rest of his soul on a platter. "No…I will do anything but that."

"You are in no position to barter, Anderson."

"Please…anything but that."

Wild snarled under his breath. "Then give me something just as valuable—a piece of information that I can use against Peter."

Nick glanced toward the solarium door, then bowed his head. No matter what he did, he always ended up hurting his brother. It all had to end. And that meant he had to get out of town—immediately.

"I am waiting, Anderson."

"Emerson Brant got an order from the Oak Park Men's Club—it is smaller than before, but they signed a contract and gave him a deposit."

"I see…it seems that no one is listening to me!" Wild exclaimed, his face blazing. Then, grabbing Nick by the front of his shirt, he added, "I want you to pledge that you will be loyal to me—and me alone—from now on!"

"You have it," Nick announced, knowing that he would be free from his tormentor the moment he stepped on a train headed out of Sandorville.

Wild released his hold and moistened his lips. "Why do I not believe you?"

Nick shrugged as nonchalantly as he could.

"I intend to see Peter tomorrow, and after my visit, I want a convincing vow of allegiance from you—or I will proceed with the next step of sending you to the stockade...do I make myself clear?"

A nod was all Nick could muster.

"Oh, yes, and if, by chance, you are thinking of exiting this town, I suggest you reconsider...I would have no qualms whatsoever about sending the police after you for...hmm, let me think...what will I tell them...ah, yes, for the burglary that I watched you commit."

Closing his eyes, Nick groaned. Although he had listened to everything Lynette had told him, he knew, now, that she was wrong—not even God could rescue him from the catacomb that he was in.

❦

Standing in the quiet factory, Peter surveyed the sleeping machines, which, over the weekend, had become frosted with a fine coating of sawdust. He was beginning to believe that the factory would not only survive, but even become successful, despite the scandals and spies. And, as he eyed his brother and best friend, who were lighting the overhead gas lamps, he nodded. Everything was good—the factory was toddling, but it was toddling on its own...he was surrounded by devoted kith, kin, and workers...and a beautiful young woman cherished him—for reasons only God knew. Yes, everything was quite good...except for the nagging sense of doom that circled his neck like a noose.

Part of his dark mood was due to the date, he knew that—July twenty-ninth would forever stab him in the heart. But it was more than just the memory of Daven that haunted him...it was as if he were being followed by a deadly presence that planned to bludgeon him the first chance it got. Then, as he glanced around the room once more, Peter saw a sight that dismissed some of his apprehension—coming toward him was Hermann Winkel and a parade of five men, weaving their way through the silent saws.

"Peter," Hermann called, "I'd like you to meet my brothers and nephews."

With a wide smile, Peter watched Hermann and his family approach, then surround him. "Guten Tag," he proclaimed, hoping that he had pronounced 'good day' correctly.

All six Germans grinned and uttered greetings in return.

"Thank you so much!" Hermann offered and grabbed Peter's forearm.

"Why are you thanking me?"

"My brothers and nephews don't speak much English yet, but you made them feel so welcome with your thoughtful 'hello'...thank you."

"Well, they are welcome."

"This," Hermann proudly said, pulling one of the men to the front of the group, "is my brother, Horst...and that," he added with a jab of his finger, "is his son, Edwyn."

Then, in the same fashion, Peter met Hermann's other two brothers, Heinrich and Helmut, and Helmut's son, Klaus. Feeling a bit ashamed of his earlier, simplistic salutation, Peter tried to form a personal welcome for each man, but with his limited German vocabulary, he couldn't offer more than a handshake and a few fumbled phrases.

"Ah, I see our long-awaited troops have arrived," Jaxson remarked as he and Nick joined the gathering.

"Ja," Hermann put in with a pleased smile, "and they are ready to work."

As Hermann repeated the introductions for Jaxson and Nick, Peter examined his new employees more closely. All of them seemed eager and sturdy. And, if they were anything like Hermann, their loyalty and energy would be endless. Perhaps now, Peter told himself, his melancholy would vanish—but as another figure entered the factory, he knew it would only worsen...

"Hello there, Leighton," the unwanted visitor proclaimed as he strolled up to Peter, ignoring everyone else.

"You're the last person I expected to see this morning," Peter returned, his jaw automatically clenching.

James Wild grinned with feigned innocence. "And why is that?"

"Because it's six-thirty in the morning."

"Ah, yes, it is rather early, but I was on my way to locate a patrolman...my home was burglarized just hours ago."

"That's too bad," Peter remarked with little sympathy.

"Yes, it is...the thief absconded with my gold toothpick and a handful of other valuables," Wild said, his eyes fixed on Nick.

Instantly, Peter's pulse began to pound as outrage surged through him. Up until that very moment, he had allowed Wild to make his harassing, snide comments, because they were only directed at him...but no one—especially James B. Wild, the third—threatened his brother. "Your thief isn't here, James. So, unless you have business to discuss, I suggest you go find your patrolman."

"Ah, but I do have business to discuss."

Looking at his German workers, Peter forced a nonchalant smile. "Hermann, why don't you take the men upstairs and show them the assembly and painting rooms…I'm sure they'd like to see what they'll be working on."

At first Hermann hesitated, then, glancing at his family, he sighed. "All right, but remember, we'll be a shout away, if you need us."

Peter smiled again, this time genuinely—his friend's statement was reassuring, warm, and somewhat humorous. Peter knew that he, alone, could physically overcome the gaunt Wild with just one punch—but defeating the man in any other way would take a lot more than any human could offer. "Thanks, my friend," Peter called as the wiry German led his parade of kinsmen toward the stairs. "Now, James, what's your business?"

"I wanted to congratulate you on obtaining, for a second time, the Oak Park Men's Club furniture order and on the remarkable sacrifice of your employees…how you ever persuaded them to relinquish their wages is beyond my comprehension."

Peter opened his mouth to respond, but he couldn't find his voice—it was as if Wild had grabbed him by the throat, barely allowing him to breathe. The man always seemed to know things he shouldn't know. "Get out of my factory—and take your spies with you!" Peter finally seethed.

Wild exhaled and plucked a spot of sawdust from his coat sleeve. "I informed you, the last time you accused me of such nonsense, that you were mistaken…these spies are just figments of your infirm mind."

"Listen to me, Wild," Peter roared, his blood simmering. "I know you have snoops everywhere, and I'm telling you to remove them."

"You? Are telling me?"

"That's right," Peter continued, moving closer to his enemy. "You might as well remove them—they're not doing you any good."

"No?"

"No. God always finds a way to transform your vandalism into blessings for us."

"Is that so? Well, Leighton, let us just see if your God can transform this into a blessing," Wild hissed as he removed a piece of paper from his breast pocket. "Do you recognize what I am holding?"

Peter's heart suddenly skipped a beat. "It's our contract."

"Correct," Wild continued, ripping the page into tiny fragments. "I hereby cancel my furniture order."

Feeling as if ice water had been thrown in his face, Peter stood speechless. *Dear Jesus,* he inwardly moaned, *what have I done?*

"I see that I have finally succeeded in muffling that foul mouth of yours," Wild replied smugly.

Stunned by the bits of paper littering the factory floor, Peter shook his head. "You've...you've just lost your deposit," he tried.

"That is true—but I can afford the loss...you, however, have lost much, much more."

Snap! The pain was so real that Peter truly felt as if Wild's noose had, indeed, snapped his neck in two. Why? he wondered as the tension began to pound against his skull. Why couldn't he have just kept his mouth shut and let Wild have his fun? Why? Now, because of his weakness, his partners, his employees, and his fiancee were going to suffer. "James, I—"

"It is far too late for apologies, Leighton...unless, of course, you invite me into your company as a partner—then I might reconsider."

His jaw clamping down tighter, Peter peered into Wild's hollow eyes. He would do anything to save the furniture order and the factory's future—anything...except sell his soul to James Wild. Even though he knew he was letting everyone down, Peter choked out his answer. "No."

Wild laughed and adjusted his long locks of hair. "My offer will expire at six o'clock this evening—after that time, it will be up to you and your God to find buyers for the table and chair sets that you have completed thus far."

Unable to react, Peter just stared as his conqueror sauntered toward the door, circled, tipped his hat, and departed. Then Peter looked at Jaxson, and the agony churning inside him increased. How could he have made such an important decision without consulting his partner? "Jax, I'm sorry...I should have discussed it with you before—"

"Your answer was fine," Jaxson cut in. "I would have slapped ya if ya had said yes."

"But I just destroyed this company's chances of survival!"

"No, you didn't!" Jaxson countered, placing his hands on Peter's shoulders. "We're gunna survive, with or without Wild—'cause God's standing with us."

"But—"

"Peter, didn't you hear Wild? He challenged God! The Lord will find buyers for our furniture...just have faith."

As Peter listened to Jaxson's reasoning, Irene Spreyer's tale of Lazarus sprang back into his thoughts. 'God is never late,' he repeated to himself. And, holding onto that thin thread of hope, he breathed easier. If the Lord could resurrect Lazarus after four days, then He surely could revive their dying factory. "You're right."

With a confident half-chuckle, Jaxson gently tapped Peter's shoulders and released his grip.

"I just...I just wish I hadn't spouted off like that," Peter mumbled, more to himself than to his friend.

"It wasn't your fault," Nick returned, his eyes downcast. "It was…it was…"

As Nick stumbled over his words, Peter grinned with appreciation—his brother's sympathy was unexpected but very welcomed.

"Well, I dunno about you two," Jaxson announced, "but I'm ready to get started on those tables for the men's club, now that we don't have to spend every minute on Wild's stuff."

Peter laughed, then, as James Wild's comments flashed in front of him, his lightened mood dimmed. "Wild might be out of our lives, but we still have to contend with his spies."

"I know," Jaxson sighed. "The order was one thing—any of Wild's snitches in town could have overheard the men talkin' about it…but nobody outside this factory knew what happened with the payroll."

"I'd give anything to find out who is betraying us."

"Me…it's me."

Confusion washed over Peter as he tried to digest his brother's statement. "What did you say, Nick?"

"Wild learned about the payroll from me."

Studying his brother's distressed and fidgety demeanor, Peter shook his head defiantly—it couldn't be true. "Nick, you know Wild has spies everywhere…you have to be careful who you talk to, especially when you're in the saloons."

"No, Peter, no," Nick groaned. "Wild learned it from me…I met with him last night—as I do every night—and I told him about it."

A freezing jolt shot through Peter and numbed him to the core. "You told him?" he asked incredulously, glaring at the stranger who used to be his brother.

"I had to, Peter…Wild was so angry 'cause I didn't do anything he—"

"Why? Why would you spy on us?"

"I started snitchin' because I was mad at ya for tellin' me about my dead fam—"

"Get out."

"But then I started likin' ya, and I didn't wanna do it any—"

"Get out!"

"Wild wouldn't let me stop. He threatened to—"

Peter trembled with fury and heartache—and he ran a quivering hand through his hair to keep himself from adding more bruises to Nick's already injured face. "Get…out…of…my…sight!"

"I…I know this doesn't mean much now, but…but I'm sorry, Peter," Nick said, then he turned and shuffled toward the factory door.

Slowly, Peter sank to the floor, and leaning against one of the saws, he rubbed both hands over his face. Just like a year ago, he had lost everything—the factory he was supposed to rebuild…the livelihoods of those who trusted him…and his family. Massaging his left palm, Peter gazed up at Jaxson. "I've ruined everything—again."

"No, you didn't…it only looks grim from where you're sitting," Jaxson returned, squatting next to Peter. "I see a factory that's free from Wild's control…and loyal employees ready to work on the orders that we still have."

"How could Nick do this?"

Jaxson sat next to his friend and shrugged. "I dunno."

"I'll tell you one thing," Peter said as streams of frustration, anger, and grief ran down his cheeks, "the next time I see a pair of those crystal-blue eyes, I'm running in the opposite direction."

Jaxson chuckled and nodded sadly. "I don't blame ya…whatd'ya say we get Hermann's kin started on those tables?"

Brushing his tears away, Peter took a deep breath. Although he was relieved that his traitorous brother was no longer in sight, an overwhelming hurt—as painful as the one Daven had left—still pierced him. July twenty-ninth. Yes, Peter thought, that would definitely be a day that would forever stab him in the heart.

❧❧❧❧❧

As she stooped to grab another dishrag to pin on the clothesline, Lynette saw a familiar pair of boots and trousers stop next to her basket and she quickly stood up. "Nick?" she questioned, surprised to see him so early in the morning.

"I…I told Peter," he replied, his clear-blue eyes glazing over with moisture.

"And?"

"And he told me to get out of his sight."

Lynette dropped the rag back into the basket, and grabbing Nick's hands, she gazed at him sympathetically. "He needs time…you've injured him and he needs time to heal…Peter will forgive—"

"No, Lyn, you don't understand," Nick returned and twisted himself free. "I don't blame Peter for bein' angry…if I had been him, I would have thrown me out the window," he continued, pacing around in a small, haphazard circle. "Peter…Peter trusted me…you should have seen his face…if anyone else had told him that I was the one snitching to Wild, he would have slugged them…he trusted me…I never knew how much…not until I saw him look at me with that…that devastated expression."

As he ambled round and round in an erratic pattern, Lynette studied Nick Anderson and repeated his words inside her head…'that devastated expression.' It wasn't a phrase Nick would typically use. Maybe his steely, crude facade really did shield a warmhearted and wise spirit…and maybe that shell wasn't as unbreakable as she had thought. Stepping over to Nick, Lynette halted his wandering and hugged him tightly. "Peter will forgive you…just give him time to accept—"

Nick shook his head and gently pushed her away. "That's the one thing I don't have. Wild's already made up a rumor about him gettin' robbed…I've been walkin' around for almost two hours now, tryin' to figure things out…and I've decided to—"

"Please don't say leave."

"Why?" he asked as he looked deeply into her eyes.

"Because there are people here who care about you."

He studied her for a moment, then smiled sadly. "After what I've done and what I'm about to do, no one's gunna care—except, maybe you…and you're better off with Emerson Brant."

Trembling with alarm, embarrassment, and yearning, Lynette rubbed her goose-pimpled arms. "I'll make that decision."

Nick chuckled. "It would have been nice to see what could have happened between us."

"And what about Peter? He cares about you," she tried, hoping the breeze would cool the blush that was pulsing through her.

"He doesn't want me around anymore."

"One day, Peter's heart will soften toward you."

"Maybe, it will," he nodded. "But it ain't likely—not after what I aim to do."

"What do you mean?"

"I'm gunna fix what I broke."

"I don't understand."

"Wild canceled his furniture order to hurt Peter, and I'm gunna make him reconsider."

A sudden shiver fluttered down her spine. "No, Nick—"

"I gotta, Lyn…for my brother."

"But, if you harm James Wild, they'll—"

"I ain't gunna harm him, Lyn…I'm gunna give him what he wants."

"Nick, you're not making any sense!"

"I'm gunna give Wild a vow of allegiance and tell him that I'll be his dedicated little puppet—as long as he restores the table and chair order and leaves Peter alone from now on."

"You can't do that, Nikolaus."

"Sure I can, I'm used to gettin' the little end of the horn," he put in with a shrug. "The Denglers…Cass Phillips…Hannibal the Bear…Wild…at least this time, some good will come out of it…I can give my brother back what I selfishly caused him to lose."

"No, Nick! Becoming James Wild's henchman isn't the answer."

"Then what is?"

"Talk to God first…your scheme may interfere with what He wants to have happen."

"I don't have the time to wait for Him," Nick curtly replied, and spinning around on his heel, he headed toward the front of the house with a quick, determined gait.

"Nick, wait!" Lynette shouted and followed after him. "You're not thinking… please wait!" she tried again as she chased him into the front yard and down the sidewalk—but her pleas were disregarded. And, as Nick moved farther and farther ahead of her, she slowed to a stop and breathed in some much-needed air.

"Please keep him safe, Lord, and open his ears," she prayed aloud as she watched Nick's tall frame turn the corner and disappear from sight, "open his ears and make Your plans known to him…and if it be Your will, please bring him back to me…I would truly like to see what could happen between us."

❦

"I do know how to get there on my own."

"I know," Jaxson said as he and Peter continued their brisk walk to the showroom.

"So why are you still escorting me?"

Realizing that his friend would be more perturbed by the truth, Jaxson just offered a shrug in response. He knew Peter was strong and dedicated and had an uncanny ability to rise up after a fall—but he also knew his friend was edgy, explosive, and in his current frame of mind, completely unpredictable.

"Jax?"

"Yeah?" he replied, hoping that he wouldn't be asked to return to the factory.

"Did…did you suspect Nick and just didn't say anything because of me?"

Jaxson let out a humorless laugh and shook his head. "No…I thought he was using you, but I never thought that he was workin' for Wild."

"I guess I was just fooling myself."

"About what?"

"I thought we were making a dent in Nick's bitterness."

"Whatd'ya mean?" Jaxson questioned as both men tipped their hats to a group of oncoming ladies.

"Well," Peter murmured, twisting his watch chain between his index finger and thumb, "I just thought that you and I were succeeding, for the most part, in being living Bibles for Nick."

"Succeeding in what?!"

"In showing Nick that God is more than just words on a page…that He really does bring peace…you know, the way you and Anna showed me."

As Peter finished his explanation, Jaxson stopped in mid-stride as if he had stepped into a puddle of glue. A living Bible?

"Jax?"

Still unable to move, Jaxson just stared into the void of failure. He had been everything but a living Bible…uncharitable…selfish…spiteful…and he definitely didn't 'do unto others.' How could he have been so blind to his own actions? His fear of losing his brotherly bond with Peter had compelled him to turn his back on Nick…he had failed to minister to another human being because, God forgive him, he was scared and uneasy and, yes, jealous.

"Jax? Are you all right?"

Realizing that their parley was causing a blockage on the sidewalk, Jaxson pulled himself from his revelations. "Yeah…yeah, I'm okay," he mumbled as they continued their trek to the showroom. "If anyone around here showed Nick a shred of Christian goodness, it was you."

Peter grunted sarcastically. "Right, that's why I told him to get out of my sight."

Halting the journey once again, Jaxson grasped Peter's arm and turned him so they were face-to-face. "Nick betrayed you!"

"I know…I just wish I had…that I had said 'get out of my sight—for awhile'… it's going to take a long time before I can forgive him, and I don't know if I'll ever trust him again, but I don't want him to disappear altogether…he is still my brother."

Jaxson bobbed his head in amazement. Maybe a year ago, he had been a good example for Peter, but now, it was his friend who was teaching him how to mirror the Bible's words. "It'll work out," Jaxson tried, resuming their hike. "Nick seemed sorry, maybe he won't disappear."

Peter replied with another skeptical grunt, then fell silent—and once again, Jaxson's heart sank with sympathy and concern. Of all the days in July, why did Nick and Wild choose this particular day to come against his partner?

As they approached the showroom's carved door, Peter reached out to grab the handle, and instantly, a cramp rippled up his right forearm. Cussing under his breath, he cradled the sore limb and looked into Jaxson's worried eyes. "This arm's been bothering me all morning—and there isn't a cloud in the sky."

Jaxson nodded. "Yeah, but there sure is a heaviness in the air."

His brow furrowing with bewilderment, Peter studied his friend. "Why do you say that?" he asked, wondering if the same foreboding that had been following him since daybreak was also enveloping Jaxson.

"Because it's true...what Quentin Fetch did to us—and most of all to Daven—will, I think, always cause us pain on July twenty-ninth."

Swallowing hard, Peter whispered, "I miss him, Jax."

"So do I...you gunna go see him?"

Peter glanced at Jaxson, then quickly averted his eyes. "I...I don't know."

"You need to go...you haven't been to the grave since—"

Suddenly, the showroom door burst open, violently jangling the overhead bell. "Thank you, Mr. Franz," the man exiting hollered over his shoulder, "I'll look for him there." And, without bothering to see if his path was clear, the stranger barreled over the threshold—and squarely into Peter. "Forgive me, Sir. I hope I didn't—" the man declared, then he cut himself off and smiled broadly. "It's you! It's really you!"

As he peered at the stranger's features, a ripple of recognition swirled inside Peter's head—he knew the person standing in front of him...but from where?

"My name's Kyle Knight," the man said as if answering the thought. "Do you remember me, Mr. Leighton? We met a couple of weeks ago in Willow Ridge...in Logan MacColl's office...I'm the court jester who spilled my catalogs all over the room...do you remember?"

"Yes, yes," Peter replied, shaking Kyle's thin hand. "Your face was familiar, but I just couldn't place it."

"I'm so glad I finally found you," Kyle announced, and tightening his grip, he backed into the showroom and dragged Peter inside with him. "I've been searching for you for over a week!"

"Why is that?" Peter questioned as he pulled his hand away and glanced at Jaxson, who had followed them into the building.

"Peter!" Del Franz called from the stairs, "I didn't expect you yet...I just told Mr. Knight that you'd be at the factory."

"Well...uh...Jaxson and I just had to...to check on something," Peter returned, not wanting to delve into the factory's latest ordeal. "Thanks, Del, I'll take care of Mr. Knight."

"Just yell if you need me," Del offered and continued his climb to the second floor.

"So, Mr. Knight, why have you been searching for me?"

Instantly, Kyle dropped his valise on the floor and, getting down on one knee, rummaged through the bag. "Please, please, please, tell me that this is yours," he pleaded as he held up a ragged-edged photograph.

His eyes widening in awe, Peter took the picture from Kyle's outstretched hand and gazed at the painted table and chairs that Max Green had so carefully photographed. "Yes, it's mine," Peter murmured, still amazed that the lost still life had found its way home.

"It is? Oh, that's wonderful!" Kyle shouted, jumping to his feet. "I found it mixed in with my catalogs."

Peter nodded and chuckled. "I had it with me when I was ordering my lumber from MacColl…he had set it on his desk and—"

"And," Kyle put in, "I buried it under all my books."

"Yeah, I guess you did…thanks for returning it."

Kyle Knight practically giggled and snatched the picture from Peter's hand. "Mr. Leighton, I did not come here to return it."

"Oh?"

"When I got back to Detroit," Kyle explained, "I found your picture sandwiched between two of my catalogs, and my boss ended up seeing it…well, he absolutely fell in love with the furniture set. He wants to buy it."

Peter smiled. The Lord was astounding—He was indeed finding buyers for their furniture…one by one. "Well, if I can persuade the photographer to finally give the set up, your boss can have it."

"No, no, no, no, no, no, no," Kyle rattled, spouting out the word as if he were a Gatling gun. "You don't understand…my boss loved your furniture so much that he wants to sell it…he's ready to print up some flyers to distribute along with his catalogs."

"What?" Peter choked out as an excited thrill gushed through him.

Kyle laughed—half joyously, half nervously. "I know that seems a bit presumptuous, but you see, my boss asked me if I had spoken to you—about us selling your furniture—and I said that I did."

"What?" Peter asked again, trying to make sense of the man's babbling.

"I realize that I had no right to do that, but my boss can be…well…and he was so anxious about putting your pieces into his catalog…and, uh…well, he offered me a really marvelous bonus for finding you…so, you see…I had no choice, I had to tell him that I had your blessing."

"What are you trying to say?"

"Well," Kyle continued, wiping a jittery hand over his face, "will you let us sell your furniture through our catalogs?"

Feeling as if he had been handed a pail of good fortune, Peter staggered backward a step, then he looked at Jaxson, who was also flabbergasted.

"Please say yes, Mr. Leighton," Kyle begged. "My boss feels that people will really clamor for these sets."

"He does?"

"Yes. That's why I have been frantic this last week…I was responsible for this great piece of merchandise, but I didn't know who made it! I retraced every step of my last trip, and thank goodness, there were only a few people who the picture could have belonged to—and you were one of them," Kyle recounted. Then, after taking a few long, badly needed breaths, he went on with his monologue, "But I couldn't recall where you said you hailed from…at least, though, I did remember that I saw you at Logan MacColl's sawmill…and he sent me here…and I have found you at last!"

"I guess you did," Peter put in with a gasp—he was as winded from the saga as Kyle was.

"So? May we sell your decorated tables and chairs? We would like at least thirty sets to start—which I can pay you for right now."

With Kyle's words, Peter's pail of abundance overflowed, and he grabbed onto Jaxson to steady himself. His friend had been correct all along…their times were definitely in God's hands…

A year ago, the Lord had arranged for Rheinhardt Furniture to have a new factory, long before the old one burned to the ground—and this year, He had devised a way to sell Wild's tables, long before the man canceled his order. It was all so amazing, Peter thought. God had been busy working on their problems—even before they became problems.

Then, suddenly, as he surveyed Jaxson's beaming expression, Peter realized that he had failed to introduce his friend. "Mr. Knight," he offered, grabbing Jaxson's arm and pulling him into the midst of his conference, "I must apologize…we bounded off into our discussion, and I never had the chance to introduce my partner, Jaxson Averill."

Immediately, Kyle's smile vanished and he scanned Jaxson from head to boot. "He's your partner? But he's…he's a…"

"Yes, he's my partner—along with Karl Rheinhardt, who's in Europe right now."

"I see…I thought you ran this company."

"Well, I'm the one who stands in the foreground most of the time, but before any major decisions are made, two partners must agree on the issue."

"Ah," Kyle said, obviously pondering the situation. And, for an endless minute, no sound emerged from anyone, then, suddenly, Kyle's grin returned. "How about it, Mr. Averill? May we sell your furniture?"

"I don't see why not," Jaxson answered in a cool and aloof tone, but as he tilted his head to look at Peter, his eyes screamed out a stern and silent, 'you took a big chance—you should've just let him insult me.'

"Well, Mr. Knight," Peter announced, "we would be honored to have our furniture in your mail-order catalog."

Kyle exhaled in relief and shook hands with both Peter and Jaxson. "Fabulous! How soon do you think we can get the thirty sets?"

"Immediately…we actually have thirty-two crated and ready to ship…however, those tables have a different painted motif than the one in the photograph."

"I'll let my boss know, but I don't think he'll mind—we'll just change the art for the flyer," Kyle said with a whoop of elation as he pressed the photograph to his chest. "My prayers have been answered…thank you."

"No, Mr. Knight," Peter countered, "I must thank you."

"I'd like to talk with both of you further and work out the shipping details," Kyle added as he picked up his valise. "Would twelve-noon be convenient? I would take care of it right now, but I'd like to telegraph my employer first—and get myself a hotel room…I came here right from the depot after one of the most taxing trips I have—"

Hoping to prevent another soliloquy, Peter held up his hand. "Noon would be fine. Jaxson and I will meet you here…my office is upstairs."

"You both have made this a great day for me…I will see you at noon."

Simultaneously and almost as if they had arranged it, Peter and Jaxson sighed, crossed their arms, and watched Kyle Knight bounce out of the showroom, then, glancing at each other, both laughed.

"You almost pushed him too far," Jaxson chided as the chuckles subsided. "You should've just said that I was one of your workers."

"Jax, he was so desperate to buy our tables he would have kissed your boots."

Instantly, a twinkle shined in Jaxson's eyes. "Did you hear what you just said? Our tables—he wants our tables!"

"Yeah," Peter replied, grinning, "I think we got our miracle."

"I know we did…we gotta go tell the men."

Placing his hand on Jaxson's shoulder, Peter's smile swelled. "I'll let you inform the men…I'm going to see Anna…it'll be nice to bring her some pleasant news for a change."

***

Filling his lungs with a deep breath and his heart with courage, Nick pounded on the large, ornate door of James Wild's Park Street home. Although he dreaded everything he was about to do, he silently admitted that his present position did have one advantage—at least he no longer had to slink around in the dark.

"Yes, may I help you," the butler asked, opening the door. Then, recognizing Nick, he added in a whisper, "Mr. Anderson, you are supposed to go to the back door, remember?"

"Not anymore," Nick declared, feeling almost ashamed of the accomplishment. "I need to speak to Wild…is he here?"

"No, he left very early this morning to take care of some errands. He did mention, though, that he wanted to inspect the work being done on his new home."

"He's not there—I already checked."

"And I know he wanted to visit the Rheinhardt Factory...perhaps he is—"

Nick cut the butler off with a cynical laugh. "That visit is long over with."

"Well, I do expect him to return at eleven-thirty...Mr. Wild is usually quite prompt when it comes to his afternoon-dinner."

Pulling out his watch, Nick clicked it open and studied the hands that still moved according to their own whims—if only he had been able to fix his own timepiece before Marion demanded the return of his tools. "What time is it now?"

"Nine-thirty."

Nick sighed. That meant he would have almost two hours to wait—all the while wondering if Wild had taken his fictional burglary to the police.

Grabbing a clean sheet from the chair next to her, Anna unfurled the linen and waved it over the stripped hospital bed. Then, as the fabric wafted onto the mattress, a faint murmuring tickled her ears. Was her father beckoning her? Or another doctor? Or was it a patient? Standing motionless, she listened for the whisper to sound again.

"Anna...Anna."

Stepping into the hospital's main hall, Anna searched for the person paging her but saw no one. Confused, she scanned the hall again, then shrugged. Maybe, she reasoned, the noise had been a remnant of someone's conversation.

"Anna."

This time the caller came into view, and Anna gasped with consternation and surprise—Peter, uncommonly disheveled, was jogging in and out of the wards, obviously looking for her.

"Here," she whisper-shouted, and as he trotted down the hall, Anna's features stiffened with bewilderment. Although his appearance was frazzled, Peter was smiling—widely—and he held a collection of white flowers in his hand. "Is there something wrong?" she inquired softly.

Peter made no response until he neared, then, with an ecstatic "No, just the opposite," he wrapped his arms around her, and lifting her off the floor, he spun around and around.

"What's gotten into you?" Anna insisted as they whirled in circles.

Without a word, Peter gently released her, held out his bouquet, and gazed at her so intently that she felt her face redden. "Anna Spreyer," he finally said breathlessly, "will you marry me?"

"Will I…Peter, what has gotten into you?"

"Will you marry me?"

Anna's blush deepened as a few of the patients and other volunteers peeked through the doorways and around the corners, trying to glimpse their tete-a-tete. "I believe I've already answered that question," she said, taking the fragrant bouquet and staring into Peter's sparkling brown eyes.

"Yes, you did, but will you marry me on August twenty-seventh?"

"August? What…what's going on?"

"That was your first choice for a date, wasn't it?"

"Yes," she replied, utterly perplexed, "but why the change?"

"Because I don't want to postpone being with you for one moment longer," Peter returned and lightly stroked her cheek. "I want to be with you…and hold you…and do this," he added, giving her an ardent kiss on the lips.

As their embrace finally ebbed, a deluge of passion swept through Anna, and she tilted her head to the side, hoping to hide her excitement—then she noticed their increasing audience. With an chagrined whimper, Anna grasped Peter's arm and quietly led him to a small, secluded anteroom next to the hospital's front doors. "Now," she proclaimed, still clutching him, "tell me what's going on?"

"I've been a fool, Anna…a complete fool."

"Why do you say that? You have not."

"Yes, I have…instead of trusting God, I let James Wild—and my fear of what he was and wasn't going to do—control my life…I forgot that the Lord's plans are written in stone…and man's are written in sand."

Although elegant, Peter's words baffled her. What, Anna wondered, could have prompted her fiance to make such a profound statement?

"James Wild canceled his furniture order this morning," he went on as if he had understood her thoughts.

"Oh, Peter, I'm so sorry…I know how much that order meant to you."

"But it shouldn't have…I put my hope on Wild, instead of God…I let James Wild manipulate me…and antagonize me…and I stupidly based my actions on what he did."

As Anna listened to her fiance's insights, she inwardly beamed. Her heart had belonged to Peter Leighton since the first moment she saw him, but as his faith continued to grow, so did her love. And the thought of being united with him, in less than a month, thrilled every fiber within her. "What brought all this on?"

"Do you remember when I told you about my trip to Willow Ridge and how I left Max's photograph there?"

"Yes."

"Well, while I was at the sawmill, a friend of MacColl's, a salesman from a mail-order company, stopped in, and somehow, my picture got mixed in with his catalogs…so, without either of us knowing it, the man took the photograph back to Detroit with him. Then, when he eventually found it, the salesman showed it to his boss—who fell in love with the furniture and who wants to buy thirty tables…the tables that Wild just said he didn't want!"

"That's wonderful, Honey!"

"Yeah, it is and I…I still can't believe it…with one wave of His hand, God just washed away Wild's plot to slither into our company."

"Just as if it were scribbled in the sand," Anna murmured, now grasping the imagery.

Peter smiled and brushed an errant strand of her hair back into place. "Exactly."

"And that's why you want to get married in August instead of October?"

"Yes," he replied, caressing her arms. "I don't want to waste any more time…and I don't want to have any more detours or delays because of Wild, or Hans, or anybody else…I want our marriage to follow only the Lord's agenda."

Rising up on her toes, Anna slid her hands behind Peter's head, and pulling him close, she kissed him…and kissed him…and kissed him, not caring who might still be watching. She knew their union would face turbulent whirlwinds in the future and waves would try to overwhelm them, but she also knew the tribulations would not prevail. She and Peter were building upon the perfect foundation—and that would enable them to weather any storm. "If you'd like," she offered, loosening her hold, "I'll ask Papa if I can take an early lunch. We could get something at the bakery or general store and have a picnic."

"I'd like nothing more—but I can't…I'm meeting the catalog salesman at noon, and…and I want to give myself enough time to walk over and see…"

Anna waited for an ending to Peter's statement, but his voice broke and faded into silence. "Walk over and see who, Honey?"

"My brother."

With a smile, Anna nodded. "I'm sure Nick would appreciate hearing the news—especially coming from you."

Peter coughed out a bitter laugh, then sadly gazed at the floor. "No…Nick's left town."

"Why?"

"He's…he's been working for Wild all this time…he's been one of the spies in our midst."

"Oh, no!"

"Oh, yeah."

Suddenly, Peter's hesitant words reentered Anna's thoughts and her spirit soared. She was truly sorry that Nick had departed, but she was elated that, after a year of battling pain, guilt, and denial, Peter was finally going to see Daven—it meant her fiance was truly healing.

❈Twelve❈

"Well, well, well…how kind of you to pay me a visit."

Nick rolled his eyes and pushed himself up from the fireplace hearth. He hated Wild's haughtiness, but he knew he had better get used to it—among other things. "Did you talk to a patrolman about your missing jewelry?"

Wild stroked his chin as a smirk danced across his face. "Maybe. Am I going to receive my vow of allegiance?"

Trying to steady his nerves, Nick reached out, and even though the movement pulled on his stitches, he clutched the fireplace's flawlessly carved mantle. "I have thought a lot about it, Mr. Wild, and I would like to offer you—"

Suddenly, a loud rapping sounded on the door, cutting Nick off from his long-rehearsed speech.

"Excuse me, Mr. Wild?"

"What is it, Robert?"

With hesitation in his every step, the butler entered the solarium, his eyes dashing from Wild, to Nick, and back again. "I apologize for disturbing you. I just wanted to inform you that your afternoon-dinner will be ready in fifteen minutes—the cook is just finishing the sauce…uh, will Mr. Anderson be joining you? If he is, I will need to inform the cook so she can—"

"He will not be joining me."

Robert smiled and exhaled in relief. "Thank you, Sir. I did not look forward to dodging any more dishes," he replied. Then, to Nick, the butler offered, "The cook is very temperamental—especially when we have unexpected visitors that she must—"

"That is enough, Robert," Wild snapped.

"Of course, Sir."

Releasing his stranglehold on the mantle, Nick grunted and wondered if he would be treated better—or worse—after he handed his leash over to Wild.

"Again, I apologize for the interruption," the butler said, bowing slightly.

Wild dusted the air with his hand to dismiss his servant, then he paused and held up his index finger. "Robert."

"Yes Sir?"

"Please inform Aaron to keep the brougham in readiness…I may need to continue with my errands following my repast."

"Yes Sir."

"That will be all."

"Yes Sir. Thank you, Sir."

"Now, Anderson, you have squandered enough of my time…am I going to receive a vow of allegiance—or not?" Wild demanded as he moved to his overstuffed chair and donned his usual, kingly position.

Closing his eyes, Nick gritted his teeth—maybe prison wouldn't be so bad after all…

"Well?"

"I have thought a lot about it, Mr. Wild," he choked out, forcing his eyelids open, "and I would like to offer you a proposition."

"A proposition? Do you even know what that word means?"

"Yes, I know what it means," Nick hissed.

"Then, by all means, proceed."

"If you give Peter back the order for your tables and chairs—and stop harassing him—I will indenture myself to you for life."

At first, Wild chuckled, then he cackled, then his amusement swelled into a boisterous laugh. "You must be mad! You will indeed indenture yourself to me for life—however, it will be in exchange for your freedom…and your freedom alone."

"Look, we both know that you can control me with your threats about prison," Nick went on, ignoring Wild's comments, "but I will despise you every second, and you will never be able to fully trust me."

Instantly, Wild's merriment vanished, and moistening his lips, he leaned his head against the back of his chair. "Go on."

Taking a deep breath, Nick slowly strolled toward his soon-to-be master. "I am offering to become your devoted henchman…to submit to your every demand…no questions asked…I will even sign a contract stating just that. But, to get my complete loyalty, you must give Peter back your furniture order—and leave him alone from this point on."

Wild stared somberly at Nick and crossed his arms. "Your proposition is intriguing—however…"

"However what?" Nick asked as he reached the overstuffed chair.

"It requires that I concede."

"Yeah…so?"

"So, my good man, I have labored at my contest with Peter Leighton for almost a year…it is not in my blood to be that magnanimous."

"I do not understand you, Wild…you are going to give up a henchman that will do your every bidding, just to continue a battle with one man?"

"Yes…I want Peter on his knees."

Nick laughed. "He has already been on his knees—talking to God…you will never beat him…why not just forget about your game with him? I am sure there is someone else in Michigan that you can find to play with."

Wild caressed his chin once again. "If I were to agree to this proposal, you would willingly do anything I ask?"

"I will not kill—but anything else…yes."

"No questions asked?"

"None."

"Hmm, most intriguing…Bryce was always willing, but he was impossible to—"

"Bryce?" Nick cut in, shuddering. "As in Leland Bryce?"

"Uh…no…um, I misspoke."

"Leland Bryce works for you?"

"I do not know to whom you are referring," Wild returned, tugging at his shirt collar.

"Well, let me refresh your memory…Leland Bryce…wanted murderer…used to work for Quentin Fetch…wants my brother dead!" Nick shouted, and as he said the words, the truth hit him like a blow to the belly. "You hired Bryce to kill Peter!"

"I did not! Peter's death would end our game—and that is the last thing I would want to have happen."

Nick stood motionless as he sorted out Wild's words, then, trembling with fury and panic, he grabbed his adversary by the collar and pulled him to his feet. "Where's Bryce now?"

"Release me at once!"

Tightening his hold, Nick pulled Wild forward until their noses touched. "Where is he?!"

"I will have you arrested for assault if you do not release me straightaway!"

"Go ahead…at least this time, you won't have to lie about your charges…now, tell me where Bryce is, or I'll beat you 'til you're unrecognizable—and I know the meanin' of that word too!"

Wild swallowed hard. "I…I do not know…he terminated his employment on Friday…he said he needed to meet with someone today and conclude a business transaction, then he was heading to the frontier."

"He needed to meet with someone today?"

"Yes…now, release me."

As Wild's disclosure repeated itself inside his head, Nick's grip slackened. Bryce was going to kill Peter—today—and all he had done for the past two hours was practice a speech that was now useless. "You just better hope that I find Bryce before he hurts my brother."

"Or what?!" Wild demanded as he smoothed the lapels of his frock coat.

"Or you're the one who's gunna find himself in the stockade!"

"That is quite doubtful—I will merely explain to the authorities that I hired a man named Wit Dearborn as my assistant and that I had no idea he was a wanted criminal using an alias."

Nick spit out a curse. "Dearborn?! The bald guy who caused Peter so much grief was really Bryce?! You rotten…"

Without finishing his rebuke, Nick spun around on his heel, dashed out of the solarium, and hurried over the front door's threshold. Then he abruptly stopped as if he had reached the end of his tether. Was he rushing off to find a dead man? Or was Peter still alive? And, if his brother was alive, how was he going to reach him in time to keep him alive? Suddenly, a smile worked its way onto Nick's face as he noticed Wild's carriage and horses snoozing in the street. That was how! Running to the unattended vehicle, Nick grabbed the railing and started to climb onto the driver's seat, but within a blink, he found himself lying on the ground and the coachman hovering over him.

"Try that again," the driver barked, "and I'll use the whip on you!"

"Wild said I could use his coach!" Nick lied, shoving his ambusher away and scrambling to his feet.

"Sure he did!" the man bellowed and swung a reckless fist at Nick.

"Aaron!"

The coachman and Nick instantly froze and peered at James Wild, who leaned against the carved railing of his veranda.

"Let Mr. Anderson take the carriage."

Although relieved by the proclamation, Nick glared at Wild and hollered, "Is this some kind of trick?"

"No, this is not a 'trick.' It was never my intent or desire to have Peter die…now, go save my favorite opponent."

Swearing at Wild's tone and motive, Nick shouted, "I know you have no fear of being punished for your games, but I'm telling you, if any harm comes to Peter, you will fear me!" Then, in one swift movement, he bolted for the brougham, leaped onto the seat, grabbed the reins, and urged the horses into a gallop.

Barely staying upright, the carriage raced down the road, violently bouncing over the wooden-block paving. And, as he pushed the team of horses to run even faster, Nick's mind centered on one question…where should he start searching for his brother? The showroom and factory were in opposite directions—which should he go to first? If he chose the wrong place, it could end up costing him precious minutes—and even worse, Peter's life.

Crushed by uncertainty, Nick cursed and yanked the horses to a stop. He had to choose, he knew that, but he couldn't budge his anxiety-crippled mind into making a choice. If only God would point him in the right direction…

Taking a deep breath, Nick laughed at himself—did that thought really come out of his head? Then, gazing up at the glistening sky, he sighed. "Okay, this is Your chance to prove that You're the wonderful God Peter and Lynette say You are…which way do I go?"

Trying to calm his pounding heart, Nick waited, but only the noise of the passing traffic answered him.

"Please…I know I don't deserve anything from You, but this isn't for me—it's for Peter…do I go to the factory? Or the showroom?" he pleaded, first gesturing to his left, then to the right.

Nothing.

"Fine! Then I'll make my own decision…I'm goin' to the factory!" he yelled as he swatted the horses with the reins.

But, instead of moving, both animals snorted and stood fixed in place.

"What's wrong with you worthless nags?! Go!"

Once again, the horses just whinnied.

With a shiver, Nick glanced upward and swallowed the lump that had formed in his throat. "Maybe I should try the showroom instead, huh?"

Instantly, the team started to pull the coach to the right.

"Okay," Nick continued with a delighted—and astounded—gasp. "The showroom it is."

<hr/>

Lifting the latch, Peter opened the cast-iron gate, but he still couldn't step inside the cemetery fence. He wanted to—he truly did—but it seemed as if a web of memories and guilt had spun itself across the opening. The meshy barrier not only blocked his entrance, it also reminded him that he had left his brother in the graveyard, alone, for an entire year.

"Hey, Daven," he called from the fence, hoping that, somehow, the greeting would grant him courage. "I…I just wanted to come and say…"

His voice breaking, Peter clenched his jaw and forced himself through the gate—if he was going to apologize, he was going to do it right…no matter how much it hurt.

"Hello, Daven," he whispered as he neared his brother's resting place, then, glancing around the area, he smiled ruefully. "Jaxson's done a fine job taking care of things here…and your maple tree is doing great," he offered, pointing to the sapling that their friend had planted near the marker. "Well, it's been a whole year since…since you were…"

Wiping away his forming tears, Peter slipped out of his frock coat and laid it and his hat on the ground—his brother deserved more than his awkward attempts at being cordial.

"Daven, I'm so sorry for what happened last year," he said, kneeling by the stone. "I had no idea that you'd get…get…and I'm sorry for not coming to see you…I…I just couldn't…I couldn't bear to come…forgive me."

Brushing at his eyes once again, Peter studied his brother's tombstone and the freshly cut vine of ivy that now encircled it. "I see you've already had a visitor today…you are definitely missed by a lot of people—me, most of all," he sobbed. "Oh, Dave, I wish I had shown you more love…I should have remembered that every day could have been your last…I've tried to do that with everyone else in my life, but…but I'm still failing."

"How poignant…and pathetic."

Instantly, Peter's back stiffened and the hairs on his arms stood on end. It wasn't the fact that he had been overheard or that someone had crept up on him…and it wasn't even the sarcastic words…it was the voice, alone, that made him shudder.

Slowly, Peter turned and peered at the man behind him—he didn't recognize the bald head or the glasses or the beard, but the eyes…the eyes, like the voice, were all too familiar. And, as Peter stared into Leland Bryce's icy orbs, he realized that this was the dark shadow that had been, literally, trailing him all morning—and the past year.

"Kinda funny, ain't it?" Bryce snickered as he leveled his pistol at Peter's head. "I wrote that you should keep lookin' over your shoulder, because, eventually, I'd be there—and guess what…here I am."

Peter searched for something to say but found no reply—his executioner was right…and no words could change that. Then, as he looked beyond Bryce for the first time, Peter's heart sank even deeper—another of his enemies hovered at the cemetery gate.

"You want me to come and keep him in place for ya?" Manning Cole hollered from the fence.

"No," Bryce loudly returned, his eyes glued to Peter.

"But you said I could help ya kill him," Cole whined, running over to stand behind Bryce.

"Look, you idiot, I told you the plan a thousand times—we're going to kill him, but not here…now, go get the rope!"

"Don't call me an idiot!"

"I'll stop calling you an idiot when you stop actin' like one."

Snorting in dissatisfaction, Cole contorted his face and glared at the back of Bryce's head.

"I said get the rope!" Bryce sneered without turning around. Then, waving his gun, he asked Peter, "You do remember Cole, don't ya?"

"Yeah, I remember him."

"I bet—that smell's hard to forget…Cole remembers you too—that's why he's agreed to assist me…you sure are good at gettin' people to hate you, Leighton."

"I reckon I am."

"And I reckon it's time we get going."

"Going? Where?" Peter asked, his brow furrowing.

"Here's your stupid rope," Cole announced as he trotted up to Bryce and held out a length of cord.

"Good…tie his hands—tightly."

Cole snickered, and walking across Daven's grave, he dangled the twine in front of Peter's face. "This is for beatin' on me at the factory…put your hands behind your back."

Drawing in a deep breath, Peter slid his arms rearward and crossed his wrists. "Where are you taking me?"

Bryce's lips curled into a wintry smile. "To Everly's…I thought it'd be rather appropriate to shoot you at the same place that your brother got shot…and on the same day…and in the same manner."

Peter opened his mouth to respond, then squelched his retort as Cole yanked the rope taut.

"You do recall how to get to Everly's, don't ya?" Bryce questioned, obviously enjoying the situation as much as Cole.

"Yeah," Peter grunted.

"Then get your legs movin'…and just so you don't lose your way or get any ideas about escaping, Cole and me will be followin' ya all the way on our horses."

❧ ⚜ ❧

Careening down the streets, Nick weaved Wild's carriage to and fro, all the while yelling and cursing at everyone to flee from his path. He knew most of the people he passed had the right-of-way, but he had the speeding carriage—and the task of saving his brother's life.

Then, as the team approached the showroom, Nick drew in the reins, and without even waiting for the coach to stop completely, he jumped from the seat and ran toward the door. Once inside, Nick spun around, scanning the showroom for his brother, but he only saw Del and Jaxson talking with a thin, brown-haired man.

"Where…is…Peter," he panted, jogging over to the trio.

"Nick," Jaxson replied with a mixed expression of relief, annoyance, and sympathy, "we have a very important meeting, you can talk—"

"Where is he?!"

"He's not here yet, but I'm sure he's on his way."

"We gotta get to him, Jaxson…now!"

"Nick, this isn't a good time for—"

Shaking his head vehemently, Nick grasped Jaxson's shoulders and peered into his eyes. "Leland Bryce has been working for James Wild!"

Instantly, Jaxson's lower jaw dropped, and a sickly haze washed over his features. "What?"

"Bryce's been workin' for Wild. He's been using the name Dearborn…you know, the bald guy who's been makin' so much trouble…he told Wild he had to meet somebody today—to finish a business matter."

"No…" Jaxson gasped.

"We gotta get to Peter before Bryce does…do you know where is he?"

"He went to see Anna…she's workin' at the hospital today."

"Well, come on then!" Nick exclaimed, taking a step toward the door, but Jaxson seized his forearm and pulled him back.

"Peter was supposed to be here at noon…he's already ten minutes late."

⚜

"Are you sure it's okay, Papa?"

"Yes," Doctor Spreyer returned gently. "As long as you and Pay-ter have sought the Lord's approval, Mama and I will happily support any wedding date you choose—whether it be in October, August, or tomorrow."

Anna giggled at her father's joke, then a somber cloud descended and her grin faded. "And are you sure it's okay that I don't wait for Hans?"

"Liebchen, your brother has never mentioned your nuptials in his letters—he didn't even address the matter when he responded to my telegram…I think his silence is our answer."

With a sigh, Anna bowed her head. "Why, Papa? Hans and I were always so close…why would he just walk away from me the way he did?"

"I don't know…I fear he's walked away from all of us."

Hearing the pain in her father's voice, Anna grasped his hand.

"One day, though," the doctor went on, "I think he will regret his decision."

"What do you mean?"

"Well, I just think there will come a time when he'll desire a family again—and he'll come home…but it won't be the home of his youth."

Anna's forehead crinkled as she tried to decipher her father's words—obviously it wasn't a good day for comprehending the men in her life. "I still don't understand, Papa."

Doctor Spreyer laughed. "Mama is so much better at philosophizing than I am… I mean that Hans has decided to live his life without us, but he doesn't realize that our lives will continue to go on too—without him…when he does, eventually, come home, he won't know us anymore…he will have missed being a part of his nieces' and nephews' young lives…he will have missed watching you grow into a vibrant woman…he will have missed witnessing your wedding and Pay-ter's inspiring strength through this past year…he will have missed spending time with his mother before…"

Her eyes watering, Anna reached her arms around her father and laid her head on his chest. "We'll just have to pray that Hans decides to rejoin us—before he misses too much."

"Ja," the doctor replied, pulling her close. "Now, I want you and Pay-ter to go ahead and continue with your lives—choose a wedding date that the two of you want. And, remember, God is the only one you need to please…not me, not Mama, and definitely, not Hans."

Wiping the teary moisture from her face, Anna smiled. "Thank you, Papa, I—"

"Anna!"

Startled by the shout, Anna glanced in the direction of the voice, expecting to see Peter, once again, at the other end of the hallway, but this time, it was Jaxson and Nick who were running toward her—and this time, it wasn't consternation or surprise that rippled through her…it was fear.

"Nick, what's going on?" she asked as they neared. "I thought you—"

"Where's Peter?!" he demanded, his face lined with dread.

"He…he went to see Daven."

"How long ago did he leave?"

"It's been well over an hour."

"Over an hour?"

"Yes—he was going to walk to the cemetery and see Daven, then he had a meeting," she returned, gazing into Nick's worry-filled eyes. "What's going on?"

Instead of answering, Nick peered at Jaxson. "You know where the cemetery is?"

Jaxson nodded. "Yeah, it's over on the east side, at the outskirts of town." Then, giving Anna and the doctor a weak smile, he offered, "We just got some news, and we gotta let Peter know about it right away."

Although Jaxson's statement sounded reassuring, his tone and countenance belied his casual words. "What news?" Anna whispered.

"We better get going," Nick put in and tugged at Jaxson's sleeve.

"Yeah, okay."

"What news?!" Doctor Spreyer bellowed, repeating his daughter's question.

Jaxson first looked at Nick, who was already trotting toward the front doors, then, turning back, he hesitated before offering, "Nick just found out that...that..."

"What?" Anna gasped with a shiver.

"That Leland Bryce is in town."

Instantly, Anna's shiver transformed into a stabbing jolt, and she grabbed her father's arm. Although her fiancé had never mentioned Bryce's death threats, she still knew he received them, having found three of the letters while tidying the guest house. And, because of those horrible notes, she also knew how much danger Peter now faced. Pulling herself from her daze, Anna watched Jaxson jog down the hall, then, as a cyclone of fear began to spin around her, she chased after him. "Jaxson, please bring Peter back to me!"

With a wave and a muffled answer, Jaxson pushed the hospital doors open and disappeared.

"Oh, please, dear Lord," Anna prayed, hoping to quiet the whirlwind that surrounded her, "don't let Bryce hurt any of them."

"Everything is going to be all right," the doctor cooed as he came up behind her and placed his hands on her shoulders. "God is with them."

Turning, Anna looked up at her father. "When Peter came by earlier," she said, her lip quivering, "he called himself a fool—but I'm the one who's been foolish! All this time, Papa, I have been postponing the wedding, just waiting for everything to be perfect—that could have been time spent with Peter! Now, I may lose him!"

"Don't give up hope, Liebchen. The Lord brought Pay-ter through the fight he had with Quentin Fetch—and He can bring him through this one too."

❧❦❧

"Get out of the way!"

Grabbing onto the metal railing that surrounded the driver's seat, Jaxson glanced over his shoulder, then back at Nick, who was loudly urging the horses to intensify their breakneck speed. "You almost hit that lady!" he barked as he tightly clutched the railing, trying to keep himself from becoming a victim of Nick's heedless driving.

"I told her to get out of the way," came the reply as Nick snaked the brougham around two more pedestrians and another vehicle.

With a grunt, Jaxson surrendered to the fact that he wasn't holding the reins, and for the first time since they had begun their search for Peter, he studied his ally's appearance and, surprisingly, was both pleased and astounded by what he saw. No matter what Nick Anderson had lied about in the past, his current expression of concern and determination was no facade—he really was worried about Peter's welfare. And, even though Jaxson was still angry over the betrayal and trickery, his heart started to mellow toward Daven's counterpart.

"Jax, is that the church?"

"Yeah…the graveyard is right behind it."

"Couldn't you people bury Daven in a cemetery closer to town?"

Ignoring the sarcastic remark, Jaxson craned his neck, hoping to catch a glimpse of Peter, but all he saw were the stoic markers.

"You see him?"

"No," Jaxson answered and pointed to the wide-open gate. "Pull up there. I'll run inside…maybe Peter's…maybe he's just sitting behind one of the stones…or something."

As Nick steered the slowing carriage next to the cast-iron fence, Jaxson hopped down from the seat and darted through the gateway. Please, Lord, he silently prayed as he rushed through the cemetery, please let Peter be here. Then, as he reached Daven's grave, Jaxson abruptly stopped and stared at the tombstone—and at the frock coat and soft felt hat lying next to it.

"Don't be his…don't be his," Jaxson softly chanted as he stepped toward the marker and grabbed the two pieces of clothing. "Don't be his," he tried again, but Jaxson's examination of the articles only confirmed what he already knew in his heart—the hat and coat were Peter's. They had to find him, he told himself, they had to find Peter before it was too late. Firmly holding onto the garments—and his resolve—Jaxson pivoted on his heel and hurried back to the carriage…or at least to where the carriage used to be…

"No…no…" Jaxson moaned, scanning the area. "Please tell me you didn't leave." Then he finally spotted the missing vehicle—Nick had driven past the cemetery and turned onto the old stage route. "Where the Sam Hill do ya think you're going?" he hollered as he sprinted for the brougham.

Drawing in the reins, Nick brought the horses to a fidgety halt. "Where does this road lead?" he asked, pointing southward.

"Nowhere."

"But it has to—"

"Peter was here all right," Jaxson cut in and held up the coat and hat. "We gotta go to the police…we're never gunna find him on our—"

"Jaxson, where does this road go?"

As he stood beside the carriage, Jaxson gazed at the two weed-covered, bone-dry ruts—the only remnants of a once bustling highway. "I told you—nowhere…it's an old stage line…now, listen, I think we should check back at the showroom, then go to the police sta—"

"No! The horses wanna keep going…Peter's down this street somewhere." And, almost as if Nick's words were a signal to start a race, the team lurched forward, running yards before Nick could get them under control.

His heart skipping a beat, Jaxson took a deep breath and jogged up to the carriage again. "What…whatd'ya say?" he questioned, still staggered by Nick's remark.

"Peter's down there," Nick yelled, motioning at the southbound ruts. "Now, would you get up here so we can go?"

"This trail isn't even used anymore," Jaxson countered, and as he looked into the distance, a familiar dread settled upon him. "It just goes to Everly's," he added in a whisper.

"What's Everly's?"

"It started out as a hotel and restaurant along the stage line—then Quentin Fetch got a hold of the place and it became Hell…he forced all the single men from the factory to stay there…and…and it's where Daven was shot."

His eyes widening, Nick gestured to the empty place next to him. "Get up here now! That's where Bryce has taken Peter…don't you see his plan?"

"What if you're wrong? Everly's is a long ways away—even by coach…if they ain't there, we'll just be wastin' our time!"

"You're the one wastin' time!" Nick shouted as the horses tugged against the reins. "Get up here now or I'm goin' without ya!"

"How can you be sure?" Jaxson replied, climbing onto the seat.

Nick shrugged. "I…I just am," he said, finally allowing the team to pull the carriage toward Everly's.

As the horses' trotting transformed into a gallop, then into a run, Jaxson eyed Nick once again. Why, he wondered, was Nick so positive that Peter was at Everly's? Although he couldn't find an answer, Jaxson still prayed that the man's hunch was correct—because, if it wasn't, it meant they would never find Peter in time to save him…just as he had been too late to save Daven.

❦

"Move a bit more that way," Bryce ordered, motioning with his pistol.

As Peter stepped slightly to the side, he glanced around the deserted restaurant. Except for a few boarded-up, glassless windows and a twelve-month accumulation of dust and dirt, the small eatery had changed little since his last visit. Everly's was still a sad, bleak, and lonely place that seemed to reflect and bemoan all the treachery it had witnessed. Even now, as a breeze wafted through its partially covered windows, the building sounded as if it were mourning the fresh blood that would soon spill over its once grand floor.

"You won't be leavin' this room standin' up, Leighton, so you might as well quit lookin' for a way out," Bryce smirked. Then, jabbing at the air with his gun, he added, "Just a trifle more to the left, if you would."

Growing tired of being maneuvered around as though he were posing for one of Max Green's photographs, Peter stood firm. "If you're going to shoot, then just shoot."

"Oh, don't worry, I will…now, do as I say!"

As he once again shuffled sideward, Peter continued to surreptitiously twist his hands back and forth, rubbing his skin raw against the rough rope binding his wrists. He had already loosened Cole's poorly tied knot, and if he could just lubricate the cord with his blood, he might be able to…

"There…right there," Bryce declared. "Don't move from that spot…I want you exactly where your brother was standing when Fetch shot him."

Bowing his head, Peter surveyed his surroundings a second time, and as he did, a strange and wonderful peace blanketed him. He had no idea if the stillness arose from the continuous praying he had done on his forced march to Everly's or from the fact that he was walking beside his brother's footprints. But he did know one thing for sure—the Lord's arm was around him. And, even though he would, most likely, step off the face of the earth within the hour, he realized that he would, at the same time, step into God's loving hands.

"That's your brother's blood on the floor behind you," Bryce put in, pointing at the large, rusty stain a few feet away.

Glancing over his shoulder, Peter studied the inky blotch that had made him double over in pain and vomit last July. "Yeah, I know," he replied with a calmness that puzzled even him.

"And, shortly, yours will be splattered all over his."

Peter just nodded.

"Did you know that I started planning for this moment the day you burned down my factory?"

"Your factory?"

"Yes—mine," Bryce fumed. "I was gunna become foreman after Fetch married Lorelei and got rid of the old man…he was even gunna give me this place…I was finally gunna be in command, but you ruined everything—everything!"

"You would've never gotten that far."

"No?"

"No," Peter replied serenely.

"I want you to stop that right now—you hear me!"

"Stop what?"

"That!" Bryce exclaimed. "Your brother did the same thing."

"What?" Peter asked, thoroughly perplexed by Bryce's request.

"He kept actin' as if nothing was wrong…as if he wasn't afraid to die—just as you're tryin' to do."

Suddenly, a warm surge rushed through Peter, and for a minute, he stopped wrestling to free his fettered arms. Daven must have tasted the same peace that now flowed within him—and that meant his brother had also stepped into God's waiting palms. Gasping out a relieved breath, Peter couldn't stop a smile from spreading on his face. He had wondered, for so long, if the Lord had been with Daven at the end and had taken his brother into Paradise…now, finally, he knew.

"I said stop it, Leighton!"

Instantly, the restaurant's door opened, scraping along an arc that had been worn into the floorboards. "Is it time?" Cole excitedly asked. "You need me to hold him in place now?"

"No! Get out!" Bryce seethed.

"But, you said—"

"Cole, when I asked you to keep Leighton 'in place,' I just meant that I wanted somebody around to help—if I needed it…now, go back outside and keep a lookout for any unwanted visitors."

"But I wanna—"

"Look, I've been waiting a whole year for this," Bryce returned as he icily stared at Cole. "So I'm gunna do the shooting…but I'll let you dump him into the South Pine River bed—then we both can watch him bleed to death…all right?"

As Cole scratched his stubbled chin and debated the question, Peter quietly inched his way toward the eatery's kitchen door. He really didn't know if the room could offer him any defense against Bryce's firearm, but he figured he could at least find something to help him liberate his hands.

"Okay," Cole answered with a shrug.

Shaking his head, Bryce watched Manning Cole exit the restaurant. "It's a wonder the idiot can put his boots on the right feet," he murmured under his breath. Then, as he circled and noticed Peter's new position, Bryce's features darkened. "I told you not to move."

Peter froze in mid-stride—the kitchen was so close, and yet he knew he wouldn't reach it before getting a bullet in his back.

Suddenly, a malignant grin formed on Bryce's face. "I just had a brilliant thought…you wanna know what it is?"

"Do I have a choice?"

Peter wasn't certain if he heard the gun explode or not, but he definitely felt the searing piece of lead pass through his right shoulder and knock him to the floor. Writhing in pain, Peter tried again to free his arms from their shackles, but his bullet-damaged limb made any movement pure agony. And, unfortunately, all he could do was watch the blood stream out of his body.

"Did that hurt?"

Peter laughed at the absurdity of the question. "Yeah," he choked out.

"Good!" Bryce's bald head hissed as it loomed over him. "That was my brilliant thought…instead of shootin' ya in the chest, I'm gunna ram all my bullets into your arms and legs…that way you'll still bleed to death, but it'll be real, real slow."

———

"Nick, slow down…Everly's is just past those trees."

"Slow down?!"

"Yes. If Bryce is there, he could panic when this thing rattles up to the door… we're close enough—we can go the rest of the way on foot."

Although he hated to give up the speed of his horses, Nick reluctantly agreed. But, before he could even tug on the reins, the horses already started to slow. "So what's the plan when we get there?" he asked, leaping off the carriage.

"Get Peter away from Bryce."

Nick rolled his eyes. "Huh, I wish I had thought of that," he mumbled, then began jogging down the left-hand rut.

As they ran in tandem along the dirt road, Jaxson cast Nick a surly, sideward glance and puffed out, "I just meant…we won't know what to do…until we get there…if they're there at all."

"Would you quit sayin' 'if'! I know Peter's—"

Suddenly, a crack reverberated through the air and both men stopped as if they had hit an unseen wall.

"No," Jaxson groaned, "we're too late."

Fearing the same, Nick sprinted toward the dilapidated buildings—and toward the brother he hoped was still alive. Upon reaching the side of the smaller structure, Nick headed for the front, but as he rounded the corner, he froze and instantly jumped backward.

"What's wrong?" Jaxson quietly panted as they both leaned against the side wall.

"Manning Cole…I don't think he saw me though."

Carefully, Jaxson peeked around the corner, then pulled his head back and swore. "We've been followin' Cole—not Peter," he whispered accusingly.

Nick shook his head—he knew the horses had led him to this place to find his brother. God wouldn't trick him like that…or would He? "No…no," Nick stammered, "Peter's got—"

Crack!

Another gunshot rang out and Nick peered at Jaxson with a petrified expression. "That came from inside!" he exclaimed in a hushed voice.

Jaxson nodded and slinked toward the rear of the building.

"Where are you going?" Nick called softly.

"Just come on," Jaxson rasped, beckoning with his arm.

Unsure of the strategy, Nick hesitated, then reluctantly followed his confederate around the decaying structure until they reached a back door that loosely hung from only one hinge.

"This used to be the restaurant," Jaxson murmured. "And this door leads—"

His eyes widening with understanding, Nick darted for the opening, but Jaxson whipped out his hand and blocked the entrance.

"Where do you think you're going?"

Nick gaped at Jaxson in astonishment. "I'm goin' in to see what's goin' on."

"No, you're not."

"What?!"

"Shut up," Jaxson hissed, slicing the air with his hand. "You're not goin' in—I am."

"This is no time to argue!"

"Nick, the windows are boarded-up—it'll be hard to see."

"So?"

"So this door leads into an entry room, which leads to the kitchen, and that leads to the dining room. I used to live here. I know my way around—you don't...besides, I won't be as visible as that big ol' blonde head of yours," Jaxson replied, then disappeared into the restaurant.

As he waited...and waited...and waited, Nick gazed upward, past the sagging exterior of the building, and peered at the crisp, blue sky. "Please, don't let him be dead," he whispered as his eyes flooded with moisture. "I know this request is for me—and I don't deserve it—but still, please don't let Peter be dead in there."

"Nick."

Not even realizing that Jaxson had emerged from the doorway, Nick blinked away his tears and stared at his ally's distressed visage. "Well?"

Jaxson swallowed hard. "Peter's alive, but he's been shot, twice, in the shoulder...and Bryce keeps..."

"Keeps what?"

"He keeps tellin' Peter that he deserves to suffer for all the meddling he did last year."

"Bryce is hurtin' Peter because he tried to make things right? That's...that's insane! He's..." As Nick heard his own mutterings, a tremor rushed down his spine, and he let his sentence trail off—he had just indicted himself along with Bryce. "We gotta get Peter outta there."

"I know," Jaxson returned.

"Do you think anybody else heard those shots?"

Jaxson shook his head sadly. "No, nobody comes around here anymore—they all say it's haunted."

"Haunted?" Nick echoed. "Haunted!" Instantly, Nick's eyes glimmered with a foolhardy yet ingenious scheme. "Make me look like Daven."

"What?!"

"Make me look like Daven…maybe I can distract Bryce long enough for Peter to escape."

"You're the one who's insane, Nick…Bryce'll kill ya the minute he sees ya."

"Maybe—maybe not…but it might allow me to get close enough to him, so I can steal his gun away."

"No. It'll only get you—"

"Please, Jaxson, please…it's the only way to give Peter a chance…let me be noble for the first time in my life."

Jaxson sighed. "It's not gunna work…you got the bruises all right, but Daven's forehead and hand were all cut up, I'm not gunna—"

"Then just fake the injuries with some blood," Nick persisted, removing his jacket.

"And where am I gunna—"

"Hit me and break the stitches on my arm…please, we're running out of time!"

"Are you sure?"

"Yes! And hurry!"

As he heard the fabric of his shirt rip, Nick gritted his teeth, bracing himself for the impact of Jaxson's…

Flinching at the incredible spasm that gushed through his body, Nick leaned against the restaurant to steady himself.

"You okay?"

"Yeah," Nick lied.

After a second, harder punch, Nick's gash reopened and his torn, white sleeve slowly turned red. "All right…here goes," Jaxson sighed, smearing some of the blood over Nick's right temple and left hand, and across the front of his shirt. Then, squatting, Jaxson grasped a handful of dirt. "Daven was darker than you," he explained as he spit onto the soil and rubbed his palms together. "Your bruises take care of your face, but that mane of yours is just too blonde…sorry." And, with the apology, Jaxson stood and combed his muddy hands through Nick's hair.

"Well? Do I look like Daven?"

Jaxson quickly averted his eyes and grabbed Nick's jacket. "You're gunna need this to hide that arm—Daven wasn't hurt there," he offered and slipped the garment over Nick's bloody limb.

"Do I look like him?!"

Pulling the jacket up, Jaxson patted Nick on the back and described the layout of the kitchen and dining area.

"Why won't you answer me?" Nick tried, turning to face Jaxson. "Can I fool Bryce for a couple of seconds or not?"

Jaxson wiped the back of his hand across his face and looked into Nick's eyes. "You...you could be Daven's ghost...okay?" he sputtered. "Now, I'll take care of Cole, and you...you do your best to bring yourself—and our brother—outta Everly's."

⁓⁓⁓⁓⁓⁓⁓⁓⁓

As he lay on the floor, Peter stared at the pistol being leveled at him once more, and clenching his jaw, he prepared for a third bullet to pierce his body.

"What's the matter, Leighton, you seem to have lost your—"

"Bryce! Leave my brother alone!"

With his firearm still pointed at Peter, Leland Bryce circled and gawked at the half-hidden figure in the kitchen doorway. "What the..."

Trying to blink the sweat from his eyes, Peter studied the image of Daven as it seemed to float into the dining room. Although it had always hurt to think of his brother, he never thought it would feel so good to see him again.

"I said leave my brother alone, Bryce—or I'll haunt you for the rest of your life."

As the apparition spoke a second time, Peter's tortured mind realized that his brother's voice was different, then the truth crystallized in his head—the specter before him wasn't Daven...it was Nick. "No," he murmured.

"What's going on?" Bryce demanded as he focused his attention—and his weapon—on Nick. "You're dead...I saw Fetch shoot you myself."

"I've come back to make sure that my brother doesn't share the same fate."

"Nobody's gunna interfere with his punishment...he deserves to suffer after what he did to me," Bryce sneered and tightened his index finger around the trigger.

"No!" Peter hollered, forcing himself to his knees. "Your fight is with me...it's always been with me...don't touch him."

Glancing sideward, Bryce narrowed his eyes. "You're right about that, Leighton," he said as he swung his pistol around and aimed it at Peter's chest.

With a deep breath, Peter readied himself for the coming shot, then, in horror, he watched his brother swoop toward Bryce. And, before Peter could move or even shout a warning, Bryce turned the gun on Nick—and fired.

Immediately, Nick clutched his side and sank to the floor.

Screaming in anger and anguish, Peter scrambled to his feet and, using all the strength he had left, slammed himself into Bryce, sending them both crashing through one of the partially boarded-up windows.

Lying stunned and motionless on the ground, Peter gazed up at the sky and prayed that he would stay conscious, even though his pain-racked body cried for relief. Then, as the buzzing in his head began to subside, he rolled onto his side just in time to see Leland Bryce rise to a wobbly, stooped position.

"Get the gun!" Bryce roared.

It was then that the battling Jaxson and Manning Cole simultaneously spotted the fallen weapon. And, in one swift movement, Cole slugged Jaxson in the gut, pushed him to the ground, and dove for the firearm.

"Shoot them! Shoot them both!"

Giggling uncontrollably, Cole picked up the gun and waved it back and forth between Peter and Jaxson.

"I said shoot them, you idiot!"

His face contorting into a snarl, Cole aimed the pistol at Bryce. "If I'm the idiot, why do I have the gun?"

"You idiot! Fire already!"

"Yes Sir!" Cole snapped—and fired the rest of the bullets into Bryce's head. "Guess you won't be callin' me an idiot anymore, will ya?" he continued as Bryce's body settled into a lifeless mound.

His mouth falling open in shock, Jaxson peered at Cole, then Peter. "You all right, Partner?"

"I've…I've been better," Peter choked out. "Nick's inside…Bryce shot him."

Jaxson nodded and took a stride toward Peter.

"Hey!" Cole barked, jabbing the pistol into the air. "I didn't say you could move."

Jaxson smiled slyly and sauntered over to Cole, balling his hands into fists. "What are ya gunna do? Shoot your empty gun at me?"

Cole's brashness promptly paled, and he stared at the weapon as if he could will some ammunition into it.

"That ain't gunna help ya," Jaxson announced and whipped his fists at Cole's face until the man's senseless frame fell to the ground. Then, hurrying to Peter's side, Jaxson asked again, "You really okay?"

"Yeah…will you get this rope off me?"

"We got a carriage just down the street," Jaxson put in as he untied Peter's hands. "I'll bring it 'round so we can get you and Nick to the doctor…and Cole and Bryce to the police."

Slowly, Peter sat up and tried to bring his numbed arms in front of him, but only the left would obey, and it, just barely. "Please, help me up…I have to get in there to see Nick."

"No," Jaxson countered. "You just stay here."

"Please, Jax…I…I want to be there…in case he…he doesn't make it."

Sighing resignedly, Jaxson grasped Peter's left arm and heaved him up.

"You better hurry with the coach," Peter returned, wavering.

"Peter, you're not—"

"I'm okay," he lied. And, without waiting for another rebuke, Peter stumbled toward the window he had broken just moments before. "Nick?" he called, stepping into the restaurant. "Nick, it's Peter."

Only silence answered him.

Then, as he caught sight of his brother's prone form on the floor, Peter cried out, "No…no…please, Lord, not him too." Shuffling over to Nick, Peter knelt and lightly petted his brother's mud-coated hair. "I'm so sorry…I'm—"

Suddenly, Nick's eyes fluttered open and he grinned faintly. "Don't worry," he mumbled, "you ain't…rid of me yet."

His heart jumping, Peter laughed in relief. "Hold on, Nick…Jaxson's getting the carriage."

"What about…Bryce?"

"Cole shot him…he's dead."

"Hmm…and Cole?"

"Don't talk…you have to save—"

"I'm okay," Nick cut in as he elbowed himself up and leaned against the kitchen wall. "It ain't too bad."

"Why? Why'd you do that? You were taking a big risk."

Nick offered a crooked shrug in return. "I had to make up for what I did to you."

With a long exhale, Peter twisted himself around and sat next to his brother. "You could have gotten yourself killed."

"I had to do it, Peter…to show you how sorry I was for betraying you."

Taking another deep breath, Peter nodded.

"I…I wanted out…I really did, but Wild kept threatening to send me back to prison."

"Wild kept what?" Peter questioned, moving so he could look into his brother's watery, blue eyes.

"Threatening to send me to prison…that's what his little story was all about this morning…he was going to tell the police that it was me who stole his stupid gold toothpick…he even said he'd arrange for the jewelry store to be robbed and that I'd be blamed for that too."

Peter's jaw clamped down tight, and he cussed between his teeth.

"It's true…please believe me."

"Oh, I believe you…what I can't believe is the arrogance of that man."

"I wish I could stay and make everything up to you."

"Why can't you stay?"

"Because of what I just told you," Nick replied, his voice breaking. "Wild won't stop until he gets me behind bars—especially now."

Closing his eyes, Peter rested his head against the wall. "God's worked mighty hard to bring us together—He won't let that happen."

"But—"

"Nick, after what's happened today, I know Wild will lose every game he plays against us."

"How can you be sure?"

"Because James Wild's foundation is the sand—not the Rock."

"Do…do you forgive me then?"

Peter opened his eyes and glanced at his brother's blood-stained body and hopeful, crystal-blue eyes. "I have to admit, Nick, it's going to take me awhile before I can completely trust you again…but when I saw Bryce's bullet hit you, all I wanted was for you to be all right—for two reasons…first, so I could tell you that, yes, I do forgive you."

"And the other reason?"

With a lighthearted wink, Peter returned, "So I could give you a tongue-lashing for getting mixed up with Wild."

Nick chuckled, then winced and clasped his hand over his side. "You know what? I'm actually looking forward to that—Brother."

❧

As he walked out onto the Spreyers' front porch, Nick donned his hat and breathed in as deeply as his wounded side would allow. Was he really part of a family now? he asked himself. He knew the answer was 'yes,' but he still couldn't accept the fact that something good had finally happened in his life. Leaning on the porch railing, Nick absently gazed at the children playing in the yard and considered his good fortune—then a faint chattering caught his attention, and turning, he eyed Anna's sisters, who instantly fell silent.

"Ladies," he offered, bowing slightly to the seated huddle, "it was a wonderful ceremony, don't you think?"

Marion clucked out a laugh and leaned back in her chair. "Wonderful? It was far from that! The groom and his brother are covered in bandages, and the best man's face is all cut and swollen…you call that wonderful?"

"Yeah, I do…it's wonderful that all three of us were here to enjoy it."

"I suppose," Marion replied. "I just don't understand why they wanted to get married so soon after that disgraceful encounter at Everly's—they could have at least waited until everyone had healed."

"I agree," Elsa chimed in. "They're having Mr. Green set up his camera for a wedding photograph right now—with all the injuries, it's going to resemble a post-mortem picture."

"Anna should have waited," Ida added with a long sigh. "And for more reasons than just a poor photograph."

"How true!" Elsa exclaimed. "This union was just too rushed."

Gretchen nodded sadly. "Our sister never gave herself the chance to consider any other…um, possibilities."

"And there are so many handsome—and rich—possibilities in Sandorville," Marion said as a sly smile formed on her face.

Instantly, Nick's eyes narrowed. "If you are so against my brother marrying Anna—why are ya even here?"

"For Mama and Papa's sake," Marion answered, wiggling her fan under her chin.

"Well, what about Anna and Peter's sake?!" Nick proclaimed. Then, noticing the volume of his question, he put in softly, "How about giving them a little encour-agement—instead of condemning their marriage before it's even a day old."

Marion lifted her nose into the air and glanced at her sisters. "Look who's giving us counsel—a convict."

Nick shook his head. It was downright unfair—all he ever wanted was to have a loving family…and sitting in front of him were four girls taking theirs for granted. "You can insult me all you want, Marion," he returned, surprised at his own com-posure, "but I am, officially, part of this family now—you might as well get used to having me around…and having me voice my opinion."

"I'll do no such thing…I plan on distancing myself from you and that strumpet in there," Marion huffed, motioning to the house, "as much as possible."

"Well, it's gunna be somewhat hard to distance yourself from me—unless your aim is to stay away from the jewelry store."

"And what, pray tell, do you mean by that?"

"Oh, just that Michael and I had quite a long talk earlier. He apologized for treating me like rubbish, and he asked me to work in his shop and repair his broken watches…I'll be starting as soon as my arm's out of this sling."

"He did what?!"

"I think you heard me."

Jumping up from her chair, Marion angrily shut her fan and glared at Nick. "We'll see about this!"

"Go ahead," Nick shrugged. "Just remember, you have over a half-dozen watches hanging in your store that need to be fixed."

Red-faced, Marion opened her mouth to respond, but only an outraged screech emerged.

"I think it'll be rather nice," Nick put in, enjoying Marion's unhappiness. "It'll give us a chance to get to know each other."

"Michael John Nealy!" Marion screamed and charged into the house. "What do you think you are doing hiring…"

As the shrieking eventually faded, Nick smiled—he had never realized, until now, how much courage and confidence Peter's support gave him. Tipping his hat at the remaining sisters, Nick circled and started to follow Marion inside, then, out of the corner of his eye, he glimpsed an all-too-familiar, long-haired figure strolling up the walkway. Firmly holding his hand over his injured side, Nick descended the porch stairs and limped along the wooden planks, purposefully blocking Wild's approach. "What do you want?!"

"I have come to congratulate the bride and groom—and to offer the new couple a wedding gift."

"This gathering is for family and friends only," Nick announced. "People who have tried to kill the groom are not welcome."

"My dear Mr. Anderson, I assure you, as I assured the authorities, Leland Bryce and Manning Cole operated under their own agenda—not mine."

Nick's mouth fell open in disbelief. "You do remember who you're talkin' to, don't ya?"

"Why yes—I am speaking to the man who constantly tried to coerce me into purchasing information about Peter's confidential business dealings."

"Nobody'll believe that."

"No? I explained to the authorities that you volunteered these details in the hopes that I would compensate you for it…Patrolman Farrell more than understood when I told him about your insatiable thirst for money and liquor…you do recall Patrolman Farrell, do you not? He escorted you home on your first night in Sandorville—after you ravaged Conner's Saloon."

Nick gritted his teeth in disgust—once again he had succeeded in destroying his own credibility. "You're still not welcome here, Wild."

"Hmm, must I remind you of a sordid incident that we have yet to settle?" Wild quipped as he polished the knob of his walking stick with his glove.

"I told you before—it ain't my fault that we bled all over your precious carriage…I ain't payin' for a new one."

"No, no…that was not what I was referring to…I was speaking about the fact that my toothpick is still missing, as are many other valuables from—"

"That's enough, James."

Startled and relieved, Nick glanced over his shoulder and silently thanked Peter for his impeccable timing.

"Ah, Peter, your brother and I were just discussing your—"

"No, you weren't, James," Peter announced, stepping forward. "You were threatening him—again."

James Wild stroked his chin with his walking stick and feigned befuddlement. "I give you my oath as a gentleman, I was not making a threat."

"If you touch Nick," Peter continued, poking Wild in the chest after every word, "you'll touch the apple of God's eye."

"And what is that supposed to mean?"

"It means, if you come against Nick or any member of my family you'll come against me—and my Father…and you will lose, just as you did this time."

Wild moistened his lips and looked from Peter, to Nick, and back again. "Gentlemen, I see no reason for this pointless conversation—especially on such a happy occasion."

"It'll be a lot happier," Nick said with a wide grin, "when you leave."

"Oh, but I cannot leave just yet…I have not bestowed my gift to the groom."

"That's not necessary, James," Peter returned.

"But I insist…you see, I wish to reestablish my table and chair order."

Uncertain if he should trust his perpetual adversary, Peter rubbed his left hand over his face and stared at Wild. "That's fine," he finally offered. "Of course, since you tore up our last contract, we will need to draft a new one."

"Of course."

"With new conditions…and a new timetable."

"A new timetable? I thought you would be anxious to diminish your stock of all those dust-collecting tables and chairs."

"Oh, they aren't collecting dust, James," Peter said, savoring every word. "They've been purchased by another customer."

Wild's expression fell into a pout. "I see…well, if you will excuse me, I do have other business to attend to…" And, as his words drifted off, he pivoted on his heel and plodded toward the street.

"It's funny," Nick whispered as he watched Wild depart.

"What?"

"That man always seemed so big to me…now, he seems so puny."

"Yeah," Peter nodded, "after you've seen the Lord at work, most obstacles shrink in size."

"I guess."

With a half-smile, Peter motioned toward the house. "Come on, Max is ready for us."

Nick glanced at the farmhouse but remained fixed in place. "Peter?"

"Yeah?"

"Here," he said, holding out a silver coin.

"What's this for?"

"It's the dollar that I stole from you when I first arrived."

Peter chuckled. "That's okay—you can keep it."

"No, I want you to have it," Nick persisted and slipped the coin into Peter's breast pocket. "It's just my way of sayin' that I'm sorry for taking so much from ya—and never givin' back."

"Nick, you saved my life—I'd say that was definitely giving back...but thanks."

"Pay-ter! Nick!" Doctor Spreyer called from the porch. "Max is waiting to take the photograph."

Glancing at his own sling, then at his brother's, Peter laughed again. "This is going to be some picture."

"Yeah," Nick put in as they walked toward the porch. "It kinda looks as if we're paralleling each other again, huh?"

As he reached the steps, Peter grabbed the railing and pulled himself up—all the while hoping that Nick was wrong...if they were, truly, paralleling each other, that meant his brother's arm was as numb—and unusable—as his.

Allowing Nick to go in first, Peter greeted and thanked his numerous guests as he ambled through the entranceway, the hall, and the kitchen, then, pausing at the back door, he surveyed the scene Max Green had arranged outside. Sitting, kneeling, and standing in front of the twin-trunked pine tree were so many of the people he cherished...Doctor and Mrs. Spreyer...Jaxson, who also held Daven's portrait... Holly Jaye and her family...Lynette, William, Bock the kitten—and Nick, who was now standing closely behind them...Hermann and his brood...Del Franz, Emerson Brant, and countless others from the factory...and of course, his beloved Anna, who, in her white gown and pink accents, took his breath away.

"Are you sure everyone is going to fit in the picture?" Peter teased as he stepped into the backyard and watched Max Green's bushy, silver hair bob here and there as the man fixed errant curls and crooked lapels.

"I'm sure," the photographer returned, bouncing over to his camera. "Now, get yourself in there, Peter—before these people fall over from me not letting them move."

It was remarkable, Peter thought as he walked into the midst of the assemblage and headed toward Anna. Absolutely remarkable. Last July, he barely had a family...now, his kith and kin barely fit into a photograph. Sighing with a serenity he had never really known before, Peter Leighton wrapped his arm around his wife and gave her a gentle kiss on the cheek, then, gazing upward, he smiled and thanked God.

The End

Born and raised in Michigan, Nancy Feldbush has always approached life with a creative flair, which can be seen in just about everything she authors. And, having worked as an Art Director, a Graphic Designer, a Copy Editor, and a Copywriter, she knows firsthand how thrilling and trying it is to transform ideas into reality. So far, her greatest accomplishments in bringing her creativity to life are her two novels, *To Repay A Debt* and *To Rebuild A Life*.

Writing, or wordsmithing as Nancy calls it, is one of the most pleasurable challenges that she has ever faced. To shape words together, then reform and chisel away at them until they make a reader sigh, or laugh, or shed a tear is her favorite way to spend time. And now, with the completion of her second book, Nancy prays that, God-willing, her hobby will become her next career.

Rivaling her joy of wordsmithing is her love of history—evident by the amount of research Nancy does for her books. Although she is captivated by the famous people of history, she is even more fascinated by the everyday individuals...the ones who toiled day by day to carve out a place for themselves—just as we do today. Mesmerized with the details of the past, Nancy can spend hours reading antique postcards and be amazed by the artwork, the author's choice of words, the strokes of the pen, and even the marks from the post office.

Surrounded by her dog and three cats, who produce the warmhearted atmosphere she needs to write, Nancy does her best to craft stories that combine her fondness of history, her faith, and her devotion to friends and family.

Moose Run
Productions

A publisher of books that offer readers a wholesome and enjoyable respite.

Moose Run Productions publishes manuscripts of various genres that are decent, uplifting, and steeped in Christian values. If you would like a **free** copy of our catalog, please visit our Web site at moose-run.com or complete and send this form to: Moose Run Productions • 22010 Highview • Clinton Township, Michigan 48036.

Name _____

Address _____

City, State, Zip _____

E-mail (optional) _____